The Watchers

The Blood Dagger: Volume Two

Misty Hayes

The Watchers - The Blood Dagger: Volume Two by Misty Hayes

ISBN: 9781732140516

"Fairy tales are more than true: not because they tell us that dragons exist, but because they tell us that dragons can be beaten."

-Neil Gaiman

Chapter 1

Corinth

I'D GONE AND GOTTEN myself captured by the enemy. Not on purpose, mind you; that part had come about when I felt the all-encompassing need for fresh air. I had been grabbed and then carted off to what I believed was a warehouse or abandoned factory. I wasn't exactly sure which, because it was pitch-black in the space I now occupied. But I didn't need my eyesight to know this place was filled to the brim with tetanus-y, sharp metal things. The rodents and bats were most likely plague-ridden—I hated bats.

"Oh sure, you're scared of *bats*, but vamps … no problem," I mumbled.

Speak of the devil—little feet followed by a tail scampered over my foot. I let out a loud yelp that echoed around the cavernous room.

Way to sound manly, Corinth.

I was tied to a metal chair bolted into the ground. There was a silver lining to all of this though. I still had my watch, the one Larna had given me, with all the gadgets a secret agent might need. I wasn't quite ready to push the ol' panic button quite yet though. I'd like to say I'd gained a little bit of dignity since becoming the *"Chosen One."* Why in the world a mystical dagger would choose *me* as its defender, well, was beyond me. That and the fact that a mystical dagger could *choose* anything at all should have been my first indicator to just go with the flow.

Only dead fish go with the flow.

Larna and I had become the dynamic duo—well, okay, maybe not so much the dynamic as the hiding-out duo. Ever since I'd taken possession of the blade, I had inadvertently made myself a target. If there was an Olympic sport for lying low, we'd have won gold. So after months of hiding, I had felt the overwhelming urge to clear my head and stretch my legs. In my defense, I couldn't take the cabin fever one more day.

A voice broke the thick silence, causing me to jerk painfully against my bonds.

"You should be scared."

Funny how quickly the body reacts when it fears for its life. I tried unsuccessfully to control the sound of my breathing. The guy was a Brit. That part didn't surprise me; we were in England. I would argue my accent was cooler, as I had a Texas twang.

The sound of his voice came from above, but this time, when he spoke, I could tell he had moved closer. "Where's your girlfriend?"

"Um, who—?"

Hot breath hit the back of my neck, causing me to cringe. The ropes bit into my wrists, and something warm and sticky slid down my arms. I tugged my shoulders up, trying to protect my neck in anticipation of what was about to happen.

Blinding light hit me square in the face, and I was lit up like a Christmas tree. Blinking away the black splotches from my vision, I glanced down, managing to make out the outline of my shadow. In the harsh light, it was as sharp and clear as a black-and-white photo.

A nervous laugh bubbled up out of me. "Does my hair really look that bad?"

"You're a funny guy, huh?" He swung the flashlight beam away from me in order to illuminate something across the way. "Check that out."

I followed the path of the light, grimly aware of the gloating way in which he'd said that. And I definitely didn't want to see what he was trying to show me. I looked anyway, instantly regretting it. When my eyes locked on the object, my heart shot up into my throat. It was one of those steel surgical tables on wheels—the kind in the movies where the medical examiner conducts autopsies on people. Except this one looked extremely unsterile. Were those straps?

I knew there was stuff in here that could give me tetanus.

The uncleanliness of my environment didn't irk me as much as the rather large needle did. My eyes drifted to it, and then down to the bag it was attached to. Something told me it wasn't saline. When he threw the light back in my eyes, I found myself unable to keep them open any longer. A stray tear rolled down my face. I wasn't crying; I just couldn't see anything … and needles sucked.

"If you tell me where the dagger is, we can avoid all this unpleasantness," he said. "Your girlfriend has a price on her head too."

"Funny thing, I don't know who you're talking about."

The funny thing was that Larna *did* have my blade. I had left it with her back at the hotel before slipping out of the room, which made this moment both a blessing and a curse. If I'd had the blade with me when I'd gotten nabbed, I might have put the smack-down on them. Of course, now they didn't have the one thing they needed—besides me. My high school crush had gotten the blond dude and I'd won the consolation prize—a knife.

My arms were bound behind me, which still afforded me the opportunity to use my watch. Realizing it was time to call for help, I wrapped my right hand over my left forearm and went for the button—

But before I could push it, the bounty hunter's hand was on mine, ripping the watch savagely off my wrist. "I think I'll relieve you of this fancy-looking timepiece." He chuckled, and I could hear the amusement in his voice as he added, "I've heard about you. Made a name for yourself, haven't you?"

Even though I couldn't see him, I knew he was studying me. I could feel those creepy eyes of his raking over me.

"Not what you imagined, right?" I lifted my shoulders in an exaggerated shrug. "I may not be a muscle-bound jock, but I bet I can still kick your ass."

"I'll be famous grabbing you," he said darkly, ignoring my taunt. "There's quite a price on your head, you know. Clan Deimos … they're paying a pretty penny. Really don't see the point. You're a tiny scrap of a thing. And talk about it being too easy plucking you up. There are photos of you everywhere. Some are calling you a vampire hunter." He snorted in derision. I also detected a hint of something else: a silken threat woven with threads of greed. Money was always a good motivator.

Once I was on that table, something told me I wasn't getting off it again.

I cracked an eye in the harsh light, catching a glimpse of a brown hiking boot. "What's the price on my head up to now?" I asked, stalling.

"Five hundred thousand," he answered quickly.

Yeah, definitely all about the money, which was not necessarily a bad thing—he had to keep me alive for a payday.

I whistled. "Up from last month."

The bounty hunter's dark outline shrank and receded as he shoved his face closer to mine. In the direct beam of light, I could now see that his eyes were in deep contrast to his dark skin. They were the lightest shade of gray I'd ever seen. Even though he looked to be in his early thirties, he was probably going on five hundred.

And then the light winked out again, drawing me back to the present, dousing me in total darkness. This time it felt final.

Rough hands tore at my bonds, and before I knew it, he was dragging me across hard concrete, and then hauling me onto that steel table, using inhuman strength to do it. Eight months ago, Al had broken my arm. Well, technically, I'd broken my own arm in order to save my little sister's life. It had taken time to heal. Ever since then, I'd been working out to gain strength and muscle back. Larna had also convinced me to incorporate boxing into my training regimen. I may look scrawny, but I had packed on a lot of lean muscle because of it.

Using the element of surprise, I struck out blindly, catching him on the side of his face. As soon as he staggered back, I started yanking off the strap on my left arm. Once I was free, I threw a leg over the table only to catch a vicious blow to the stomach. As I doubled over in shock and pain, he shoved me back down, strapping me once again to the tabletop in a fraction of a second.

"You have a strong right," he grumbled, "but not strong enough."

"No offense …" I wheezed, "but you don't have a strong anything …"

His eyes flashed—the telltale sign of impending vampire *Sight*. His face lit up in the darkness. It was the eeriest shade of blue I'd ever seen, making him look that much more menacing. I wondered if his compulsion would work on me. Larna had tried to compel me back when she confessed the truth about being a vamp, but it hadn't stuck. I was hoping it wouldn't now either. My stomach did a frantic flip at the prospect of not knowing what would happen. Would he take control of me? Was this how I would die? Being turned into a mindless zombie that felt no pain... Actually, that part didn't sound too bad. If I could pretend to do whatever he asked, he might be less guarded, maybe make a mistake. All I had to do was wait for an opportunity to present itself.

I felt the bizarre pull of compulsion as he whispered, "No hard feelings, mate." Mind control felt foreign and wrong—a mental invasion of the worst kind. If he was trying to be stealthy inside my head, it wasn't working. He was Godzilla, except instead of a village, he was stomping through my most precious thoughts and memories. I gasped in fright at the mental invasion.

Once he thought he had me, he whispered, "Tell me where the blade is."

I sagged back, letting the cold steel from the table seep through my shirt. I shivered uncontrollably—that is, until something happened that I hadn't been expecting—

I arched up off the table, my eyes matching his in intensity and fire and something else. To my sudden and overwhelming surprise, I found I could see. At first, I thought someone had switched on a light. Except that wasn't the case at all, it was still dark, but I could see as clearly as if it were daylight. I sucked in a sharp breath, glancing around in astonishment. We were in the basement of a mechanical room; that much I knew for certain. There was oversized, dank machinery; concrete conduits and metal piping overhead that snaked through the rafters in the ceiling. I listened to the soft plink of condensation dripping from the pipes across the room; heard the tiny susurrations made by the bats that I now knew were hanging above me. The tang of mildew and mold overpowered the rest of my senses. I was surprised at how much I'd been missing out on by being human—if this was vampire *Sight*, that is.

The bounty hunter's face went slack, and he dropped his hands from around my neck. The sudden movement drew my eye back to him. He slumped over right as my eyes flared brighter, his *Sight* dissipating and mine increasing.

My voice came out in a dry rasp as I said, *"Untie me."*

He reached over and pulled at the leather straps on my wrists, doing exactly as I had asked. Holy Caesar's ghost—this was new and completely unexpected. I had the power of vampire compulsion.

As soon as I was free, I ducked out of his grasp, hopping off the table as quickly as my body would allow. I was stiff from being tied up so when I hit the ground my legs almost buckled out from under me. My *Sight* sputtered and winked out like a dying battery on a flashlight. I couldn't hold on to the compulsion. There was too much raw power flooding through me and I had no idea how to control it. As soon as it fled, the darkness spiraled back up to greet me like an old friend. Darkness and I were most definitely not friends.

A spike of fear shot up my spine as I staggered, my legs bumping against the edge of the gurney. The stretcher slid forward on squeaky wheels. I put a hand out on it in order to right myself. Where was the exit again? The voice inside my head screamed for me to get out now. I should have been running, rather than stumbling around in confusion, but I felt disconnected from my own body. This was my waking nightmare. An extra dose of anxiety hit me as I imagined my captor regaining use of his faculties again. I imagined his skeletal hands coming to claim what he thought was rightfully his—*me*.

And then my fears turned into reality as something hard hit the back of my head and I fell to a knee.

Before succumbing to the dark once again, I heard a new voice say, "What *are* you?"

Chapter 2

Corinth

As I came to, my chest tight with anxiety, I felt a tug just above my right elbow. A tingling numbness ran down my arm, all the way to my wrist. For one terrifying second, I thought they were getting ready to chop my hand off—maybe torture the information out of me—until I realized the thing wrapped around my arm was a constricting band, the kind of tool nurses used to find a vein to take a blood sample. My stomach dropped. I knew what he was about to do. Were they going to sell my blood, study it, or drink it? Something told me all of the above.

Someone spoke, but it wasn't the same guy who had tried to compel me. I guessed the one who bashed me on the head. His voice was deep and brash where the first guy sounded nasally, like his nose had been broken one too many times. "How did you turn compulsion around like that? You're not a vamp ..." He drew air between his teeth, making a weird sucking noise that suggested he might enjoy draining me dry. "I heard stories about you; never believed them until now though."

When I spoke, my words came out slurred. "Now you're just flattering me ..."

He gave an amused grunt. "I'm going to make a lot of money off you. Thought I'd drain you first... not kill you, of course. Mr. Stanton wants you alive." He said it so nonchalantly it gave me chills. "Your blood on the black market will sell for a lot of money. Wonder if it tastes any different." I heard the soft rustle of clothing, which I assumed was him shrugging. "Or maybe they want it for other things. I'm not going to try your blood after what I just witnessed. I ain't that stupid. I do have to admit, I'm intrigued." He sniffed loudly. "It doesn't smell any different."

"It tastes as bland as cardboard. It would be a waste of your time—"

A finger found my vein and I tensed, expecting the worst. Then I heard the sharp squeal of metal scraping against concrete as he moved his chair. The sound reminded me of being at the dentist's office—a really messed up dentist's office with unsterile equipment.

The first kidnapper, the one I'd whammied, had come out of his trancelike state, because I heard him moan and then say, "What happened, Marv?"

"The kid pulled one over on you. Got ya good, Cal." Marv snorted. "We heard all these sorts of biblical striking-us-all-down rumors about you. You know what they say about rumors though—they're spread by fools and accepted by idiots." He patted the crook of my arm like he was checking out a piece of meat from the butcher. "But if you tell me where your friend is, the girl, I promise, I'll make this is as painless as possible. I got my marching orders like everyone else, but we could make a deal on the side if you just tell me where the blade is."

I'm glad I couldn't see what he was about to do. I hated needles—needles and bats.

My voice sounded tiny as I whispered, "Could you at least sterilize that?" A bead of sweat slid down my head then off the side of my nose. Never fails you get an itch when you know you can't scratch it.

Where are you, Larna? Now would be a great time to show up and rescue me.

Marv leaned closer and his hot, stale breath hit the side of my cheek. "Maybe after draining you, you'll be a little more apt to talk. We're reasonable; I mean, we have to get as much out of you as we can."

I didn't make a peep as he jammed the needle into my arm, but I really wanted to.

If I couldn't see the amount of blood leaving my body, it meant it wasn't happening. My kidnappers were next to me. One of them yanking the needle out of my arm and then pulling the constricting band off. I let my head loll in his direction, feeling drained, no pun intended. Was that two bags or only one? Somewhere I think I lost track of how much he'd taken. How long had I been here? It felt like an eternity.

His shadowed face dropped closer to mine. Either I was seeing double, or they were both looking down, taunting me in tandem. "You sure you don't want to tell me where that big boned girl is? The one with the short hair—she's a spitfire of a thing. What's her name again, Marv?"

Marv said, "Larna Collins."

"Yeah … that's her … We'll find her eventually. We know you were staying at the Crescent Hotel."

"*She's not big boned!*" I yelled, anger surging up inside me. "You *really* don't want to mess with her, guys. She's a badass …"

If there was one thing I was certain of, it was that they would never get me to rat on Larna. My only form of solace was that she was somewhere safe. We had prepared an exit strategy, if things went sideways. Keeping Larna out of harm's way was the only thing getting me through the next jab. A wave of nausea hit me, bringing me crashing back to reality. I could really use some food or one of those juice boxes.

If I couldn't escape, I would make them kill me. It would be better than being handed over to Gabriel Stanton and tortured. "Why don't you just use your *Sight*—compel it out of me?" I goaded.

He smiled, clucking his tongue in annoyance. "Listen, kid, you don't have to be the hero here."

Because they'd taken my watch, I assumed Larna had no idea where I was or what was going on. Imagining her out there fighting a horde of Deimos made me more light-headed than losing blood to this schmuck.

"I don't think there's much left in you …" His voice faded as my attention was suddenly diverted to the sound of liquid sloshing around. I heard squeak of a cooler lid opening.

"You know, how about you come back in a few hours? Let me lift some weights or eat a pizza … I'll donate all the blood you want," I babbled through another wave of dizziness.

My captor reached down to grab something off the

table, and when he did, I got a good look at his face. He had wild eyes, and he looked a lot younger than I originally thought, with dark, curly hair protruding out from underneath a black baseball cap.

"Larna was poking her nose around here a little while ago. My partner dragged some other kid outta here—just for this very occasion. It wasn't hard finding another skinny twit about your size. Put a hood on him, to make it look like we were taking you somewhere else in order to draw her away. Can't have her interrupting all the fun, can we?" He sniffed loudly, adding, "She took the bait and left you here all alone. Guess we don't need you to talk anymore … We'll just make her tell us where the dagger is—she probably has it on her. We'll search your hotel room next …"

It felt like what little blood I had left in me drained from my face at this revelation.

The table moved, wheels squeaking and pulling across the floor like a bum wheel on a shopping cart. The needle was ripped from my arm once again. I screwed my face up, inhaling sharply at the sudden sting it left behind as he tapped his fingers against my left arm this time. I didn't think I could take any more. Larna was in trouble because of me—I had to find a way out of this.

"Can we talk about this? I'm feeling a lot chattier now that you mention it—" A wave of vertigo hit me. For a second, it got so intense I thought I had fallen off the table. Being in the dark wasn't helping either. But he didn't let me escape into my own head long enough before the needle was back in my arm.

My voice came out shallow and reedy as I breathed, "You wouldn't want to waste an opportunity to get more money, would you?"

How many pints of blood did it take for someone to bleed to death?

"What d'ya mean?" I could hear the eagerness in the sound of his voice now.

"You're about to ..." It suddenly became harder to take in oxygen as I stammered, " ... k-k-kill your best chance at making more money."

He fell silent. And the pause went on for so long I thought he'd disappeared, maybe to leave me to die in peace, but the sound of his voice brought me back from the edge of my stupor. "You know you may be right; you don't look so hot—"

The sound of a door creaking open on dry hinges stopped him cold. My first thought was that Larna was here, that she'd found me. My heart skipped a beat before thundering loudly in my ears.

"No one's supposed to be back yet." I felt the air rush past me as he zipped off to check on the disturbance, finally leaving me alone to bleed out on the rusty table in peace. But before I could drift off completely, I heard a loud thud and then the sound of shoes slapping and slipping across concrete. The sound of several people grunting and breathing heavily seemed to be evidence of a scuffle taking place.

I was hallucinating. Didn't loss of blood bring on hallucinations? A flash of Jacob Marley, complete with rattling chains, crossed my vision. I imagined him whisking me away to the past so I could see all of my transgressions in Technicolor. I knew what he'd show me: my dumbass not pushing the button on my watch—or me going for a walk because I needed some fresh air ...

Even though I had complete faith in Larna winning a fight against these dudes, it didn't alleviate the sudden onset of dread that had taken root in my chest, and the fear resting in my gut as heavy as a boulder. In a last-ditch effort to break free, I yanked against my bonds. I bit the inside of my cheek to keep from crying out, the pain knifing through me where the needle had been inserted into my vein.

Someone screamed, and I heard a heavy thud followed by a grunt, and then nothing. A few seconds later, lights flooded on above me. I slammed my eyes shut and then slowly let them adjust to the brightness. When I cracked them open, I couldn't tell if my blurry vision was from poor eyesight or if the cluttered network of piping in the rafters overhead had been installed with no real aforethought or planning. I might have been in shock. Was this what shock felt like?

A familiar face dropped in front of mine, and I blinked rapidly, making sure I still wasn't just seeing things.

"It's been a long time."

I let out a deep sigh, sagging back against the table to finally let the strained tension drain out of me. There came a slight tug on my arm and then the sweet relief of the needle being removed.

"Your timing is impeccable, Al." The pounding of my heart thundered in my ears, until it finally got so loud I decided the darkness wasn't such a bad thing after all.

Chapter 3

Corinth

I WOKE UP TO a muscle spasm in my left arm. Every part of me was sore, but at least I was alive. With great relief, I realized I was no longer on the table with the squeaky wheels. The pressure from the constricting band and the straps left phantom pains in my limbs. Sunlight streamed from the window through a slit in the curtains, reminding me of the bright flashlight that had been shoved in my face back at the warehouse. I cringed at the sudden thought, breathing hard against the wave of panic.

I wasn't in the Crescent Hotel, which meant I'd been moved to another one. I curled my outstretched fingers around the hilt of my blade, which sat on the nightstand between two queen beds. Hugging the dagger to my chest, I felt like a part of me had returned. I also didn't need to turn my head to know Larna was on the bed next to mine. I knew the curves of her face better than my own, down to every line and freckle. The curvature of her jaw always made me want to run my hand along it. Even the worry lines etched into the corners of her mouth and around her eyes were cute. These days, they seemed to be a permanent feature.

My first thought was thank God she was alive. My second was me wondering why Al wasn't here with us right now. To be clear, I was very much okay with that. For almost a full year, we'd been on our own. It was nice having Larna as a roommate, and honestly, I wanted us to be more than that. That was my problem: I felt guilty for even thinking about my best friend in a romantic way. The guilt stemmed from how I'd seen her look at him back when we were fighting Gabe at the cemetery. Something momentous had happened between them. It had brought them closer together because of it. That type of attraction was the stuff of legend. I know, because I felt that way about her too. Technically, I had asked her out long before Al came into the picture … so these thoughts of mine were completely normal. *And* he was the one who had upped and left us eight months ago. I was okay with being the swooper. He'd been the swooper when she'd arrived in London last year. Turnabout is fair play. Even though Al and I had worked well together in the past, that didn't mean I was his fan. He had still left us high and dry for months.

I snuck a quick glance at her. She looked older. And that was saying something, because she aged really, really slowly.

"*Coffffeeeeee …*" I begged.

There one second and gone the next, she moved with inhuman speed to stand over me. "You were in and out of it for a long time."

I relinquished my hold on the dagger only long enough to scratch at the scabbed-over cuts on my wrists. They itched. When I noticed her watching me, I dropped my arm back down. Sometimes the dagger made me feel like an addict reaching for their vice. I didn't want her to see the level of need I had for it in my body language.

"Where's Al?" I finally asked.

Her eyes widened, and her mouth opened and closed like a fish sucking air. "Alastair?"

"Well … by the look on your face that answers my question…" I let the sentence trail off and then, when I saw the glimmer of hope fade from her eyes, added, "He showed up during the final act to rescue me like a knight in shining armor. You're telling me he left again? That *a-hole* …" I said the last part trying to lighten the mood, but Larna flinched, letting me know it was out of line.

The last thing I wanted to do was make him look like the hero, but the part of me that wanted to put her at ease was too great. The incessant way she tried to tell me different meant how much she really needed him. It was exceedingly frustrating to want her to be happy—and not be the one who was the source of that happiness.

She plopped down at the end of my bed, and I almost flew off the other side. It was all that hard muscle she'd packed on. If someone had told me a year ago that she was going to be ripped, I would've laughed them off the face of the planet. Of course, the same could be said about me—minus the ripped part.

"I'm *so* sorry, Corinth. I thought that bounty hunter was taking you somewhere else. It turns out they were trying to lead me away so they could separate us. They tried to grab me. I almost … If Alastair hadn't been there to help—" Her voice hitched, and after she composed herself, she added, "Why wouldn't Alastair say something? No text, phone call, or communication in months, and now he suddenly shows up in time to save your bacon? Where's he been all this time? What does he have planned? Why wouldn't he tell me?"

"Didn't he say he was doing something for your father? Maybe this has something to do with that … or maybe brooding and mystery are a package deal when it comes to him." I tried to give her a reassuring smile, but I think it came out more as a grimace. "They fooled me too. I think we need to come up with a new plan though. This lying-low thing is *not* working." I stretched an arm over my head, noticing the nasty bruise in the crook of my elbow. It'd started to turn a gnarly purple and yellow that reminded me of the color of a faded tie-dye T-shirt. "Too bad I don't heal like you guys do, huh?" I said, half joking. "And what's the deal with Gabriel upping the price on my head?" I pointed to my face. "Pretty soon I won't be able to show this mug outside ever again. It might even be worse than having paparazzi stalk me." I paused and then said, "There's something else I didn't tell you."

Her head snapped up. "What?"

"One of them tried to compel me … and something happened." I rubbed my eyes, still not sure I even believed it myself. "I could see in the dark like it was daylight out. Everything was sharper and clearer. I felt more focused than I've ever felt in my entire life. It was almost as if I sucked the *Sight* right out of him like a leech—and then I compelled one of them."

Larna jumped up, pacing at this sudden revelation. "Why didn't you mention this first thing?" She seemed worried. After a few seconds of silent ruminating, she said, "You were able to compel a vampire … That's *huge*, Corinth …" She whirled around to face me. "What did you make him do?"

I shrugged. "I told him to untie me—and he did."

She held up a hand as if coming to some sort of realization. "Wait, you didn't have the blade on you. And if the dagger is supposed to imbue you with its magicalness—how were you able to reverse the compulsion? Or better yet, how are you able to use a vampire's *Sight* against them when you aren't even a vampire?"

I sat up straighter, wincing at even that small amount of movement. "Maybe it's a close-proximity thing? Or maybe the dagger changed me as soon as I took it from you at your mom's house? Or maybe I'm just really good at soaking up magic," I added dryly.

Larna raised an eyebrow. "You're telling me you don't think it's weird—all of this?"

"I have a magical dagger that gives me powers. You're a vampire, and you find that strange?" I ran a hand through my hair, mussing it up in agitation. "I wouldn't have even made a convincing street magician a few months ago. Hey, Mom, look at me now, I'm a vampire hunter …" I let the rest of the sentence hang in the air at seeing the look on her face.

Good one, Corinth … way to alienate your best friend, who just so happens to be a vamp.

"I didn't mean it like that. I would never hurt you."

She bit her lower lip and, after a painfully long pause, nodded. "I'll go get you some ice for your arm."

I stood to go to her, but as soon as I did, the room spun for one sickeningly long second. Larna was beside me in an instant. I admit it was cute the way she had to stand on her tippy-toes to help guide me back down to the bed. She was so short. I let my head fall back on the pillow, closing my eyes. When I opened them again, she was still leaning over me.

"Will you stop it?" I tried to cover my face, but she gripped my wrist and pulled it away right as my stomach growled.

It had been instantaneous, her hovering over me with nothing in her hands, and then, in that same millisecond holding out a carton of apple juice. Street performers everywhere would pay for this kind of flair and spontaneity. If I hadn't known any better, I'd say the drink had materialized out of thin air. I wasn't surprised by this sort of behavior. If you weren't privy to the whole vamp-speed thing, you'd never notice the hairbreadth's movement in the first place. Vamps were sneaky fast. Once I had recognized what that tiny pop of pressure was behind my eyeballs, I could sort of sense it coming. It was still not humanly possible to see everything in that peculiar blur of motion. No mortal brain could register that kind of speed.

My arm shot out right as she dropped the carton, her way of testing my coordination and agility, and I caught it deftly in one hand. She nodded her approval.

After struggling with the straw for one embarrassingly long second, Larna gently took the juice back from me and stuck the straw through the foil opening. It was small gestures like these that made me think she cared for me in the same way I cared for her—as in, more than just friends.

She handed it back to me. "Here."

I nodded gratefully, finishing it in two gulps. "Got any more?"

The pressure behind my eyes returned. This time, she was standing over me with a bottle of water. She dropped it. I grasped at empty air right before the bottle hit my stomach, groaning at the sudden unexpected weight.

"One out of two ain't bad," I muttered, and then drank it down, wiping my mouth on the sleeve of my shirt. "I think I lost weight on the donating-all-of-the-blood-in-your-body diet."

"I can see right through your jokes," Larna quipped, "and your ribs."

"I'm not that skinny," I muttered.

She grunted her disagreement, stalking to the other side of the room, and then sliding down the wall to the carpeted floor. *All doom and gloom*—her current mood, thanks to Al. I couldn't help but notice that she didn't use the bed next to mine. This was a rare moment to glimpse past that hard exterior of a wall she'd erected, locked, bolted, and threw away the key for since Al had left.

We were silent, thinking about the new turn of events, until I finally realized something. "Wait, how'd you find me if you never saw Al in the first place?"

She gestured to my wrist from her spot on the floor across the room. "Your watch went off. I was across town, dealing with the other bounty hunter, before I knew you were still back at the warehouse."

"Al must have gotten it back from the guy who grabbed me, and then signaled you with it. What about the cooler with my blood in it? Did you get it back?"

She whipped her head around to meet my stare, her eyes stretching wide. "What cooler? Two vamps were dead when I showed up, but there was no cooler ..." Her voice trailed off as she thought.

Using the bed frame for support, I stood and then slowly shuffled over to her, feeling a lot like someone who'd put way too many miles on their body for an eighteen-year-old. Slumping down to sit beside her, I draped my arm around her shoulders. She stiffened for a quick second and then melted against me. We still fit together. Moments like these made me think we could give us a second shot. We'd shared a pretty incredible kiss on our first date. I felt like we should explore more of that—

I shot a glance back to the dagger on the nightstand.

Dread welled up in the pit of my stomach. I licked my lips, which suddenly felt more like dried beef. I couldn't ignore the deep-seated hatred for a creature I *shouldn't* hate. I mean, I hated Gabriel Stanton, but for good reason. The urges for violence ran through my body like currents in an electrified fence.

If someone got close enough to me, they'd get fried. I knew it—I felt it deep in my bones.

What is wrong with me?

I couldn't get two feet away without having that incessant need to possess the dagger. I didn't even know how I'd managed to go for a walk without it. The itch was as convulsive as a worm wriggling in my gut. This feeling was exactly why I didn't pursue having the talk about a future with the *love* of my life. What was the point if I couldn't control the violent urges running through me?

I was so intently focused on the blade; I didn't realize Larna was staring at me until she spoke. "You think Alastair stole the blood because he was compelled to do it?" I could hear the tension tight in her voice.

I didn't want to be the bearer of bad news, but I also didn't think he'd been compelled either. "I can't be sure, but he didn't have to save my life. He could have just handed me over to Gabe," I said. "I think he took it for another reason, and that reason has to do with your father's last request."

Larna leaned her head against my shoulder and nodded as if willing herself to believe me.

We sat on the floor, silently comforting each other when I said, "Can we talk about the elephant in the room?" My eyes shot away from hers and back to the blade on the nightstand. "*Please?*"

She took notice, her eyes flashing. "You want me to tell you I'm concerned about that thing? Well, I am. I'm worried," she said. "That weapon has some strange power over you—I thought you were going to strike me down in the cemetery after you stabbed Gabriel with it. If I really believed you'd be safe at home, I'd send you packing right now. There is nowhere you can go without being found by someone wanting that damn blade. What you said about being a vampire hunter, that wasn't a joke."

"Finally, some honesty," I grumbled. "You think we're in over our heads? Because you're totally right," I teased. "But you're not the only one who is worried about someone else."

This time, she sat up and turned to me, hazelnut eyes meeting mine.

"I mean Vinson, by the way. I'm totally worried about that guy. Have you seen how much hair gel he uses? That can't be good for his hair."

She punched me on the shoulder, and I feigned a wince—okay, sort of feigned, it did hurt.

"I'm terrified Gabe will get his hands on you. Back at the warehouse, those guys threatened you." I cleared my throat. "They were planning on torturing the answer out of me. That psycho is obsessed with you. But I need you to know something … I will *never* sell you out. Not in a million years. They can play the most horrible instrument on the planet, the pan flute, until my ears bleed, and I'd never give you up."

I felt her body shake against mine, half-laughing, half-crying, as she swiped a hand under her nose.

"We can be each other's saviors," I said, "together." There are moments when you feel the electricity or spark with someone. It's a hard thing to find. When you do happen upon it, it's not something you should take for granted. I wanted more of this same feeling.

A second later, the moment was gone and she was pulling me to my feet. It still amazed me how strong she was. She led me to the bathroom and turned on the shower.

I pulled my stained and filthy shirt off, watching the steam fog the mirror. When I caught a glimpse of myself in it, I flinched. Now I knew why she looked so worried. My eyes were red rimmed and puffy, and I could see the outline of my ribs. The way my pants hung off my hips was an extreme indicator that I should eat soon. I'd been getting a lot leaner due to the working out, but now I just looked like a junkie—a junkie with a modicum of abs. I hadn't lost all of my gains.

Larna sucked in a deep breath at seeing the bruises and cuts on my chest. She placed a warm hand between my shoulder blades. I stilled, and gave a little gasp as her fingers skimmed over my injuries. Even though she was just taking inventory, her fingers left a tingling sensation across my chest in their wake.

"Your ribs are bruised. You have some abrasions that need some Neosporin, but other than that, dehydration is your biggest worry. I'll get you some more water and food."

I reached out, placing my hands on the tops of her

shoulders to look her in the eyes. "I'm fine." She watched as I reached down to pull my socks off. "You can stay in here with me if you want. But these pants are coming off in about two seconds."

Larna's cheeks flushed slightly. "Oh, yeah … sorry." She inched toward the door, but stopped and turned back to me, swallowing heavily. "You know it's okay if you're scared."

I was going to think of a joke or play it off but I realized we'd been through too much together. The way her face contracted a touch, a tiny shift in her countenance—well, to me, that shift spoke volumes. A rip could grow if you didn't patch it right away. She looked small and frail and fragile. Maybe she wasn't quite as shut off like a fortress of solitude as I had first thought. She always had such a presence about her, even when she was just my Larna Collins from small town, Texas.

I towered over her in the cramped space and, because I couldn't help it, I reached a hand out to trace a finger lightly along her jawline.

She jerked beneath my touch, squeezing her eyes shut—they trembled as moisture glistened beneath long eyelashes. And then, just like that, she was gone.

Chapter 4

Larna

BEING CRAMMED INTO THE same room with someone who had just shown romantic feelings for me was a little awkward. Corinth had been pretending to sleep for an hour, and I had been staring at my laptop without actually reading anything on it. My mind was playing leapfrog, jumping from thoughts of Alastair and then back to thoughts of Corinth. Why hadn't Alastair stayed? It was a nagging question that wouldn't let up anytime soon, I guessed. He'd been gone long enough for me to consider the possibility that he was dead. It was why recently I'd allowed myself to think about Corinth in a different light—the kind of starry-eyed way that led me into making mistakes, like not keeping a better eye on him.

And then there was the way Corinth put his hand on my chin. I liked it. That feeling left me confused and guilt-ridden.

Alastair and I had shared so much before he'd left— including that fleeting kiss at the churchyard. My heart yearned to know more about him, but he wasn't here; he'd left months ago and failed to stay in contact for whatever reason. I kept telling myself that my emotional turbulence had resulted from working so closely with Corinth over the past few months. Everything had been so much clearer back then.

But, when Corinth told me Alastair had saved his life back at the warehouse, I felt that spark for Alastair rekindle.

Even as hardened as I'd become over the past year, the thought of that kiss with Alastair before he'd left still buoyed me. It also left me in a state of worthless frustration. The mental image of Alastair cooking shirtless back at Nan's farm—before I was turned—was one of my most pleasant memories. Not because he had stellar abs (which he did), but because he had been so light and carefree—so full of life—and seeing him lose some of the heavy burden he always carried around with him was everything. I trusted Alastair, but that didn't mean I wasn't angry with him. He'd told me he needed to take care of something for my father. Alastair had a price on his head too. I prayed he hadn't been compromised. There was no one to watch his back.

My mind wandered back to the moment when I found Corinth on the surgical table. I shivered at the recollection. As soon as I'd gotten him back to the hotel, I'd filled him with as much fluids as I could get into him. I knew he would recover when he was able to keep it down. Corinth kept trying to convince me he was okay, but I knew better. The fake smile was his way of trying to deal with everything. We'd trained, hunted, and lived together, relying on each other for survival. He'd transitioned from computer geek to formidable fighter. With nothing better to do since we'd been in hiding, Corinth had trained day in and day out with the blade—and it showed: muscle corded his arms, back, and chest. I was impressed with how he'd gone from scrawny to lean.

I switched gears, thinking about Gabriel and his price on our heads. I was even more determined to find and kill him. My father's thirst for revenge and violence made a whole lot more sense now. I understood why he'd risked both my head and his to get at Gabriel, and in a weird way, I respected it.

My father's cabin had been gifted to me, but because we had been operating below the radar as of late, I wanted to make sure we didn't go there unless it was absolutely necessary. It was my place now, and I needed to make sure it stayed hidden—that, and I was afraid a place my father had lived in would bring back too many painful memories. I wasn't quite ready to confront them just yet.

My stomach rumbled, bringing me out of my reverie. We had been stuck inside this hotel room without any source of food. It was a good thing Paul and Vinson weren't as sought after as we were, and could help us remedy that. They were our only access to the outside world. Corinth was just as hungry, the sound of his stomach growling matching mine in intensity.

And then a knock sounded at the door. I was on my feet, gun in my hand, all in an instant. Surprisingly, Corinth was almost as fast—the dagger already in his grasp, he was quickly behind me a second later.

I put a hand out to motion him to put his weapon away. I didn't need to glance out of the peephole to know who it was. Paul had this particular aftershave he used, mixed with his choice brand of cigarettes, both of which made his scent unmistakable. I opened the door and quickly ushered him inside.

Paul's eyes darted from me and then back to Corinth. Once I closed the door and locked it behind me, I turned around and was met by Paul's twitching mustache and then his smiling face. It was like that thing had grown twice the size in a short amount of time, like a living organism.

His gaze fell on Corinth. "You look like shit, mate."

Corinth pointed at Paul's mustache. "Speaking of shit—what's that thing on your face?"

Paul snickered at his own expense, chucking a brown paper bag onto the end of the bed. "Curry for the lad, and type A for the lass."

I tucked my pistol back into my waistband, eagerly pulling the bag open and digging inside until I found what I was looking for—a container that held the one and only source of sustenance I needed right now. I tossed what remained inside of the bag to Corinth. His eyes were wide with hunger as he threw himself back down onto the bed, pulling out the naan bread and pitching it into his mouth. I don't think he even chewed before swallowing.

"You hear anything?" I asked, chugging down the contents inside the container. The refreshing warmth sent a shiver of pleasure down my spine. At one point in time, drinking blood would have grossed me out; now I only considered it like nectar for champions. It was what fueled me—what helped me keep Corinth alive. I couldn't apologize for that. I wondered if Corinth thought it was gross. I never heard him complain, but I did catch a few furtive glances in my direction from time to time.

The old Larna would have sent him packing a long time ago. My attempt at trying to keep him out of battle was only half-hearted though.

The darker side … *oh*, it wanted to *play*.

It was the part that lay dormant, patiently waiting for its call to action. The thing inside me wanted Corinth close, and that's what worried me most. Maybe his feelings for hunting vamps were just as intrinsic as mine were for ingesting iron. These were the dark thoughts I tried to keep at bay: There had to be a reason why everyone was so curious about his blood. It *must* taste different. He was different. I hated myself for not shutting these thoughts down quicker. What was wrong with me?

There was more than enough darkness to go around. He had his own lurking inside him too. I could sense his deep-seated need for the blade. We had only scratched the surface of what he was capable of. I was certain he was a lot more powerful than any of us knew, his abilities seeming to be like a string with no end. Sometimes I'd notice him get this strangely vacant look on his face. He'd already brought up the words *vampire* and *hunter* in the same sentence. What was I supposed to do with that?

Paul broke through my thoughts as he said, "No word from or about Alastair, but the price on your head went up." He shot a worried glance at Corinth. "The kid's too."

I handed the now-empty container to Paul, who would dispose of it for me—it wasn't a good idea to leave behind blood in hotel rooms, for the obvious reasons and also because we could be tracked by other vampires. They could sniff this stuff out from a mile away. I wiped a hand across my mouth, already feeling much better.

Paul twisted his hands together in agitation. "What did you two do?" he asked, concern creeping into his voice. "Vamps from all over the country are swarming around here like angry hornets. You kick the nest over or something?"

In between another big bite of chicken tikka, Corinth said, "Something like that."

I shot an angry glance in his direction. "*Yeah*. Corinth decided to get captured by the enemy."

Before Paul could answer, an alarm of warning went off in my head. The feeling of someone approaching our door from outside launched me into action. I quickly threw a finger in the air to stop them from saying anything else and shot forward, grabbing my gun from my waistband. Crouching beside the doorframe, I listened. Someone was out there, trying to mask the sound of their footfalls—and they were highly skilled.

Paul saw me react and moved at the same time, pulling something from the inside lining of his coat. He swung his arm down in one fluid motion and flicked his wrist, extending a folding baton to its full length. A deadly weapon, but still not as effective as a gun. In addition to being a badass, I knew he carried it to keep a lower profile because he still drove his cab—the Beetle.

He flicked a quick glance at me. "Vinson is meeting us. Could be him."

Whoever it was, they were now on the other side of the door, and they spoke through it. "Open door. I can hear you breathing."

Paul pulled the door open wide.

Even though Vinson was average build, he still made the hotel room look smaller as he marched inside. He was wearing camo pants, and I could just barely see the end of his rifle sticking out from underneath his long trench coat. He eyed my gun, Corinth's dagger, and Paul's extended baton, giving a quick nod of approval.

We filled him in on Alastair rescuing Corinth; Vinson

remained as inscrutable as he always did while he listened. After a few seconds, he said, "Alastair knows what he is doing."

I crossed my arms over my chest. "So you *have* heard from him?" It was annoying how I couldn't keep the apprehension and hope out of my voice.

Vinson grabbed a spot in the corner of the room, like a spider taking up residency, mimicking me by also crossing his arms over his chest. "No. But I did find Gabriel's weapons stash."

The wind rushed out of me as I felt both disappointed and elated that he had found one of Gabriel's hideouts. It was huge news. I ran a hand through my hair, suddenly feeling more optimistic. "Did you see Gabriel?"

He shook his head. "But he will come running if you take out his supply."

"So you're suggesting … what? We take out his facility. Isn't that an incredibly bold move?" Corinth asked. "Why not just take him out at his manor? At least we know he lives there."

Vinson glared at Corinth for a full minute before he said, "Very bold." His eyes narrowed. "And stupid. I have been watching heavily guarded manor—he is not there. You two not only stirred pot, you spilled it all over place and stomped around in its mess. Your only course of action is to take fight to him."

"How do you know this is his weapons stash?" I asked uncertainly.

He rolled his eyes as if I shouldn't even bother questioning him. "There is no one outside of warehouse. Many surveillance cameras on perimeter. Vehicles bring weapons in and out."

"How do we get in?" I asked. It made sense to bring the fight to Gabriel. We had been lying low for too long. Corinth had still gotten caught. None of us would be safe until we took him out. It was what my father had wanted. Not to mention we couldn't keep hiding forever. An image of Corinth splayed out on the table in the warehouse flashed behind my eyelids. Sometimes you had to fight in order to keep the ones closest to you safe.

Vinson pointed his chin at me and gave me a wicked grin. "If we highjack vehicle on way in, we can assume their spot. They won't see us approaching until much too late."

Corinth skillfully spun the dagger up into his hand, matching Vinson's wicked grin with one of his own. "I'm down."

"No. You're staying here." I threw him a glance and said sternly, "You need to rest."

He waved the blade at me. "I'm the one with the magical deadly weapon."

Vinson squinted at us both. "The kid will make good distraction. He comes with us."

"Fine," Corinth said, bouncing on the balls of his feet. "I'll be bait. Everyone knows what this baby face looks like, anyway. Of course, I would go so far as to say no one will be asking for my autograph anytime soon."

"What do we do after we get in the building?" I asked.

Vinson turned those wickedly, frightening eyes on me and growled, "Don't die.

Chapter 5

Larna

WE PACKED WHAT LITTLE we had and left it with Paul so we could regroup later. His job was to make sure the cabin was ready for guests. It would be our meet-up spot if things went sideways. He was also our getaway driver. It felt like old times again. Corinth pulled his bullet proof vest on and then threw a shirt on over that. He sheathed the blade and tucked it into the side of his belt.

"Why do you keep looking at me like I'm going to break?" he asked, glancing at me out of the corner of his eye. "I'm no porcelain doll, sweetheart."

"You sure about that?" I asked. "I saw those bruises … I just want to make sure you're okay with all of this …" The knife Alastair had given me was tucked into one of my vest pockets. I felt for the cool bone handle. Curling my fingers around it, I silently willed it to bring me calm before the storm. There was something comforting about having it in my grasp. It was like Alastair was here with me, rallying me on. Wherever he was, I hoped he was okay.

"I'm fine," Corinth said more loudly than necessary,

bringing me back to the present.

My gaze snapped to his honeyed eyes. "You've been through a lot in the last few days. You're still recovering—"

He cut me off, repeating, "*I'm fine.*" It came out sounding angry and rehearsed, as if he was trying to convince himself but was losing the battle.

Vinson walked into the room to grab the rest of our gear as Corinth pushed past me, but before he could storm off, I grabbed his arm. "You gotta do better than that, Taylor."

He ran a hand through his mop of hair, causing it to stand on end. I remembered how I used to love it when he did that. As a matter of fact, I still did. I had known him so long; his body language provided me with all the information I needed to know. It was telling me that he was frustrated, tired, and scared.

It took him a second, but when his eyes finally snapped up to meet mine, the fire in them was enough to convince me that he was ready. I let him go, trying to tamp down a sudden urge to knock him out and leave him behind. Yet here we were, about to rush right into the frying pan once again. I took only a small amount of comfort in knowing we might never get out of that pan alive. Maybe then I wouldn't have to deal with my burgeoning guilt. I missed Alastair. He had been gone so long, but now that I knew he was alive, well, it made that sinking feeling in the pit of my stomach that much worse. Was he still out there somewhere, fighting for our cause? Should I be doing more to find him? Were my conflicting emotions for Corinth only brought on because we relied so heavily on one another? I cursed myself inwardly for my ambivalence.

Vinson brushed past me, pulling me from my thoughts and back to the task at hand.

We needed something a little stealthier than the Volkswagen, so Paul had rented us a sleek SUV and left his baby parked at the cabin.

As we piled in, Vinson spoke up from the front seat. "You two are distraction. Once we're inside, you're on your own. I'll take out as many as I can. Once they see him, they'll go сумасшедший."

I didn't know what that last part was, but I was pretty sure it meant "crazy."

Corinth and I exchanged a glance. "He's talking about my fan club, right?"

"Get your head in the game," I told him. "This is no time for jokes."

He flashed me a lopsided grin. "There's always time for jokes and *games*."

After thirty minutes on a deserted highway, we were eventually deposited out onto a dirt road. Another half hour went by, and Paul finally pulled over in the middle of nowhere and swiveled around in his seat. "This is the spot, gentleman ... *and* lady."

Grabbing my bag of goodies—by *goodies*, I meant "dangerous weapons"—I threw it over my shoulder and got out.

Paul nodded at each of us in turn. "I'll see you lot soon. Okay?"

Paul was the one person who seemed to bring back the most painful and yet achingly satisfying memories of my father. His story of how my dad saved his life struck a chord. I had had so few of those moments with my father, and now I wanted to hoard those recollections like a pirate hoarding treasure. Paul was proof of how unyielding, brave, and amazing my father had turned out to be. Even as a blood-craving vamp. It gave me hope that maybe I wouldn't turn out so bad either. Paul was my father's best friend, and that made him as close to family as Corinth was to me.

He stuck his hand out for me to shake, but instead, I yanked him into a tight hug. After a second, he pulled back to clap me on my shoulders, his mustache twitching and eyes shining.

"Thanks, Paul … for everything. We'll see you soon."

Not wanting to draw out the moment, because this wasn't going to be our last goodbye, I turned around before he could say anything. It wasn't his style to respond, anyway; he was the strong, silent type.

"Oi!" He called out after me. I turned back to see him pulling out a pack of smokes from his pocket. "Alastair knows what he's doing, love." He threw a cigarette into his mouth. "Don't you worry about him—he'll be back when he's good and ready."

I nodded my thanks as he turned to walk back to the SUV, grumbling under his breath, "I still think this plan is the worst."

Keeping the headlights off, he maneuvered back onto the roadway without a backward glance. His headlights disappeared around the corner, shrouding us in darkness.

Corinth said, "Someone please explain to me why I'm always the victim in these scenarios?"

"Because you volunteered, and you're so good at it," I quipped.

He stuck his tongue out at me and moved to the center of the roadway, Vinson following him. "You need to make it look convincing," Vinson said in his stilted English. "They will be distracted by smell of human blood."

Human, all alone … Who could resist such a tempting snack?

Even though the stars had been swallowed up by the night sky, I could still see Corinth's eyes on me all the way across the road.

He knew I could hear him whisper, "Get a look at Sirius, Collins." He drew in a sharp breath. "All stars shine, but not like the Dog Star."

Sirius is one of the brightest stars out there. Corinth always pointed to this star first, it being his favorite. It came from the Greek word Seirius—meaning "scorching."

I heard the soft thrum of bronze clearing leather as he drew the dagger out of its scabbard.

A moment later, Vinson joined me in the overgrown brush across the road. We wouldn't be visible from the path in this spot. Someone could be standing on top of us and they wouldn't see us. I tried concentrating on anything other than the fact that I was sure the blade would end up turning Corinth into a mindless zombie.

Above us a shadowed outline of a plane cut a path through the darkened sky, reminding me that we were still on the outskirts of the city, even though it felt like we were on another planet altogether. The crickets seemed to keep better company than Vinson. In fact, he was so quiet I wasn't sure he was even breathing. Yes, that included using my super-hearing. His skill level when it came to stealth was one I'd never achieve.

Meanwhile, Corinth had propped his head up on an arm. An hour passed with still no sign of oncoming traffic, and in his impatience, he sat back up, playing with a blade of grass and occasionally slapping himself, cursing about mosquitoes being worse than vamps.

With nothing else to do but dwell on thoughts of the past, my mind flung me into a barrage of vivid memories of Corinth lying on the table in the warehouse—his face drained of color from extreme blood loss. It made me shudder, thinking about how slack and lifeless he'd been when I'd carried him out of the warehouse. I shook my head, trying to shake off the macabre thoughts. *Did Alastair steal his blood?* Even though Paul had told me to trust Alastair, I found I was doing the opposite. I had this nagging feeling that maybe he had been compromised— ever since Gabriel had compelled him to do his bidding, it had become a very real possibility that it could happen again. This was my biggest fear. He had intentionally left us out of his plan. Did he not trust me?

Thoughts of Alastair were only going to distract me further from the task at hand, so I tuned them out and sought the source of my *Sight*. I immediately drew comfort from the sudden arrival of its presence. Did Gabriel feel like this when he sought his *Sight* too? Had this darker side overtaken him? Or was it more gradual? What if his other half was the one controlling him? Maybe over time this was what happened to everyone who was turned. *No ...* he *was* a psychopath hell-bent on tormenting everyone in his path. There was no remorse or humanity left in him. He'd proven that when he'd brutally killed my father in front of me. There was a tiny niggle at the back of my mind, though, that said if I wasn't careful, I could become him.

As two more hours passed, I could sense Corinth's tension from all the way across the road. Even though he looked like he was at ease, his rigid posture said otherwise. He slapped at a spider and then stretched out, placing his hands behind his head to gaze up at the dark, cloudless sky.

I wondered if he was thinking about our name-the-stars ritual. We'd gotten good at identifying the constellations. Now, as I also gazed up at the tree-lined sky, I realized we were on opposite ends of the spectrum from each other—he was slayer and I was vampire—and yet I felt more connected to him than ever before. He didn't quite fit. I didn't quite fit. How had he used vampire *Sight* without the blade? As vampires, we had this strange ability to tap into a kind of sixth sense. It was what separated us from humans. Well, that and the drinking blood part. I'd been thinking about this a lot lately. I sensed the supernatural in him. Even though we shared most everything with each other, I hadn't been able to find the right words to admit any of this to him. Was it the dagger's control I sensed?

Vinson finally stirred, and because I'd forgotten he was beside me, I almost went flying into the air like a startled cat. He whipped his head around and put a finger to his lips.

I took a moment to listen and then heard what he'd heard: the sound of a car's engine, followed by tires on gravel. We crouched down lower, and I coughed, giving Corinth the signal.

After a sharp intake of breath, I smelled fresh blood. It instantly put me on edge as Corinth flipped back over onto his stomach, hiding the blade underneath his shirt.

The color of the car was a deep green so rich it

blended in perfectly with the night around us. It came to a complete stop in front of Corinth, its headlights lighting up his body in an eerie afterglow. It upset me to see him in such a vulnerable position. I knew it was ten times harder being the cover than playing the bait, but I didn't even know I'd inched forward until Vinson motioned for me to stop.

I could just make out the outline of three people's heads inside the car. When no one made a move to exit, I realized they could be calling for backup. If they did that, we were done before we even started.

After what seemed like an eternity, the right-front passenger stepped out. She was petite and mousy and not at all like I expected one of Gabriel's people to look like. Of course, he had tried to recruit me—and I definitely didn't look like one of his cookie-cutter models, with their made-from-the-same-mold rock-hard abs. This woman appeared to be as unassuming as a teacher. I guessed she had been turned in her mid-twenties, and her brunette hair was stretched into a tight bun at the top of her head. The form-fitting black attire showed off her trim figure. She sniffed at the air like a bloodhound, and then turned excitedly back to her companions, who were still in the car, to give them a quick thumbs-up.

Spinning back around to her prey, she inched closer, but this time a lot less cautiously, while the others stayed put, guarding their precious cargo, no doubt.

The woman was almost close enough to touch him now. She cocked her head to the side, listening, and so did I.

Surely Corinth's racing heart was going to give us away.

Her mouth twitched up at the corner, but the smell of his blood proved to be too much for her to resist, because with surprising speed and strength, she was flipping Corinth onto his back. I hadn't noticed the thin blade clutched in her pale hands until it was too late. My insides turned to ice, and I quelled the cry of warning that bubbled up in my throat.

This had all been part of the plan. I had to trust Corinth could take care of himself for now. Fighting the impulse to go to him first, I took the lead, jumping up from my hiding spot to fly toward the back passenger. Hopefully, our appearance would be enough of a distraction for Corinth to react.

I was pretty sure that Gabriel's vehicles had bullet-proof glass, so I didn't go for my gun immediately. Instead, I let my *Sight* take over. By the time I arrived at the car in my current state of rage, I ripped the back door open, glad that modern door locks didn't have anything on vampire strength. It must have been quite the sight, because even the passenger looked too stunned to react.

The driver, a wily-looking teen with honey-colored skin, stomped on the gas as Vinson popped the driver's side door open, catching him by surprise. The goal was to keep the car in as good a condition as possible so we could use it to drive into the compound, hopefully without them noticing a few minor dings and dents. At this rate, we would be lucky if the car stayed in one piece. I felt fairly certain that I could fix the door later.

Vinson grabbed the steering wheel with both hands, yanking on it at the same time as he clocked the driver across the face. The kid's head bounced off the steering wheel, causing him to reflexively stomp on the gas. The screech of tires tearing at gravel was deafening as the car shot forward—right for Corinth.

Please hold out until I can get to you.

As we rocketed forward, I clung to the car's roof, giving the guy in the back seat enough time to recover from his initial shock. I would have gone for my own weapon, but I was hanging on for dear life. There was a bright flash and then the sensation of being hit in the chest with a baseball bat. The blast was enough to knock my already-tenuous grip loose. Centripetal force kept me glued to the side of the car as it swerved to the right. The young driver overcorrected, proving that gravity was fickle as we careened first one way and then back the other, reaching dangerous speeds. I tumbled over the top of the roof and went airborne. You don't realize how long a second is until you're cruising through the air without wings. I flew right over both Corinth and the woman currently attacking him. As if in slow motion, I watched the bun-headed woman start to plunge the thin blade down toward his chest.

And then Time's hasty return brought me crashing back down to the earth like a bottle rocket. I skidded and rolled across gravel and dirt, skinning everything right before blacking out. When I came to, I couldn't feel anything below my waist. Patchy black spots floated across my vision. The only thing I could move was my head, and I almost wished I couldn't, because Corinth was getting his ass handed to him. There was nothing I could do but stare helplessly at him while my body went through the slow and painful process of healing.

Wild, wispy tendrils of hair clung to the vamp's forehead as she crouched over Corinth. No longer a mousy teacher, she was a demented wolf with eyes flashing her murderous intent. I'd never seen him beat a vamp using pure strength. I had to hand it to him; he was holding his own against her.

Even after eight months of learning to adjust to miraculous healing, it was still odd—that sharp tearing of muscle and sinew, of tendons kneading and knitting themselves back together again. Intense pain tore through me and then rapidly vanished, as if I'd never been hurt in the first place.

Please, Corinth, hang on until I can move again.

I was so focused on Corinth it wasn't until I felt the cold steel press against my temple that I realized I'd made a grave error. With eyes crossed slightly, I fixated first on the chrome barrel of the handgun and then the person holding it. The back seat passenger who I'd been fighting was wearing one of those brightly knitted red beanies. His eyes lit up like dwarf stars.

There was a tiny millisecond of space right before he pulled the trigger that I managed to operate in. The small smile playing on his lips said, "I won." But in that same infinitesimal moment, my *Sight* took over—primal, alien instinct—giving me more than enough time to slam my palm against the side of the gun. It exploded in his hands, the discharge singeing the side of my face. A cloud of gunpowder smoke drifted past me, carried on a gentle breeze. The guy on top of me tried to push himself back down at the same time as I let out a roar of rage and kicked up. My foot connected with his groin and he grunted in pain. I had spent hours and hours practicing drawing my gun from my vest—and because of this training, my Sig was in my hand, lightning quick as I emptied a full magazine into his gut.

The overly bright red beanie soared into the air in a hauntingly bizarre tableau as he fell backward, as still as a corpse.

Without wasting another second, I turned to Corinth, who was now losing ground. It brought back flashbacks of Gabriel standing over my father with his sword pointed at him.

Blood dribbled down his arm in a steady stream. I was going to witness another death of someone I loved, and I wouldn't be able to stop it from happening, just like last time.

Chapter 6

Larna

SHE PLUNGED HER KNIFE down right as Corinth's eyes filled with lightning and fire and doom, the kind of end-of-the-world glory you only see in movies. I almost skidded to a halt at his complete overhaul in appearance. Actually, if I hadn't been heading in that direction like a torpedo, I might have tucked tail and run away in the opposite direction. Somewhere in the span of a few seconds, he had managed to make it to his knees, which was impressive considering he'd been on his back only moments before. Even though it was apparent Corinth was stronger than usual, he was still weakening.

The knife missed its intended target, burying itself all the way up to the hilt into the hard-packed dirt beside Corinth's thigh. The mousy-looking woman-turned-wild-animal let out a feral scream.

I willed myself to move faster, feeling the effects of my newly healed legs returning to full strength. At least I still had eyeballs in my sockets—his normally chestnut-colored eyes were completely gone—replaced by blinding light as bright as a thousand blow torches. It definitely wasn't

Vampire *Sight* possessing him.

I also assumed the vamp knew who she was fighting and had decided to try a different tactic. So when she abandoned the buried blade, I tried to shout a cry of warning. The woman let out a high-pitched wail and went straight for Corinth's neck, her teeth latching on to him with so much force that I thought she might have snapped him in two.

Corinth's arms flailed uselessly out to his sides as the woman's hold tightened. I collided with her, and it felt like hitting the side of a building. We toppled over one another, a tangle of arms and legs, until we fetched up in a ditch at the side of the road. Up close, she was smaller than I originally thought. Underestimating anyone in the vamp world was a huge mistake. Strength was gained through age and experience, not youth or size. You could be big or tall or small or scrawny and still be powerful.

Her hair hung down in wet clumps, framing a pear shaped face. She swatted at a lock of it as she got back to her feet. When her eyes flicked to meet mine, the maddening grin she wore, widened. By the way she was smiling, I figured Corinth's blood tasted as rejuvenating as every vamp had been imagining it would. It took me a moment to realize what she'd done. Corinth's blood. This had been the question I'd asked myself over and over again. What happened to a vamp when they sampled it?

I cracked my knuckles, ready for the fight, but instead of her coming at me again, her grin melted and she bent over at the waist, clutching her abdomen in apparent pain. She let out a spine-tingling howl and fell to her knees. "Help … me …" she gasped, spitting up blood. It dribbled down her chin as I stood rooted to the spot, unable to do anything except watch in captivation as her entire body shook with tremors. She curled into a ball, seizing until finally—after what seemed like an eternity of pain—she went still, her chest rattling as she tried to suck in her last breaths.

The sudden alarm of my inner voice struck as the hairs on my arms and the back of my neck stood on end. Everything inside me screamed not to turn around.

I did anyway.

Corinth was behind me, a hand clamped to the wound on his neck where the vamp had latched on to him. I stood mesmerized by the light dancing in his empty sockets. It almost made me want to sway like a cobra before a snake charmer. The edge of the blade glinted in the moonlight as his fingers tapped against the handle. I didn't dare move or breathe. The holes in his head, black as night, sent a shiver of dread running through me. Without eyes, I couldn't tell if he could even see me or not. It made me think of a character from a video game I used to play, *Mortal Kombat*—Raiden, God of Thunder. There was no slight curve of his lip, the sign of his usual cocky smile, only the hardening around the edges of his mouth to show confliction on who he might kill first. Ice-cold fear paralyzed me at seeing that hostile expression painted on his face.

Maybe he sensed the *other* inside me, as I sensed the *thing* inside him. There was a sudden uneasiness of my *Sight* unfurling, as if it, too, recognized something very wrong.

Corinth spun the dagger up into his hand and I flinched. I couldn't kill or hurt him no matter what he did to me. I wanted to put a hand out to try to talk some sense into him; however, the words I wanted to say evaporated on my tongue.

Fortunately, he didn't seem that interested in slaying me just yet. His head swiveled slowly as it settled on his intended target: the not-so-threatening elfin vamp at his feet. She was still down for the count, but now she only seemed fragile and weak.

I don't know why I didn't stop him as he marched past me to kneel next to her.

Violence was more my thing than his.

I mean, yes, he would do what he had to do to stop a threat, but he wasn't a cold-blooded killer. He was sweet and funny and kind. He was *my* Corinth. I'd accepted violence as part of the package deal when I'd been turned. Vampires craved each other's blood, always chasing that feeling of youth and vitality, and not just because we needed it in order to survive. It was addicting and vital and out of this world. Corinth, on the other hand, didn't need to kill, and he certainly didn't drink blood for sport or survival.

An urge to stop him swelled up inside me like a raging storm. I knew in my heart that if I didn't stop him now, I would lose him forever. Besides—call it self-preservation— if he started offing vamps, he might just start taking a liking to it. Would *it* consume him? So far, he'd only killed Sherry. She'd been determined to take me out, and even though he had killed her to save my life, I think that act had tormented him more than he let on. He'd tried to kill Gabriel, but had failed in doing so.

I wouldn't let him kill her.

He turned his head toward me, as if he knew I would try to stop him. I inched nearer, hoping he could see my empty hands. When I was close enough to touch him, I crouched down. His hand stilled midair. The skin around his mouth tightened a considerable degree, a sign that he still perceived me as a threat. I listened to the slowing of the woman's heartbeat. She was dying. This was a definite violent reaction to drinking his blood. I ashamedly admitted to myself that this could have been me. I'd thought about sampling it on more than one occasion; Corinth had even offered to donate some to me when I was at a low point. I could have said yes.

I heard Vinson behind me, deliberately not masking the sound of his footfalls so that I knew he was approaching. I put a hand out to stop him from coming any closer. If anyone could pose a threat, it was Vinson.

Corinth's head jerked around at Vinson's sudden arrival. I took the distraction to wind my fingers around his hand still on the handle of the dagger. His eyes had been replaced with radiant light so hypnotic I almost got lost in them. He tensed, and I could see the sharp lines and contours of his shoulders set back in determination. I wondered if this was what it felt like to be on the other end of my *Sight*—like a moth to a flame.

"Don't go all dark side on me, Taylor," I urged. "Come back, bud."

He gave a minute shake of his head, as if he recognized my voice, but the squaring of his shoulders told me he wasn't quite ready to come back just yet. My hair stood on end as the air thickened around us with the sudden influx of static electricity. I had this strange feeling that if I took my hand off his, I'd be blown to bits. Bringing him back from these trancelike states seemed to get harder and harder. Maybe this would be the last time before he vacated the premises for good.

"I know you're in there, Corinth." I motioned to the dying vamp at his feet. "Look at her."

He turned and then cocked his head to the side as if he was indeed studying her.

"You got her, Ringer." The word Ringer threatened to get caught in my throat. "Remember ... your handle for every game you play—Ringer," I echoed. "I used to change it to Flinger when you weren't looking, because I knew how much you hated it."

Corinth squeezed his eyes shut, his knuckles turning white against the bronze handle. I found my own fingers tightening around his. I needed to ground him to something other than the blade—hoping he would feel the warmth in my gesture. I could see fluttering behind his eyelids, as if he was trying to recall the memory. It seemed like an infinitely long time, but eventually, he opened his eyes, and when he did, I realized with great relief that they were back to their normal coffee-colored hue, albeit now swimming with tears.

I threw my arms around him, and he returned my hug with surprising strength. I pulled back, searching his eyes. "You all there?"

He arched a grateful eyebrow. "Thanks to you."

I felt relief but also an overwhelming sympathy well up at the thought of him dealing with this all on his own. At least I had had help with my change. It was why my connection with Alastair was so profound. We were made from the same mold. I didn't want Corinth to fall into the same vat and come out all warped like me.

"Your blood is toxic ... Your eyes did this weird thing ..." I let the sentence trail off, thinking about the implications. It was obvious that this was not just about a dagger, unless it could change his genetic makeup; there was something else going on with him that we needed to get to the bottom of. I kept an arm wrapped over one of his shoulders until the tension started to drain out of him.

He swallowed heavily and then glanced down at my hand still on his.

I sensed Vinson behind me, and I wondered if his face was stoic as usual, even after having witnessed Corinth's newfound abilities.

Suddenly the woman at Corinth's feet bolted upright, scrabbling at her throat in terror. She seized his shirt in one hand before letting go and falling backward into the waist-high grass. I listened to her heart as it slowly stopped beating.

Vinson leaned over me, looking down at her with steely coal-black eyes. "Lesson learned. Don't drink kid's blood." He disappeared and then reappeared next to the car we were about to procure. It had rolled to a stop in a ditch behind us, but was thankfully still drivable.

As Vinson worked on cleaning up our mess, I helped Corinth back to his feet and then grabbed our bags from the spot we'd hidden them in. Pulling out a first aid kit, I met Corinth across the road to lead him around to the front of the car so he could see by the headlamps. I didn't need them, but I figured it would make him more comfortable. He reached out, plucking a stray leaf from my hair, and then held his arm out for me without comment. I could see where he had cut himself and that it was now filled with gravel and dirt from the scuffle.

I was more worried about the bite marks on his neck, so I started with that first, gently moving his head to the side so I could get a better look at it. The sight of his blood was a lot less appetizing now that I knew what happened to a vamp if they sampled it. He didn't flinch at my touch—he only closed his eyes and let me work.

After a while, he said absently, "You know, you're just as skilled in the medical field as your mom."

I placed gauze on his neck and started taping it in place, smiling sadly at the mention of my mother. I used to sit glued to my seat for hours watching my mom patch people up at the hospital. "Yeah well, you're giving me enough practice these days." I paused briefly and then added, "I thought I was going to be a doctor one day. Whenever I visited my mom in the hospital, I'd ask her a ton of questions about treating patients ..." My voice trailed off as I met his empathetic gaze. He seemed to know exactly where I had been going with that statement. We'd both expected different things after high school.

"It doesn't look too deep," I noted crossly. "You're lucky."

He nodded his thanks but was oddly serious, perhaps deep in thought about what had just happened to him.

"You scared me back there ..." My hand stilled on his chest and I gestured to his eyes. I was afraid of what I might see in them, so I glanced away to add another piece of tape to the bandage on his arm. It wasn't until I felt him push a locket of my hair behind my ear that I finally looked up to meet his intense gaze.

My cheeks lit up, and I backed away from him, clearing my throat. "That was quite the meteorological effect you had going on back there," I persisted, trying to coax his thoughts out of him once again. "You want to talk about it?"

He lifted his shoulders. "I'm—"

But before he could finish what he was going to say, Vinson appeared out of thin air to stand beside me. "Let's go."

"Do you think they heard us?" I asked Vinson.

Vinson grunted. "I'd be surprised if Queen of England didn't hear us."

I motioned to Corinth's blade, strapped at his thigh. "Maybe not use the dagger until we can figure out what's going on with you."

Corinth said, "Way ahead of you there."

He had grown the past few months. "You wear confidence well," I told him.

Corinth winked at me. "I wear a lot of things well—including my birthday suit."

"There he is … He's back." I muttered to myself, "Why was I even worried?"

We loaded our things into our commandeered ride, and I got behind the wheel. I wanted to call it all off, but we needed to make a stand. This was about getting Gabriel's attention. Our message: back off or we'll keep coming after you. We were going to at least put a dent in his enterprise.

It was time to make a stand.

Corinth popped his head into the back seat before he got in, glancing around. "Looks cozy," he said. "You sure you're up to driving on the other side of the road?"

"Get in," I barked. "Did you find anything in the car?"

Vinson was already in the front seat next to mine by the time Corinth shoved himself into the back seat. He held up a remote for me to see. "Only this in console. All three clan members are dead, so we can't ask them what they were doing. Most likely they were going in to pick shipment up and take out."

Corinth raised a teasing eyebrow as he watched me pull the driver's seat all the way up to the steering wheel. "Maybe they called for an Uber?"

"I guess we'll find out once we're inside," I said through clenched teeth.

Because Vinson had been here before, he knew exactly where to direct me. He pointed to the road in front of us. As we headed out, I couldn't help but feel the paranoia start to creep in. There could be low-lying aircraft, drones, or an army of vampires clad all in black blocking our path. To my relief though, nothing like that awaited us. In fact, when we pulled up to an ordinary-looking gate with no signs of life nearby, my anxiety only seemed to increase. There were no lights on or around the place to suggest this was a business. Maybe Gabriel had gotten word by now that we were coming. Or maybe they had heard us and were all lying in wait … Maybe we'd roll right on in to an ambush as soon as we got in.

I pushed the button on the remote anyway.

Chapter 7

Corinth

MY NECK STILL BURNED from where I'd been bitten. I couldn't help but shudder at what had happened to that vamp after she'd sampled some of my blood. I wasn't sure exactly what had happened when she had tried to kill me—I snapped. Sweat pooled under my arms at the thought of losing control. How could I watch my comrade's backs when I was a possible threat too? One thing was for certain—I would have to deal with this later. For now, I needed to stay focused on the task at hand. Larna trusted me to hold it together.

The soft hum of the motor starting up and sliding the gate open on well-oiled hinges brought me out of my rampant thoughts. *Access granted.* Inside the gates, well-worn tracks paved a path for us through overgrown grass and thick weeds. We didn't speak, mostly because I could feel the tension building between us. My chest tightened at the thought of the unknown.

Once around the side of the building, the graveled path led to an enclosed circular lot. The structure we'd arrived at was massive and had at least three levels to it—

not including a possible basement. Vinson had given us what little intel he'd gathered from his recon missions. The layout inside was still a mystery.

Even though fifty thousand layers of paint had been slopped over ordinary beige cement siding, the building itself looked solidly built. It was all concrete and brick and rebar. At the back, where we'd come to a stop, was a service entry for trucks and cars. Ramps led to a set of closed-off freight doors.

Vinson pointed at the ramps. "They drive in through there."

Larna glanced at Vinson. "Should I drive up now?"

He shook his head. "Nobody move."

A few minutes went by as we anxiously sat waiting on something to happen, and then a soft scrape in the quietude brought me fully to attention. The doors rolled to the top in a high-pitched whine of metal on metal. After a second, a guy wearing all black poked his head out to wave us inside.

Your car service is right on time, sir. Nothing unusual going on here …

Once we pulled all the way inside, the doors closed behind us with an eerie finality.

No turning back now.

Large open space, polished concrete floors, warehouse full of unpacked crates—evil lair—check. In some ways, Gabe was just as predictable as he claimed *we* were. This act of defiance was about our unpredictability.

As the sound of the engine faded away, we heard the scuff of work boots squeaking across polished concrete floors, heading in our direction. Suspicions might have been high, since we weren't getting out of the car right away. Scanning the area, I noticed the row upon row of wooden crates of varied sizes stacked throughout the complex—a labyrinthine maze full of supplies. Vinson pointed to a set of double doors twenty yards ahead of where we'd parked. "Whatever you do, don't go that way." He nodded to another set of doors about thirty yards in the opposite direction. "I'm going in there. Stall them as long as you can."

"Indiana Jones would have had a field day in here," I whispered under my breath.

Larna's eyes darted around the warehouse, analyzing and assessing. "No, Indy would probably be more concerned about what was inside those crates—whereas *we* should be more concerned about our exit strategy."

My eyes stayed locked on the big red EXIT sign above the door Vinson had said he would be going through.

Noticing the direction of my gaze, Vinson said, "That door leads to roof—meet me up there in twenty minutes."

By my count, there were twelve guards patrolling the immediate area—all of which had big ugly-looking machine guns. I adjusted the dagger at my hip, but I didn't unsheathe it, opting to use my handgun instead. The loss of control I'd felt earlier was enough to convince me of that. I wasn't sure if I could control it enough not to hurt Larna in the chaos.

"Welcome to the hornets' nest," I murmured. "We'll stall them as long as we can, Vinson."

"Remember what I said," he whispered sternly. "Twenty minutes *exactly*."

I spoke out of the side of my mouth. "Yeah, yeah … We're the distraction. You sure you know what you're doing?"

Vinson slung his backpack over his shoulder and gave us a maniacal grin. "I'm not idiot with explosives."

I didn't like the fact that he had enough C-4 strapped to his back to take down the entire building, but *he* sure did.

The guy who let us in had decided to investigate, probably wondering why we were just sitting here. His curly dark hair flopped into his eyes as he strolled closer to the driver's side window, where Larna sat.

Waving his hands in the air at us, he shouted, "Jessie, you're in the wrong spot again, mate; you're supposed to load up over there!" He pointed across the way, toward the other end of the warehouse. When he was close enough, I could see half his face was disfigured by a zigzagging scar down the side of his neck; it stood out against copper-colored skin. I guessed he'd been injured before he'd been turned. His close-set eyes narrowed as he rapped on the window.

Larna gave Vinson a small nod right as she opened her door. The scarred vamp stepped back, motioning with his rifle for her to get out. We were enemy number one, our faces plastered everywhere. Hence, *distraction*. He took one flustered look at her as she pulled the door open, and his face morphed, his mouth dropping open. He started to shout a cry of warning, but Larna's knife shot through his throat before he could even get one word out. Add another scar to the collection, except this one probably wouldn't heal. His knees buckled, and I watched in rapt awe as she grabbed the muzzle of his weapon to silently guide him to the ground. It never ceased to amaze me how proficient she'd gotten at fighting.

I hadn't even taken a breath before she was on the

move again, closing her knife, the one with the bone handle, to stow it back in one of her vest pockets.

Two more vamps popped out of nowhere, pointing their rifles at us as they shouted in unison, "*HOLD IT RIGHT THERE!*"

Vinson had already vanished without me even seeing him move; as smooth and stealthy as a military-minded ghost. The only sign he'd slipped through the set of double doors in front of us was that they now stood slightly ajar.

The timer on my watch was set for twenty minutes— I started it, thinking this would probably be the longest twenty minutes of my life. Two more goons ran toward us as I spilled out of the car, pulling my cap down low over my eyes.

I lived for the dramatic reveal.

In the privacy of many, many hotel rooms over the past eight months, I'd learned to get comfortable with guns. Disassembling, cleaning, dry-firing—it's good training to practice with no bullets so you don't trick yourself into jerking the weapon off target at the last second when you do use live fire. Falling to a knee, I swung my pistol out in front of me: elbows locked, finger on the trigger, lungs emptied. I closed an eye, centered the three dots on the first bad guy I saw, and gently pulled back on the trigger. I missed. Vamp super-speed be damned—I should have been aiming for the future, not the present.

Bullets started flying—and so did I, quickly ducking back behind the car as a hail of gunfire ricocheted off the car's trunk, where I'd just been standing a moment before.

Larna was up and over the hood of the sleek sedan, beside me in a flash of movement as more rounds slammed into the spot she'd just occupied. "I knew it was bullet-proof," she hissed. "We got more company. I don't think we can hold them off much longer … How much time is—"

"You keep messing up my hair moving that fast!" I shouted out of the side of my mouth. "*Not cool!*"

"You're wearing a baseball cap, *Ringer!*" she bantered.

Back in slowville, where I lived, I managed to lunge forward, throwing myself behind the hood of the car, using the engine block for cover. Popping back up, I shot off a few more rounds. Even though I was trying to use my ammo sparingly, I still managed to empty my entire magazine in what felt like seconds. A dude with a crown of ginger hair poking out of the back of his black hat hit the ground hard. I took the smallest amount of pleasure seeing his buddy's face go red with rage.

That is, until he swept his gun in my direction and opened fire. Larna saw it and pulled me out of the way right at the last second as the bullets smacked into the sedan.

I dropped to all fours, shoving my gun under the car to aim at the pair of legs opposite us. I fired, and then I heard a squeal of pain shortly after.

Larna, deep in concentration, slid from one knee to the other; an expert markswoman. I couldn't help but notice her level of skill as she closed one eye and emptied the rest of the magazine, taking down two more vamps closest to us. It went on like this as we played a deadly game of "Pop Goes the Weasel" until she grabbed my shirt collar, hauling me into the back seat of the sedan.

She jumped behind the steering wheel as another hail of gunfire struck the windows. Fortunately for us, they only rattled ominously and didn't break. There were so many rounds flying I was pretty sure the car, doubling as a reinforced tank, wasn't going to hold together for much longer.

Larna turned the engine over and it sputtered back to life. "*Hold on!*" She hit the gas hard. The car careened sideways, and for a split second, the wheels spun as if in a cartoon, slowly gaining traction and then surging forward as the tires left behind a trail of burned rubber in their wake.

We almost plowed through a couple of vamps, but they had jumped out of the way at the last second to avoid the impact.

Because bullets were flying and chaos reigned down around us, Larna hit a crate the size of an elephant, and the car slid to a bone-crushing halt against the side of it, a cache of heavy-duty-looking artillery spilling out like candy from a piñata. My head smacked into the back of a headrest, and sharp pain lanced down my neck. The ginger with the unruly mop of hair I'd shot earlier, grabbed a bazooka from the pulverized remains and took aim at us.

"The car is reinforced, but not *that* reinforced," Larna cried. "We need to move! Now!"

It was both terrifying and captivating, the power she possessed. By the time the pain in my head subsided, she was already out of the car and dragging me to safety right as our stolen ride exploded. The world tilted around me like I was in one of those spinning funhouse tunnels. I was out cold, and it could have been minutes or only a few seconds, but the sound of an alarm going off finally brought me back to the waking world once again. When the incessant beeping didn't stop, I looked down in a daze to discover the timer had gone off on my watch. Twenty minutes was up.

"It's time to split!" I yelled, holding up my wrist.

She emptied the rest of her gun into the head of one of the goons who had come running around the side of the crate.

The next thing I knew, my legs were being pulled out from under me.

I saw a burly black beard first, followed by gargantuan thumbs as they clamped around my throat, squeezing viciously. I thrashed out as my attacker pulled me roughly to my feet, my toes barely scraping the ground. Black Beard pushed me up against the now ruined and crumpled hood of the sedan, ripping my cap off with a grunt of satisfaction.

In a quicksilver flash of movement, I spun my blade up into my palm.

As soon as Black Beard recognized it, he froze, his eyes churning bright with *Sight*. He tried to compel me, and I felt the all-too-familiar pull, but like the last vamp who tried this, the sensation was soon drowned out by my own anti-*Sight* reflected back on him. I gave him a vexing grin as his face relaxed and he dropped me like a sack of potatoes. Slack-jawed and open to suggestion, he awaited my command right as three more goons showed up, all with their weapons trained on us.

Fueled by my newly appropriated power and the intense influence of the blade, I breathed, "Kill as many as you can. Protect us at all costs."

I should have felt bad I'd commanded a suicide mission—but this was war.

Black Beard shot to attention, turning on our aggressors, now his, right as I fell to the ground, curling into a ball. Larna threw herself on top of me, which I found funny because she was half my size. Bullets ricocheted off the ground, bounced off the car, and smacked into Black Beard in a deadly cacophony that reminded me of being back in the cemetery with Larna. Amazingly, our unlikely hero was still standing, rifle empty, when the barrage finally ended and Larna rolled off me.

I stood back up on wobbly legs, realizing I had been gripping the hilt of the blade so tight my fingers hurt.

The flood of energy and adrenaline seeped out of me. I remembered how taxing compulsion was on the body. Whatever amped-up juice it had provided was now long gone, and so was the power supplied by my blade.

We were surrounded, with no hope of escape.

Chapter 8

Corinth

IF YOU DECIDE TO attack a base full of armed super-villains, always find cover, especially if you're human and you can't heal like one of them. A bullet flew so close by my head I swear I felt my hair move. Shock happens. Put that on a T-shirt.

One minute we were out in the open, and the next, we were huddled together behind a wooden crate in the corner of the warehouse, having been funneled here like cattle to their slaughter.

Larna inspected the rest of her gear and then chanced a peek around the side of the crate. "Ten more just showed up … at *least*. You got any more ammo?"

I flung myself down beside her, fumbling with the Velcro on my vest in order to yank a magazine out of my pocket and slam it into her hands. She reloaded the fresh mag as another hail of gunfire erupted around us.

"Where's Black Beard?" I growled. "Or better yet, Vinson?"

"Who is Black Beard?" she asked as she fired two more rounds blindly around the side of the crate. "And Vinson is supposed to be on the roof, where we should be right about now. But unless you have a way past all those guards out there, we're trapped."

"Black Beard—the guy I compelled. Here. I've got three rounds left." I handed her the gun and she tucked it into her belt. There wasn't enough room for me to start shooting, so I stayed down and let her take over.

I rested the dagger on my lap, holding it reverently in the palms of my hands. It was time I took them all out.

"Vinson better hurr—" Larna started to say, but her voice caught as soon as she saw the blade on my lap. "As much as I want to see you throw down some thunder and lightning, I also *really* don't want to be caught in the crossfire."

I wasn't sure if I would take her out in the process, a prospect that left my mouth dry as a bone. I felt something wet on my head and ran a hand through my hair. It came back slick with blood. The bullet must have grazed me, or maybe it was from when we crashed. Either way, I had been banged up pretty good.

I ground my teeth together, looking down at the blade. "I hate that there isn't an instruction manual for this thing." Another barrage of gunfire smacked into the wall near my head, and I ducked lower. "But it would appear we might be out of options."

Larna pulled the pistol with the remaining three rounds from her waistband as if she were the last surviving samurai. "Not if I can help it."

Before she could jump out in a blaze of glory, the shooting suddenly stopped, and everything went deathly still.

With a quick glance around the corner, she turned

back to me, her eyes round as saucers. "They're just standing there—"

A deep, resonating voice rang out, interrupting Larna. "Corinth Taylor," a woman's voice said loudly, "further bloodshed will not be necessary."

The way she said my name made me think she might have known me, so from my crouched position, I risked a glance out. A striking woman stood in the center of the warehouse. A throng of bad guys all dressed in black surrounded her. Wearing a long flowing crimson gown, she looked completely out of place. The dress hugged her curves in all the right places, though. If I hadn't just survived a deadly fire-fight, I might have found her ridiculously attractive.

I didn't, though, find her attractive.

Hoping I sounded just as authoritative as she did, I shouted, "I see my reputation has proceeded me … You know my name, but I don't know yours."

I guess I still needed a confidence boost, because Larna rolled her eyes at me.

The woman's commanding voice carried throughout the warehouse, sounding ominous. "I am Imani." She said her name as if I should know who she was. "You're surrounded. There are more guards on their way. Come out now and I will guarantee your safety."

As I thought about it, I realized her name did sound vaguely familiar. And then it hit me. I turned quickly back to Larna. "That sociopath who compelled my sister, Zoey, back at the cemetery. Remember the chick wearing that red dress?" I motioned to the other side of the crate and mouthed, "*That's her.*"

Larna's frown deepened as she nodded. "Now what?"

I gave her an exaggerated shrug. "Do you think Vinson set timers on all those explosives?"

"Good question," she said.

I yelled out around the corner of the crate, "I have a firm rule against trusting anyone wearing that amount of red!"

I heard a flurry of motion and footsteps shuffling closer as Imani said, "I just want to talk. I can't guarantee your safety when the others arrive. Give up now."

I poked my head out briefly to get a better look at her. She stood out as bright as a beacon on an open sea of darkly clad enemies. I had the same impression the last time I saw her. There was no forgetting those Amazonian legs and rich black skin. The smallest hint of a smile played on cherry-red lips. I wondered if this was her intention—wearing the opposite of Deimos' usual clan attire to show her position and separation from the rest of the group. Maybe Gabe worked for *her*. Either way, I had a feeling I didn't want to mess with her.

She snapped impatiently at someone. It took three of their biggest and baddest to haul a struggling Vinson through the set of double doors he'd run into when the shooting had started.

Oh no, this is bad. Very bad.

He was bound and wrapped up like a Christmas present. My heart plummeted at seeing him trussed up like that. They dropped him unceremoniously at Imani's feet. He thrashed against his bonds as the three who carried him out stayed close, the fear evident on their faces. Vinson wasn't one to trifle with and they knew it.

Shooting a worried glance at Larna, I whispered, "This is not good." I drew the dagger up to my chest and squeezed it tightly, willing it to come up with a plan so I didn't have to.

"If you don't come out, I'll drain him right here in front of you, Corinth … I really would like to keep this civil."

Larna raised her gun, ready to unload the three remaining bullets on them, but I dove toward her to grab her arm. "Are you trying to get yourself killed?"

"We don't have a plan B," she murmured. "Better me than you."

"More bloodshed isn't going to help us get Vinson back. Plus, there are a lot more out there than three vamps. We have to think of another way out of this."

Imani snapped impatiently. "Have it your way."

From my crouched position behind the crate, I watched with growing dread as the three goons picked Vinson up and presented him to Imani like he was a fine bottle of wine. Without preamble, she pulled off her five-inch stilettos. Even with her shoes off, she was tall. I suddenly realized I didn't want to know what she was going to do.

Imani rolled her shoulders back and, with calculated coldness, said, "A woman's shoes are her best asset." Her eyes flicked back toward us to make sure we were witnessing what she was about to do. Once she was satisfied that we were watching, she drew back the sharp point of her heel and slammed it into his thigh.

I was sure it had to be excruciatingly painful to have a lady's stiletto shoved into your leg, but he didn't scream or shout. In fact, the only way I knew it affected him was from a deep blue vein popping out on his forehead.

I, however, jerked back as if it was my leg she'd stabbed. Throwing a hand over my mouth, I exchanged another glance with Larna. I'm sure the expression on her face matched mine in abhorrence.

We couldn't let him be tortured. Since Jack had been killed, Vinson had become our most trusted ally. And even though he'd never say it to me, I considered him my friend. I was pretty sure the only reason he stuck around was out of loyalty for Jack. Those two had had a special bond. Whatever Jack had done to earn that trust from him had to have been huge. I knew there was a story there, but I never pressed. Whatever his motivation for helping us, he was still a part of this team. It was high time I stepped up.

Imani had stopped talking, but I could still hear the impatience in her body language: a tapping of a long red fingernail against her patent leather heels. She snapped her fingers again, and the guy to her left handed her his gun, and when she aimed it right between Vinson's eyes my heart shot up into my throat.

I blew out a deep breath, knowing exactly what I had to do and not liking it one bit. Clutching the dagger between slick fingers, I leaped out from behind the safety of cover, raising my hands over my head. "Don't kill him," I said loudly. "I'm coming out."

Imani smiled coolly at me, her eyes sliding to the blade in my hand. She handed the gun back to the goon on her left, and ever so slowly, pulled her heel out of his thigh, the small smile turning into a sadistic grin as Vinson struggled against his captor's hold.

I scanned our surroundings, searching for a way out. There were about fifteen vamps surrounding us. Three were crouched near the demolished car, two more against the wall on the opposite side of the warehouse, and the rest surrounding Imani and Vinson.

We are so screwed.

Larna was a few feet behind me. I was glad I couldn't see her face, mainly because I could feel her eyes burrowing into the back of my skull. She was probably beyond pissed at me for giving myself up. I just hoped I could get them both out of this, myself be damned.

There was only one play I had left.

"Well, well, well … the—" her eyes flicked over me, assessing "—*boy* of the hour." She licked her blood-red lips as if in anticipation of devouring a tasty snack.

As I inched closer, I noticed her eyes were swallowed by black. She looked both seductive and deadly. She'd given me the same kind of scrutiny back at the graveyard.

Anger bubbled to the surface, but I didn't feel the torrent of power that usually flooded through me when I took hold of the blade. All that was left was a woozy fatigue.

"You were at the church with my sister." I flashed a wicked grin. "Please tell me Gabe has a nice scar on his back." My eyebrows shot up, bragging. "You know … from when I stabbed him with the dagger and he ran away like a coward." I looked her up and down before saying, "I seem to remember you running scared too, sweetheart."

She tapped a long red fingernail against the side of her pistol, arms crossed over her chest. After a second, she let out a chillingly cold laugh while the rest of her entourage glanced nervously between each other. I didn't think they liked the fact that I still had my hands on the infamous blade.

Imani didn't seem worried in the least, though, as she eyed me with one side of her mouth snaking upward. "You seem different than when I saw you last."

I may not have been stronger than these bozos, but she wasn't going to win the battle of snark against me. "I've been doing a lot of yoga lately. There's this great video you should watch—"

Imani threw her head back, and a lock of dark, wavy hair fell to the side. "I like you." She turned to the two vamps closest to us and motioned to them with her gun. "But you talk too much."

The short one with blond hair swept back into a long ponytail grabbed me. I could practically hear his teeth clacking together as he yanked the dagger from my grip. He slow-blinked a few times, probably expecting to be struck down where he stood. When nothing happened, he gave me a rough shove into their newly formed inner circle.

I stumbled forward, shooting him an angry glare over my shoulder. "I'll go with you, Imani … I won't fight. Just let them both go." I swallowed hard, turning back to face her. "You have the dagger and me, just like you wanted."

The urgent concern in Larna's voice wasn't lost on me as she hissed, "*Corinth, what are you doing?*"

Larna tried to break free at the last second, vaulting forward, her gun back in her grip at the same time as the second vamp cold-cocked her from behind. She fell to her knees, and then he was savagely yanking her back to her feet, relieving her of her pistol. I watched with growing dismay as he grabbed a pair of heavy-duty-looking handcuffs from his belt and wrenched her arms behind her back to snap them on her wrists.

I stepped toward them, but rough hands on my shoulders stopped me. Through clenched teeth, I said, "Y'all seem to be awfully frightened of us." I whispered menacingly, "Good. You should be."

Blondie gave me another hard shove as Imani beckoned for him to bring me closer. I couldn't help but notice the glare Vinson gave me from his place at Imani's now-bare feet. He was livid, his face a shade of plum that belonged only on a piece of fruit.

She seemed to entertain my negotiation until she cooed, "No deal." Her lips parted and her teeth flashed dangerously—a face that said she ate babies for breakfast. The dried blood on the side of my head seemed to draw her interest. Feral eyes skimmed to it and then to the bandages on my neck and forearm.

Vampires suck. Literally. If most of my friends weren't vamps, I'd wipe every single one of them off the face of this earth.

Recognizing that look on her face, I murmured, "Why don't you try a taste?"

Imani held up a finger to quiet me. "Maybe later ..." She inclined her head toward Larna. "For now, Gabriel Stanton wants the girl alive." She waved a dismissive hand at Vinson. "Kill the Russian." Then her eyes leveled on me. "We have some things to discuss before I turn you over to Gabriel."

Imani pointed to the blond with the long ponytail, motioning for him to give her the blade he'd taken from me. Her minion snapped to attention, handing it over as a look of relief washed over his face.

She took it from him with delicate pianist's fingers. I didn't like the worshipful glint in her eyes as she studied every inch of it.

Panic twisted inside me, spiraling up my chest; constricting my throat. Why couldn't I turn my powers on and off whenever I needed them? What was the point in having stupid abilities if I couldn't use them? The dagger was mine. It had chosen me. I didn't like seeing her talons on my blade.

Ponytail pulled me roughly away from the rest of our group. It was enough to send me into a tailspin. If they led me away from Larna and Vinson I had a feeling I'd never see them again. There are times when you have to fight. This was one of those times. I kicked out at the vamp that had started to haul me away, readying myself for the fight of my life, but someone sucker punched me in the gut—someone supernatural, because I hadn't seen it coming or even felt the usual signs accompanied with vampire speed. I sank to my knees, gasping in pain, but still managed to throw a terrified glance over my shoulder. *What did I just do?* In my stupid thirst to prove myself, I would have agreed to just about any moronic idea. *Give yourself up to the bad guy, Corinth … stellar idea.*

The goon who'd punched me grabbed my other arm to haul me roughly back to my feet. His gargantuan forehead looked like a blurry smear in my vision as he punched me in the gut again. I doubled over, wheezing, "That … all you … got, Potato Head?"

As soon as Larna saw him hit me, she tried to break free, but her captor yanked hard on the handcuffs, bringing her to her knees. The last thing I saw were her eyes blazing in anger as two more thugs jumped on top of her, trying to hold her down.

"Corinth, I'll get us out of this!" she shouted, but then her voice, thick with emotion, was fading as I was hauled through a set of double doors on the opposite side of the warehouse.

Imani held her shoes in one hand, and my dagger in the other, leading the way; her dress fanned out behind her just like a devil's pitchfork.

Chapter 9

Corinth

WE WERE IN AN underground tunnel or basement. My best guess was a maintenance area or a bomb shelter. It smelled musty and stale in this part of the facility. This had to be how they got out of the building in such a stealthy fashion. There were no windows down here; fluorescent lights flickered in an unnatural hue above us. As we made it halfway down the hall, Imani stopped and held up a hand, her eyes darting to the shadows down the corridor. The two vamps holding my arms let me go, and I slid to the floor in an exhausted heap. Even though I was sitting still, everything around me spun and tilted.

Imani cocked her head, listening, though whatever she heard wasn't audible to my ears. Then immediately she was shouting, "*Take Cover!*" Her cry was suddenly followed by a low rumble that worked its way up to a thunderous crescendo. I'd never been in an earthquake before, but this was exactly what I imagined it might feel like. The ceiling seemed to bulge and pulsate overhead. I kept thinking about creatures popping out of the walls—and throw in a poltergeist or two for good measure. Just as the lights broke apart, Ponytail and Mr. Potato Head turned and ran. Bits of glass and plastic and concrete hit my shoulders as debris rained down around us. This wasn't an earthquake.

This was *Vinson. C-4.*

The blast came from above. Mortar and stone and cement cracked under the sudden and intense pressure. The two turncoats had made it all the way to the exit doors by the time a massive chunk of concrete broke loose and crushed them flat. They were fast, but not that fast.

Imani's eyes found mine. There was a moment's hesitation as she considered what she should do: come after me or run for her life.

I tried to stand back up, but when the ground shook again, I stumbled and fell back to my knees, using one hand to hold on to the wall for support. Emergency lights flickered overhead, winking on and off again.

"I'll only slow you down," I said, coughing out about a pound of dirt. "It's me or the dagger. Choose wisely. But you're not getting both."

Imani's eyes flicked to my blade, still clutched in her grasp. I guess she decided to opt for self-preservation, because I watched as she disappeared and then, like a flickering mirage, reappeared at the end of the maintenance tunnel we had been heading down. It was only a fraction of a second by the time she made it to the doors when a tremor started up again, and this one sent her rocketing back toward me, bare feet flying over her head and red dress flowing up like a kite behind her.

Quaking, quivering, the earth cracked open underfoot, and my heart beat quickened, matching the irregular pace of the flickering lights. I tried to get back up, only to stumble into the wall—or maybe the wall hit me … Either way, the lights finally winked out, dousing me in complete darkness once again. *Story of my life.*

Chapter 10

Larna

THE MOMENT THEY SNAPPED the cold, hard steel around my wrists, I knew it was going to end badly. I'd never seen Corinth look so terrified. It hurt to watch, and it was even more gut-wrenching that that guy kept hitting him in the stomach. Currently, though, I was in trouble on my knees next to Vinson. The cuffs they'd slapped on me were made of some kind of heavy-duty material, because I couldn't break them no matter how hard I tried. The rest of what was left of clan Deimos had formed a tight circle around us.

I took a vicious blow to the stomach and gulped for precious oxygen, my watch pinching painfully against my skin, reminding me of the panic button. I pushed it, knowing it probably wouldn't help, but I couldn't think of a better idea at the moment. Paul was the only one who could help right now. A tiny part of me held out hope that Alastair was still in town and that he'd come running. Since he'd been gone, there had been times, during my weakest moments, that I had thought about doing just that. What stayed my hand was the fact that his mission was probably more important than mine. Trust and loyalty were hard, and he'd definitely earned both of those. Alastair had protected me on countless occasions, shown me compassion, and helped me transition from self-conscious to bold. Besides, I couldn't always rely on him to get us out of a jam.

Vinson was gagged by duct tape. Chains and rope covered every inch of his body, but he managed to waggle a finger at me, the only part of him that was free, and his eyes flicked to mine. He was trying to tell me something.

The vamp who kicked me said, "Who's going to off the Russian?"

My eyes darted back up and my breathing quickened. The vamp who spoke looked more like a math teacher than a cold-blooded killer. He wore thick-rimmed glasses, the kind only worn for fashion, and had a head of patchy hair that poked out in all different directions.

"Firing squad for the Russian?" He pulled out his magazine, eyeing the rest of his bullets. "Anyone got any more ammo?"

The guy who had snapped on my cuffs looked like he was my age. He would have fit right in at my high school—actually, he reminded me a lot of Colton, Madison's boyfriend, except this dude had a head full of dark hair, and Colton was blond.

I tried to wrench my hands free, but the cuffs bit painfully into my wrists. I let out an involuntary gasp, and the dark-haired vampire, seeing my pain, started in on me again, landing a savage blow across my shoulder. I gritted my teeth as a spasm worked its way up my neck.

He pushed his face closer to mine. "You killed my sister."

I managed to give him a thin-lipped grin before snarling, "You're going to have to be more specific … I've taken out a lot of y'all today."

He kicked me again; this time, I felt a rib break. I was lucky there was a hard lump in the back of my throat, or I would have given him the satisfaction of crying out. The cold glint in his eyes told me he enjoyed seeing other people's pain. I didn't plan to oblige him.

"Starting to remember yet? You stole her car." He crouched down beside me, leaning in closer to whisper in my ear, "I'm going to kill that freak … the skinny kid with the dagger. I don't care how much Stanton wants him alive. That mutant will get what's coming to him even worse than what I'm going to do to you."

His eyes flashed as he stood back up. I risked a quick glance back to Vinson right as he managed to form the letter *C*, and then hold up four of his digits. His stony black eyes were wide, urging me to understand. As soon as he saw that I was paying attention, he lifted his eyebrows and nodded, again showing me *C* and four fingers.

And then there was a shift in the air right as a concussive heat wave hit us.

My tormentor dropped his gun in sudden fright. Seeing my opening, I propelled myself back to my feet, hands still restrained behind me as the world around us turned into a conglomeration of fire and chaos. A section of corrugated steel and metal cracked overhead, accompanied by a horrible screeching noise right as a section broke loose from the ceiling, swinging down like a deadly pendulum, heading straight for us. Timing it perfectly, I barreled myself into the guy's chest as the backswing of jagged metal sliced right through the top of his skull. *What a way to go.* I turned my head away from the carnage and cringed. The combination of the sudden upheaval and my wicked grin caused the rest of our rapt audience to run.

Flames licked at the roof, spreading across the ceiling as the earth roared its displeasure beneath our feet. My balance was already off, thanks to my hands bound behind my back, so when the ground shook and reinforced masonry broke apart, I found myself tripping over Vinson's still-prone form. He grunted, wriggling against his bonds, looking a lot like a magician trying unsuccessfully to free himself from a straitjacket. Climbing shakily to my knees beside him, I turned around. Facing the opposite direction and blind to what I was doing, I began working at his bonds. My sweat-slicked fingers kept slipping off the ropes as I jerked, wrenched, and tugged at them. It was a painstaking process that left my fingers raw and swollen, but finally I felt the rope give in right as another explosion shook the foundation to its core.

An iron support beam broke loose and hit the ground, hurtling toward us like a missile. I watched in stunned captivation as sparks shot up from the beam's underbelly. It was a fast, strong, locomotive of pure devastation, and the razor-sharp metal looked as deadly as a carving knife. There was nothing I could do to prevent it from mowing us down. My choices were bleak: throw myself out of the way at the last second and let it wipe Vinson off the face of the planet—or block it with my body; maybe save his life. He'd do the same for me. I would never be able to live with myself if I jumped out of the way like a coward. So I closed my eyes, and braced myself for the impact. The steel javelin hit me, knocking the breath from my lungs, and punching a hole right through my abdomen. I gritted my teeth against the agonizing pain as the force of it slingshotted me away from Vinson, in the opposite direction. Oddly enough, as I slid across the warehouse floor, still skewered by unforgiving metal, I had one last fleeting thought: *Vinson really knows how to take a building down.*

I think I saw Vinson freeing himself right as I plunged through the heart of the inferno, flames accepting me into their blistery embrace.

An image of my father hit me: his smiling face and also my mother's—when they had been happiest together. And then my mind shifted back to thoughts of Vinson. I knew he would probably think he had failed his mission. He hadn't come out and said it, but I think Vinson had made my father a promise to keep me safe. Those two had had a special bond, and now I guess I'd never find out why or how that had come about.

The metal still in my stomach was at least five hundred pounds of pure steel. The force of resistance was too much for me to stop it without the use of my hands. Instead, I was an unwilling participant along for the ride. It flung me against the far wall, pinning me in place as helpless as a fish on a hook. At least this part of the warehouse hadn't been completely consumed by the fire yet.

I sucked in a deep breath, intending to use what little strength I had left to push the steel back, but my hands were still pinioned behind me, and instead of pulling in oxygen, I got a lungful of searing heat. It stunned me, tears springing to my eyes. Pain is misleading, complex, and volatile, not just a mere reflexive response to an injury. In my case, I couldn't feel anything below my waist. There had been a serious disconnect from wound to brain—at least, that was my guess for the lack of pain. I read somewhere that if you didn't look at an injury you wouldn't be able to feel how badly it hurt.

Now, I found that I could only gaze up at the warped ceiling with a cold despair spreading through my veins. The fire crawling across the rafters was hauntingly beautiful. The iron was twisted and deformed, as bright as a solar flare—melting like crayons, from Mississippi mud to rust red to, finally, molten yellow. It reminded me of the end of one of Paul's lit cigarettes. It was a blessing being pain-free, and also horrifying. An angry squeal of metal on metal came from above, as if even the building were crying. Another beam collapsed in on itself, as fiery orange sparks shot out in all different directions. At least this would be the last thing I saw, something so stunningly warped and yet oddly comforting.

I smiled at the thought that if Vinson made it out alive, he would have to live with the fact that I saved his life. I reached for my *Sight*—not because I thought I could save myself, but because I didn't want to die alone. A twist of familiar presence stirred inside my chest, and I felt only its sorrow. I could almost hear it say, "I'm here. You're not alone."

I was surprisingly dry-eyed. In the end—I was glad for its company, but saddened that my *Sight* would die with me.

Another block of concrete cracked under the pressure directly over my head, and this time, as it came crashing down, there was nothing I could do but close my eyes.

When I didn't feel the impact like I expected, I cracked them back open again.

Someone was standing over me; I could see black combat boots and hear labored breathing.

"*I'm here.*"

I fully expected it to be Vinson who had spoken, but when I saw who was standing over me, I thought I really had died. Either that or this was the best hallucination in the entire world. My heart gave a jolt, and then it started to flutter rapidly against the backs of my ribs, like caged hummingbirds.

Even though he was giving in to some extreme exertion, I'd have recognized those features anywhere. Exceedingly bright blue eyes met mine. His blond hair hung partially over an eye making him look younger than he actually was—the contours of his face, even shadowed by rising flames, were still a sight to behold. A vein popped out on his forehead, and with a final grunt of effort, Alastair heaved the two-ton block of concrete he'd stopped from flattening me aside, as if it didn't weigh a thing.

And then he was kneeling by my side, damp and sweaty hands exploring where the hunk of metal had entered my stomach. A muscle ticked along his strong jawline as he assessed the damage.

After eight long months, there were no cordial niceties or greetings, no hug or "Hey, let's catch up" as his eyes zipped back and forth, the wheels spinning in his head as he rapidly thought through his options. "As soon as I wrench this out of your stomach, you'll start losing a lot of blood. I'll have to put a lot of pressure on the wound." Alastair squinted down at me, the concern and emotion churning in those remarkable blue eyes of his. "You'll have to help me," he said hoarsely. I could tell he was trying to hold back a flood of emotions.

And then he was lifting me gently into a sitting position so he could inspect the cuffs at my back. I let out a strangled cry; even that small amount of movement was excruciating—there it was, the pain returning. I just kept thinking over and over again, *You shouldn't have looked.*

His brows furrowed and he pressed his lips into a thin line. If my hands were free, I would have reached up to trace the outline of his soot-smudged cheek. "I'm sorry, Larna … I have to get these cuffs off," he said, regret for what was to come lacing his voice. "What are they made out of?"

I shook my head, finding it frustrating that I couldn't brush away the tears now welling up in my eyes. "Go … find … Corinth," I panted. "*Leave me.*"

He rolled his eyes at me as if I'd suggested something so foolish that it wasn't even worth a reply. He replied anyway. "Like hell."

My own eyes flashed dangerously back at him. "They took him … He needs help …"

He spoke more to himself than to me as he blew out a frustrated breath. "Where's the key?" He wheeled around, scanning the immediate area.

I nodded in the general direction of where Colton's doppelganger had been crushed by the thing that probably now had me pinned against the wall. Payback, I suppose.

Alastair spun around. The raging inferno rose up before him like a firestorm. He had to shield his eyes against its blinding intensity. Spurred on by the fire's path of destruction toward us, he turned back to me, making his mind up. "I'll break them myself."

My head sagged against his shoulder as he sat me up—this time, I found I was too weak to even respond.

"Hold on... Stay with me, Larna," he pleaded.

I managed to gasp, "Leave me … Go while you still—"

"One … two …"

He pulled on *two*. Ass.

Chapter 11

Corinth

IMANI SAT WITH HER legs crossed, and her frayed and dirty dress fanned out around her. She stared at me with unblinking eyes. We were surrounded on all sides by uncompromising rock and also probably a thousand years' worth of dirt and dust and mold. Our escape had been cut off by the explosion, causing a subsequent cave-in around us. The air was thin. Luckily, though, there was an emergency flood-light that had survived the blast and had fortuitously for me, kicked on. Soft light illuminated Imani's face, making her look strangely striking in its orange glow.

I swiped a hand across my brow, peering down at my watch in frustration. The face was cracked and the digital display broken. I pushed the button for the umpteenth time. Nothing happened. Hitting it with the palm of my hand didn't help either. So much for indestructible secret agent watches. Maybe Larna and Vinson had made it out. There was always hope. They had a much better chance at escaping, not being surrounded by a ton of brick and mortar and all.

My dagger sat in between Imani's talons.

There were several reasons why I didn't try and take it back from her. One, we weren't going anywhere. Two, I didn't want to risk potentially starting another cave-in by fighting her for it, and three, she wasn't a threat—right now.

I was pretty sure she wasn't going to try and kill me with it. Gabe needed me alive. It was funny how everyone who came in contact with the ancient relic was either frightened or awed by it. Imani only appeared inquisitive, turning it over and raising a dark, manicured eyebrow as she studied it. I wondered idly what she was thinking.

"It's no good without me," I told her, taking a guess as to what was on her mind. "That dagger and I are kind of a package deal."

Her eyes flicked back up at me.

I threw my watch and it hit the wall near her head, and I had to admit, seeing the look of surprise on her face made me feel better. It wasn't that juvenile.

If she was annoyed by my actions, she didn't show it. Instead, she purred, "You're not what I expected."

"Expecting Hercules, with the big muscles?" I asked dryly.

"Something like that." Her tone was measured, and the slow enunciation of the word *something* wasn't lost on me.

I said, "Well, get used to disappointment, sweetheart."

"I'm not the one trapped with a bloodthirsty vampire. You're snack sized at the very least." She let the insult sink in before adding, "It's likely I'll survive a long time down here … but you…"

I had the sick mental image of being a sardine in a fish

tank with a shark. But my give-a-crap meter had broken along with my watch. Her drinking my blood was a sacrifice I was willing to take—she'd die and I'd get my dagger back: win-win.

"What are you waiting for?" I goaded.

She shook her head and laughed, definitely not provoked.

My chest felt heavy and constricted. I tried to ignore the anxiety building as I ran a hand through my hair, dirt and ash falling out of it like little snowflakes. It made me realize how much I needed a shower. I explored the cut on my head, where the bullet had grazed me. It was tender and swollen. The rest of me was still intact, so there was that.

I caught her watching me out of the corner of my eye, and when I looked back up, she was seductively tracing her middle finger along the edge of the blade. I wanted to charge her, take it back forcibly. But I made myself sit still and focus, willing myself not be drawn in by her taunting. Her eyes raked over mine, daring me to do something about it—maybe see how far I'd go to get it back.

I knew she was trying to push my buttons. *It was working.* The way my heart knocked annoyingly against my ribcage was proof of that. She must have heard it, because her smirk widened. Unable to take it any longer, I stood back up and started pacing. Being tall had its disadvantages. The concrete, rocks, and plaster overhead only seemed to leave me with an overpowering sense of claustrophobia and did nothing to help ease my anxiety.

After a few minutes of silence dragging on between us, I said, "You can wipe that narcissistic grin off your face." I spread my arms out wide. "Well … you wanted to have a chat. Let's chat."

Imani picked up the already-ripped material of her dress and tore at it. When she finished, it resembled a T-shirt more than a dress. I cleared my throat and glanced away. Even her underwear was red.

"Gabriel will be here soon," she said in a drawl that I didn't find becoming at all.

"If you think he gives a damn about you, you're a lot dumber than I first thought," I spit.

"Maybe," she shot right back.

Maybe I could press this issue more. Her answer revealed a lot. Gabe was definitely not on her Christmas card list. I prodded at a large chunk of concrete, only to realize my mistake too late. A hunk of it broke loose and came crashing down right as a hand shot out to pull me out of the way at the last second.

On the ground in a tangle of limbs, I felt her hips shift beneath mine, and the tip of my dagger prick my chin.

The cave-in stopped just shy of both our feet, the space now cut in half.

"Comfortable?" she said with icy malice. Those incredibly dark eyes tried to pull me in, but I cleared my throat, quickly shuffling back as far as I could go. There wasn't much space between us to move now.

I answered way more childishly than I wanted to. "No. I'm not comfortable if you must know," I huffed. "Gabe only cares about numero uno. You get that, right?"

It was embarrassing how easily my breathing changed from shallow to erratic. A tiny drop of blood trickled down to the tip of her finger from where she had nicked me. She smiled and pulled the dagger deftly back onto her lap like she was playing keep-away from a two-year-old. Those eyes were like bottomless pits.

Careful, Corinth, you might fall in.

I stood back up to yank my bullet proof vest off. Underneath, sweat soaked every inch of my T-shirt. "What I wouldn't do for some painkillers and a cheeseburger," I muttered, and then turned back to her. "So, what's up with you and Gabe? Y'all two a power couple or something?"

Imani cocked her head to the side. "Fine … let's talk." She gestured around us. "Before this, you were destined for a long life in cramped living quarters, to be studied like a rat." She placed a long red fingernail against her bottom lip. "Now you're destined for a much shorter lifespan and even smaller living quarters, it would appear."

The thought of being a lab rat for the rest of my life made the hairs on the back of my neck stand on end; they felt like little needles against my skin. That was never going to happen on my watch.

I clamped my teeth together and hissed, "Sounds quaint."

The sound of her laugh echoed hauntingly in the confining space. "You're a mystery. You aren't one of us, but I saw you use the power of *Sight*. I've never seen anyone do that before. You compelled another vampire … I thought Gabriel Stanton was the only one who could do that, but you aren't a vampire." Her eyes narrowed like a hawk's. "What *are* you?"

I shrugged. "You seem like a gal who likes a good mystery."

Something told me I wasn't getting out of here. We had been buried under so much rubble with no signs of rescue. After a beat, I could only find myself telling her, "Thank you."

Her eyebrows rose in question, and then her mouth

fell slightly open in surprise.

"It must be the lack of oxygen … but—" I sighed in disappointment at myself for confessing this to her "—thank you for saving my life."

She laid my dagger down by her side, probably all the trust I'd get from her, but I'd take it. It might be my only chance at getting it back. "We can't have someone like you getting crushed by a rock, now can we?" she said slowly.

I lifted an eyebrow. "I totally agree," I said. "Now, what are we going to do about oxygen deprivation?"

Imani scooted closer, and I sat down across from her, conceding. My eyes roamed to the dagger near her thigh, then slowly up to her rust-red lips, and then finally to those ink-black eyes. She curled her fingers around the hilt of my dagger and placed it back on her lap.

Curiosity getting the better of me, I asked, "How long can you survive without air, anyway?"

"We still have the same reaction as humans to lack of oxygen, but I can survive a lot longer than you can." She became quiet for a minute and then, as if on a whim, said, "If you're going to die anyway … well …" She arched a flirtatious eyebrow. "Then why not have a little fun?"

A sarcastic laugh bubbled out of me. "You've got a lot of nerve." I laughed again, shaking my head. "You try to kill my friends, kidnap my sister, threaten me, torture Vinson … Yeah, that sounds like a great idea."

Have a little fun? The idea was preposterous, but a tiny part of me thought if I was gonna die … how would I want to go? I shook my head. *Stop it, idiot. Of course, you didn't worry about that with Larns, did you?* I blamed my racing, rampant thoughts on lack of oxygen, and hormones. My eyes flicked back to the dagger in her lap. If I had it, I was absolutely positive I could kill her with it. The idea of sitting in this tiny tomb with a dead vampire wasn't so appealing either.

I rubbed a hand across my neck, trying to loosen the tightening muscles, and then a coughing fit struck. I was shaking uncontrollably by the time it was over. Imani was kneeling over me with a strange expression on her face. I had no idea where she'd come from.

I couldn't ignore how hot it was now, with the body heat increasing between us to an almost unbearable degree. "Is that a look of concern on your face?" I asked, clearing my throat, and then inching back. She'd been so close I could have stolen my blade back. But, man, had she distracted me. She closed her eyes and pulled her long legs underneath her, revealing well-toned thighs.

"Where are you from?" I croaked. "I mean, I don't really care—"

"Egypt," she answered, so softly I almost missed it.

Now that Imani mentioned it, she did look like the Egyptian statues I'd seen in museums. With round dark eyes, black skin, and wavy hair. "Did you hang with the pharaohs? Nefertiti invite you over for a spot of tea?" I gave her a lopsided grin, but when she didn't answer, I said, "You aren't Nefertiti, are you?"

She shook her head. "No, I am not Nefertiti."

"How old are you, anyway?"

"It's not polite to ask a lady that."

"Screw polite." It was out of my mouth before I could stop it. I was dying. What I wouldn't give for some water.

She moved in a flash. I flinched, expecting her to slash my throat. Instead, she rested her head against my chest, listening to the sound of my galloping heartbeat. I tensed, and then the walls spun for one nauseatingly long second before coming to a dizzying halt.

"What are you doing?" I asked quickly.

I felt her smile against my chest, and when she pulled back to study me, she didn't look like a heartless monster, the way I'd seen her back in the warehouse, she looked like someone concerned about how much longer I had left to live.

Chapter 12

Corinth

"THERE IS SOMETHING ABOUT you. I don't know what it is …" Imani wiped a hand across her damp brow. "Seeing that you haven't much time, I'll tell you what I know. There are stories from some who say vampires were created by Dracul."

"Dracul—you mean, like Dracula? Or do you mean that Romanian ruler, what's his name … Vlad the Impaler?"

She inclined her head. "You pay attention in history class. But, no. He was ruler during the mid-fourteen hundreds. I'm talking about the real Dracul. The name likened to the Devil. I believe the first vampire was created by something else, something *stronger*. Your fiction novels and history books have some of it right, but most of them are wrong—dead wrong. I went to Gabriel about my theory because he had access to the blade I'd been searching for for a very long time. The first of us were considered abominations—a blight to the human race." She shook her head, then pinched the bridge of her nose, as if deciding where to start. "It only took me four centuries to figure out. Explaining it in a matter of minutes is next to impossible."

"Four centuries? You're kidding, right? Okay, well, give me the *Cliffs-Notes* version. Where do I come in to all of this?"

"Gabriel..." she started to say, and then stopped, glancing down. I wondered if she was still trying to decide on how much she should confide in me. Now was the time I pressed for answers.

"You know ... I think you *want* to tell me ... It's why you decided to have a chat first before turning me over to Gabe. Now's your chance," I urged. "Tell me, please, Imani."

"What lies within you is the capacity to destroy or bring life." Her eyes flicked down to the blade in her lap. I could see written in the deepest parts of her irises all the vast knowledge she possessed. This is why Gabe was using her ... She was a resource unlike any history book. Hell, she *was* history.

"You have no idea how important you are," she whispered. "Do you?"

Geeks don't get put in charge of the important stuff. Heroes do. I am *not* a hero. I wanted to laugh at the absurdity of it all. Nerds play video games, sitting behind computers, letting their avis slay the evil in the world. It was hilarious to even consider.

"The dagger is a vital tool," she said. "But the blood running through your veins is the key."

Chapter 13

Larna

I WAS LYING ON a hard surface, covered by a thin sheet. As life slowly flooded back into me, I realized, thankfully, that the hard surface was not an autopsy table, but in actuality a pool-table-turned-makeshift-gurney. For the life of me, though, I couldn't remember how I'd gotten here.

"How bad is it?"

A familiar voice brought me fully out of my stupor, my heart racing.

Alastair was here.

I mean, not in the same room, but he was here with me now and he hadn't left. For one brief, confusing moment, I had thought I only imagined him coming to my rescue. My eyes shot open all the way, and I blinked rapidly, trying to clear my head and take in my surroundings. Even though the events that led up to this moment were still fuzzy, I knew I didn't want to tug on that strand of memory just yet. Something told me it was going to be a traumatic one. I just wanted to live in this tiny moment of reprieve—knowing Alastair was under the same roof as me again.

Relief washed over me as soon as I recognized my dad's cabin.

I'd only been here once before, with Vinson.

Twisting my head to the side, I saw bloodied towels, gloves, and medical equipment … The fishing line gave me pause, along with a huge-looking staple gun. It looked like a scene from one of those horror movies where unlicensed wannabe doctors stole kidneys from unsuspecting tourists. I felt like Frankenstein's monster, covered only in a sheet. A bone-chilling cold swept through me. I hadn't felt this horrible since being turned; maybe it was the loss of blood or being that close to death. Whatever it was, I could barely sit up on my own. When I did, I found the tremors to be almost too unbearable. I stretched my legs out, slowly pulling the sheet back around me, shivering. Only a small amount of embarrassment burned my cheeks at the thought of Alastair or Paul seeing me in my underwear— they'd saved my life, so I wasn't going to complain now. Next to the tray, I saw a Styrofoam cup full of blood waiting for me. It was still warm, and my stomach churned at needing fresh blood in my system. I took it between trembling fingers and drank it down in one gulp, instantly feeling better.

I pulled the sheet back, noticing the fresh bandage covering my chest and abdomen. I winced at the onslaught of sharp, searing pain, and a sudden flashback of being shish-kabobbed hit me. I shuddered at the recollection. All I wanted to do was to lie back down and go to sleep for a million years. Memories of the past had already started swelling deep inside me, slowly seeping back in.

Not yet—I wasn't ready to remember everything.

I heard a conversation from some other part of the cabin and I found it to be a much-needed distraction from my current situation.

This time, it was Paul who spoke. "I tried to do what I could, but she's in a right state..."

"Any word from Corinth or Vinson?" I heard the worry and strain dripping like acid out of Alastair's voice. And then what I had been trying to keep at bay sent my stomach crashing up into my throat. Corinth and Vinson weren't back. *Corinth* was still in an incredible amount of danger. I doubled over, whimpering in misery at the thought that I'd abandoned him.

There was the imperceptible sound of someone shaking their head and then a moment later the sound of a door creaking open.

I heard Paul say, "I'm going to make another sweep. I'll call if I find them, but I used up all our fresh supply. You'll need to help her if I don't make it back with more blood soon."

The door slammed closed, and I heard the unmistakable sound of the Beetle sputtering to life and the engine fading away.

Corinth and Vinson were missing—I had to help.

I planted my feet on the ground, and clutched at my side, gasping in pain. When the agony subsided, I turned around, wrapping the sheet around me like a toga, and then hobbled over to a chair in the corner of the room, where someone had laid my clothes out for me. Injuries be damned, I was going after them. As soon as I changed, I went in search of weapons. I hadn't been able to spend a lot of time at my father's cabin, for fear of another vamp clan finding it, so I wasn't sure what Paul or Vinson had stocked up on. Knowing my dad, he had some high-tech gear waiting for me.

I stopped at the threshold of his bedroom, finding myself unable to step inside it. From the doorway, I could see it was sparsely decorated: a thick red-and-black checkered blanket covered the twin-sized bed in the corner of the room. It smelled like him in there. Worn leather, gunpowder, and something else I couldn't quite put my finger on. He didn't just stay here from time to time; he had made this his home. He had put down roots. This was why I had been avoiding this place. I didn't want to face the loss and guilt. Those feelings already clung to me like old friends. Thinking about it sent a longing ache for the past running through me like a fissure. I wondered what would happen if the figurative crack burst.

The unmade bed hadn't been touched since he'd died. Pillows lay scattered on the floor, reminding me of the time I first saw him in that dingy apartment in downtown London. Paul had told me no one stayed in this room but me.

A single framed photo sat beside the bed on a small nightstand. It was what finally brought me hobbling all the way into the room without even realizing it.

I was about seven when the photo had been taken. Sitting on a swing with my legs straight up in the air—the biggest grin on my face. I remembered that day. After Dad took the picture, I flew off the swing and banged my knee all up. He'd consoled me by taking me to get ice cream. It was a good memory even though I'd been hurt.

I found myself standing in front of an unopened cardboard box at the foot of his bed. Throwing the lid open, I discovered a spare set of watches like the ones my dad had given us. Beneath the watches were three blue plastic containers that all contained brand-new pistols. The smell of stringent oil and grease assailed me as I inspected them. They were all fully loaded and ready to go. I grabbed a duffel bag by the bed, moving more slowly than I would have liked; I began to shove supplies inside it. As soon as I threw the bag over my shoulder, I winced under its full weight—a sign of how weak I still felt.

The motels he'd chosen to stay in had always been a means to elude Gabriel. But this place had been my dad's space. I half expected him to walk through the door to tell me to put my shoes on and go get my clan.

I put a hand on the photo and whispered, "I'm working on it, Dad."

I turned to leave, but instead of being met by my reincarnated father, Alastair was in the doorway, his arms crossed over his chest as if he couldn't decide if he was angry or relieved.

I sucked in a stunned breath, dropping the duffel bag.

I could've had my memory scrubbed and wiped, but I could never forget those hauntingly intense blue eyes of his. Now that I had the chance to study him more closely, I realized in the time since he'd been gone, he looked like he'd aged. And normally, they would have blinded me with their brilliance, but now they were red-rimmed and glassy with fatigue—the truth of how hard he'd worked to keep me alive was evident. His dark-wash jeans were stained with my blood. A damp lock of blond fell over one eye. The way he was looking at me stole my breath away—as if he were just as spellbound at seeing me as I was at seeing him. It was funny how time couldn't dim our chemistry.

I drifted closer as if an invisible magnet had been

placed between us, drawing me enthrallingly toward him. "After all this time—" My voice caught and I stopped within a hairsbreadth of him.

His face was still crumpled with sorrow and empathy after he had watched me take in my father's room for the first time.

But I was already almost past him, ready to run the entire way back to Gabriel's warehouse, barefoot if I had to. Even though Alastair looked exhausted, he still put a firm but gentle hand on my shoulder, trying to guide me over to my father's bed.

His baby-blues flashed under a creased brow as I gave him a stern glare. He held his hands up in surrender. "Where do you think you're going?" *That's how I remember them: big and bold and bright and endless.* "The building came down. I barely got you out..."

I had heard him use that same pacifying voice on me in the past, back when I was human, when he had tended to me like a babysitter watching over a disobedient child.

I ground my teeth together to keep them from clacking, so as not to prove his point. "I'm going to get my team back."

"You almost bled out. It was a lucky thing Paul had spare blood on hand … If I hadn't given you a transfusion on the way here, you'd be dead. You need to rest—"

"Are you coming with me?" My voice broke as a tremor ran through my whole body. "Y-y-you should have gone after him."

Alastair was in front of me now, blocking my exit. "I haven't heard from Vinson. He'll make contact when he's able."

"*MOVE.*" My *Sight* had taken over, and the dark void

was on sudden violent display. "If Corinth is dead, it's on *me.*"

I'd rather deal with anger than grief. If Corinth *was* dead, I'd never forgive myself. I let him risk his life. I was angry and I needed an outlet to pin it on. After almost dying, the fear of never seeing Alastair again, and everything else I'd been through, I snapped. He'd been gone eight months. No word. Nothing.

I pulled my fist back and let it fly. The sound of his nose breaking told me how mad I'd actually been at him. He staggered back, a hand to his face at the same time as I doubled over, the sudden wash of icy-hot pain rooting me to the spot. Barely above a whisper, I managed to ask, "How did you find me?"

He held up his watch and flashed me a grin; despite him being so tired and the fact that I'd just hit him, it still lit up his entire face. "You pushed the button."

I squared my shoulders; ready for the battle I knew was coming. Instead, he was wrapping surprisingly warm arms around me. Maybe he expected more of a fight, but my anger fizzled and then slowly drained out of me as he pulled me closer against him, his grip firm and unyielding. He rubbed his hands along my arms, down my back, and over my shoulders until my shivering finally stopped. I felt every ripple and bump of hard-packed muscle in his torso and chest as he pressed against me. Now that I was in his arms, I realized I didn't want him to let me go. Not ever again.

Any thoughts of shoving him out of the way fled. His chest heaved up and down as he breathed my name, "*Larna,*" against my ear, nuzzling the side of my face with his. "I thought you were dead back there."

"*Me?*" I said, frustrated. "I've been worrying about you for months."

Each rise and fall of his chest proved to me he was alive. *He was okay.* It was also as soothing as a hammock swaying in the wind. I was frozen, rendered motionless, and purified of the capability to draw in a deep breath. The desperate need to maintain physical contact wasn't lost on me. Warm, ragged breaths hit the side of my face, my neck; my eyelashes—his breathlessness meant vulnerability and desire, and I felt my heart swell at finally getting confirmation that he felt the same way as I did about him. I didn't mind the discomfort from my wounds now. My own need matched his in intensity as I pulled him closer, letting the warmth of his body seep into mine. I needed *him*. He smelled like he always did, of his old-man deodorant mingled with sweat, smoke, and blood. It was good to know I hadn't imagined something between us all those months ago. I *had*, however, played this reunion out over and over again in my head.

And it was all so strange and intoxicating, the feeling of everything being right in the world. As if he'd never left.

I let out a strangled sob before saying, "I missed that old-man deodorant of yours."

"I'm sorry I was late."

He laughed softly against my hair, ruffling it as I nodded against his chest. "You did cut it a little close."

Guilt threatened to send me crashing into a blubbering heap at his feet for forgetting about Corinth for this one tiny moment. I pulled back from him, panicked. "I haven't seen you in eight months. You have no idea what's going on. You could have died. This whole time … no text or word or phone calls … What if you had been compelled?" I breathed, "You could be compelled now. I mean, how'd you find my dad's cabin?"

He stepped back, his hands still on my shoulders as he searched my eyes. "Vinson told me the address. I don't have any memory gaps—I'm not being compelled or mind controlled. I am in control of my own faculties, I swear."

He turned and moved back into my dad's bedroom, grabbed the duffel of supplies I'd gathered, and walked back to the door of the cabin and pulled it open. Without a backward glance, he stepped through and vanished. The door swung wide as the wind picked up, whipping leaves around in a vortex. I had this sudden feeling of dread that if I walked outside, he would be gone forever this time.

Following slowly in his wake as if in a dream, I inhaled the windswept earth into my lungs; he was there, waiting for me in the driver's seat of a silver Mini Cooper. I had no idea where the car had come from, but I was grateful he had it.

As soon as I jumped into the passenger seat, he said, "Let's go find our friends."

I couldn't admit to him that I had had a fleeting moment of apprehension when he'd walked out and left me. He really did have this horrible habit of toying with my heart and not even knowing he was doing it—or maybe he did.

Chapter 14

Corinth

I WASN'T DEAD. GRANTED, I didn't feel so hot. Imani hovered over me, her dark eyes wide and lovely, with raven hair draped over my face like a curtain. She sat back on her heels, examining a broken fingernail once she knew I was okay.

Something had changed. I felt more alert and my breathing wasn't as shallow. "What's going on?" I asked, sitting up. I hurt everywhere, especially my chest, where I'd been trying to pull in oxygen for the better part of an hour.

She put a finger to her lips and cocked her head to the side, the corners of her eyes quivering as she strained to listen to something I couldn't hear. "Somebody's coming," she said. "There was a cave-in on the other side. The rubble shifted in our favor."

When I glanced down, I noticed her hand still resting on my chest. I coughed and looked away. She seemed to sense my growing discomfort and edged back to give me some space.

"I see it now … where I was blind before."

I sat up straighter, suddenly curious about why she

was looking at me with a weird sort of reverence. "See what?" I asked.

"Why you're so special," she said simply.

I started coughing as dirt and soot settled deep into my lungs. "My mother says I'm special … Sorry, Sheldon Cooper fan here."

"I've been around enough shamans, priests, voodoo doctors, faith healers, and hypnotists—even the Pope—to recognize a sign when I see one. I am an expert in religion."

I held up a hand. "Wait—did you say the *Pope?*"

"Yes. Pope Leo XIII, to be more specific. Dying, coming back to life, wielding ancient artifacts; spiritual individuals—" She stopped suddenly to pick up my blade.

Even though she'd saved my life, she was still willing to hand me over to Gabe, where I'd live to be the ripe old age of a lab rat. This was my only chance to get her to see reason. She might be swayed to switch sides, and I was only too ready to convince her.

"You said my blood is the key? What does that mean?" I asked quietly. "If what you say is true, you don't believe I'm destined to be a lab rat." I tried to clear my parched throat. "I know I'm meant for something else—something more—and I know you're searching for proof."

She'd all but admitted as much.

Her hands started to shake, a sign that told me to keep digging. She was right on the verge of telling me everything. I could see it in the way she avoided eye contact.

"You said it yourself. You're an expert on religion. You know everything there is to know about *my* dagger." I made sure to stress the word *my*. If I kept saying it, maybe she'd start believing it. "It's meant for me. You know it is. I can feel it. What you said about my blood … are you referring to lineage?" Hazarding a guess, I said, "*You know what I am, don't you?*"

As if the very mention of me being *something* else was enough to bring it out of me, I felt the sudden change in atmosphere—which should have been impossible; we were below ground, buried underneath a ton of rubble.

The air was charged. It threatened to suck the remaining oxygen out like a vacuum. Imani's eyes widened as she stuck a hand out, trying vainly to feel for the ozone as thick as a blanket wrapped around us. It started out as a dense haze that flickered to life like clouds being backlit by lightning in a thunderstorm.

It wasn't until I looked down at my hands that I realized my fingers crackled with that same lightning—an impossibility fifty feet under a pile of rubble. Mother Nature had decided to possess me, and I liked it.

It had been the same back when I'd almost killed the vampire who'd sampled my blood. Imani barked out an astonished yelp, dropping my blade. It clattered to the ground at my feet as a pungent zing of ozone struck—the telltale sign of an impending rainstorm. Retrieving the dagger, my gaze flicked to hers right as the feral look in Imani's eyes returned. *Kill or be killed.* She flew at me, wrapping her hands around my throat, cutting off precious oxygen. I returned her snarl with one of my own, angry for being stopped from taking back what belonged to me. My veins sizzled as the supercharged energy snaked its way through them, as uncontainable as bottled lightning. The sparks arced off the tip of the blade, curling, twisting, and coiling around my wrist like fire from a welder's torch—

And at that same time, a loud knocking came from overhead, someone's desperate attempt to get to us. A fragment of light knifed through the crack in the stone and mortar above. Whoever was out there was close to freeing us.

Even with all that commotion, Imani's eyes stayed locked on mine.

The ringing in my ears had been replaced by the sound of my own hammering heart—the force inside of me threatening to unleash itself in an almighty display of devastation.

Imani's eyes went wide. "*Impossible.*"

Dirt and debris pelted us from above, peppering my hair and dusting her long black eyelashes gray. White light rippled across the handle of the blade as Imani whispered, "You're too dangerous. I'm sorry, but this has to be done."

Imani's hands pressed unforgivingly against my windpipe. Even though she was trying to kill me, I still found myself grinning back at her, my power reflected deep in her inkblot irises. Through her eyes, I could see the ribbons of deadly light snaking out of empty eye sockets. A part of me, the part that was still human, screamed at the sight.

She seemed to come to the conclusion that she was damned either way, because as suddenly as her fervor started, it stopped, and she relinquished her hold on my neck. I pressed the tip of the blade to her chest, the cold metal kissing bare skin right above the plunging neckline of her dress. All I had to do was push a little further. The sudden urge to end her right here and now was almost impossible to resist. It was what I was meant to do. She wasn't going to stop me.

No one can.

You will not kill her. Resist the urge. Fight it.

You are not meant *to be a cold-blooded killer.*

I heard Larna's pleading voice inside my head, begging me to come back to her. My heart lurched. I really wanted to come back to her. I could see the memories on the backs of my eyelids: a vision of me sitting on Larna's front lawn, morning's dew-soaked grass drenching the seat of my pants, and me not caring … and then it shifted to my kiss with Larna on our first date—it had been pleasant and delicate and fleeting. The unexpected way in which I'd planted one on her had been all too sweet, the kind of unforeseen kiss that people told their grandkids about years later. It still lingered in my memory.

Put the blade down, Ringer—Larna would say.

My fingers tightened around the hilt, digging against the solid metal. I willed the pain to ground me, to keep me centered and focused in the here and now. I didn't have to kill Imani. I didn't *want* to kill her. I saw how frightened she was of me.

I let out a hissing gasp, sagging back against the wall. Dropping the blade down to my side, I thought, *this was a win. My win.* It meant I controlled my own destiny; no one else—not the powers that be or my bloodline or the dagger.

The commotion outside increased, bringing me crashing back to reality and the problems still at hand. It was only a matter of seconds before we were either released from our tomb or crushed by concrete.

The real question was, who would be on the other side to greet us?

Stones and bricks collapsed like a stack of cards right as a hand reached down, yanking me miraculously clear of the cave-in.

The last thing I saw was Imani's red stained dress and bare feet before she was buried alive.

Chapter 15

Corinth

ASH AND SOOT TICKLED the back of my throat, and smoke clogged my nose. Fortunately, whatever fire prevention system had been in place was now working, because water trickled from the ceilings, keeping the rest of the flames at bay.

I found my grip on the hilt of my blade had tightened to a bone-crushing caliber.

Vinson raised an eyebrow at seeing my white-knuckled hold on the blade. "Gabriel's clan is right outside freight doors. Unless you can take out his entire brigade with your soulless lightning eyes … we must go. Now."

I glanced down to see the last remnants of hot silvery light fizzling out of my palms. Whoa … no wonder he was looking at me like that. "Soulless? Come on, man." I shrugged in conceit of that description, squeezing my eyes shut as sweet relief flooded through me. "I think this might work."

The very fact that I had been able to pull myself back from the brink of killing Imani was the best news I'd had all day—I mean, besides not dying.

Blowing out a cleansing breath, I sheathed the blade at my hip. It felt good having it back, strapped to my thigh again. For the first time since it had been taken, I was able to feel a little of the built-up tension drain out of me. By the amount of devastation around us, I was surprised I was even still alive. The tiny opening Vinson had pulled me through was no longer there. The upper floors had collapsed, caving in all the way to the subbasement, where we'd been trapped. I tried to scramble down to see if Imani was alive, but Vinson pulled me back.

The slabs of concrete had to weigh at least several tons. If I stepped or even breathed wrong, this whole place could come down around us. There was no way we could get her out without more help.

"We can't just leave her down there …" A pang of pity and remorse rose up inside me, along with the feeling of having missed a golden opportunity. "She's got the answers I need."

Vinson growled, "She deserves nothing less."

I turned in a circle, scanning our surroundings. "Where's Larna?"

"She got hurt … Then we got separated. I went after red bitch." And as if I were merely an afterthought, he added, "And you."

The pit of my stomach dropped out as panic twisted my gut. "How bad?" My mouth was so dry the words had become drastically harder to get out. "Vinson … how bad …was … she hurt? How long have I … been trapped down there?"

"Bad," he grumbled. "Hours." He cocked his head, listening. "They're coming. We go now."

I spun my dagger back up into my fist defiantly. "I'm

not leaving without Larna."

Vinson said something in Russian and spit on the ground. When he saw I wasn't budging, he lifted his wrist to show me his watch. The display was blinking the word "LARNA" and the coordinates of her dad's cabin. We had all memorized the address in case we got separated from each other—turns out that had been a good idea on her part.

I breathed a sigh of relief. "You could have just told me that," I muttered. *Smart thinking, Larns.*

"Love is foolish. You are foolish. Now we go."

My cheeks flushed in embarrassment. "Is that your idea of a pep talk?"

"I placed charges on upper floors, but we must go that way to get out. How long can you hold breath?"

I had an idea what he was about to do, but something told me I didn't have much choice or say in the matter. "I don't like where you're going with this." I grabbed the edge of my T-shirt, tore a piece off, and then tied it around my head, over my mouth. Smoke and soot had started to work its way down into my lungs again.

Vinson studied me as if calibrating my height-to-weight ratio and then, without another word, plucked me into a fireman's lift, ignoring my weapon as he did so. My already-bruised chest did not thank him for that. This was so humiliating. I was tall, which made it that much more awkward for him to carry me. Also, the way he took off felt like being on top of a runaway locomotive. The sensation left me feeling ill. I willed myself not to throw up, as from the edge of my vision I kept catching terrifying glimpses of orange and red glowing embers: signs that the inferno was eating its way through the warehouse.

He was moving so fast now I was pretty sure his feet weren't even touching the ground. When we hit what I thought was a stairwell, I really started to panic. My vision blurred, and the heat felt blistering against my forehead and cheeks. I knew I should've gotten a haircut. It was only about thirty seconds before I realized I couldn't hold my breath any longer. My stomach heaved and my lungs burned, and unable to take it any longer, I sucked in a gallon of smoke. This was way worse than inhaling water. My head exploded with pain. Everything went pitch-black for a fraction of a second, and then came crashing back to me in flashes of light and fire, the rush of wind whipping in my face. I think we were suspended in midair for a full minute before Vinson landed heavily on something that shuddered and shook under-foot. Metal shifted and swayed—scaffolding maybe, or a fire exit, I wasn't sure which.

When he fell to a knee, I almost toppled over the side of the railing to plummet hundreds of feet to my death, but he regained his balance and took off again. A few seconds later, glorious fresh air was hitting me full in the face. I'd never been so happy to see sky. I loved oxygen.

As soon as my airway cleared and I could push cold air down my throat again, I threw up. Glancing around, I swiped a hand across my mouth. "Where are we?"

"On top of roof of attached structure we just came from. Gabriel has place surrounded."

Vinson vanished, and then reappeared carrying a backpack. It was the same one he'd brought with him. I watched, numb and disconnected, as he started emptying out the contents.

Clutching my dagger in one hand and my stomach

with the other, I said, "You have a way out?"

He gave me a maniacal grin, one that told me I wouldn't like the answer. I much preferred scowling Vinson over smiling Vinson any day of the week.

He pulled out a bunch of bungee cords and ropes and a harness. "Number one rule: Always have an exit plan."

"Oh … no way, I'm out." I slapped my hands together. "I'm not doing that," I said. "Besides, why can't you just spider monkey your way down the side of the building with me on your shoulders?"

Vinson growled something in response and tied some of the rope onto another piece of metal at the edge of the structure, then tested the knot. Satisfied with his handiwork, he jumped into one of the harnesses and then threw me the other one. "If I fall, I won't have enough energy to heal myself *and* keep you alive."

I made sure the dagger was tucked safely away before saying, "Well, why didn't you say so?" Shoving my feet through the loops, I yanked the straps up, cinching it around my waist. I'd seen rock-climbing equipment before, but I had never attempted anything like this, mainly because I hated heights and I liked living.

"This is your figure-of-eight descender." Vinson pointed to a metal device on my harness. "Feed rope through it to lower yourself to ground. Use legs to push off wall." He grunted. "A monkey can do it." He pointed to the knotted part of the rope near my harness. "Brake hand here." Then he pointed to the rope at my back. "Don't take your hand from this part of rope. Keep it near your hip."

Hasty instructions were worse when you had a concussion and smoke inhalation and your life depended on paying attention. I was very motivated to get to safety as we moved quickly to the edge of the structure. I made the mistake of looking down and seeing the eight-story drop below us. The ground pitched and rolled like a yacht in the middle of the ocean. I staggered back a step, putting a hand to my head until the vertigo subsided.

Vinson climbed over to the edge, grabbed the rope, and nodded for me to follow.

I reluctantly crawled over the side, mimicking what he did as he threw his feet out into open air and then disappeared in a whir of metal and burning rope, expertly scuttling down the side of the wall like an aerial acrobat. When he hit the ground, he motioned for me to follow.

I kicked my legs out over the side of the roof, said a little prayer, and then pushed myself out into open air. *You can do this. Nice and easy.* The feeling of free-falling to my death made me blanch and my stomach heave. "This is a bad idea," I whispered. "Title of my autobiography... Sure, let's commit arson and take out Gabe's entire armory—it sounded like a swell idea at the time."

When I glanced back down, Vinson let out slack from the line and motioned for me to keep going. Balancing myself against the side of the wall, with feet straight and harness achingly tight, I used my brake hand like he'd shown me, ever so slowly inchworming my way down the side of the building. It probably looked Spider-Man cool. Okay, I'd settle for geriatric Spider-Man cool. I definitely had swagger. Readjusting, balancing and creeping along, I worked my way down. This might have been mildly fun if I wasn't afraid of plummeting to a horrible and painful death.

Once I thought I'd gotten the hang of it, confidence bolstered me along, and I started moving faster. The sensation of being weightless wasn't so bad. I felt myself grinning despite the danger, barely touching the balls of my feet against the wall as I bounded down.

Jump ... Lower ... Jump ... Keep hand on brake ... Move.

Vinson must have sensed my confidence boost, because he started letting out more slack in the line, and because boldness was a bitch, my legs, which had been okay only a moment earlier, suddenly gave out from underneath me. Unable to stop my downward spiral, the ground rushed up, but before I was turned into a pancake, I slammed painfully against the side of the wall, breath leaving my lungs as the line snapped taught upon impact. *Please hold my weight.*

Vinson pulled the line tight until I could get myself back under control. Sweat beaded my forehead as I stabilized myself and straightened my wobbly legs back out in front of me. This time, when I started my descent, I used a wee bit more caution. After what seemed like an eternity, my feet hit the ground, and I released the harness, my legs shaking uncontrollably.

The sun cut a path through the tops of the trees, and the plumes of smoke lightening the darkened sky to a purple haze. From this side of the facility, it was all forest and cover. The start of the new day in all its wonderful glory said, "Rise and shine! You didn't die!" Burned plastic, chemicals, and gas permeated the ozone, proving just how much damage we'd really done. Gabe was gonna be mad at us. It almost hadn't been worth it. If Larna hadn't made it out, I would have been singing a different tune.

I brushed the dirt from my clothes. "Please tell me you have a Maserati waiting for us around the corner."

Vinson marched past me and stopped so I could catch up. "We walk."

I fell in line behind him and muttered, "I follow."

We entered the dense copse of trees right as a helicopter buzzed tantalizingly low over our heads. The search party had arrived. I don't know why the word *'party'* was attached to searching for anything—this was definitely *not* a party. Picking our way deeper into the woods, we kept a close eye out for any of clan Deimos's arrival on foot.

Five miles from the warehouse, the brush and woods started thinning out.

I rubbed a hand absentmindedly over my shoulder—there was a tight band of pain all the way across my chest that wouldn't let up. I concentrated on putting one step in front of the other as my exhaustion seemed to go bone deep. I'd only gotten thirty minutes of sleep the night before last. Maybe this was how zombies were made.

Now that I had time to think, I tried to play out the conversation with Imani again. My blood was the key to something. And then there was the look in her eyes. Even though I'd been able to stop that force inside me from taking over, I still kept worrying about the next time it would happen. Maybe I wouldn't be able to stop it. And what was with all this strange energy surrounding me? I stopped my mind from wandering anymore when I thought about laser beams shooting from my eyes.

Damp leaves stuck to the soles of my boots and to my pant legs. I imagined sinking down into the soft earth, never to be seen or heard from again. At least I would get some rest. When I finally stumbled out onto asphalt, out of the thick blanket of forest, I couldn't hide my groan of relief until I turned to see the look on Vinson's face.

His usual scowl had deepened and he was frowning, in concern or annoyance, I couldn't tell which. "A car is fast approaching."

I rested a weary hand on the hilt of my blade. I knew I didn't have much choice in the matter, but I really felt like, this time, I wouldn't be able to fight if my life depended on it.

Vinson pulled the arms of his sleeves up and pushed the button on his watch. It was close to five in the morning. We couldn't stay out in the open. The chances of being spotted by Gabe's people increased tenfold, and with a helicopter searching the area, it made our situation that much more precarious. Vinson's eyes flicked to my hand on the blade. He twisted his wrist around for me to see the display on his watch. It showed a rapidly approaching green dot that read "LARNA." And then a silver dot on the horizon was screeching around the corner.

I could see the passenger waving furiously from out of the car window. As soon as they were close enough for me to make out, my legs started moving of their own accord. Even though I was tired beyond belief, I still managed to speed up as I watched the rescue party's blessed and well-timed arrival.

Unfortunately for me, the helicopter swooped down; buzzing so low I thought it might scalp me. Its sudden appearance made me think it had some sort of stealth mode in place. A spike of adrenaline and fear tore through me, and my curses were swallowed up by the thundering blades beating at the air.

Vinson, who was, of course in front of me, turned

around right as the chopper dropped down between us, cutting off my escape to the rapidly approaching getaway car.

Blades whirred, thumping the air with so much force I was sure it would open a portal to another dimension.

All of our hard work escaping, only to be caught once again.

I wondered how I hadn't heard the sound of the blades lashing the air earlier. Now, though, I couldn't even hear the thundering of my own heart—I only felt its erratic stutter–stopping rhythm in tune with the thumping of the blades ... so close now I could see the people inside the chopper scurrying around, getting ready to jump out—

I staggered back, putting a hand over my face right as Larna came into view from the other side of the flying behemoth, a tiny dot of arms and pixie black hair sticking up.

Chapter 16

Larna

CORINTH WAS ALIVE, BUT he was about to be caught by the bad guys. A helicopter swooped out of the clouds like an invisible wraith—its sudden appearance making my heart rate skyrocket. I reached into the bag of goodies I'd taken from my dad's cabin, pulled out a hand cannon, and took careful aim at the chopper's rotor. Alastair's grip tightened on the wheel as he accelerated at breakneck speed.

As soon as we were close enough, I fired a volley of rounds at the sleek, black chopper. Bullets pinged off the blades, striking home. Black smoke roiled from the engine, and the pilot banked off to the right. Amazingly, it was enough to make them back off—I didn't think I had done enough damage to take it down, but something told me they didn't want us dead because they weren't firing at us. The bird circled around right as Alastair drove us right through the wall of thick black smoke it left behind.

We swerved to a halt, rubber still burning on asphalt, so Vinson and Corinth could jump inside.

"*Go, go, go!*" I shouted.

Alastair was already slamming on the gas as Corinth swiveled around, looking out the window to get eyes on the chopper, but it had already disappeared into a cloud of fumes and exhaust.

I turned to evaluate Corinth. Every inch of him was covered in soot, scratches, and bruises, and he had a knot the size of a goose egg on his forehead. Even though he appeared utterly sapped, he still slapped me on my back in greeting. After his reception, he promptly slumped over and was out cold in seconds.

I gave him a worried glance in the rearview mirror.

"He has smoke inhalation and concussion," Vinson said in answer to my gaze.

I couldn't help but feel bad that Corinth couldn't heal like we could. "You should probably try and keep him awake."

Vinson gave a small shake of his head. "I don't think I could wake him if I tried."

When I turned to Alastair, his face was a mask of concentration, brow furrowed and jaw clenched tight as he flew down the road, hitting curves at speeds dangerously close to tipping us over. I held on to the door handle and gritted my teeth.

After doubling back and retracing our route a few times over to ensure we hadn't been followed, we managed to make it back to the cabin in under a couple of hours. All the while, Corinth slept soundlessly next to Vinson. I didn't like how still and quiet he was.

The helicopter never returned for round two.

Vinson deposited the still-slumbering Corinth into

my dad's room. I knew he needed the rest more than anything else right now, but I was worried for him when he didn't wake even with being carried inside like a ragdoll.

The cabin was a three-bedroom, two-bath split with a cozy living room and fire-place. Surprisingly, it wasn't heavily fortified. Paul told me my dad had been in the middle of renovating it for that very purpose. Having had the chance to explore a little more, I found that my favorite spot in the whole place was the enclosed back patio. On a lazy Sunday, I could imagine myself enjoying a cool breeze coming from the oversized windows but, because we were on high alert, they remained locked and secured. My father had loved the outdoors. The cabin was built in the late eighteenth century, but Dad had worked hard on updating it, making it his own private sanctuary.

Eclectic, mismatched barstools and worn leather couches made up the living room, along with the pool table that had been used as my makeshift gurney. No point in getting blood all over the nice furniture.

I felt a sting of tears at the backs of my eyelids. There really hadn't been any down-time to stop and take it all in. I guessed now that everyone was safe for the time being, things had started to hit me. I swiped at my eyes in irritation. The house was full, and I didn't want anyone to see how much it affected me, being here. My father's space made me miss him terribly.

Alastair and I hadn't said a word to each other since we'd gotten back. The reasoning behind this was simple. He owed me an explanation, but because it wasn't out of the realm of possibility that he could be compelled, I wasn't sure if I could trust him just yet.

A small rap on the doorframe to the outside patio

brought me out of my reverie. I glanced up to see Alastair's gloriously brooding face studying me. It was a look that was undeniably *him*. It reminded me of the time when he was outside Gabriel's manor, on the stone walkway. I had thought I was watching him without his knowledge—that is, until those unnaturally blue eyes had snapped up to meet mine, proving me wrong.

I nodded at him. He joined me at the tiny two-seater breakfast nook on the back patio. There was a marked difference in his appearance since yesterday. As he sat down across from me, I tried to discern what that difference was. There was an up-to-no-good smile on his face. The youthful spark was back in his eyes. It stole my breath away momentarily. My heart lurched agonizingly in my chest. I couldn't believe I'd almost forgotten what an impact he had on me. He was absolutely striking.

I traced the outline of my mug's handle, suddenly wondering what it would be like to run my hands into his hair, and push that shock of blond back from out of his eyes.

The warm steam rising out of the cup drew my eye. It reminded me of being back at Nan's place—a time when we had truly gotten to know each other.

"Thank you … for showing up when you did," I told him, hesitating.

His lively blue eyes matched the lightness of his mood as he said, "It would help if you guys didn't get into trouble on the regular."

I picked up my teaspoon and pointed it at him. "Don't give me that all-knowing grin. I had it under control … and when I didn't have it under control—I still had it under control."

"Your idea of control is a lot different than mine," he said wryly. His eyes flicked to the cup near my hand. "Got any more?"

I gestured toward the doorway that led into the kitchen on the other side. "Fortunately for you, Paul stocked up on tea and Toblerone—it's in the cupboard above the fridge."

Alastair disappeared and then returned with a steaming mug and the candy bar that had been stashed next to the tea. He tore open the package, broke off a piece, and pushed the rest toward me. As he took a bite, he said, "I'm surprised you're not grilling me for answers."

I raised an eyebrow. "You're right; I could really use some answers on where you've been these past eight months, but it might not matter what you tell me if I can't trust you."

"Ah …" Understanding lit up his eyes. "You still think I'm being compelled."

"Are you?"

"As I said before, no. But it's good to be wary." He let the silence stretch between us, taking a sip of his tea. After he savored it for a moment longer, he cocked his head to the side, studying me. "Vinson said you saved his life back there," he said. "Do you know what that means?"

I shook my head, surprised that he actually sounded impressed. I found that his opinion of me, after all this time, still mattered greatly.

He leaned back and crossed his arms over his chest. "It means he'll be loyal to you up until the end. It's why he chose to help your father. Jack saved his life too."

This bit of information surprised me. I didn't know that much about Vinson and I found myself wanting to know more. "How did he save his life?"

Alastair took another bite of chocolate, weighing how much he should tell me, I guessed. When he finally spoke, he said, "That's not my story to tell. I'm afraid you'll have to ask Vinson." He paused. "I miss your old man though. You know … you remind me of him, now more than ever. Did I ever tell you about the first time he and I met?"

I sat up straighter and shook my head, finding myself suddenly very interested in what he had to say.

Alastair glanced up, but he was looking past me, seemingly reliving the memory all over again. "It was at Nan's place. Jack had decided to come traipsing onto her property, looking for me, but he didn't know it was me he was looking for. Gabriel told Jack he knew someone in his network was giving away information to another clan. Jack was supposed to gain Gabriel's loyalty when he came back with the traitor's head in hand—*my* head. He didn't have a face, only a location—Nan's farm. At the time, I was still Gabriel's driver." He nodded at me. "You remember?"

I mirrored his nod, trying to imagine my father and Alastair meeting for the first time. It must have been entertaining, because he had a crooked smile playing across his face as he remembered the recollection. "Well, Jack remembered too. As soon as your father saw me, he knew I was the one giving information to Nan—Gabriel's arch-nemesis. Jack and I had this standoff as soon as we saw each other … He had this conflicted look on his face, like he didn't want to kill me, but he had no choice. Gabriel had threatened to turn you if he didn't cooperate, to destroy his whole life for disobeying. If he didn't come back with *someone's* head on a stick—he would have turned you …" Alastair rubbed the back of his neck. "Lucky for both of us,

Nan was there to put a stop to it."

There were many days I tried to imagine my dad's "other" life, away from us. How he was living, what he was doing, who he had met before I knew he was fighting to protect me. I also didn't want to think about the fact that my father had to bring back someone's head to Gabriel. The choices he'd had to make to keep me safe had to have been terrible. My dad had told me he did a lot of things he wasn't proud of. I guessed this had been one of those instances.

I wiped a hand under my nose, glancing down at my now-lukewarm tea. "Let me guess, Dad tried to take your head off with his vambraces?"

Alastair barked out a laugh. "Understatement of the year…"

"That sounds like Dad all right," I whispered. I couldn't help but notice I'd used the present tense. I felt the raw emotion building up in the back of my throat. Suddenly I didn't want to talk about him anymore.

"Thank you—for sharing that with me," I said softly, and halted before adding, "Do you think that's why Gabriel wants you dead? Because he knew your intention was to betray him?"

Alastair's eyes flashed as brilliantly as any jewel I'd ever seen—eyes that could suck the blue right out of the ocean. He reached into his pocket and pulled out the timepiece I knew he carried with him everywhere. His eyes flickered to mine as a look I couldn't decipher crossed his features, but it was gone in an instant, replaced by acceptance.

"In the century I've been around, I've never allowed anyone to—" Alastair cleared his throat, as if it was too hard to finish that line of thought, and then he changed direction. "So, how are you feeling?" He pursed his lips. "You really had me worried there."

I unconsciously put a hand to my stomach, the phantom pain of being skewered all over again hitting me. The bandage was gone, and so was the giant incision the metal had left behind. I shuddered at the sensation and I wondered if I looked pale, because he reached a hand out to gently place it over mine. A jolt of electricity traveled all the way up my arm to the tips of my cheeks. His eyes were full of longing and hope. My heart contracted at seeing that look he was giving me.

"Your father made me promise to protect you," he said quietly. "Before he was killed, he asked me to seek out a clan called Eleutheros. Their leader's name is Sozo. It took me a long time to find them, and even longer to gain an audience with him. That's why I've been gone so long. Your father died before he could give me any more information about them." He swiped a hand through his hair. "I've always been a spy … a loner; it's what I do. Your father knew this. It's why he asked me to seek out this clan in the first place. You have to understand, Jack wanted to be on the same chessboard as Gabriel." Alastair shook his head. "He was obsessed about getting one move ahead of Gabriel. He predicted we would need to be a part of a stronger clan in order to take Gabriel down. He needed to be sure we could trust them … All that time he spent away from you—he was trying to gain an audience with these people."

I sat back, putting a hand to my mouth in thought. After a brief pause I took a sip of tea and, despite it being cool, I found I needed the mint to soothe my parched throat. "What did this Sozo have to say?"

"I would never have agreed to leave you and Corinth, but I believed your father. Gabriel has something planned … and not just for you … for him too. Like, end-of-the-world big." He held up a hand as if he knew I was about to bombard him with questions. "All I know is that we need time to plan and your father thought the answer might rest with this clan. They can protect us. Whether you believe we need their help or not. I think there was another reason he wanted me to seek them out, but I never found out what that was."

My blood ran cold at the thought that Gabriel might have something end-of-the-world planned for Corinth. I didn't need protecting, but Corinth sure did. Nothing was going to happen to him on my watch.

Even though I knew I shouldn't ask this before I knew he hadn't been compelled, I said, "You stole Corinth's blood, didn't you?"

There was only a moment's hesitation. "Yes."

I tried unsuccessfully to keep the anger out of my voice. "Why?"

Alastair let out a frustrated sigh. "It's complicated … Besides, you think I'm being compelled." There was an edge as sharp as a razor in his tone. "How can you trust anything out of my mouth right now?"

My fierce desire to protect Corinth overrode the logical part of my brain that said I should wait to question him further. He was pushing me. I fell for the bait hook, line, and sinker anyway. I had to know the answers to the burning questions. "You had no right to make that decision on your own," I snapped. "Tell me why they want his blood."

Alastair tried to pull my hand into his; imploring me to understand, but I tugged it away from him. He rocked back slightly, as if I'd pushed him. I could hear the hurt in his voice when he spoke. "You have to believe me. This is our only option. I should have come to you but there was no time. Do you know what Corinth is capable of?" Alastair's hands slapped the tabletop, and his eyes hardened like chips of sapphire ice. "Because I sure don't—"

I sat back, stunned. I'd never seen him this angry before. "What if they use it to hurt him?" My words came out in a rush and a lot louder than I wanted them to.

"Sozo gave me his word that wouldn't happen." His voice was strained as he added, "This is our *only* option."

I couldn't hide my skepticism. "And you believe him? You were probably compelled to say that—"

Alastair leaned closer, his tone frosty. "When vampires as old as Sozo give their word, they mean it." I was surprised at the harshness with which he had spoken to me. Alastair had always been calm and in control around me. Something was wrong. He was scared.

The anger melted out of me, leaving me feeling deflated and resigned. I'd never seen him this troubled, and it worried me. "Let me guess … these people have agreed to give us asylum and you said yes, without consulting us in the process or keeping us in the loop."

Alastair nodded unapologetically. "The question is, are you coming with me?"

Chapter 17

Corinth

I WAS DREAMING. BAREFOOT, standing alone in a field of soft, cushiony grass—not the scratchy kind of grass like back home—I wiggled my toes between the soft tufts as a ripple of tranquility ran from the soles of my feet to the tops of my shoulders. The weird thing was that I still felt the aches and pains of the past few days. My head was pounding, and there was considerable pressure in my chest. I rolled my shoulders back, trying to alleviate some of the tightness. My chest burned as a wave of dizziness washed over me. The sun seemed to help, and even though it was soothing against my skin, I still had to squint against its brightness.

Beyond the field of grass, yellow daisies dotted the rolling valley of hills. It seemed to stretch on forever. I was in the middle of a meadow inside a Thomas Kinkade painting. Why couldn't I have dreams like this all the time? Maybe I should start sleeping again. I wasn't one for romantic gobbledygook, but I had to admit I was impressed that something this striking had come from me. There were no people, blaring radios, or congested traffic—open space without any signs of technology was a rare thing to come by these days.

It smelled like fresh laundry drying in the sun. The only thing that would make this more relaxing was if I had a steaming mug of coffee in my hands.

There was something about this place that made me want to abandon all restrictions. Like I felt that if Larna were here with me, I might even ask her to dance— something I would normally have shied away from because I had two left feet.

My legs seemed to move of their own accord as I marched myself across the field to stop in the center of the meadow, turning around in a slow circle in order to take everything in. But as soon as I ended up back where I started, I nearly jumped out of my own skin.

Let me preface this by saying I don't have random dreams about strange men.

But when one appeared out of nowhere, it became slightly concerning. A tall stranger stood in front of me, where no one had been moments before. Also, when I say tall, I mean he was at least seven feet—professional basketball player height. I wasn't used to seeing anyone with a stature larger than my own six-foot-four-inch frame.

The man had on a tan linen suit and a fedora. Sandy blond hair touched the tops of his shoulders, and thin lines creased his forehead and mouth. I guessed he was at least forty. He had a friendly face. His eyes glowed gold like lanterns set adrift in the night sky. There was also a strange familiarity about him that I couldn't quite put my finger on. I'd seen him before; I knew it. Maybe it was in the way he was grinning at me, as if he were greeting an old friend.

"Hello—" I started to say, but a sudden stabbing

sensation hit me right behind my eyeballs. I sank to a knee, grabbing my head in between my hands.

This had to be me incorporating real-world pain into a dream. So focused on my misery, I didn't realize the man had stepped closer, until he touched my shoulder.

At first, I attributed my worsening condition to the stranger's presence.

It was why I flung my hand down to my side where I normally kept my dagger. It wasn't there and neither was my sheath. My lungs would be squeezed to an orange-juicy pulp at any second. I wheezed noisily, trying to suck in precious air.

The stranger, seeing my sudden mistrust, slowly backed away and said, "I need to heal you. Your lungs suffered major damage."

I grimaced up at him from my crouched position on the ground. He flashed me a reassuring smile, the kind of smile that could thaw the North Pole. He was looking at me like a veterinarian might look at a rabid animal.

"How could you poss—" I stopped in order to pull in a shallow breath "—know that?" I was panting like I'd just sprinted a mile. Maybe he was right about my lungs being damaged. *It's just a dream.* I would wake up and feel fine.

Without realizing he'd even moved within arm's reach again, he brushed a finger lightly across my forehead in a surprisingly compassionate gesture. And just like that, my headache was gone, along with the band of tightness in my chest and around my back.

I felt more alert, as if he'd injected my favorite thing directly into my veins—caffeine.

His kind smile grew wider as soon as he saw the relieved look on my face.

More than a little gob-smacked, I whispered, "Who *are* you?"

"I'm Dave." He said it with no other explanation, as if I should know him just by his first name. There were a million Daves out there. I didn't want to be the bearer of bad news to let him know I didn't recognize him, but then a sudden terrifying thought struck me—what if I was dead?

I had this mental image of my grandpa meeting me at the pearly gates. "Please tell me I'm not dead," I whispered, standing back up.

"You are not dead," Dave reassured me. "I wasn't able to make contact until you harnessed power from the blade," he said. "I sensed it the minute you did and then tracked you down in your dream."

I bent down, plucking one of the daisies from the well-manicured lawn at my feet. "Strangest dream *ever* …" I surveyed him from under my brow line, barely making eye contact. "Have we met before?"

Dave watched me twirl the flower in my hand, a million different emotions flitting across his features—so many, in fact, I couldn't discern one from the other. "In time I will tell you everything, but today, I came to warn you. If I can find you, the others can too."

He'd gained my full attention. My eyes darted from the flower up to his eyes at the mention of *warn* and *others*. Talk about eyes being the window of the soul—his were an infinite universe made up of the stuff astronauts wrote home about: new discoveries of empires and frontiers.

My jaw dropped open as I gasped, "Others? What *others*? What does that mean?"

"It means you are in grave danger. My strength is limited. If I had not risked healing you, the smoke inhalation would have damaged your lungs permanently. I will try and make contact again. I've managed to ward your mind from further intrusion—*temporarily*. If I can gain some of my strength back, I'll tell you everything. You have my word."

And then I awoke in a tangle of sheets; the feeling of grass between my toes still lingered. It was dark and I was confused and fuzzy headed. I put a hand to my forehead. No more goose egg.

Patting the rest of my body, I realized there weren't any more bruises either, and I felt rested for the first time in months—which was saying something.

Dave had done this to me. How was it possible to dream-hop and heal people by a single touch? He had come to warn me about a threat and said that he would be back with answers. *Why couldn't he have answers now …?* I fumbled around, groping in the dark for an end table or something that might resemble a lamp. As soon as my hand hit something solid, I felt for a switch. When I found one, I twisted the knob, and soft light flooded the room.

To my great relief, the blade was on the nightstand, sheathed safely inside the brown leather scabbard. The straps that normally tied around my thigh were wound neatly around it. I guessed Larna wanted to make sure to have it ready for me in case I needed it in a pinch. *She got me.* I rubbed my thumbs into my eyes, trying to relieve the sudden flood of emotions. Larna was okay. That was the most important thing. I knew we were at her dad's cabin, even though I had never been here before. This had been our meet-up spot, so it was safe to assume that that's where they'd taken me. At least we'd escaped out of Gabe's douchey clutches.

Scanning the room, I noticed a picture of Larna next to the lamp I'd switched on. The photo showed her to be about seven or eight-years-old, with her short legs extended out midflight as she swung herself on a swing.

I let my mind wander back to where I didn't want it to go. What threats could be worse than Gabe and his legion of bloodsuckers? The hard thump of my pulse beating urgently against the side of my neck seemed to be a premonition of what was to come.

I forced myself to get up on shaky legs, stumbling to the open door of the bathroom to flip on the lights. My mouth fell open at the image staring back at me in the mirror. No dark half-moon circles under my eyes; my chest was bruise-free, and the skin on my neck was smooth once again, as if no bite marks had ever existed. The only thing out of place was my hair, sticking up every which way.

Dave's power was definitely of the supernatural variety. Meeting him had really happened. Maybe he wasn't telling me the truth. An urge to call my dad struck. He was a religious man, and he had a lot more knowledge on miraculous healing, although I wondered if Dave could just be some ancient vampire gifted with extraordinary powers we didn't know about. I shuddered at the thought of someone stronger than Gabe out there. A sudden image of silvery light shooting out of my fingertips came to me. I thought back to Dave's words: harnessing the power of the blade. This guy had been my source on all things dagger related, and I'd let him slip through my fingers. I felt more than frustrated.

Splashing cold water on my face, I glanced at myself

one last time before slouching back out into the bedroom to throw on a fresh change of clothes that had been laid out for me. Lastly, I fastened the leather sheath to my thigh and then wrapped the straps around my leg, securing it snugly into place. *Ah, that's the stuff.*

In the living room, I found Paul, Al, and Larna all waiting expectantly for me. It figured they already knew I was up and around—they could hear a ghost fart in Canada with their supersensitive hearing.

Their jaws collectively dropped at seeing my appearance.

"What's everyone staring at?" I asked, feigning innocence to draw out the moment. I liked attention way more than Larna did. "Y'all should be used to the strange."

Paul's mustache twitched as he reached for a cigarette, muttering to himself, "You lot *are* the strange."

Larna was in front of me before I could blink or back away or, more appropriately, run, her hands exploring every inch of me for wounds I knew no longer existed. My cheeks flushed when her hands brushed lightly against my neck. I stopped her from probing any further, circling my fingers around her wrist.

She pulled out of my grasp to grab my forearm where I'd cut myself with the dagger. "You've been out of it for twenty-four hours." She ran her fingers softly along my skin, leaving goosebumps along my arms. She sounded almost breathless when she spoke. "How did you do it?"

Al stood in the corner of the room, watching me. I took the tiniest bit of pleasure in seeing his pupils narrow down to the size of tiny pinpricks—as close to a feral cat's eyes as I'd ever seen. He looked as uncomfortable as I felt, his lip curling up as he watched Larna's fingers skim over my ribcage. I caught one of her hands and flattened it against my chest, halting her father inspection.

She opened her mouth to ask more questions, but I stopped her with a look. "If you want me to—I can strip down to my underwear," I said roguishly.

Larna cast a worried glance in Al's direction.

Oh, great, I've already been replaced by this schmuck. I didn't trust Al. He could be compelled for all we knew.

"This is serious," she chastised. "You can't be turned, because of how toxic your blood is to a vampire, so this must be a side effect from the dagger." She inched back, putting a finger to her lip in thought. The tone of her voice suggested she was still stunned by my appearance as she said, "I don't understand how you could—" Her hazel eyes flickered to mine. "What happened? Corinth, *is* this a new ability?"

I wasn't sure if Larna had told Al about my anti-*Sight*. He hadn't been there when I'd made those discoveries.

I could still feel Al's heated glare on me as I turned back to Larna. "Can I talk to you alone?"

She nodded, grabbing my hand to lead me back to the room I'd just vacated. When she shut the door behind us and twisted around, her forehead was creased with a *V* right above her nose. I loved it when she made that face. Her concern made it that much cuter.

"Have you tested yourself since you woke up to see if you can heal like one of us?"

I plopped down on the bed, putting my head in my hands. "I'd really prefer not to have any more bloodletting happen to me right now." I risked a glance back up at her, trying to control the concern creeping into my voice. "There's something I couldn't tell you in front of Al."

Larna perked up as her green-and-brown flecked eyes flew to mine. "What is it?"

"This is going to sound crazy, even for our standards, so I'm just going right into it—a tall guy who said his name was Dave showed up in my dream." I clarified, "*Not* a figment of my imagination, Larna. This guy healed me with a single touch." I snapped my fingers. "And just like that, the pain was gone. I know I sound like a faith healer's dream right now, but this guy also told me there are people after me. He said it was because I harnessed the power of the blade, or something like that, and he warned me against further attacks."

Larna bit her bottom lip in thought. "Do you think it was real or incorporated into a nightmare? Maybe you were able to heal yourself on your own, like, with the dagger's help? Or maybe he's a manifestation *from* the blade?" She held up a finger. "The real question is, do you believe him?"

"So you believe me?" I asked, letting out a relieved sigh. "I thought it was going to take longer to convince you that this guy isn't just a figment of my imagination. He's real. He told me he would be back to tell me everything when he had had a chance to fully recover … and that's when I woke up … without a scratch on me."

She straightened to her full height, which wasn't saying much, and then pointed to the dagger at my hip. "Since the very first time you laid eyes on that thing, weird has become the norm."

We didn't say anything for a few minutes as I let everything sink in. A lot had happened. It was already hard enough to process, but I had to address the issue at hand—because I couldn't take the silent brooding any longer.

"Is Al back for good?"

As if I'd said the very thing she was worried about most, she sank down beside me on the bed, folding her hands in her lap. "He says he is … but I need you to use your hocus pocus on him … We have to make sure he hasn't been compelled."

I held up a hand, pretending to be offended. "First of all … *hocus pocus*? Do I look like a wizard? Really? And second …" I shook my head. "Nope, you're right, I don't have a second … It's definitely *hocus pocus*," I breathed. "What has he been doing all this time?"

"He claims my dad sent him to seek out another clan for protection. I guess we're doing this whole clanning-up thing. The problem is that we don't have a lot to go on with these people, except for Alastair's word—which I *do* trust, by the way," she added pointedly. "We can't do this alone. Apparently, Dad thought there might be something bigger at play, and you're right smack in the middle of it. Alastair said some pretty scary things."

The hairs on the back of my neck rose as I thought about Dave and his sudden appearance, and Imani's last confession before she was buried under the rubble. This was about my blood. It couldn't all be just coincidence.

I said, "As I recall, Gabe wants you just as badly as he wants me … which is *gross*, by the way. He'd old. There's a reason he needs us; we just have to figure out what that is."

Larna glanced away, and then slowly leaned into me, pressing her body so closely against my side I was sure she was trying to keep herself from breaking apart.

Throwing an arm around her, I listened to the slow, steady sound of her breathing as she slid an arm around my waist, sucking in a hiccupy breath. "I thought you were dead back there when that building came down." She laid her head against my shoulder.

"Yeah … let's not do that again anytime soon," I whispered into her hair.

She laughed softly, sitting back up to study me, the way she sometimes did when she thought I might be hiding something from her. Those dark, avocado-flecked eyes threatened to pull me in and never let go.

There was something that had been bothering me. I felt like Larna should know about Imani and our conversation, so I lowered my voice, whispering, "Imani told me my blood was the key. I don't know if I believe her or what it means, but I thought I should mention it."

Her eyebrows drew together as she considered the implications of what I'd just said. "Alastair stole your blood and gave it to this new clan … Your blood can kill a vampire—maybe that's what she was referring to. I mean—the key to what?"

I shook my head, trying to think it through, but something at the back of my mind kept telling me we still didn't have all of the correct puzzle pieces in order to put it all together just yet. "This other clan … they team Gabe or what?"

She shrugged. "The jury is still out on that. Supposedly, Alastair made sure Eleutheros—that's their name—gave their word not to harm you. That's why I need you to do your reverse compulsion. Make sure they aren't sending him here for ulterior motives."

I flashed her a lopsided grin. "They should have just sent Bella Thorn after me; I wouldn't have said no to her." Larna's frown deepened, which told me she didn't think I was funny, so I slapped my thigh and added, "I say we go meet this new clan … see what they're all about. The enemy-of-my-enemy-is-my-friend rule might apply here." I added quickly, "That is, if Al checks out."

"You sure?" she asked, searching my eyes again for signs of any doubt.

I nodded in earnest.

"Okay, let's talk to Alastair," she said.

We were seated in the living room. After explaining our situation to Al, he stood slowly from the worn leather loveseat to glare at me from underneath pensive brows. "Corinth can compel vampires?" He shook his head in disbelief. "That's new."

Larna gestured at me from across the room. "He can't turn it off and on like a switch; it only works when another vamp tries to compel him first." She gave me an impressed grin. "He doesn't even break out into a sweat. We think it's a defense mechanism. My theory is the blade supplies him with certain abilities when he needs it most."

I said, "Well … that part about not breaking out into a sweat is sort of an exaggeration. I mean, I do get extremely tired afterward." I widened my eyes at Larna and said loudly, "*Larna*, you've told him too much already."

Al barked out a laugh. "You realize how crazy all of this sounds, right? The dagger is an inanimate object. It doesn't have feelings. Did that change while I was gone?" He turned his quizzical glare back on me. "Does it sing and dance too?"

His superior attitude was really getting to me, so I let the sarcasm drip from my voice like acid to match his own.

"It's more like Stephen King's Christine—an evil car hell-bent on seeking revenge from those who bullied its owner."

Larna's mouth dropped open.

It was at this point that I knew I'd overstepped my bounds. I probably shouldn't compare the blade to a malevolent killing machine.

"Okay, obviously, I didn't mean it like that … I don't want to kill y'all." I laughed uneasily, pressing my palms against my eyes. "We can sit here and talk about theories and what-ifs all day. What we *do* know is that Al can't be trusted until we make sure he hasn't been compelled." I said, "Let's just get this over with."

Al crossed his arms over his chest, suddenly looking very uncomfortable. It was probably the Christine remark that set him on edge. "If I agree to this, I need your word you'll only verify that I haven't been compelled. I don't want you poking around in my head any more than you have to." He added louder than necessary, "I need your word on that."

"Oh, trust me … I do *not* want to dig around in your noggin' any longer than I have to," I muttered. I was, though, going to dig around—a little. "I promise," I lied.

Chapter 18

Corinth

AL PULLED SOMETHING OUT of his pocket and ran his thumb across it.

I glanced at his cupped hand, unable to see what he was holding. "What's that?"

He looked down, blinking as if he didn't even realize he had anything in his grasp. After a second, he held it out to me so I could get a closer look. An ornate silver pocket watch sat in his palm. The intricate and delicate floral pattern wound itself around the clock-face. It looked like thick, gnarled roots. It was an eye-catching timepiece that I'm sure had to be worth a fortune now. I'd seen it before—the night I stabbed Gabe in the back. I remember Al kissing it for good luck. It meant something special to him. I was suddenly extremely curious as to why. He plucked it back up into his fist before I could study it any longer.

I scanned the wooded area surrounding the cabin. I could see why Jack had chosen this place to call home. The enclosed deck was great for watching wildlife. A red bird darted out of the knobby branches of an old oak tree. If this were Texas, you'd hear the cicadas chirping from miles away. Here, though, it was much quieter. I imagined Robin Hood hiding out among the canopied forest with a nocked arrow held at the ready … Enter stage left the merry band of thieves running away from Gabriel Stanton and his marauding gang of evildoers—my thoughts drifted to the tall stranger, Dave, and his warning against a looming threat.

When I was ready to talk, I turned back to face Al and found he was studying me, his eyes glowing with curiosity.

"What don't you want Larna to know?" I asked him, with the same amount of interest he was showing in me.

He took a slow sip of his drink of choice, which was vodka, without answering my question.

"You know the tough-guy routine doesn't work on me. I babble a lot," I said. "I can keep myself talking for hours … I'll win the battle of wits—"

"You think this is about winning?" Al swirled the alcohol around the lip of his glass. The way he did it, so smooth and imperious, with a graceful poise, almost made him seem even more threatening and alien. Was he trying to make a point?

I tried to hide my sudden unease with a shrug. "Isn't it?"

His drink came precariously close to spilling over the edge of the glass, defying every single law of gravity. They were unnerving, those unnatural reflexes of his. I supposed that was what he was going for—to put me off my game. Maybe he knew I didn't plan on sticking to just one question. Or maybe he was the one who was sweating it right now. *He should.*

"This is about Larna," he whispered, more to himself

than to me. Then his steel-blue eyes snapped to meet mine. "You like her, don't you?"

I hadn't expected him to be this direct, so I felt embarrassed when I started opening and closing my mouth, incredulous, searching for a quick retort. When I couldn't find one, I clamped my teeth together. I *really* wanted to tell him yes, to back off and let me pursue her, but there was something preventing me from saying it out loud. I needed to know exactly what he thought about her first—and there was only one way to do that.

"Look, I know you don't like me," I said, rattled. "I don't particularly like you … so why don't we get this ov—"

"I'm curious as to what I did to offend you," Al said, interrupting me. "It has to be pretty big for you to dislike me so much."

My words were leapfrogging over each other before I could stop myself. "You stole my best friend and let her get turned into a blood-craving leech. You ran off when she started counting on you … and then show back up, only to ride in on your high horse..." *Ugh. Yeah, I am that guy … the jealous, insecure one.* I hated myself for admitting that to him.

Al rubbed a hand across his face, his eyes flicking back to the watch still cradled in his hand. "You think she's a leech?"

"Nooo … I didn't mean it like that." I knew I didn't think of her that way. *What is wrong with me?* I looked away, disgusted at myself. "Maybe *I'm* the leech," I said, self-deprecatingly. "Larna is the farthest thing from a parasite; she's saved me countless times. This isn't entirely all *your* fault. I get it … Larna didn't need to get mixed up in all this, did she? I can't help but feel you and Jack let this happen on purpose."

Al leaned back, studying me. I could tell there was something seething just below the surface of those overly bright blue eyes. Guilt maybe.

After what seemed like an awfully long time, he blew out a frustrated breath. "I didn't *steal* your girl, mate. But you are right about one thing; I should never have underestimated Gabriel the way I did. That's on *me*. Larna should be happily oblivious to the existence of us *leeches*." He put extra emphasis on that word before forging on. "And I admire you for thinking you're being strong in the face of danger. I get it. I was human once … but both of us know you aren't as brave as you put on." Al scratched the bridge of his nose, barking out a laugh that sounded a lot like irony. "Actually, I pegged you for a coward when I first met you."

"And you still do." I pressed my lips together in irritation, shaking my head as comprehension dawned on me. "Of course you do."

Al raised an eyebrow. "I don't think you're a chicken, but I don't think you've graduated out of the bird family yet either." He leaned across the table, looking me in the eye. "Come on, level with me. How'd you do it? How'd you heal yourself?"

I rubbed a hand over the spot on my head where the bump used to be only a few hours ago. I wasn't going to let him in on anything until I knew I could trust him, maybe not even then. "I told you—I woke up like this."

"Uh-huh," he said, not sounding convinced in the least. "That might be true, but you're still keeping something from me."

"Why don't you tell me the real reason why you

left?" I countered.

He smiled, but it was humorless. "The issue at hand is if you compel me, I'll have no control over what you plan on asking me. Seems a bit unfair, don't you think?"

I matched his infuriating grin and put a hand on the hilt of my dagger. "Damn right it's unfair."

His eyes flicked down to the blade. "You made good and sure everyone on this entire planet associated with a vampire clan knows who you are. This is your only chance at finding asylum. You would really be that selfish? We can't fight Gabriel's people forever … and with that price on your head …" He let the sentence trail off, making sure it was perfectly clear what he thought would happen sooner rather than later.

I was doomed. Al blamed me for the hot water we now found ourselves in. This was his way of trying to get us out of it; except I was pretty sure he was throwing us right back into another pot of boiling water.

"Okay, fine," I grumbled. "I give you my word."

His gaze stayed locked on the blade at my hip. "Something we used to do when we were kids to prove our word was taking an oath."

I put my hand out to shake his, thinking that's what he meant by *oath*.

Al shook his head and laughed. "Proving your trust takes more than just a handshake." He nodded at the dagger. "A blood oath. With your new healing ability, this shouldn't be a problem, right?"

If I didn't do this, he would call my bluff—I still didn't want him to know about Dave until I knew I could trust him, so I shrugged and said, "I've had these abilities for days … I can't control them, anyway. Besides, you heard Larna, the dagger probably responds to my needs."

"Convenient answer," he scoffed. "Look, I understand your need to keep me in the dark because you think I might be under compulsion … I'm not, by the way, but that doesn't mean I believe you." He inclined his head. "Bird family, mate."

Seeing as how he was starting to make me mad, I growled, "Okay, fine. Let's do it."

Al opened and then closed his mouth as if what he had to say was important. After a second, he said softly, "You know, you're wrong."

I raised a questioning eyebrow. "About what?"

Al downed the rest of his drink before saying, "I *don't* dislike you."

I gave him what I hoped was a vexing grin and added an infuriating wink. "So, what you're saying is that there's a chance we'll be besties in the near future? I wasn't going to ask first, but since you brought it up … my answer is no; I reject your friendship," I said. "No hugging it out with you."

"Do you ever shut up?" he muttered, rubbing his head in apparent annoyance.

"Rarely." I spun the dagger up into my fist, and as it left the scabbard, the ringing echoed hauntingly in the still air around us—a reminder to him that I, too, had unnatural abilities.

Unflinching and unimpressed, he held his hand out for me to make the first cut. I leaned toward him, the thought of hurting another person not giving me pause like it should have. I was pretty sure the blade was playing on my emotions, because sparks of silvery light shot out of my fingertips, dancing across the blade's razor-thin edge.

Anger was a strong fuel. When Al saw the unexpected special effects, his inhuman eyes shimmered and flickered, bringing his *Sight* to life—defense mechanism. It was disconcerting, seeing unyielding blue eyes pierce me as sharply as my dagger.

Slowly, and almost trancelike, I dragged the edge of my blade across his palm before I realized what I was doing. It felt as natural as breathing, making someone else bleed. It was only a shallow cut, but blood blossomed to the surface immediately. I could ask him anything in the entire world. He would tell me whatever I wanted to know. *Do* whatever I asked him to. The temporary sting from the cut was well worth it as the steel bit into my skin.

Al nodded, satisfied, and then clasped his hand in mine.

After we shook, I pulled my hand back, wiping the red onto a hand towel on the table.

He eyed his own wound, shaking his hand as if that would help it magically heal like he'd been used to for over a century. "This is *the* weirdest sensation." His eyes, still shining with his *Sight*, flickered to my hand. "Doesn't look like you can heal on your own either... You have enough electrical energy running through you to power an entire village." His gaze darted to mine. "Your eyes flash like lightning," he said in both awe and something else, maybe scorn. "But ... it only responds to your *needs*, right?" When he struck, it was as quick and sudden as a serpent attacking its prey. It hit me—that strange paralysis threatening to drag me under—as lulling and taxing on the body as any drug I'd ever felt. It always happened this way, an alluring loss of control. Control is what I'd give up gladly. I had this tiny fleeting thought that maybe I should.

That is, until his *Sight* wore off, like poison being drawn from a wound.

And then it morphed.

Alastair's brows furrowed in concentration and distress, but it was too late. I forgot how much I missed this, my own *Sight* flaring to life like a flame to a kerosene-soaked wick. I could end him without even lifting a finger.

An evil laugh bubbled up, escaping from my throat, sounding foreign to my own ears. *Larna, why did you leave me alone with Al?* I thought I'd been able to master this feeling.

A drop of sweat slid down Al's forehead as his eyes followed my every move, ticking back and forth like a pendulum. Having no control over your own body was incredibly frightening. *Good.* His eyes darted to my dagger. Normally, by now I would have a blank canvas to work with. It made me wonder just how strong Gabe had to have been in order to compel Al. Pretty damn strong.

I could end his existence—thereby making me stronger than Gabriel Stanton.

Would that be such a bad thing?

Gabe's face twisted and melted in my mind's eye, transforming into Al's face—were they one and the same?

Both vampires had wreaked so much havoc in Larna's life. *Larna.* Her name triggered something inside me. *What am I doing?* The sudden feeling of betrayal was as jarring as jumping into the middle of a frozen lake. She wouldn't want this. I tore myself free of the blade's influence, and also my macabre thoughts, looking away briefly to blow out a shaky breath in the process. When I glanced back up, Al's face was blank. He had the same vacant look on his face, exactly like the day he broke my arm eight months ago. No one was at home. This time, it was me who did the controlling and not Gabe. I felt a very sudden appalling guilt for duping him in this way.

But my curiosity won over, so ignoring the oath we'd just taken, I went straight to the heart of the matter. "Do you love Larna?"

Asking it out loud, even though I knew he wouldn't remember it, still made my cheeks flush with heat, an embarrassing emotion that proved how much I needed to know the answer.

"Yes." Al's monotonous tone and glassy-eyed stare made it seem like his version of being in love was as exciting as picking out a pair of socks to wear for the day.

An anguished ache welled up in me at finally knowing the answer to that question.

He loved her.

Too bad I did not feel any better now that I knew the answer to my question. The rock in the pit of my stomach grew to the size of a boulder. My fingers twisted tighter around the handle of the dagger, cutting off blood flow. I knew he liked her, but … *love?* Why didn't he just pluck the blade from my hands and stab me in the heart with it? I'd feel better than I did right now. I could make him forget he loved her—just give him a tiny suggestion otherwise …

The blade seemed to hum in tune with my rising resentment.

Feeling the all-too-familiar crackle to the air, I snarled, "Then why did you leave?"

If he noticed my change in demeanor, he didn't show it. Instead, he spoke in a deadpan tone and without conviction. "Jack asked me to finish what he started. He suspected Gabriel might thwart his plans to end clan

Deimos—he made me promise to seek out one large enough to protect his daughter."

"Did Jack think this clan was trustworthy?"

He gave a minute nod. "He would never have sent me otherwise."

To finally get answers to the questions that had been eating me up these last few months was a relief and also a blow. It felt like he'd punched me right in the gut. At least he had been telling the truth. "Should we trust them?" I asked, suddenly winded.

"I don't trust anyone," he answered simply.

I scooted my chair back, making sure to keep eye contact. "Do you think we should join this clan?"

"Yes."

"Elaborate," I ordered.

"We have no other options left. Even though it was a ballsy act of defiance, you made too many enemies when you botched the attack on Gabriel's armory."

When Al's eyes fluttered closed, I knew I had to hurry up. I was losing my hold over him. I gripped the dagger tighter. This was the longest I'd ever compelled someone. The bead of sweat on my forehead was an indicator I'd better wrap this up soon.

I drew in a deep breath, forcing myself to clear my mind. "Why did you take my blood back at the warehouse?"

There was no denying that he had done it, only an explanation: "Sozo needed a sign of trust. We need their help. It was his one condition. My assumption is that he will use it to study you like everyone else wants to. You are an oddity."

I caught myself from closing my eyes against the sting

of that one word. It was as close to *freak* or *loser* as you could get. I'd never been lumped into that category before. I was the funny guy everyone liked. It reminded me of seeing the torment bullies had put Larna through over the years. I hated it then and I hated it now. The need to protect her from those dill weeds was still ingrained in me. *Oh, how the tables have turned now though.*

With surprising dexterity, I twirled the blade in my hand, balancing it skillfully across my knuckles and then flipping it back over into my palm. *I'll show you oddity.* "Do you know *what* I am?"

Al shook his head but didn't offer up any further enlightening details.

"Have you been compelled by anyone other than me?" I asked, trying my best to hold on to the compulsion before it sputtered out.

There was fire now in his eyes, where it had been glossed over just moments before. "No," he said defiantly. "Not since Gabriel."

I pressed a hand to my forehead. It felt clammy. I could get one or two more questions out maybe. I needed to know if I could rely on his instincts to know if he trusted me to watch his back. Feeling as if my tongue weighed a thousand pounds, I mumbled, "What do you *really* think about me?"

A muscle jumped out on the side of his jaw, and for a second, there was no reaction at all until he finally spit out, "You're in way over your head; you're untrained; you don't take anything seriously, and you use humor like a shield. I also think there's a strong possibility you'll get yourself killed in the not-too-distant future. But ..." he added, "you are most definitely *not* a coward. You have more heart and spirit than anyone I've ever met before. I also think that if the dagger *is* more than just a mere object … then it chose wisely."

I slumped back, finally releasing my hold on Al and on the dagger. It clattered to the tabletop with a loud thunk. I had wanted to ask him about his pocket watch, but I had done enough prying for one day. I don't know how long I sat there, my arms extended out in front of me with my head bowed, breathing deeply, until I heard Al speak as if from far away.

"You look like someone just punched you in the gut."

My eyes flicked to his. He was slow-blinking at me in confusion, having returned from his torpor. "Did I punch you in the gut?" he asked.

Fatigue sunk its talons in deep, refusing to let up. *Drag me on down into obscurity.* I shook my head sleepily. "What do you remember?"

"Nothing …" Al let the sentence trail off, glancing down to the fresh cut on his hand, and then, after a second, he nodded as if having an epiphany. He stood, picking up his empty glass, and then held his hand up so I could see it. "This cut was a reminder that I willingly agreed to let you compel me. If you had tried to mind control me and I hadn't been cut, I would have known there was something wrong. I told myself I'd never be compelled against my will ever again."

I nodded in sudden understanding. "So … there's no such thing as a blood oath." I laughed softly to myself. "You had me cut myself so you could make sure once you came out of it, you'd know you had been compelled. The only memory loss suffered was from the questions I asked you, right?"

A ghost of a smile flitted across his face. "Having you cut yourself wasn't just about making sure I'd know when I was compelled … It was to see if you could miraculously heal yourself." He turned to leave but twirled back around to face me, a serious expression on his face. "Did you get the answers you were looking for?"

I gave him a defeated shrug. "Yeah, I did." *And then some*, I thought. "We're going to meet Sozo."

Chapter 19

Larna

THE WHOLE CABIN SMELLED of fresh bread and stew. Alastair was in the kitchen, humming softly to himself, his mood so light I froze in place with my mouth hanging open. I had never seen him in such a good mood before. I knew he was glad Corinth and I had decided to go with him. Corinth had shared very little of their conversation with me other than to say we could trust Alastair. No matter how hard I tried to wheedle answers out of Corinth, he wouldn't budge. I was also teeming with curiosity about their conversation. I'd only promised to give them privacy because Alastair had asked for it. I had yet to ask Alastair, because I knew he wouldn't remember much of what was said. Compulsion *is* amnesia.

Only Corinth knew the details of their conversation, and he seemed to want to take it to his grave.

Alastair must have sensed me watching him, because he turned to me and flashed one of his half-dimpled smiles. My heart lurched, transporting me back to Nan's place, when we were just getting to know each other. He had let me vent and cry and regale him with tales of my troubled childhood, all the while being my figurative rock to hold on to.

I watched, mesmerized by how fast he chopped celery, his arms a blur—the only sign he was holding a knife was the quick flash of silver glinting in the light. Even though I was just as fast as he was, I was absolutely positive I would never be able to possess that kind of speed or precision. Pieces of the cut-up celery disappeared from the carving board to plop into the stew, almost as if by magic.

Alastair would make a good sleight-of-hand magician—if spy or cook didn't work out.

When he was finished, he poised the point of the knife on the tip of his index finger. After balancing it there for a few seconds, he flipped it into the air and caught it by the handle behind his back. He was way better than any expert hibachi chef I'd ever seen. Actually, I shouldn't have been surprised at how excellent his knife-handling skills were. I was transported back to that night at Gabriel's manor when we escaped. The way he'd taken down Jeremy with that infantry sword had been beyond frightening. *Boy, things sure have changed.*

I laughed at the look on his face, and for the briefest of seconds, I felt some of my burden lift from my shoulders. It was foreign, and I immediately felt guilty for that tiny second of freedom. Alastair saw my smile falter, and his own grin slipped too, but only for a moment. I watched him work as I padded closer to stop in the doorway. He cleaned the dirty dishes, salted the stew simmering on the stove, and finally dried his hands on a towel tucked into his belt.

The kitchen was too small for the both of us to fit in, so I stayed put, blocking the entryway. "You made bread?"

He gave me a sideways glance, nodding in affirmation. "From scratch." His gaze flitted down, and when he looked back at me, his flaxen hair hung in his eyes. "Did I ever tell you I lived in the south of France? That's where I learned to cook."

I perked up at this new bit of personal information about him. He was such a mystery that when he shared something like this, I couldn't help but feel grateful.

"Did I ever tell you bacon sizzling in its own fat is simultaneously my favorite smell and sound?" I joked.

Alastair snorted. "I believe you have. You and I will get along just fine, then …" He let the sentence trail off, plucking the hand towel from his pants and throwing it onto the countertop.

"France sounds lovely. I'd love to visit," I whispered, "but I don't think it's gonna happen anytime soon."

Alastair must have seen the distant look on my face, because he materialized beside me as a whoosh of air whipped my hair into my face. He laced his fingers through mine. His touch was as galvanizing as a cool breeze on a hot summer day. I let him silently lead me over to the chair in the corner of the room and I took a seat, grateful for the distraction, while he grabbed a folding chair from the patio to join me a second later.

Alastair's inscrutable gaze landed on Corinth, who was sprawled out on the deep sofa in the living room, a light blanket wrapped around his ankles.

After a full minute passed, Alastair finally shook his head. I wondered what he was thinking, but when he turned back to me, he was grinning, his smile radiant. "You'd love France. It has such a long history of romanticism and mystery. Once you live somewhere like that, you'll never want to live anywhere else," Alastair said wistfully. "Best wines in the world, people and food. Plus, it's nice that they don't ID." He gestured at his face, and as soon as he did, I caught the sight of a fresh cut on his hand and I shot to attention.

"Your hand … what happened?"

"Oh, this …" He tucked his wounded hand under his other arm, hiding it from my sudden scrutiny. "It's nothing … It was my idea, actually. I wanted to see if Corinth could heal himself on his own … with or without the power of the blade." He ducked his head. "I kinda tricked him into it. He still has the cut, by the way."

I glanced at Corinth's still-dozing form. "What if the injury has to be severe in order for him to heal? Or what if the dagger affects him like one of us—if he gets cut by it, does he heal? I don't think I've ever seen him get sliced by the blade before."

Alastair shook his head. "I know when people are intentionally evasive. There's something he's not telling us." Alastair looked at Corinth to make sure he was still asleep, lowering his voice. "You've been around him since he's had the dagger … I don't want to overstep here or upset you." He glanced down, almost afraid to deliver bad news. "But doesn't he seem a bit off to you?"

He'd hit the nail on the head. It wasn't just me who had noticed the changes in him. A flashback of Corinth's eyes disappearing, being replaced by lightning, hit me, and my heart skipped a beat.

"I was hoping it was something Corinth and I could work through. Sort of like when you helped me when I was turned." My eyes popped open again and I met Alastair's concerned gaze. "I can only imagine how he feels right now."

"We'll figure it out. All of us … together," he reassured me. "You do trust me, right?"

I nodded. "Implicitly." After a brief pause, and barely above a whisper, I said, "But don't make promises you can't keep." He glanced away as I added, "You must really believe this clan is our only option if you let Corinth compel you. No telling what secrets he found out from that figurative vault you've got locked up tight."

Alastair scratched the side of his face, suddenly looking tense. A sliver of alarm twisted my insides at the look in his eyes—it was the furtive glance away and a change of topic. He was hiding something, and I thought I knew what it was—he believed Gabriel was stronger than we were. I wasn't sure how to approach this bit of information. I guess I already knew how true it was.

He said, "Nah, the kid isn't that good … Even if he can compel vamps, I'd wager he still has a lot to learn."

"What's that smell?" I turned to see Corinth sitting up, his head swiveling in the direction of the kitchen. "I'm starving," he said. The disheveled mess on top of his head made me smile. It was the little things—things that gave me hope that he was still his geeky, over-caffeinated self and not a vampire slayer. As I sat studying him, I realized I loved Corinth but I was not *in* love with him.

I glanced to Alastair. The fluttery tingling in my stomach transported me back to the day out in the hedge maze at Gabriel's manor. I had had that feeling way back then. Love was a funny, fickle thing. Was this love? *I think it is.*

Alastair had gotten up and checked on the bread and stew, taking a sip from a full spoon that had been cooling on the stove. After nodding in approval, he doled out the food in a bowl, tore some bread off from the fresh loaf, and handed it to Corinth.

He caught my eye and pointed to the pot on the stove to indicate there was more, but I shook my head to let him know I didn't want any.

I glanced over to see Corinth greedily digging in, dipping the bread into the stew with reckless abandon. After taking his first bite, his eyes snapped up toward the ceiling as if he were looking directly up into the heavens. "Holy moly … this is *divine*." When he went back for seconds, he abandoned the spoon altogether, slurping it directly from the bowl, all the while making appreciative gurgling noises at the back of his throat.

Alastair's eyes slid to mine, and he shrugged, giving us his white-toothed grin. "A recipe has no soul; you, as the cook, must bring the soul to the recipe."

Between mouthfuls of food, Corinth said, "This definitely has soul all right." He swallowed heavily, adding, "I figured we're leaving soon … so how about we have a movie night? Or play some poker? We need to unwind before we head out into the unknown."

I looked at Alastair and then back to Corinth. "Um, not to rain on your parade, but don't we have way too much to prepare for—?"

"I think it's a great idea," Alastair said, cutting me off before I actually could rain on everyone's parade.

Suddenly suspicious, I said, "When do you ever agree with Corinth on anything?"

Corinth pointed his spoon at Alastair. "Two against one."

"Oh, I get it. Corinth compelled you to cook and agree with everything he says. That explains Alastair's good mood all of a sudden."

Alastair, sounding offended, said, "I'm not always in a bad mood."

"Yeah, you are. Your middle name is Broody. Alastair *Broody* Iszler." Corinth shoved a piece of bread into his mouth and swallowed without chewing. "But Larns … seriously, I didn't compel him to do anything. That's all him."

It was my turn to share a glance with Corinth. "Since when did you two start getting along?"

Both Corinth and Alastair rolled their eyes as the front door flew open and Vinson stomped in—cloaked in fatigues that made him look like a tree accepted him as one of its own. His raven hair was slicked back, barely touching the tops of his shoulders. When his eyes stopped on Corinth, his lip curved up in disgust. Corinth's dagger was strapped to his thigh, but it was over flannel pajama pants, and he wasn't wearing any shoes.

Alastair was the closest to being combat ready, in dark-wash jeans, black boots, and a navy T-shirt. Because Vinson had been out on watch, we had all relaxed. If it hadn't been secure, he wouldn't have come storming in the way he did. He would also never leave his post without the firm assurance that we were safe for the time being.

Vinson's eyes roved over Corinth, and his sneer widened as he honed in on the dagger and then on Corinth's bare feet. "It's wonder you are still alive."

Corinth waved a hand as if he wasn't concerned. "Good timing. I was just telling everyone we're having a poker night." He said, "You in?"

Vinson ignored him, marching over to me. He slung his rifle across his back, and reached down to pull me to my feet. I thought I was in for it—he was going to wipe me off the face of the planet. Instead, he clapped the tops of my shoulders in a surprisingly warm greeting, saying something in Russian. He wasn't smiling by any means, but for some reason, he still exuded a sense of companionship and trust and amicable acceptance that surprised me. Something I'd never felt from him before.

"What you did was stupid. Very stupid ... but also very brave," Vinson told me.

Everyone had gone suddenly quiet; when I glanced around the room, they were both staring at us with their jaws on the floor. I'd never seen Vinson touch anyone unless he was going to kill them. Apparently, no one else had either.

Vinson pressed his lips together, uncomfortable with the extra attention, and turned on his heels to march into the kitchen without another word.

I was more taken aback by his show of solidarity. He had never treated me like a peer, but I knew that something had changed between us.

"I've never seen him do that. Not even with Jack," Alastair said, the awe evident in his voice. "I told you he didn't take it lightly."

Corinth polished off the rest of his meal and said, "Larna, how badly were you injured?" He answered his own question before I could. "You look okay now—"

"I got skewered by a giant piece of metal," I said with a shiver.

Corinth sprang off the couch like a jack-in-the-box. "I was so worried about dealing with Al I forgot to ask about you ... I'm so sorry ..."

I waved off his concern. "I'm okay—I healed."

Corinth gave me an apologetic grimace, dropping his gaze from mine. He looked like he was going to say something else, but he pressed his lips together as if he was angry with himself, and then murmured, "I'm going to get dressed."

When he came back a half hour later, he was wearing jeans, his favorite Converse, and a hoodie—and he reeked of alcohol. Corinth didn't drink. He always joked that caffeine was his main squeeze, that there wasn't room for any more love in his life. Not even for Irish coffee. His hair was still a mess, going every which way, even after trying to brush it out of his face.

Vinson was brooding in the corner of the living room with a glass of vodka; Alastair was leaning against the wall by the kitchen, and I sat slouched on the loveseat, glad for the momentary respite. The only thing that would make this moment better was if my mom and dad were here too.

"Ready to lose? I found these cards in a box," Corinth slurred, holding up a deck of cards and a bowl of popcorn as he situated himself on the ground next to the small wooden coffee table.

Alastair edged his way into the living room before moving to the door. "It's my turn to check the outskirts of the property. Get started without me." I started to get up to join him, but he shook his head, motioning for me to stay. "I got this shift. Vinson said we're in the clear and I've already packed." Before I could respond, he slipped out into the shadows of the night like an apparition. My father had set up motion sensors and cameras around the cabin, and I had connected the digital alarm to my fancy spy watch. With a couple of new upgrades, I could now observe any movement alerts just by the press of a button.

This type of equipment made our lives a tad bit easier when it came to stealth. Dad would be proud.

Corinth shuffled the cards while I listened to the nightlife around us. There was something soothing about being away from all the hustle and bustle of the city. I tried to hone my abilities like Vinson. He seemed to be able to sense things where I couldn't. I took a deep breath as a tree branch scraped its long nails against the tiles of the roof. It evoked an image of skeletal hands digging down into the cabin; tiny bugs pecked at the glass, ever searching for a way to get inside to the light. An owl hooted somewhere off in the distance, sounding forlorn and indignant. It made me think of the many nights I had sat at home alone while my mom worked the graveyard shift. It was the reason why Corinth always snuck into my house late in the evenings. He would tell me he wanted to show off by naming every constellation, but I knew it was because he wanted to keep me company.

"Come on, Vinson, you know you want to play," Corinth goaded.

Vinson's answer was a scowl of indignation.

I turned to Corinth. "How much have you had to drink?" I cocked an eyebrow at him. "You want to talk about it?"

Corinth shuffled the cards, ignoring my stare. He bent them mercilessly, and in their protest, they fluttered out of his hands, landing at his feet. I watched, trying to stifle a giggle as he groped at the rogue escapees, slow as a sloth. "I never claimed to be good at cards. But, hey," he barked out, "trust me with a deadly dagger ... *great* idea." He gave an involuntary shudder, suddenly looking ashamed. "And then you got hurt because I just *had* to give myself up."

Ah, the real reason he had partaken in drinking—he blamed himself for me getting hurt. It had never occurred to me until now, but maybe he was scared of being surrounded by a bunch of vampires. How would he be able to control his own urges to strike them down?

Corinth must also be worried sick about his family. Gabriel had already kidnapped his sister. If I wanted my mom here with me now, smelling of dirt and grass after a long day of gardening, I couldn't imagine what he was feeling. He lived for his family.

Vinson inched closer, bringing me out of my ruminations, clearly curious about what we were doing. I wondered if he had ever done anything remotely fun in his entire life besides demolitions expert and assassin.

Corinth, having shuffled the cards, started to deal them out to first me and then Vinson—he left his cards on the tabletop. Once he had given us five each, he said, "*Texas Hold 'Em*. I found it appropriate we play a game that reminds me of home."

Add homesick to the list of reasons why Corinth had been drinking. I wondered if there was something else going on besides these things—even though anyone of them could lead to extreme stress. Now that I studied him closer, he *did* seem different after his conversation with Alastair. There was a subdued quality about him, and the vivid color of his chestnut eyes seemed to have dimmed. I didn't think it was because of the alcohol.

I eyed the pair of twos in my hand and then chanced a glance at him. "I think this is the first time I've ever seen you drunk."

"Well, then, we're even, because I've never seen you

drunk before." His words slammed together almost to the point where I couldn't make out what he was saying.

"Technically, it would take a whole keg for me to get drunk," I said, gesturing to myself. "Fast metabolism." I arranged the cards in my hands methodically, stalling. "So, why *are* you drunk?"

Corinth rolled his eyes to the ceiling but didn't feel the need to elaborate.

"And since when are you ever silent?" I put my cards down, waiting for him to look back up. "I expected a retort about how great I'd be at a party or something along those lines."

Corinth looked me in the eye, his lazy smile wilting. "Fine. I might be a little buzzed." He put a hand over his head and made a circle motion around himself. "This is a no-judgment zone. You can't use this against me when I'm sober."

I made a cross over my heart with all the seriousness I could muster. "No-judgment zone. Got it."

He gave me a solemn nod, leaning closer as if he were about to reveal the juiciest of bit of gossip. I could smell the vodka on his breath when he spoke. "I've been gone almost an entire year. A year. My family needs me. I thought I would … we would … If I'm not there to protect them …" His voice broke and he put a hand to his chest. "What if that douche nozzle takes them? What then? If he does, I'll give him whatever he wants, Larna." He hung his head. "I'll turn myself and the dagger over like I did before—for *you*." He glanced at me briefly before his dark eyes flicked back down. "If you got hurt like at the warehouse …" He licked his lips. "Some of our most important choices in life have a timeline." His gaze flickered to mine briefly before moving away. "Nothing is more expensive than a missed opportunity."

I wrinkled my forehead in confusion. I felt like he was trying to get something important across to me, but I had no idea what that was. "What are you talking about? What missed opportunity?" I said, "Corinth, what happened between you and Alastair?" I couldn't take seeing him so dejected, so I slid off the loveseat, scooting next to him on the floor to drape an arm over his shoulders. The warmth radiating off him was familiar. Comfortable. The only thing different about him was how his hair smelled. It wasn't minty fresh, exactly how I remembered. But because his brand of shampoo wasn't so easy to come by, the only scent that clung to him now was plain old ordinary soap. It wasn't bad, but it wasn't him either.

He looked down, and suddenly his face was inches from mine, his gold-flecked, albeit glossy, eyes swimming with the effects of alcohol—that which now gave him the courage to skim his fingers along the side of my cheek. I shivered under his touch. I knew I should have pulled away, but his doe-like eyes were too wide and full of pleading. There was just so much history between us, and this felt comfortable and familiar.

Corinth whispered, "Do you think if we hadn't come to England … that things would have been different between us?"

How did I answer that? I couldn't lie to him. The painful yearning in his expression was almost enough to make a liar out of me though. I swallowed hard against the burgeoning emotions rising up inside me. What was wrong with me? I wasn't attracted to Corinth, right? "I—I don't know. Maybe at one point in time …" Again I swallowed past the lump of truth lodged in my throat. The last thing

I wanted to do was hurt him. "But now, Alastair—"

As soon as his name was out of my mouth, Corinth launched himself to his feet, a hand on his head as something flickered in his eyes. He sucked in a disquieting breath and then changed the subject. "That was inappropriate … sorry … I'm just worried about my family."

And that was the problem. He *was* my weakness. I realized I would give up just about anything to make sure he was safe. I blew out a deep breath, my voice shaking with conviction. "Your family will be safe. I promise, Corinth."

He ran a hand through his untamed hair, turning away, and that's when I noticed movement out of the corner of my eye. Vinson was watching us with a curious expression on his face.

Corinth followed my line of sight, his eyes widening in surprise. "That's impressive, dude," he said, "the way you never breathe … I forgot you were even in the room."

Vinson's eyes narrowed to tiny slits, kind of like how I would imagine a hawk might look right before it devours a mouse. And then he turned that gaze on me. "This is important to you? That his family be safe? And yours?" It wasn't spoken in a sarcastic tone. There was no hint of a teasing. He was serious. As if the concept of having a family to care about or vice versa was a foreign concept to him. I was so surprised by his quasi concern that I forgot to answer, and it wasn't until Corinth nudged me that I remembered Vinson was still waiting on my response. "Uh, yes, it's extremely important—" I glanced back to Corinth "—to both of us. But my mom is out of the country, traveling. I've been in contact with her. It would mean a lot to me if you could keep an eye on his family."

Corinth was nodding vigorously. "You have family, Vinson?"

I knew Vinson would never give up any personal information about himself—he wasn't the sharing type—but when he spoke without derision or a hint of scorn, I was nonetheless still shocked.

"Family used to be important to me—long ago... a long time ago. January seventh, 1895— дьявол—Grand Duchess Alexandra Feodorovna, she did not want me to forget day I was reborn." He inched closer, almost gliding on the balls of his feet as he moved into the room. "I had family once. I was married … Alexandra didn't care." He stopped speaking abruptly, as if this was all there was to the story.

I dared not move or breathe for fear he might decide not to share any more with us. Corinth sat rigidly straight too, probably thinking the same thing, because I heard his slight intake of air. Vinson had always been aloof. To be honest, I didn't think I'd ever find out anything about his former life. He'd always made it clear that he was a soldier first and nothing else after.

When he spoke again, his voice sounded almost gravelly—I guessed from disuse. This was probably the most he'd ever spoken to anyone in a very long time. He nodded at Corinth. "I see way you two make eyes at each other. I will go watch kid's family and yours. Just until I know they are safe … and then I come back."

After a few seconds of me floundering for words, I finally managed to squeak out, "Vinson … that means more to us than you will ever know. Not that I'm looking a gift horse in the mouth or anything, but why would you do that for Corinth?"

He thrust his chin out. "It's not for kid. For you."

My heart swelled almost to the point where I didn't think my chest could contain it anymore. I had always considered Vinson as a one-man show, operating out of respect for my father and a thirst for revenge. And maybe that had been true at one point in time, but now, I felt a shift in his attitude. Maybe he wanted to be a part of a team, or maybe it was something else—*family*.

Corinth seemed just as stunned as I was, his mouth hanging open. I watched him stand, using the coffee table for support. "Vinson … I don't know what to say." A tear rolled down his cheek, leaving a salty trail in its wake. He swiped at it, surprised at his own vulnerability. "Look, is there anything I can do for you in return, Vinson? Anything at all? Just name it."

Vinson nodded. "Do not ask about my family again. I have none."

As he turned to leave, I blurted out, "You do have a family." I said quietly, "*We* are your family."

Vinson's body stiffened like a rod, but he didn't turn around to face us; instead, his head drooped and he spoke in a frighteningly whisper-soft voice. "Do you know what my wife called me as she choked on her own blood? As she lay dying in my arms after I killed her?"

I swallowed heavily, suddenly not wanting to hear it, but finding myself needing to know the answer anyway.

"She called me a монстр … *monster*," he growled, translating the last word into English for us. "That is what I am. I have never denied it. Keep that in mind when you say such things." Vinson turned on his heels and disappeared without another word.

Corinth ran a hand down his face in apparent relief,

as if someone had lifted the Great Pyramid of Giza off his shoulders.

We both had witnessed the pain in Vinson's voice, and his mention of killing his wife had struck a chord. Maybe this was his chance to atone for what he'd done … or what he thought, anyway. I couldn't imagine the kind of torture he'd put himself through for who knows how many years.

I nodded at Corinth. "I need a drink now."

"That shell sure is hard to crack, but, boy, is he the scariest person I know." Corinth raised a hand. "I'll be the first to admit I'm a fan though." He threw a finger in the air as if remembering something important. "Did he mention a grand duchess?"

I watched him race into my father's bedroom, and when he came back out, he was holding his tablet in hand.

He repositioned himself on the floor in front of the table next to me, his thigh brushing against mine as he handed me the device. He raised an inquisitive eyebrow. "Come on, you know you want to know more."

I was suddenly glad we'd been able to get Wi-Fi this far out. Dad had made sure to have superior tech in this place. I think he controlled all the air traffic in the area for ten square blocks. It was probably why we hadn't been overrun by clans clamoring to take us down, I think.

"This seems like an invasion of privacy," I noted hesitantly, but I couldn't quite hide the curiosity creeping into my voice at the same time.

Corinth plucked the device from my hands. "I'm only looking up public records; that's not an invasion of privacy. It's on the internet for all to see."

I couldn't help but inch closer so I could see the

screen as he put a finger to his lip and started typing "'Grand Duchess' 'Russia' '1895" and pushed enter. What popped up in the search engine left me speechless.

Corinth scanned through several of the first articles that showed up. "Alexandra Feona …" Whispering to himself, he said, "1895… Russian royalty … From what I can gather, grand duchess is a courtesy title usually given to daughters of the emperors, or empress regnants of Russia …" He kept scrolling down the page until he finally stopped. "Here it is—Alexandra Feodorovna—that was who Vinson spoke of; she was the wife of Nicholas the Second of Russia." His mouth dropped open as he kept reading. "As in Tsar Nicholas? Like Nicholas the *Bloody*?"

My eyes skimmed over the article and I started reading aloud: "'Bloody Sunday happened on January twenty-second, 1905. Unarmed and innocent demonstrators were gunned down, and the townsfolk blamed it all on Nicholas.' I don't remember Nicholas the Bloody—who was that again?"

I could sense the nerd in Corinth rising up to meet the challenge. He thought of himself as a bit of a know-it-all. "He was an Emperor of Russia in the eighteen hundreds. His reign saw the fall of the Russian Empire—it was pretty violent. Apparently Soviet historians portrayed him as a weak and incompetent leader. More importantly though, are his ties to Rasputin, who, at the time, was believed to be some sort of prophet or healer." He threw a finger in the air. "Or *vampire*, perhaps? I remember all of this from a history program we watched in class. Rasputin was like Bruce Willis in *Die Hard*. Alexandra ended up treating this guy like family because she believed he was clairvoyant or something. I think it was the secret police who tried to assassinate him. They laced his wine with poison, didn't die; shot him, and then when he didn't die of a gunshot wound, they threw him into a river." Corinth ran a hand through his hair, all wild dark locks. "History makes a lot more sense when you know there are creatures out there that have the ability to heal."

I sat back, thinking about how it made sense. Vampires had been around for centuries; even back then there had been signs of their existence, and civilization as a whole could never piece it together. "That means Vinson was or *is still* connected to Russian royalty."

Corinth shook his head. "I don't think so. He's military or secret police—has to be. Vinson's always been a soldier. Maybe he worked for Alexandra or Nicholas or even Rasputin himself?"

I said, "Or maybe he was the one who threw Rasputin in the river."

We sat together, thinking in silence until Corinth finally said, "That's the first time I've heard Vinson talk about his personal life. Ever. I feel like I owe you a thank-you, too."

His eyes had started drooping closed, so I patted him on the leg. "Get some rest—we leave in the morning, and you still have to pack and sober up."

Corinth mumbled something about having coffee ready in the morning and then disappeared into my father's old room, closing the door behind him.

It wasn't long after when I heard the sound of the door lock being disengaged on the front door. I knew there was no threat on the other side, so I didn't bother getting up when it creaked open. I had already packed my meager belongings in one backpack.

Alastair slipped back in, greeting me with a nod as he joined me in the living room, sinking into the deep folds of the sofa beside me.

"Did you get it taken care of?" I asked.

He nodded. "I sent word for Sozo to expect our arrival in a few days, but I didn't want to let them know our whereabouts or when we'd be coming exactly." He twisted around to face me with all the blue-eyed intensity he could muster. "Even though I think this clan is our best bet, I still have reservations about giving away too much information ahead of time. These people are secretive and rarely venture out. They would have made an exception by arranging transport for Corinth, but I didn't want to give anyone an opportunity to give out our location before we even get there. Also, I wanted a chance to train Corinth before—"

"I've been training him," I interjected, almost a little too defensively.

Alastair held his hands up. "I meant no offense," he said. "You've done a great job." He cast a glance down for a moment as if he were considering something, and when he met my gaze once again, his eyes were unnaturally bright. "Don't tell him I said this, but he's not the same scrawny kid as when I left. He's stronger—a lot stronger, actually. More capable. But we're throwing him in amongst a horde of vamps—a few days will give me some time to train him in basic weapon handling. He needs to be clear-headed. That's his weakness … I think I can help him with that."

I knew deep down he was right. Corinth's real

problem was the blade's influence on him. He had always been bad about focusing on one task and finishing it. If he could master the dagger, he would be more powerful than any of us—I was sure of it.

I gave a quick nod in agreement.

Alastair sagged back in apparent relief. "I'm not going to lie; it's going to be a difficult journey. I've set up certain check-points along the way to make sure we're not followed." He added, "Bring extra socks and your hiking boots."

I blew out a breath, curling my fingers around his. His hand tightened around mine, and we sat in companionable silence. Alastair brushed his thumb along my wrist, leaving a warm tingling sensation across my skin.

After we sat in silence for a moment, I finally said, "Why isn't Vinson coming with us? I mean I'm very grateful he's going to look out for Corinth's family, but Vinson would rather be storming a castle any day of the week than babysitting." I held up a finger. "This is not me complaining, by the way. I know how important this is to Corinth."

Alastair ran a hand through his blond locks. "The clan we're going to is a peaceful one. They don't condone violence." He scratched his chin. "Vinson's reputation has preceded him, so they chose not to extend an invite to him. That and …" His voice trailed off in thought.

"And what?" I asked slowly.

"I've been working with Vinson for a long time. I get the impression he doesn't like being in confining spaces. Not that where we're going is confining or cramped in any way. It's just that as soon as I mentioned 'underground' facility to him, I could tell he was … *uncomfortable* to say the least." He saw the look on my face and clarified, "Don't worry, there will be plenty of room for all of us."

I thought about going to a place that even Vinson was afraid to enter and I shuddered. He wasn't afraid of anything. "You're not really helping your case," I muttered, a nervous laugh bubbling out of me. After a second, I switched gears. "You don't remember anything Corinth asked you?" I got the distinct impression that whatever prompted Corinth to get drunk was something Alastair had told him when they'd had their talk.

Alastair crossed his legs and tugged at a shoe-lace on his boot before flipping his hand over to stare at the remnant of the blade's mark. "Not a thing." I could hear the relief in his voice as he added, "I'm kind of glad I don't remember."

He got up and left me alone for a second, returning with the vambraces my father used to wear on his forearms. He retracted the blades several times, testing them out. It instantly transported me back to the day my dad gave me the dagger at Nan's place, and my throat squeezed up, constricting and raw.

Alastair held them out to me. "I can teach you how to use them … if you want."

I shrank back from his outstretched hand, trying not to let myself get sucked into a whirlwind of forgotten memories. It was everything I could do not to think about my dad. His presence was still here. Every inch of this place was him: from his gun cleaning solvent, to the leather duster he wore; even his fancy high-tech equipment had a certain electrical scent that was him. There had been no time to grieve, not really, until now. Corinth had kept me too busy. It wasn't long before I felt the hot sting of tears on my cheeks, my vision blurring through half-swollen eyes.

Alastair pulled me into his embrace. He wound a hand through my hair, gently rocking me. The slow rise and fall of his chest, and his strong, steady heartbeat under my cheek calmed me. I thought back to Alastair's story about meeting my dad for the first time, and a pang of guilt welled up. It was cathartic putting my weakness on display for Alastair to see, mainly because he didn't feel ashamed for doing the same. When I finally pulled back, I saw the anguish and torment on his face. I'd never asked him how he felt about my dad's death. He had lost a good friend, and he hadn't had the chance to deal with my father's death properly either. Sorrow welled up inside me, looming large and extremely contagious.

I shoved my emotions back down. I had to be strong for what was next, so with a quick nod, I pulled back and took my dad's blades from him.

He gave me a quick nod of approval. "That's exactly what your old man would have wanted."

After composing myself, I said, "So, what's this clan really like?"

Alastair hesitated before saying, "They're all about science and tech—your dad would have loved it. That's part of the reason why he sent me to them in the first place. They have the skills and know-how to give us a fighting chance to take out clan Deimos."

"So you think they'll help us?" I asked slowly.

I guess he must have heard the hope in my voice, because he gave me a quick reassuring nod. "All I care about is getting both of you out of the bullseye. I found a photo of Corinth on one of Gabriel's people not too far from here. He's getting closer, and he won't stop until he has the dagger back."

Chapter 20

Corinth

I DIDN'T ASK FOR a dose of anxiety with my pancakes, but I got it anyway. The fact that this new clan, Eleutheros, had asked Al to give them a sample of my blood left me with a bad taste in my mouth. Last night, I had started to tell Larna about my conversation with Al, when I was half out of my mind with heartache and booze. The way she'd shut me down was enough to put me in a sour mood. It wasn't up to me to tell her how Al felt. I couldn't even tell her how *I* felt. I definitely didn't want to handle anyone else's emotions on top of my own. On one hand, I wanted Larna to be happy, but on the other, not with Al—with *me*. It was selfish, I know. It was eating me up inside that I didn't confess all of this to her a few months ago.

Before I knew how Al truly felt about her.

I wished I could take back asking him if he loved her. I'd shamefully considered making Al forget his feelings about Larna. What kind of low-life tries to take away someone else's love? I mean, how petty was that? But she was one of a kind. Funny, daring, brave—before and after she'd been turned. She was the kind of take-no-shit cool that secure dudes went after. Someone who makes you laugh so hard you can't breathe. And gets your humor on a level no one else on the entire planet ever will. That's why I used to sneak into her room at night on the pretense of naming constellations. Not just to keep her company because she was scared to be all alone in that big house, but because I couldn't stand to be away from her for even one night.

I had had the opportunity when Al was gone to tell her all of this, and I'd wasted it.

Seeing her cuddled up on the couch with him made my stomach curdle. There was a part of me that wanted to pull her aside and tell her everything I'd just thought, but when I saw the look on her face as she rested her head against his chest, the truth died on my lips.

She had never looked at me like that. The longing, contentment, and adoration ... devotion ... whatever word you used to express emotions running so deep you can't imagine your life without that person in it. Love. The truth sat within those brownish, green-flecked eyes of hers. I loved her—and I'd do anything to see her happy. I don't think I'd ever seen her look that blissful before. It was time to step out of the way. *Time to let her go.*

My thoughts segued from Larna to the tall dude in the Tommy Bahama suit. He seemed friendly enough now, but what was his end-game? And then there was Imani. She had told me some pretty unbelievable stuff when we were trapped together. I wondered what she meant about my blood. I had ultimately decided I couldn't wait for Dave to show up with answers he claimed to have. I was hoping Sozo might have the answers I was seeking.

We packed light. Where we were going, they wouldn't let us bring any weapons—except my steel, that is; it was coming with me regardless of what anyone said. They could pry it from my cold, dead fingers, and then I'd still come back as a zombie and take it from them. Hopefully, that wouldn't be a real prediction.

The plan was to have Paul drop us off at Paddington Station, where we'd take the train to St. Erth in Cornwall. It was a village on the coast of the Celtic Sea. I was really looking forward to a drastic change of scenery, something other than motel-room menus and generic water-color paintings. According to Al, Eleutheros was situated in a remote forest near that area. This clan was impossible to find unless you knew exactly where to look, but Al had told us about an alternative route into the compound he'd ferreted out. He didn't want any surprise ambushes by the enemy.

Larna sidled up next to me as I finished zipping up my duffel bag.

"It'll be almost like we're on vacation," she joked.

"Forced cheerfulness doesn't look good on you, Collins." I threw my bag over my shoulder. "Trains, Celtic Sea, weird cultish clans … exactly the kind of vacay I crave." I turned to walk out of the room I'd called home for the last two days, and threw her a glance over my shoulder. "And don't think I don't know what you're trying to do."

"Do?" she asked with feigned innocence. "You mean, distract you with the idea of an all-expenses-paid vacation?" She said. "Did you get our tickets?"

I held my phone up so she could see the screen. "I selected 'quiet' for the coach type, but that's not guaranteed. Hopefully, we can get some rest before we go spelunking down mountains and into caves."

"I can't believe the word *rest* just came out of your mouth," she quipped.

"Not *spelunking?*" I bantered. "Because that was clearly the better word choice out of the two."

Vinson met us at the front door, interrupting our verbal judo. After eyeing us for an appropriately awkward amount of time, he said, "This is where we part ways."

I dropped my bag, lifting my eyebrows and opening my arms wide. "Bring it in."

Vinson's lip curled at the mere suggestion of touching him. "You will most likely perish without me—but I must admit you're not completely useless." His gaze slid to Larna next. "*Trust no one.*" In his usual ill-tempered fashion, he turned around and marched back outside.

"Did he just compliment *and* insult us at the same time?" I asked wryly, and then I added, "I'm taking that as a compliment."

I bowed my head to say a little prayer for his safety while he watched out for my family. When I opened my eyes again, I caught Larna staring at me with an expression of curiosity; there was softness in it too. She knew I believed in a higher power, but she had never really seen me explore it before. When it came to my family, I'd take whatever advantage I could get.

With quiet intensity, as if she wanted to convince me of something, she said, "He still has the watch. If anyone can make sure your family is safe, it's him."

Al threw the front door open, interrupting us. "You guys ready? We need to get a move on."

I glanced between them, sensing the rising tension, so

I took my cue to move outside and load my stuff into the ride Paul had rented for us, the silver Mini Cooper Alastair had driven to rescue me. It was burned after the helicopter chase, so we would need to get rid of it soon. We couldn't all fit in his Beetle. I glanced at the ugly beater parked in the circular driveway, nodding to him across the drive.

He saw my greeting and waved at me with his cigarette in hand.

As I loaded my stuff, he made his way over to me, taking a drag of his cigarette and blowing out a long curl of smoke. "'Our battered suitcases were piled on the sidewalk again; we had longer ways to go. But no matter, the road is life.'" He finished his cigarette, sucking in a deep breath, and in a raspy voice added, "Jack Kerouac."

"I dig it." I gave him an appreciative nod and threw my hand out. He grasped mine in his, giving me a firm handshake. "Listen, if I don't make it back, I just wanted to say thanks for everything. You're a good man, Paul."

He gave me a toothy grin; surprisingly, I could see it past his mustache. "Don't worry, I'll keep the home fire burning for you lot until you return—you *will* return, no question."

Chapter 21

Larna

ALASTAIR THREW A GLANCE at the door Corinth just exited through. "How's he doing?"

I blew out a troubled breath. "Holding up … but this whole dream-mind-healing thing has me worried."

I had confided in Alastair about Corinth's dream because he needed to know. Corinth could be mad at me for betraying his trust, but there were bigger issues at hand, like the fact that he might try and slay both of us when we weren't looking. I tried to shake the disturbing thought from my head. *He would never hurt either of us, right?*

"I should've thrown the dagger into the ocean when I had the chance," he said gruffly. "You and I could be halfway to Switzerland by now."

I could sense sincerity in his voice and it made my heart ache. Even though I knew it was impossible, the thought of leaving everything and everyone behind sent a shiver of excitement coursing through me. I knew it wasn't an option, of course. Gabriel would find us no matter where we went—and it was time we took the battle to him, but, man, a secluded cabin and a ski resort sounded amazing right about now. I'd never seen the mountains. The closest I'd ever gotten was a trip with Mom and Dad to Austin, Texas, through hill country: gently curving roads dissected by giant oaks, rolling rivers, and fields of bluebonnets so bountiful you'd think you'd stepped right into the heart of the ocean. I could only imagine seeing the enormity of a mountainside and feeling the exhilaration of insignificance. There's something addictive about the connection of Mother Nature's biggest treasures. Maybe it's because Mother Nature could smash you like an ant.

The whole point of seeking out this clan was to gather an army willing to help us take down Gabriel once and for all.

"Something tells me the dagger wouldn't stay in the deep blue sea for very long," I said, my voice clipped.

Speaking of skiing, I couldn't help but notice how Alastair's eyes were as glacial as a mountain peak. They pulled me in, and I found myself drifting closer to him.

When he spoke next, he enunciated each word, making sure to get his point across to me. "I will make it my personal mission to end Gabriel as quickly as possible."

I glanced down to my feet, but when I felt his hand on mine, my eyes flew up to meet his gaze; the intensity of the way he was looking at me made my heart leap in my chest.

"You guys have been spinning on a hamster wheel for eight months. It's time to put a plan in place. It's what your father would have done."

I nodded, feeling marginally better for the first time in months about the direction we were headed in. "You think we're making the right move?"

With conviction, Alastair said, "I know we are."

Chapter 22

Corinth

MY WINDOW SEAT ON the train showed a world outside filled with streaks of cotton balls dabbed into a backdrop of brilliant blue. I would have taken more time to marvel at it, but I was way too busy filling my cranium with information provided by Wi-Fi—that, and I was trying to keep my head down. Al had shown me a photo he'd taken from one of Gabe's goons near the cabin—the picture was of me, stolen from off one of my mom's old Facebook posts. The fact that these bad guys were following my mom on social media filled me with an ever-increasing dread. This was getting way too close to home. There was nothing I could do to help my family if something should happen. I felt the blanket of fear lift slightly at knowing Vinson was on his way to check on them.

We were hurtling away from my family and to our first stop at Plymouth.

Larna was busy whispering conspiratorially into Al's ear. It made me wonder what they were talking about. They were back to being nauseatingly cuddly with one another, which is why I was giving them their space. I knew they were playing up the couple's ardor for show, but it was still excruciating to witness. People generally became supremely uncomfortable (like me) watching make-out sessions in public, so it left Larna and Al with a lot of room to study the folks around us. They weren't making out just yet, but they might as well have been. We had a corner section to ourselves. We couldn't get private quarters, because they had all been booked in advance. That was why we'd chosen a spot at the rear of the train by the exit doors. Easy to jump on and off, and no one could approach us from behind. Public transport was a risk, but we didn't want to waste time by driving and we had to stay off the roads.

I was comfortable in letting them take over the first watch without feeling the need to be on guard. I trusted both of them with my life. Being so engrossed in my phone, I didn't realize the train had stopped and people were getting off. We were already at Plymouth.

An attendant came by to check our tickets to make sure we were in the right seats. I noticed a large group of young girls dressed in school uniforms get on and crowd into one spot, huddled so close to each other they could have been cemented together.

My dagger dug painfully into the side of my stomach, hidden beneath my shirt. We'd been able to get through security fairly easily—vampire compulsion wasn't such a bad thing—especially when Larna and Al had my back. I studied our surroundings, thinking about how an innocent-looking kid could be a five-hundred-year-old vampire.

The one who had snatched my sister, Zoey, eight

months ago had looked twelve years old.

Pulling on my headphones, I tried to tune out the background chatter, but it wasn't long before I found myself watching the group of girls. Not in a creepy way, mind you, I just missed normal. I'd gone to a private school and worn similar clothes; which in turn made me think of my family—who had repeatedly called me since I'd been gone … especially Dad. I was determined to call him on the next stop at Truro, mainly because I wasn't sure when I'd be able to talk to him again, and because I had this feeling that something was off. I'd very recently learned not to ignore my intuition. My family was a religious one, and having grown up in church, I knew a little bit about scripture. Mom and Dad even named me after a chapter in the Bible: Corinthians. There weren't many people out there with my name, and I liked it like that. It was why I didn't go by Cory. I was a believer in God myself, but learning about the existence of vamps had turned everything I thought I knew upside down. I hadn't called my father back, because I'd sort of led him to believe I was going to college with my girlfriend in Europe. *Ugh.* I hated lying. I wasn't any good at it.

And I hadn't exactly prepared the come-clean-on-the-wielding-an-ancient-magical-artifact conversation.

I was still a teen. The only thing I should have had to worry about was what color of Converse to wear that day. I mean, the answer is always red. My Converse were packed away, taking up valuable but necessary space.

The train lurched forward, almost sending one of the schoolgirls into my lap. When she fell back, to invade my personal space, her dark braid whipped me in the eyeball. She turned around, giggling, mocha-colored eyes meeting mine with a sense of mirth that told me she might have done it on purpose.

I pulled my baseball cap lower on my forehead.

This action only seemed to send the rest of her entourage into more fits of snickers. I didn't need the extra attention, so I planted my face close to my phone's screen and turned up the volume on my headphones. You could never go wrong with the Cary Brothers. This crowded train was starting to irk me. I must have been pretty zoned out, because when I felt someone tap me on the shoulder, I jumped.

"Making the girls swoon, I see," Larna said with a hint of a smile playing across her lips.

I pulled my headphones off as she inclined her head toward the group of still-gawking teens. I threw a glance at the girls. That brought on another round of titters and chuckles.

"It's the hair," I said dryly. "Gets 'em every time."

Larna raised an eyebrow. "You're wearing a baseball cap."

"I see you and Al are getting along *very* well," I muttered, changing the subject. "You two make a cute couple." The immaturity in my voice made me cringe inwardly. When I was met by silence, I turned back to her to see her grimacing, as if she felt guilty about something.

"I'm sorry, Larns. I didn't mean to sound so … childish."

Her eyes darted to Al, who was reading a magazine with the word *Physics* on the cover. Her meaning was clear. She was worried about my feelings: How I would react with her newfound exploration of whatever it was they were. I didn't think there was a label yet. If there was, I didn't want to know about it.

"You do realize we're always gonna be friends, right? Nothing's going to change that. Not ever. You're not getting rid of me that easily," I said finally. I sighed, a sigh that said I'd given over to the friend zone, begrudgingly, but she didn't need to know that. I hoped she didn't interpret it like that. Again, it sucked taking a step back. She was my best friend, and I didn't want to lose what we'd worked so hard to build over the years. I realized it would be devastating to walk away from something so good. I didn't think I'd ever stop loving her. So if friendship was all I could get out of her—I'd take it.

As if I'd said the thing she needed to hear most, she squeezed her eyes shut. I couldn't help but notice the corners of her eyelids fluttering, emotion she couldn't hide from me. She had been equally worried about losing me too.

I reached over to my bag on the seat next to me and grabbed two energy drinks, presenting her with one as a peace offering. She accepted it with a grateful nod, not because she really enjoyed caffeine, but because she knew our friendship was still intact.

We stopped at Truro, and I followed the crowd of people out onto the platform. The air was muggy, a sign that we were getting closer to the coast. Larna gave me a quizzical eyebrow-raise through the glass partition. I lifted my chin and held my phone up, indicating I was going to be a minute. She could probably eavesdrop on my conversation if she really wanted to. But I hoped she would respect my privacy.

Alastair appeared to be reading a magazine, but I knew he wasn't really interested in it. He was concealing his face, keeping an eye out for passengers who might be a little too interested in three teens on a train. No one was interested. Not that I could tell, anyway.

This stop was longer than the rest, so I felt confident the train doors wouldn't start closing for at least five more minutes, and if they did, I could easily hop back on from my close proximity. No one seemed concerned in the fact that I had gotten off, so I felt confident that we hadn't been spotted by clan Douche-mos. A sudden influx of passengers swarmed around me, chittering and barking. I put a finger in my ear, trying to hear over the noise of rush hour, and dialed Dad's cell number and waited, feeling the ever-increasing flutters of anticipation growing in my stomach.

The line clicked over and I heard his voice come through the line. "Hey, kiddo," he said. "Long time since I've heard from you, bud." The eagerness in his voice only increased my anxiety. "Where you been? How's studying going?"

"As far as studying can go ... pretty well," I lied. "How's the fam? You keeping a tight house back home?"

"Oh, you know me ... It's sick over here. Sick as in the cool kind of sick—not the actual-sick sick," he chuckled at his own humor. "When are you coming back home for a visit, kid?"

"Not sure just yet ..." I cleared my throat, already missing him. "Listen, I have a quick question. I'm doing this—" I paused "—*project* on our family tree. How far back can you trace our genealogy?"

"Project on our family tree, huh?" I caught the hint of skepticism in his voice, but he sounded happy to be of some help. "It's about time you asked. You sound like Grandpa. He used to be really big into that sort of stuff."

"What did Grandpa say?" I pressed, hoping he'd hurry and get to the point.

There was a soft rustle of material and static on the other end, and I pictured Zoey in the background, hanging off my dad's arm like a monkey, scrabbling to get at the phone to talk to me. I smiled at the thought.

"I'll let you talk to your brother in a minute, Zoey," he muttered under his breath, proving me right on my musings. "Um …" He stopped, letting the silence stretch on for a second or two too long. In that briefest of seconds, I could tell something was bothering him and he wanted to ask me something.

"Dad?" I asked. "Everything okay?"

Everything around me seemed to melt into the distance; the background noise of strangers bustling and moving by me muffled to the point where I could only hear the thundering of my own heartbeat. Sweat popped up on my forehead. What if Gabe had his sights on my family before Vinson could arrive? What if he had sent people to my house already? How would I get back home in time? Panic's icy grip threatened to pull me under until I heard his barely audible voice come back on the line. I glanced up to see if Larna had witnessed my panic attack. If she had, she didn't show any signs of it; her head was resting comfortably on Al's shoulder, eyes slightly closed.

"Sorry, Cor, your sister is distracting me. Supposedly, your mother's side can be traced back to the Scots in the fourteen hundreds. She never did confirm any of that though." I pictured him scratching his head in thought like he always did.

"What about your side?" I asked slowly, noticing that my galloping heart rate was finally getting back to a steadier rhythm.

"This is for a school project, right?" he insisted. "You *are* in college, right?"

The conversation between my dad and me the night Zoey had been kidnapped flooded back to the forefront of my memory. He had seemed like he'd known something back then, but I'd never pushed him for answers. At the time, I had thought it was because Larna's compulsion had left him confused and forgetful. That kind of control messes with the mind in ways I still didn't understand.

"What aren't you telling me, Dad?"

He cleared his throat and said something that came out inaudible. A blast of the train's horn covered the rest of his words. The sudden swell of people closing around me, bodies pressing against mine, people shoving past, made it impossible to hear the rest of what he said. I pulled the phone closer to my ear as the crowd scrambled to get on board before the doors closed.

"Can we talk later?" I yelled through the earpiece, but his response was swallowed up. I caught his last words: "Be careful, Cor."

By the time I flew through the closing doors, I realized I'd lost the connection.

"You okay?" Larna sat up straighter as I plopped down beside her. "You're sweating more than me, and that's saying something."

"I just wish I had some more answers. I think my dad was trying to tell me something, but I couldn't finish the rest of our conversation. Why did I wait this long to talk to him?"

Larna snorted. "Welcome to the party, pal," she said. "A father being evasive … I wouldn't know anything about that. I'm sure he's just missing you." Larna placed a gentle hand on my arm. "Seriously, though, there was so much I wanted to ask my dad before …" Her voice caught. "Your father is alive. You still have that chance. Don't forget that, okay?"

"You know I love when you quote *Die Hard*," I said, deflecting.

What I was really thinking about was unsheathing my blade and going to town with it. Gabe had gotten me so worked up I was having panic attacks. The dagger's influence over me was starting to feel more like a burden rather than a gift. I guess that was the thing about heavy burdens—it was how you distributed the weight that really mattered, which was some heavy shit.

I adjusted my cap on my head, lowering it over my eyes. The train was packed with loads of people now. The way Al's eyes kept darting over the crowd wasn't lost on me. The closer we got to St. Erth, the more anxious I felt.

"I completely forgot to tell my dad that I love him … and I didn't even get the chance to talk to the rest of my family. I'm a horrible son," I whispered. "I keep having this sinking feeling that I won't get to tell him again."

Larna shook her head adamantly. "You will get to tell him—see your family—if it's the last thing I do. I promise you that. You're a good son. You're keeping them safe and kicking ass."

I barked out a laugh. "Yeah, you're right, but Vinson is the one kicking ass and keeping them safe."

A moment later Larna disappeared to grab us some snacks. While she was gone, I took the opportunity to lean over to Al, who was still reading the same magazine. "I know you're not reading about physics. What's really behind that cover?"

Al didn't look up, but a ghost of a smile flitted across his face as he lifted a thin book from behind the cover. I read aloud, "*Marvel Cinematic Universe Chronological Guide*." I threw a hand to my head. "Seriously, Al? You can't just watch one of those movies?"

He cleared his throat, slipping the book back behind the magazine about science and tech. "I like to read. Besides, this Captain America guy … he's about a century old but doesn't look it, *and* he grew up in New York—sounds like my kind of guy."

When Larna came back, she found me laughing hysterically in the corner of my seat and Al glowering down at his magazine. I guess I had to hand it to him for trying to be interested in something Larna enjoyed.

There weren't many more stops until we reached our last destination, so I pulled my phone out again and started doing as much research as possible before being disconnected from society. I was pretty sure where we were going, we wouldn't have internet access.

Chapter 23

Larna

I COULD FEEL THE FIGURATIVE precipice that Corinth stood on, mainly because I was right there beside him. He was a bundle of raw nerves, glancing down at his phone and checking to make sure his dagger was still at his waist. The last time he did it, I caught the flash of his flat stomach and arching hip bone. In such a short amount of time, he'd really transformed himself. Corinth was in way better shape than when we had first started all those months ago. He wasn't awkward in his own skin anymore. I hadn't noticed the dramatic change from concaved stomach to muscled abs, until now. I was a horrible person for leaving him out in the cold. I knew he had feelings for me. I'd always equated them to simple fondness and maybe a modicum of attraction. But since we'd been so close the last eight months, it had been hard not to turn around and find him there, so achingly close at every turn. Then I couldn't help but think of Alastair. Why was I even thinking about Corinth's abs? He was my friend, and I was glad we'd established that with our previous conversation.

As we made our way outside to the final platform, I

noticed how quiet and peaceful everything seemed to be here. Gabriel would have all the train stations and airports watched, and yet there was no sign of threats or anyone following us. Or perhaps Gabriel really didn't know where we were headed. That last thought was comforting. Maybe we had finally one-upped him for a change.

I sported the same haircut since being turned—jet-black, sharp, and edgy, with blond highlights—none of us had changed our appearance, least of all Corinth. I had suggested he shave his head, but he had flat out refused and used some not-so-nice choice words to show his displeasure about me even suggesting it.

At least Alastair was here with us this time. It felt good to have the team back together again. I also felt confident this was what my father would have wanted us to do: gather intelligence, strengthen our allies, and develop our ace in the hole—Corinth. The idea of actually doing something was what helped buoy my spirits.

"What's this place like, Al?" Corinth asked, stepping quickly after me to catch up.

"Not what you'd expect," he said cryptically over his shoulder.

"How incredibly vague of you," Corinth muttered.

Alastair stopped, scanning our surroundings as if he had X-ray vision, with a frown on his face, a permanent feature he'd wear until we got to where we were going. It wasn't necessarily a bad thing; he did have our best interests at heart: surviving.

"What is it?" I asked, glancing around.

We had emerged from past the exit and out into the oppressive sunlight. A small convenience store was situated off to our left. The lack of anything out here was not what

I had been expecting. There were only a few houses; an industrial estate and some flat fields. I hadn't realized how far inland we were still. It was unseasonably hot, and the muggy air clung to our skin as we wound our way down to a set of stairs.

Corinth took a moment to inhale the humidity into his lungs. I could tell he was deep in thought about something. If I didn't know better, I'd say he was enjoying his last breaths of freedom. The closer we got to this clan, the less we'd have of it.

"Anyone else think it's oddly quiet around here?" he said slowly, turning back to face us, putting a hand on his belt. "I mean, it's a hard-knock life when you're not bashing in heads on an hourly basis, but this is a little too convenient." He had his aviator sunglasses pulled down the bridge of his nose. "Am I right, Al?"

I knew he was anxious about what these people thought, and most of all, what they'd do when we arrived.

I answered for Alastair. "Definitely too quiet."

"This *is* too easy," Alastair grumbled.

Once we were sure we weren't being watched, we set off toward the signs pointing in the direction of Trencrom Hill.

"What's Trencrom Hill?" I asked, glancing at him out of the corner of my eye.

Alastair shrugged out of his backpack, pulling a bottle of water from inside its depths, and handed it to Corinth. "Here," he said. "You're going to need this." His eyes flicked to the distant horizon. "It's a hill fort—it has some pretty amazing views of the entire countryside. We're walking from here on out. You can get to any point by car, but we have to steer clear of the roads. I'm pretty sure the

Mini Cooper was burned after the helicopter escapade. There are too many clans out there looking for us, best not to chance being recognized. Also, I think this will give me a good opportunity to train you two."

"'Where we're going, we don't need roads …'" I said, giving Corinth a playful shove.

Corinth snorted, letting me know he appreciated my *Back to the Future* quote.

Alastair rolled his eyes. "It's a wonder you two survived for eight months before getting caught." He added, "You two are going to quote movies the entire way, aren't you?"

We both said yes at the same time.

On our way out, I trailed behind Alastair and Corinth, thinking about how glad I was that Alastair had agreed to train us. I had only just started to reach my full potential.

A little over an hour later, we made it to the path leading up to Trencrom Hill. I could just make out some of the fortifications and stone outcroppings where the outer wall had been constructed.

Alastair regaled us with the history of the area as we started our ascent. "There are hundreds of stone circles, monuments, and enclosures throughout Cornwall. The clan's been here since the Iron Age."

Monolithic boulders and stones surrounded us on all sides of the well-worn path. Some of these outcroppings were as tall as houses. The further we hiked, the more I started to notice how certain outcroppings of rocks had been placed strategically, one on top of the other. They looked like flattened marshmallows. I found myself idly wondering how they got to be like that. Some of the stones had been formed in giant circles with nothing in the center of them. It was both eerie and peaceful, being surrounded by so much history.

The steep terrain and altitude made it harder to navigate for Corinth. By the time we'd hiked thirty minutes, he had finished off a bottle of water and was panting with exertion. Alastair and I were barely out of breath.

A group of tourists ahead of us looked fatigued as we filed past them.

After we'd gone a little further, I stopped dead in my tracks in the center of a Neolithic enclosure. We had this area all to ourselves. There was a sort of heaviness in my chest where there hadn't been before. This would be the spot for a magical portal to open to another world. The thin trail wound its way through a set of boulders to the beyond. And when I say *beyond*, I meant I had no idea if it would lead us into another dimension.

I said, "The stones arranged in circles are like Stonehenge, right?"

"Yeah. Trecrobben is what the locals call it. Some of the formations were used for offerings a long time ago … in exchange for healthy crops, fertile land, and good fortune. There aren't many structures still standing, but the two boulders up ahead are considered a gateway."

With mouth slightly hanging open, Corinth said, "Gateway? That sounds mildly interesting … I can see why this hill would have been the perfect line of defense. You can see everything from up here." Even though he was wearing sunglasses, he still put a hand to his forehead to shield his eyes from the bright sun. "So that's Mount's Bay over there to the south, and St. Ives to the north?"

"Yes," Alastair pointed to the south. "That's St. Michael's Mount."

The wind was blustery this high up. I turned to see Corinth trying to shove his wild hair out of his face. Being so close to the ocean, it would've been tempting to hit the beach with a good book. Unfortunately, prolonged exposure to the sun only seemed to irritate me these days. Since being turned, daylight made my skin itch and eyes hurt. By the look on Corinth's face, he would have suggested different though.

"This is the first time I've ever seen the ocean—I mean, besides Galveston, but that doesn't count. The water there is as clear as mud." He said in awe, "I've never felt so small and insignificant in my entire life."

Alastair clapped him on the shoulder. "That's St. Ives Bay. It's quite the picture, isn't it? Corinth could only nod as Alastair added, "You've got a lot of living to do yet, mate."

"God willing," Corinth mumbled, moving to stand beside me. "I can see why there would be a secret clan here now."

Alastair meandered over to one of the giant standing rocks, shaking his head, and then turning back to us. "We still have another full day of walking. This is only the fort. The cairns mark rock basins known by the locals as the Giant's Chair, the Giant's Cradle, and the Giant's Spoon." He nodded in the direction we'd just come from. "If this were a sightseeing tour, I would take you there first."

This was the first time I felt that Alastair might not dislike Corinth: the iciness had thawed a little. Maybe it was the childlike wonder on Corinth's face at seeing the ocean for the first time. We were at the beginning of our lives, while Alastair had already lived through a full one already.

Not being the only one to worry about Corinth's back was also a bonus. Now I knew how my dad and Alastair must have felt when I was running around like a seal in a shark tank.

Across the open valley below us, waist-high wheatgrass bent with the wind. It looked as if an artist was sweeping their paintbrush across canvas. Little purple flowers popped up from between crags of rock, and soft golden sunlight glinted off the blades of grass. Alastair seemed just as moved as I was, coming up beside me to brush his hand against mine. I sucked in a stunned breath to share a glance with him.

We decided to stop for a quick break. Alastair and I shared a pint of blood while Corinth polished off a leftover sandwich he'd wrapped up from the train. After that, we carried on until we reached our stopping point, far, far away from civilization.

Corinth's gaze flitted from the canopy of plant life and trees above our heads, a small smile curving his lips in amusement. "That giant rock right there, jutting out like that, it looks exactly like a duck's mouth."

"That duck's mouth is going to be our shelter for the night," Alastair said, moving past Corinth. "Let's get in a quick training session before we lose the rest of this daylight."

I was flat on my back, lying in a carpet of pine needles and dead leaves, staring up into the darkening sky in a daze. Having taken a vicious blow to the femur, I was in a considerable amount of pain. That's what I get for trying to block one of Alastair's flying kicks with my leg.

His face was pinched with concern as he stuck a helping hand out toward me. "You okay?"

I took his gracious offer of assistance, getting up to brush the dirt and debris off my pants. "Oh, just dandy," I muttered. "Thanks."

Corinth was in the clearing under the overhanging rock collecting firewood for the night. I kept catching his glimpses. I couldn't tell if he was only empathizing with me for getting my butt whooped, or if there was something else weighing on his mind.

Alastair came up to stand behind me, his breath hitting the side of my neck, ruffling my hair. A twist of nervous pleasure spiraled up inside me. "Use the bottom of your foot to stop my forward momentum." He bent down and pulled my foot up, his fingers lightly skating over my ankle to point at my heel. "Keep your toes pointed, and sweep all the way through, using your heel as a hook. Spinning like that puts power behind the impact." He let my foot drop back down to the earth. "Remember—there are no boundaries when it comes to fighting." He circled back around to stand in front of me, motioning for me to come at him. "Shall we try again?"

I remembered a long time ago when I wouldn't have given myself enough credit to even try something like this. In gym class, I'd always been picked last. Any kind of physical exertion would have left me winded and useless. How things had changed.

But before I could complete this thought, Alastair was coming at me. I rolled to my left, barely avoiding being bowled over.

I heard Corinth gasp somewhere off in the distance, and I assumed he was witnessing Alastair's supernatural display of agility and speed. Or maybe he only saw a black blur, like I did. The wind left my lungs in a rush as he landed on top of me, a guttural groan escaping from my lips. I imagined it probably sounded like a wounded moose.

I grappled for his fist, catching it at the last second before he broke my nose. Luckily, my grip strength had improved. I was holding on to his arm like it was a life raft when he flipped his entire body over me—with me still hanging on to him. Everything ground to a halt, like gears on a clock breaking. I felt for my *Sight*—it rested at the center of my core like a sleeping dragon, and I dove into its folds of blue haze, breathing it in, awash in its glorious power.

And then his words came rushing back to me: there are no boundaries when it comes to fighting. So I bit down on his hand. He let out a yelp of surprise, which was enough of a distraction to let me wriggle myself out from underneath him. It wasn't pretty, but it didn't have to be. Somewhere at the back of my mind, I knew I was just as fast as he was, maybe faster.

Here—in this place—I owned time.

I created victory.

This is where the land of abundant confidence lived. I wished to crush my opponent. Maybe I'd turn him into a mimosa and add one of those little frilly umbrellas on top.

Alastair expected me to meet his fury head-on because that's what I'd been doing since we'd started sparring. But I was faster, stronger, and more confident now. Plus, I didn't want to look like a punk in front of Corinth.

I saw it at the last second: his knee slamming into my abdomen. I went flying, only stopping because I hit a tree. I heard a crack and I really hoped it was the tree and not my back.

Alastair saw his opportunity and he went for it, but so did I.

I flung myself to my feet in a backward push-up right as he struck out. It was a move I didn't think he had expected out of me, so when I planted my feet firmly on the ground; grabbed his wrist, and then flipped him end over end, forcing him to his knees; he only blinked up at me, too stunned to move.

I wished I could have snapped a picture of his expression so I could sell it on T-shirts. He'd used the same maneuver on me before. I had control of his wrist. If he moved—I'd break it. Of course, he could have tried to grit through the pain and break it himself, but a useless arm meant losing this round. I used the brunt of my weight and the boney part of my forearm to slam it into the back of his shoulder. It dislocated from the joint with a loud *POP*. Alastair groaned and then grudgingly tapped out. It was all I needed to let go. The sound of his heart thundering against his ribcage lured me in like rhythmical drums, melding with my own racing heartbeat.

He glanced back at me with a look of astonished pride on his face. I had to admit it felt good beating him.

I could hear Corinth cheering in the background as Alastair muttered, "I guess I'll move you up to the advanced class."

The part of the trail we were on was heavily wooded. I could tell there was a lot less foot traffic this far out. Corinth threw himself down in the clearing under the overhang of rock, picking through his pack as we settled in for the night.

I plopped down beside him, eyeing his bag. "I can carry that for you."

He rolled his eyes. "If Reese Witherspoon can backpack for ninety days, so can I."

"Yeah, but Reese is a badass," I said with a grin.

"You are absolutely right." Corinth pulled an energy drink from his bag, and some sour candy, but before he could eat it, Alastair plucked it from his grasp to replace it with a granola bar and a bottle of water.

"We have a long, hard trek ahead of us—"

Alastair started to say, but Corinth stopped him with a look. "I really hate you right now."

We didn't have much room. I had packed a sleeping bag for myself and Corinth for our hastily made campsite.

I sensed something was wrong at the same time Alastair did.

His head swiveled around, scanning the immediate area. There was a soft plink of a rock being kicked, its forward momentum sending it skittering down the path where we'd come from. Light footsteps followed shortly after, proving we were right to be on guard. Alastair disappeared out of thin air, and Corinth flipped his dagger up into his hand. His quick reflexes and alertness would have impressed me more if I wasn't so worried about Gabriel walking around the corner at any moment.

My intuition was telling me this wasn't a vamp. It was a lone traveler who wasn't trying to mask the sound of their approach. I nodded at Corinth, giving him the signal to stay vigilant, and then took a running leap, jumping into a giant oak to wind my way around it like a squirrel, all the way to the top. If something happened, I'd at least have a good vantage point—I could get to Corinth and Alastair quickly with the canopy being so thick. Vinson had taught me that much. Swinging from one branch to another, I felt a lot like the female version of Tarzan. And then I realized Tarzan was a fictional character, but he was still human, restricted by gravity like everyone else. I was some*thing* else entirely, something not quite human that could move incredibly fast. So fast, in fact, that it almost felt like flying. I realized this was the first time I'd had the chance to really let loose. I'd been lying low for so long, so afraid of being caught by the wrong clan, that I had forgotten how amazing it felt to explore these supernatural abilities of mine. It was freeing being in the company of winged creatures. I barely disturbed birds roosting in their nests, chirruping exuberantly to one another as I slipped past virtually undetected. They were saying: "Look at all those suckers down there!" This was why birds sang so loudly, they felt unrestricted exploring places humans normally didn't go.

I stopped as soon as I heard the sound of voices up ahead, and lowered myself down, pressing myself flat against the trunk to wait.

One of the voices was Alastair's. The second was definitely male, older. I heard the raspy tenor in his voice from years of use and he also had a slow, shuffling gait.

Alastair had the situation well in hand, his own footfalls loud and clunky, telling us he was headed in our general direction. His eyes flicked up. I knew he sensed me hiding, watching over him from above. I caught his quick wink as they came strolling into view.

The man Alastair was with had graying hair poking out from underneath a fisherman's cap. His skin was tan, rough, and gnarled, shaped by weather and the outdoors. When he smiled, I caught a flash of overly whitened teeth—most likely dentures.

As soon as I knew we weren't in any danger, I flew back to camp, branches and leaves and debris falling around Corinth as I dropped back down out of the dense foliage to land next to him—

He had already moved, drawing the dagger up at the same time as I landed. The tip of his blade kissed the hollow point of my neck. But that was only part of what made the hairs on my arms stand straight up. The other part was how his eyes looked: like they had been swallowed up and replaced by silver strobes of light—light that proved to do the opposite of its intended purpose. Whatever possessed him seemed to be sucking his humanity from him. There was one chilling second when I was absolutely certain he was going to slice my jugular wide open. I imagined the razor-sharp edge burning through my skin—

And a second later, he was blinking back that strange light, his brain quickly registering it was me and not some other threat he had to dispatch. A flash of mortification flickered across Corinth's face as he dropped the blade back down by his side, right as Alastair and the stranger came into the clearing.

I leaned up against one of the giant boulders in our camp so I could hide the fact that my whole body was trembling from the rush of fear and adrenaline coursing through me.

Alastair gestured at me as the stranger got close

enough. I caught snippets of their whispered words: "girlfriend" and "Laura." My cheeks reddened at the mention of *girlfriend*. I knew it was a cover, but I liked the sound of it on his lips—very much. It was one tiny glimpse into what could be.

When they got close enough, the stranger stuck his hand out, flashing me a warm smile. "Name's Thatch, ma'am. It's a pleasure to meet you." He turned to Alastair, elbowing him in the ribs. "This her?" He whistled and turned back to me with wide eyes. "You a professional rock climber or something? Looks like you could go toe to toe with a grizzly."

My first thought was that he was comparing me to a grizzly, and I wasn't sure how to take that. The second was that Thatch would get along with Nan. Of course, everyone got along with Nan—until you didn't.

I took his hand in mine. His grip was firm and callused, and the scent of pungent fish and creek water clung to him, reminding me of how Corinth's dad used to smell on the rare occasions when I joined their family on camping trips. I used to hate the outdoors and anything to do with sweating in general. Now, I realized my opinion had changed. I liked the solitude.

Alastair dropped his gaze, clearly embarrassed about having been caught talking about me. "Yes, Thatch, that's uh ... *Laura*."

I wrinkled my forehead at the name. A lot of people, at first glance, mistook Larna for Laura. And even though I knew Alastair had just made it up, I still felt a prickle of annoyance at the name he'd chosen. "Yup, that's me ... I'm *Laura*."

I felt Corinth's eyes on me, but I found I couldn't

look at him just yet.

Thatch turned his attention to Corinth next. "And you must be …"

Corinth stepped forward to shake his hand, catching on quickly. "Luke."

Thatch's eyes flitted to the blade in Corinth's hand. "That's some knife," he said, whistling. "Any friend of Izzy's is a friend of mine."

Corinth sheathed the blade back at his thigh, regarding Alastair with an amused grin. "Izzy? Of course … good ol' *Izzy* is what we call this guy."

Thatch elbowed Alastair playfully in the ribs again. "So, this is the lot you said you'd bring by? Well, I'm impressed … I bet the boys fight over Laura like geese fighting over bread." He gave me a one-eyed squint, studying us each in turn for a moment longer before adding, "By the surprised looks on your faces, I suppose Izzy didn't tell you I was coming."

Corinth shook his head. "Izzy didn't tell us anything … but it is a most pleasant surprise, sir, to meet you."

I could practically hear Alastair's teeth grind in aggravation at Corinth's inflection on the name Izzy. I had never heard him use it before. I assumed he didn't want to give real names in case word got back to clan Deimos somehow.

Alastair guided Thatch over to the campfire Corinth had started to put together. "Thatch has been hiking these hills for over fifty years. I met him on the trail a few months back."

"Don't be modest, young man," Thatch said. "Izzy helped me out of a pickle. I'm not as spry as I used to be. Took a horrible tumble and hurt my hip. If it hadn't been for his help, I'd have given up the ghost right then and there." He pulled a leather rucksack from around his shoulder and started to rummage through it. "Izzy heard me moaning like a shrew. This one isn't a giant"—he thumbed a hand at Alastair—"but he sure does pack on some muscle. Picked me up no problem and took me back home." Once he found what he was looking for, he clucked his tongue and then pulled out an old metal pot from his bag.

Thatch saw the puzzled looks on our faces at seeing the pot and said, "It's a percolator … what you kids call a coffeemaker. With the advent of fancy technology nowadays, you've probably never seen one of these before." He said, "Well, don't just sit there, Luke. Go get us some more wood for the fire."

Corinth's eyes widened as if seeing a priceless artifact. I watched as he immediately jumped up, running off down the path without another word.

I thought about a time back before the dagger had come into our lives. At least back then, Corinth didn't have to worry about running his best friend through with a blade. I shuddered. And as if I were reliving a better time, I found myself saying, "Cor—I mean, Luke's dad used to take him camping when he was little—" I choked on the word *little* and cleared my throat to try again. "He used to tell me that the only good thing about being outdoors was enjoying fresh coffee over an open flame. He sure does love his caffeine."

Thatch nodded as Corinth emerged from the woods with an armload of kindling for the fire.

As soon as he saw the small brown bag Thatch held in his hands, he licked his lips and threw the firewood down. I watched as he fished a lighter out of his pocket. It looked like one of Paul's. "It's a good day when someone brings magic beans."

Thatch chuckled. "You are correct, lad. These particular beans are quite rare."

I positioned myself close to the mouth of the half shelter, silently brooding about our journey in the morning, and also trying to keep an ear open. At least it was dry and relatively warm with the giant rock hanging over our heads. Tonight neither Alastair nor I would be sleeping. We'd be watching for signs of danger. I felt my mood start to slip at thinking about what was in store for us—and more so for Corinth.

Thatch jumped up with a lot more enthusiasm than I thought possible as soon as he saw that the fire was lit. I watched him work, placing the percolator on top of a flat rock over the flames. "Coffee boiled is coffee spoiled. If you leave it on the fire too long, it'll ruin the taste. A perfect cup of joe has to be made just right."

Corinth rubbed his hands together, hanging on to Thatch's every word.

When the water started to boil, Thatch used a towel from his bag to pluck the pot up and began pouring us each a cup. I was surprised he had four tins stored in his bag, as if he had been ready for our arrival.

I sat back, sniffing in the dark roast before taking the first sip. He was right, it was definitely the best cup of coffee I'd ever had: bold, rich, and blended to perfection.

Corinth kept moaning in joy as he slurped it down.

"How far are you kids hiking?" Thatch asked, regarding our meager belongings with a frown.

Alastair said, "We've got a ways to go."

"You should have better equipment."

"We're stopping for supplies later," Alastair answered as smoothly as a car salesman.

Thatch nodded, sipping his coffee in silent contemplation, but I could sense he knew we were keeping something from him. He seemed like the perceptive type, like nothing ever got past him. I wondered if Alastair had compelled Thatch at some point, or was planning on doing it. Thatch just so happened to have four cups with him in his bag—that wasn't just coincidence.

"Have you heard the tale about these parts?" Thatch asked finally.

Corinth yawned. I watched him stretch out on top of the sleeping bag, arms behind his head, deep in thought.

It was pitch-black, only a few stars dotted the night sky. The moon didn't offer up much help by the way of natural light. I could see perfectly fine in the dark, but Corinth couldn't. He seemed exhausted from our trek and I didn't blame him. We'd been up since four this morning packing and then in transit—and training after that. I kept finding myself giving him furtive glances, thinking about his reaction and eyes lighting up the way they did as I dropped down beside him, scaring him.

Thatch set his cup down to warm his hands on the fire as he started his tale. "Legend has it there used to be two eighteen-foot-tall giants. Cormoran and Cormelian lived among these very hills." He gestured above us. "The stones and cairns, those up there"—he pointed to the protrusion above us—"folk say they were brought here by these giants. Some say it was to mess with the small folk— for a bit of sport." Thatch shrugged. "Whatever the reason, a young lad named Jack got fed up dealing with these meddlesome giants. Deciding to take matters into his own hands, he devised a plan to get rid of them forever. Jack dug an enormous hole in the earth, then concealed it with leaves, branches, twigs—anything that would hide the truth from the giants in hopes that they would stumble into it and fall to their deaths. Then one day, it worked— Cormoran stepped into it and did just that." Thatch spread his hands toward the fire, warming them.

"That sounds like a morbid take on 'Jack and the Beanstalk'," I said, gazing into the embers of the fire for so long my vision started to blur.

"Aye, exactly." Thatch turned to Alastair. "One last story and I'll be heading home. It's getting late."

"We'd love to hear more," Alastair agreed.

Thatch beamed back at us, clearly happy we wanted to listen to more. When he spoke again, there was just the right amount of intrigue and enthusiasm that made him a good storyteller. "You'll have to forgive all my tales about giants, but a lot of us around here believed they used to roam these hills as real as you or me." Thatch pointed at Alastair in exaggeration as he continued. "Bolster, another giant, fell in love. But he didn't fall for another giant; he fell for a small folk, like you or me. Her name was Agnes, and it wasn't long before he professed his true love to her. To prove his loyalty and affection, he told Agnes that he would complete a task of her choosing. Agnes told him she had just such a task, the ultimate test of true love. Bolster was to fill a hole at Chapel Porth using nothing but his blood to do it. You see, he was a tough giant, more fearsome than any around. Plus, he had more than enough blood to spare. But what Bolster didn't know was that very same hole led straight to open sea—that there would be no real way for him to fill it. Bolster opened a vein and let his blood flow. And it flowed and flowed and flowed until he eventually bled to death."

I found myself casting another glance in Corinth's direction, thinking about how Thatch's story sounded eerily familiar. Corinth was staring off into the fire with a strange look on his face. I wondered if he was thinking the exact same thing I was. The flames flared and ebbed, leaving half his face distorted in shadow. I shivered, thinking back to him on the surgical table, losing his blood in much the same way Bolster had, except *his* blood had been stolen.

Thatch continued as if he hadn't noticed Corinth's sudden change in mood. "The hole is still there at Chapel Porth—and the red rocks are said to be still covered in the giant's blood."

"I think I'll turn in," Corinth said abruptly, and I noticed his face stood out stark against his dark hair, as if the thought of losing that much blood had made him ill again.

Thatch stood and so did Alastair.

I said, "Thank you so much for your hospitality."

Thatch bent down and took my hand in his. "It was an honor, Laura." His gaze flicked from me to Corinth. "You lads and lasses be safe."

"Sir?" Corinth asked, stopping Thatch. "You think you could spare some of those magic beans?" He held up his phone. "I'll trade you a phone for them."

Thatch laughed, and it came out sounding like an owl hooting as he handed Corinth the small brown bag from his satchel. "Enjoy, lad."

Corinth tucked it reverently back into his own duffel

before saying, "You, sir, are a saint."

Alastair offered to walk Thatch back, but Thatch wouldn't hear of it. He kept saying he knew the lay of the land better than anyone who'd ever walked these hills, but once he was out of range, Alastair left to follow him discreetly until he made it back home safely.

When Alastair returned, I raised a questioning eyebrow at him. "Izzy?"

"I didn't want to give him my real name." Alastair dipped his head. "It's an old family name."

Corinth hooked an arm under his head, staring up at the rocky outcropping above us. "Family name, tell us more," he pressed. I didn't have to see the look on Corinth's face to know he was trying to distract himself from Bolster's story by provoking Alastair. "Tell the truth, Al; you compelled Thatch didn't you?" he insisted. "You use people."

"Corinth, what's your problem?" I asked, aghast at his attempt to get under Alastair's skin.

Alastair appeared beside me in a rush of wind, waving off my concern. "He's right. I did. I needed to make sure we weren't being followed. It didn't put him in harm's way. I just asked him to keep an eye out for strangers along the trail ... nothing that would get him into trouble."

"From who—Big foot or *your kind*?" Corinth said, digging deeper. His eyes flew to mine. I guess he saw the aversion on my face, because his eyebrows drew together in regret. "Look, I'm sorry. I just need some sleep. It's been a long day," he mumbled.

Alastair rubbed a hand across his mouth. "Don't forget, we have training in the morning—you'll be way too tired to be in a mood, that's for sure."

Corinth closed his eyes. I could tell by the way he pressed his lips together that he was regretting his words now.

I lifted my sleeves, revealing the armor on both my wrists.

Alastair eyed them approvingly. "Those look good on you—your father would have been proud you decided to take them up."

His hand skimmed over my arm; I felt a fluttering sensation dance through my stomach as he pulled my hand toward his, turning the device over.

"You flick your wrist, and the blade ejects from here." He pointed to the back, to a metal mechanism that I knew housed the concealed blade. "The key is to keep them hidden. Use them as a last resort." He held up a finger. "Oh, and keep your fingers clear of the blade. We can't grow back limbs."

"Good advice," I said, grinning back at him.

Alastair gave me a sideways glance. I couldn't help but notice the glint of something in his eyes, an unnerving directness that made my cheeks burn. He leaned toward me, his breath rustling my hair. "I'll show you some defensive tactics with them tomorrow if you want."

My voice had decided to conveniently flee, so I found myself only nodding in affirmation.

Alastair leaned back and closed his eyes, listening for what I assumed were signs of threats. Like maybe an eighteen-foot-tall giant. I shuddered at the thought as my eyes roamed over to Corinth once again.

We sat in companionable silence for a while longer until I said, "So … Izzy is a family name?" Alastair didn't say anything at first, only studied me with a tight jaw and narrowed blue eyes—his tough-guy act. I didn't let it deter me. If he wanted to share something personal with me, he would.

When he finally did speak, it was in a whisper-soft voice, and because I hadn't been expecting it, I almost jumped out of my own skin. "My mom used to call me Izzy."

It made me smile, picturing him grabbing the end of his mother's skirt when he was a little tot. "Why did your mom call you that?"

"My last name—Iszler. Where I grew up, the townsfolk used to call all of the Iszler kids Little Izzy."

"Your village was in Germany, right?" I asked slowly.

He nodded. I didn't want to press him; it was important he talk about his family in his own time and when he was ready.

I picked at the leather straps on one of the vambraces in thought. "You know—when you lose someone close to you, I've discovered that sharing a story about them helps keep their memory alive."

Alastair's hand found mine, and my pulse quickened. He avoided my gaze, but he gave my hand a quick pump. "Perhaps another time." He stood quickly but didn't turn around to face me. I could see the hard line of muscles on his back and shoulders. "I'll take the first watch."

My gaze rested on Corinth's still form, a shadowy lump in the darkness, his heartbeat slowing, along with his breathing. He was fast asleep, even after all the coffee he'd ingested.

I shook my head, moving past him into the night. I couldn't quite hide the smile in my voice when I spoke. "You stay with Corinth. I'll take the first watch, Little Izzy."

Chapter 24

Corinth

AL WOKE ME UP at the crack of dawn's ass for our morning training session. I was so delirious I tried plugging my phone charger into a tree and broke it.

"Straighten your back leg!" Al used the flat part of his foot to push me off-balance. "See what you're doing there. Your stance is all off. Your hips should be level with the ground while your front leg acts as support. You look like a wounded donkey. Concentrate on two things. Breathing—keeping your mouth open—and hitting the correct poses. Katas are about repetition. He put a hand to his head in frustration. "You are a terrible student."

Seeing Al standing there mocking me—with the trees spread out around us on all sides, enclosing us in a boxing-ring-like arena—I started to get angry. It was the stern expression on his face, like he was tormenting me for provoking him last night. I get it; I was a jerk, but that didn't mean I was going to apologize.

"Keep your weight above your heels. Move, step, turn—here." Al pointed at a nearby tree. "Use this as a punching bag. Practice your footwork and kicking. See what's more powerful—"

I held up a hand. "Whoa, whoa, whoa ... You want me to start punching and kicking a tree? Come on, man, I'm beat, and we have a whole day of walking ahead of us."

"Zero point two seconds."

I drank a sip of water, some of it dribbling out of the side of my mouth as I said, "Excuse me?"

"That's how fast a normal technique takes to execute. It's a blink. Vampires are faster than a blink. Do you think you can beat us if you don't train for speed?"

I felt my defiance deflate like a balloon. He was right. I had no chance of surviving against a vampire attack with my limited human strength and lack of super-speed. It had happened to me back at the warehouse.

As if reading my thoughts, he said, "You may not always have your blade. If something happens, you need to be able to handle yourself without it."

I blew out a troubled breath. "You're right ... I'm a terrible student. I promise to start working on form and technique with gusto, the likes of which you've never seen before. I've been fighting this—you—everyone for far too long."

Al flashed me a rare smile, and this time it felt genuine. "*Now* you're learning."

After I'd spent the better part of the morning stretching out the soreness in my stiff muscles, I finally moseyed back to our campsite.

Larna was resting on a flat rock in the shade of a giant oak, her legs tucked under her reading something. Once I got close enough, I saw that she was combing through her father's old journal. The pages were so worn and tattered that they had started to break apart at the binding. I couldn't help but notice how cute she looked sitting there, her eyes moving rapidly over whatever was written on the page.

Al was in the process of feeding the fire more sticks and branches. It hissed its thanks, smoke barreling back up into the air as it flared back to life. Birds chirruped softly to each other from out of the tree-tops. It was peaceful this early; normally, I slept right through the morning.

I was instantly transported back to a hot summer day in Texas, camping out with my old man. He used to have to drag me away from the confines of my room, telling me I had to learn how to appreciate nature properly. I hated it at the time because he made me leave every single one of my electronics behind. Funny, now I'd trade just about anything to be back with him one more time, sweating my butt off in a tent with an inflatable mattress. I didn't want to be the weak link of the group and admit to Larna how homesick I actually was.

"How much further do we have left?" I asked, wedging myself beside her on the rock. Our thighs touched, and I could feel the warmth radiating off her skin, even through the thick layer of material of her camo pants. I shifted uncomfortably, painfully aware of how much sweat was slicking the back of my T-shirt to my skin.

Larna glanced up from her reading, blinking at me as if she hadn't even heard or felt me sit down beside her. "Alastair said one more day. We could have pushed on, but we'll still have a distance to travel once we get to the cliff. We're going to a cave and then straight down. Apparently, it's the supersecret entrance Sozo gave him—so, no one else knows we're coming."

"So a cakewalk—" I said, my voice thick with sarcasm. The sudden smell of cooking meat stopped me cold. "Do I actually smell *hot* food?"

Larna flashed me a quick grin. "Alastair caught fish."

I gave a derisive snort. "Of course he did. I would complain about the guy being able to do everything, but I'm starving—so I'll jump on the Al bandwagon this one time."

Larna nudged me playfully with her shoulder. We sat in silence, watching the sun filter through the saplings— the soft rays of light playing across her face softened the harsh lines around her mouth, and raven-colored hair. Even her coppery gold highlights twinkled like sun dappled waves in the ocean. I found myself staring at those long, dark lashes of hers too. This was the most relaxed I'd seen her in ages. She seemed so serious these days. A second later, when she turned away, the hardness in her eyes had returned. It was the face of someone who had the world sitting on top of their shoulders. I knew what that felt like. We opted to keep each other company without the need to carry on a conversation. Our silence spoke volumes: we were going to get through whatever happened next as long as we had each other.

Al checked the white, flaky innards of the fish across the way; I could hear it bubbling and sizzling as it cooked. Breakfast of champions.

My mouth started to water at the thought of eating meat. It had only been a day and a half but, between working out and hiking, I was starving.

Among the peaceful backdrop, the wind nuzzling the leaves, it was enough to lull me into a comfortable stupor as I waited for the food to cook.

Larna broke the silence after a while. "Your dad would

be stupid excited if you told him you were outdoors."

I dug my nails into my palms as anxiety rushed up to greet me. *Go away.* On the inside I was freaking out, but on the outside, I managed to flash a small grin. "I was just thinking the same thing. I was fine being sedentary back then, but now that I have this blade … I don't know. The thing called to me for a reason." I swiped a hand through my hair, distressing it to a fine point on top. "I *swear* it's testing me, toying with me … to see how far it can push me before I break."

I watched Al reach over to pluck the succulent morsel from the fire. He plated it on a napkin he had in his pack, and then appeared in front of me in a blur of movement that made him look like a flickering hologram.

I accepted it with a nod of thanks. "Y'all don't want any?"

Al grabbed a thermos from his bag and unscrewed the top. "We're covered."

He handed the bottle to Larna first so they could share.

I would never get used to the fact that they drank blood. It was disgusting. For them, they didn't see anything wrong with it; they gained years of life back. Would I go to those lengths in order to find youth? I knew a lot of people who would. There was a small part of me that wondered what it would feel like to take a swig of liquid life. Just a tiny taste … I shuddered and the blade at my hip hummed: *It's wrong. They're wrong. Enemy. Fight. Seek retribution.* Retribution just so happened to be sitting two feet away from me. I tried to shake the words out of my head. This thing wasn't going to mess with me anymore—except I felt a little warning bell at the back of my mind that said, *I haven't even started messing with you yet.*

I pulled the small brown bag of coffee beans from my duffel, inhaling the heady scent, hoping it would distract me from my dark thoughts.

A few minutes later, Larna appeared by my side, startling me out of my daze to hand me a fresh cup of coffee. Accepting it gratefully, I drank it down, burning my tongue in the process. So engrossed in enjoying every last drop, I didn't realize she was still standing in front of me until she cleared her throat.

I glanced up at her and saw a flash of uncertainty cross her face as she stared at my blade. "Last chance to turn back."

For the second time today, I noticed how the sunlight haloed her head. It made her appear angelic and fragile. This was the first time in a long time that I had thought of her as anything other than fierce. Everything had changed the night I'd killed Sherry. College. Job. Girlfriend. None of that stuff sounded appealing anymore. And that was the problem, because I knew what did—*a reckoning*.

I picked at the handle of the mug in thought. "Oh yeah, hiding for the rest of my life with a five-hundred-thousand-dollar bounty on my head sounds like fun." My stomach churned and acid rose in the back of my throat. Something told me I wouldn't be able to quit my new day job quite so easily.

There was a small part of me that felt like if someone did relieve me of the dagger, it would be comparable to lopping off a body part. It was a part of me now, whether I wanted it or not.

Larna turned to me, her lips set in a hard line and her eyes dark with concern. "Yeah, I don't want to turn back either."

Chapter 25

Corinth

OUR TRAINING SESSION FOR the evening had ended with me on my back once again. Al's boot was disturbingly close to my head, and he had a derisive smirk plastered on his face at having bested me for the eleventh time. He'd managed to land one of those spinning kicks to my stomach. And now, I really wanted to wipe that grin off his face—and so I did. When he glanced down at me, I had my dagger clutched in one hand, pointed directly at his goods.

He backed off slowly, his eyes widening in surprise. With a tight-lipped smile, he said, "It's about time."

We'd been sparring for a few hours, and every single one of my muscles was on fire. Even my palms were heavily callused from practicing weapon strikes, defensive maneuvers, and the thousand and one ways to disarm someone of their weapons.

I shoved my dagger back into its sheath, panting. "What … time … is it?"

"Almost eight o' clock."

"As in p.m.?" I asked with a feigned gasp. "It's way

past my bedtime."

He cocked his head and smiled smugly at me.

"I didn't sleep last night—" I started to say, but stopped, wincing at the first signs of a gnarly headache coming on.

"I noticed," he said. "You were moaning and groaning all night."

"Where's Collins?" I asked, glancing around.

Al's eyebrows drew together as I clarified, "That's Larna's last name, if you didn't know."

"I know what her last name is," he answered hotly. "She's getting packed. Tomorrow, things might get a bit dodgy."

"Dodgy? I don't think I like the sound of that."

Al raised an eyebrow. "I don't either, especially because I'm probably going to be the one carrying you."

"Oh, no ... Larna will do *all* the carrying."

The next day, by the time we reached the bottom of a steep cliff, I reeked of sweat, dirt, and exhaustion. Not showering for a few days left me feeling gross and irritable. I missed my mint shampoo, and of course, hair gel.

It'd been a rapid incline the entire way. I didn't take much pleasure in knowing we would eventually have to go back down. Descending should be the easy part, but we had encountered so many jagged rocks, steep grades, and boulders as big as the ones in Thatch's stories that it would prove challenging to traverse. These rocks were the kind even giants would have a hard time carrying, which led me to believe the tales he had shared with us were probably true.

We were headed toward the caves at a massive cliffside, and the closer we got to it, the denser the vegetation and forest became. If the plant life had teeth, it would've eaten us by now. I'm ashamed to admit Al and Larna had to help me most of the way, and I was still covered in scrapes and bruises. No wonder no one wandered off the beaten path.

I swiped a hand across my forehead, turning to Al. "That was the easy part, wasn't it?"

Al was gazing off into the distance, ignoring me.

I followed his line of sight, noticing how expansive, dark, and open the ocean looked from here. It was the color of an impending thunderstorm—all blues and grays. "Why didn't we just come by boat? Or have this clan come and get us?" I asked.

Al's eyes drifted to where Larna sat crouched over her bag, making adjustments before we started our arduous climb.

Comprehension dawned on me and I rolled my eyes. "Seriously?" I said. "This is about spending more time with Larna? Because they have date nights for that sort of thing ..."

He shrugged. "Not the only reason." He pointed to the coastline, where tumultuous waves were breaking against snaggle-toothed rocks that looked like the backs of giant sea turtles. "Those rocks are man-made—from years ago—to keep boats away from this side of the land. There are hundreds of them out there, and they're all equally as sharp and jagged."

Larna, having lightened her load, came up beside me; her hair was a dark tangled mess.

Al gestured to a gap in the cliff's wall. "We're heading that way."

I put a hand to my forehead, squinting off into the distance, unable to keep the incredulity out of my voice. "We're not climbing that right? The last time I checked, we didn't bring rock-climbing equipment." The sea cliff had to be at least as tall as the Wall from *Game of Thrones*. Because I knew all things *GoT*, I knew that fictional wall was at least seven hundred feet tall.

Al gave me a sidelong glance. "No, we won't be going all the way up." He pointed to a rocky ledge about fifty yards up. "There's a way in, but it's not easy to get to."

"Nothing ever is. Let's get this over with," I said gruffly, marching past Larna and Al to take the lead.

A giant fissure ran vertically through the entire length of wall, from top to bottom. It was filled with thick vines, moss, vegetation, and lichen. And it was also probably teeming with other things like spiders and bats and giant fire-breathing dragons. I was going to need to be hands-free to climb this monstrosity. Adjusting the duffel's strap across my body, I suddenly realized how off-balance I felt. Why had I packed so heavy?

Al scrambled up over a rocky outcropping to the tiny ledge. Below that was a sheer drop-off to ocean and then death. I think if you hit water from a certain height, it would be like hitting pavement.

He grunted and, with considerable effort, heaved aside a heavy curtain of foliage, revealing the opening to a cavern. Hidden in plain sight—it was like the beginning of an action-adventure movie. I regretted not bringing my replica Indiana Jones hat.

Al fished a rope out of his pack, motioning me to come closer. I did so, reluctantly, as he reached around my waist to tie it around first me and then him. I was going to joke about being attached to his hip, but I found my one-liners momentarily unnecessary. I hated heights.

As I started, I quickly discovered that getting a firm grip on something other than slime or moss was going to be the challenging part. The cold, oppressive skeletal hand of fear started to take hold with each skid, misstep, and crumbling of rock. The volatile sound of breaking waves over jagged rocks below us wasn't helping. I had this weird ragged pant-cough that wouldn't let up too. By the time we stopped to take a breather, I realized the shaking of my hands wasn't from exertion, but from the massive amount of adrenaline and fatigue coursing through my body.

Al was ahead of me, perched on the side of a thin ledge—like an expert rock climber who liked to look death straight in the eye and flip it off. I was not one of those guys. Of course, I didn't have super-strength or healing either.

I did take a small bit of comfort in the fact that if I did fall, either one of them would easily be able to lift my body weight.

Al pulled me up to sit beside him. I took the moment to let my heart rate drop back down as Larna followed last, jumping up beside me, nimble as a cat. I was surprised how we all managed to fit in such a cramped spot. My long legs dangled out into open space on the thin lip of the ledge. There was something freeing about being so high up—up here, your problems don't seem quite so pressing. I could sort of see why people did this for a hobby. I risked a glimpse down. The colors melded in nature's tableau—green and blue and gold: the land, the sea, the sun. I could barely make out the whites of the waves as they broke over jagged cliffs below us.

Larna spoke up beside me, almost making me jump out of my own skin. "Corinth, Alastair will take the lead and help you through into that cavern. I'll be behind you just in case you slip." She gestured to my bag. "Give me that."

"Normally, I'd argue, but..." I shrugged out of the duffel and handed it to her, watching as she deftly strapped it to her back.

Without the extra weight, I felt much lighter and more confident.

Al reached into his backpack to pull out a headband with a light attached to it. He plunked it onto my brow and switched the light on. "Larna and I can see in the dark, but you'll need this."

I used the ledge and wall as a support to crawl back to my feet, noticing the thick crevice we'd be going through had about a thousand years' worth of plant life inside of it. "Today I am thankful both of you can lift a bus with your bare hands." The darkened cavern seemed to drop off into nothingness. "My panic word is *banana*," I muttered.

Larna repeated, "*Banana*. Got it."

"I prepared for this a few months ago." Al tugged the rope attached between us off. "I pre-rigged a rope-and-pulley system up here. I just need to go and grab it," he said. "I'll be back with the harness."

Al disappeared through a gap in the side of the wall, as agile and surefooted as a spider monkey leaping from a tree branch. He looked extremely comfortable for being so high up in the sky.

"So you think this pulley—?" I started to say, but my foot hit a patch of moss. I slipped, falling backward. The first thing that ran through my head was that there was no rope attached to me—Al had taken it off just seconds before.

Larna's mouth dropped open, forming a giant *O* right as the sudden feeling of free-falling hit me.

I threw my hands out, trying to reach for a handhold or anything as I shouted, "*Banana!*"

A hand snatched me out of death's grasp at the last second. I heard a snap come from my shoulder as I slammed against the side of the cliff; luckily, I didn't feel any pain just yet. Dangling in the air with nothing but your incredibly well-muscled best friend holding you up puts things in perspective.

"*I got you!*" Larna said, gritting her teeth.

She tried to pull me up, but my bag, which had been strapped to her back, suddenly came loose. It sagged off one of her shoulders, dragging her dangerously closer to the edge of the narrow ledge. By the grimace on her face, I assumed it was painful.

And then the duffel was slipping off her shoulder to plummet past me. I turned my head, catching a glimpse of it as sank into the swelling, churning waters below. Larna let out a loud battle cry, swinging me up and around like a pendulum as hard as she could; flinging me through the opening of the cavern, where Al had vanished only moments before.

The headlamp on my head popped off, hurtling into the space ahead of me, lighting a path of stone and rock and inky blackness in its wake. Just as I thought I was going to spend the rest of my life plummeting, my backside connected with earth, and then the wind was knocked from my lungs.

If there hadn't been jagged rocks scraping, burning, and shredding holes in my skin, the slide might have been fun. Instead, my body was the ball in a horrifying game of pinball as I tumbled my way into the depths of endless subterranean abyss. A giant rock materialized out of nowhere, jutting up from the earth in front of me like an iceberg. I tried to backpedal, but it was all I could do not to hit it full force. Spinning and sliding out of control, I floundered uselessly as gravity flipped me onto my backside and sent me tumbling headfirst down the tunnel. This was more frightening than it sounded. Blind to what I was doing, I dug my nails and hands into the hard-packed earth, trying to ignore the searing sting in my fingers as I struggled to turn myself back around. This was a blind topsy-turvy carnival ride that I would never pay to go on. Centripetal force squeezed my insides to slush as I pushed myself around, wildly twisting and thrashing in terror. Fortune was on my side as I managed to somehow fling myself around, feet first at the very last second. Better to break an ankle than my neck—

And then I was slamming into something soft and spongy, and it miraculously broke my fall, without breaking me.

Rolling over, I waited for precious air to rush back, and my aching muscles to stop screaming.

The dagger!

My hand flew to my hip. To my great relief, I found it was still there. Finally managing to take in a lungful of stale, closed-off air, I laid my head against the cold, spongy earth, thanking my lucky stars—and also the word *banana*.

Staring off into space, perplexed and dazed, I realized it wasn't as dark as I expected it to be in a cave. Soft natural light filtered down through the crags of worn-over-time holes in the cliff above. I ran my hands along my body, checking for more serious injuries. Surprisingly, the only spot where my skin had been sandblasted off was at my elbows and knees—wounds that had already stopped bleeding.

Al dropped down beside me from out of nowhere, cool hands exploring my clammy skin for wounds. His sense of urgency and concern sobered me. It took me a minute longer to find my voice, and when I did, I managed to croak, "I'm all right, I think—just scraped my elbows."

Larna's panicked voice echoed loudly from above us as she materialized from the same place Al did. She squeezed herself in front of Al. "I didn't have a decent grip ... and my hand slipped." She still sounded panicked. "I had to drop your bag. I'm so sorry, Corinth. I took a chance throwing you through the opening," she said breathlessly. "Are you okay?"

"Worst slip-and-slide *ever*," I grumbled, and with a strangled moan, said, "The magic coffee beans were in that bag."

Larna leaned back on her heels, sighing in relief. "We followed as fast as we could—almost caught you, but you were really moving."

I tried to sit up but found everything hurt, so I slumped back down into the soft surface I'd landed in. Fortunately, Larna and Al were already helping me to my feet right as I was seriously considering taking up real estate. Mud coated my hands, my jeans, my hair, but luckily not my favorite pair of Converse. I rolled my shoulders back and let out a gasp. Larna moved up beside me, her hands gentle and cool and also caked in mud. It felt surprisingly good on my raw skin as she explored my shoulder blade, clavicle, and back.

She nodded, satisfied. "I don't think it's broken or dislocated."

I readjusted the sheath at my hip. "At least I still have my Converse."

We carefully made our way across what felt like thick shag carpeting—and then it hit me that this was what saved my life. Algae, mushrooms, and thick moss covered the cavern walls and floor. Straight up ahead was an opening to a larger network of tunnels. Al took the lead. I followed, trying to keep up with his hurried pace as he moved through the largest opening to our right, apparently now on a mission. I was glad he knew where he was going, because I sure didn't.

"This place is creepy," Larna whispered softly as she trailed behind me.

I said softly under my breath, "*I second that.*"

As we left the comfort of streaming sunlight, the dark became oppressive and the air thinned out. I felt the beginnings of fever spiking through me. My elbows stung where I'd gotten road rash. It was right about this time that I started kicking myself for losing the headlamp. Larna helped guide me, a hand on my elbow as I stumbled through the dark.

After walking for about an hour, the tunnel deposited us into a larger cavern. Every inch of space was filled with mushrooms. They were glittering blue patches of bioluminescent light. It was strangely hypnotic and exactly how I imagined another planet might look.

Larna dropped her hand from my shoulder. By the soft glow coming off the walls, I could see her admiring the shimmering fungi with her mouth slightly ajar.

Upon closer inspection, I realized that not all of the mushrooms were glowing. There was a section of fungi that darkened a spot on the wall where Al had stopped. As

I joined him, his voice carried around the cavernous space, making him sound haunted and forlorn. "Bluefoot mushrooms." It was the first time he'd spoken in over an hour. He pulled his backpack off and filled it with the fungi. "I used to cook with these when I lived in France … They taste great in omelets."

I plucked one off the wall because I had worked up an appetite, and popped it into my mouth and then immediately spit it out. "Gross. That tastes like dirt." Taking a quick swig of water from Larna's pack, I hissed, "You *eat* that?"

"They taste better cooked," Al said, his mouth quirking up in amusement. "But they're great protein. You should eat up while you have the chance."

"I'd rather eat sludge," I muttered under my breath.

The further we progressed, the more claustrophobic I started to feel. Being in closed-off spaces and in the pitch-dark for hours was taking its toll on me. I deposited a pebble from the bottom of my shoe back to its home, noticing for the first time how many blisters I had accumulated during this trek. I couldn't see them, but I could definitely feel them. Mental note: Converse do *not* make great hiking shoes. I had a pair of perfectly fine boots, but they were swimming with the fish at the bottom of the ocean. That morning, before Larna dropped my bag, I had switched them out, hoping the gnarly blisters on my feet might heal if I wore a different pair of shoes.

Everything hurt, but I didn't want to be the first to whine, so I sucked it up, and we continued on … and on …and on … until it seemed like we'd never see the light of day ever again. I felt something dark and sinister twisting its skeletal little fingers into my gut. That thought sent me into an even more depressed spiral, and pretty soon that depression turned into an infection. What if Al didn't really know where he was going? What if he was leading me to my death? He loved Larna—he didn't care about me. They could see in the dark—all they had to do was leave me behind, and I would be lost down here forever. It wasn't until I felt Larna's hand shift on my shoulder that I realized she was still beside me.

Still, resentment started to gnaw away at me.

When we stopped for sleep, I honestly didn't know if it was day or night. There were no lights. My cell phone had been in my bag. I let that gloomy thought dampen my spirits even more. What had I been thinking? This was where some explorer, twenty years from now, would find my corpse. I shook the thought from my head, trying to rub the cold from my arms. The temperature had dropped the further we progressed. We couldn't build a fire to keep us warm; there was no firewood.

Larna and Al's company, or lack thereof, did nothing to help alleviate my ever-increasing anxiety. At times, I forgot about them altogether. My mind wandered a lot—to the only source of comfort I could think about—the dagger. The feel of it against my hip kept me rooted to the here and now. And then, without even realizing it, I found it in my grasp. I ran my thumb along the edge of the blade, mesmerized.

The weird thing, which I didn't see until later, was that Larna and Al were unnaturally quiet too. It was as if the darkness, invisible to them, had stolen their voices just like it had stolen mine. I idly wondered, and not for the first time, if they were thinking about getting rid of the weak link in their group … me.

I fell into a fitful sleep—

Sucked into a world of chaos and darkness and death, I was bleeding out on that damn rusty table again, delirious and suffocating, blood running in rivulets down the sides of my face and over my arms, slick between my fingers, and then in a jumbled suffocating mess of twisted nightmares, I was suddenly standing alone in the middle of a grove of trees.

They surrounded me on all sides and seemed to go on forever.

Their bark was stripped of all life; wasted and emaciated branches snaking upward as if reaching to the heavens for help. There was no help for them. The sky opened up and rain came down in sheets—looking as sickly gray as the bark on the trees. I felt like I might look just as ill.

My gaze drifted down as something crunched underfoot. To my horror, I was standing atop a pile of bone and ash and utter devastation. Everywhere I looked, I saw the dead. There was layer upon layer of bones—piled so high I realized the hill I stood atop was *made* from the dead. The skulls all stared up at me through vacant holes, and a shiver of fear or pleasure, I wasn't sure which, ran through me as I suddenly had a mental image of my eyes being swallowed up, replaced by the deadly lightning—

I felt someone touch my arm and bolted upright, the remnants of my nightmare still lingering, and because I couldn't separate dream from reality, I snapped the blade up.

The anger was still fever hot and thick in my veins.

I heard someone's sharp intake of breath followed by a gasp.

Coming fully awake, I dropped the dagger down to my side, my fingers slick. My shirt was soaked with sweat, and I was woozy and light-headed.

There was the scuffle of feet, followed by the sound of Al's clipped voice. "How bad is it?"

Larna groaned, and my heart shot into my throat.

I remembered I still had Paul's lighter. I don't know how I'd forgotten about it. Shoving my hand into my pocket, I struggled for a second and then pulled it free. With a quick flick, soft flame lit up the space in front of me. Al was beside Larna, with two hands on her neck, his forehead crumpled in concern.

The dagger slipped from my grasp and, suddenly revolted at my own actions, I kicked it away from me. "Larna? I'm so sorry," I panted. "Are you okay?"

She held a hand out, motioning for me to stop. "I surprised you. We've all been on edge lately. It was my fault."

Unable to take Al's uneasy gaze in my direction any longer, I released my thumb on the lighter, horrified.

"How bad is it?" I asked softly.

"You just nicked her," Al answered brusquely. "She'll be okay."

I slumped back, pulling my knees up to my chest, disgusted with myself. I hadn't meant to hurt her. It had been the nightmare that triggered the reaction, but a small part of me wondered if the dagger had goaded me into it.

Chapter 26

Corinth

THE NEXT DAY, WHEN we exited into a courtyard filled with glorious sunlight, I finally allowed myself to stop and take in a cathartic breath of air. The darkness had sapped me. Out in the light, I eyed the dagger with wary caution. Whatever sway or hold it had had over me in the caves now seemed to have lessened.

I needed to learn how to control the blade and not the other way around.

It was the exact opposite of the caverns out here. This place was ancient and uncultivated and wild. As we emerged out into a courtyard, I discovered that the outer structure connected four walls from all sides to form a giant man-made square. Wild oaks took over the building. I say *building*, but the structure was now so overrun with plants and wildlife that I wasn't sure what it had been before being taken over. Giant roots snaked and twisted their way up and over the structure's façade, down the sides of the aged and crumbling stone, and through cracks in the outer walls. Nature's persistence, I supposed.

I blinked up at the sun-dappled trees as Larna walked

up beside me. My eyes flicked guiltily to the bandage on her neck before I said, "The way the light filters in through the tree-tops like that makes it look like diamond dust falling from the sky."

Larna looked up, her mouth slightly open. "It does paint quite the picture, doesn't it?"

I stayed focused on Al, across the way in the middle of the courtyard, unable to make eye contact with her. "I'm sorry … for hurting you back in the caves."

I felt her gaze rake over mine, but I still found I couldn't make eye contact with her. "You want to talk about it?" she asked hesitantly.

"I had a nightmare—I was just so angry," I said. "Even now, I can still feel the heat prickling my skin. I was standing on top a pile of bones and skulls and ash …" I shuddered at the thought. "It felt so real."

Larna reached out tentatively and placed a hand on my arm. "You couldn't see in the dark—being in a confined space like that will mess with your head. You've been through a lot. Cut yourself some slack."

I swallowed hard. "What would I do without you?"

She flashed me a quick grin. "You'd definitely get into a lot more trouble."

But before I could respond, she was darting off to join Alastair across the courtyard. I made my way over to them, noticing how much of the environment had regained possession of the structure. Maybe this place had been a market at one point in time. People setting up stands and shucking bananas, or pots and goats, livestock auctioned off during the day and festive parties thrown at night. I imagined it all lit up, the smell of fresh fish being cooked so real my mouth started to water.

I turned in a wide circle, taking everything in. Lizards zipped through the wide cracks in the walls, giant spiders scuttled down the sides of the building, and flying insects buzzed annoyingly close to my head.

Larna was up ahead, staring at a carving in the side of a stone monument. As I approached, I saw that the carvings were actually Celtic knots. I thought I had read somewhere that the interlocking designs on Celtic knots were a symbol for interconnectedness and continuity. It reminded me of the symbol of the ouroboros; the snake swallowing its own tail. Goose bumps pebbled my arms. The symbols in this place meant something to the people who had carved them so long ago. Was I one of the few people who had visited this place since it had been abandoned?

Completely engrossed in my surroundings, I had forgotten about our real purpose for being here. When I turned in a circle, I realized Al had disappeared from my sight.

The main edifice had the most shelter and enclosed space, so I wandered in that direction, deducing that he was probably inside.

I jumped when a scurrying rodent darted across my path, so fast that I barely had time to discern what it was. Once inside, I saw that the building hadn't fared any better than the outside. Spotty patches of roof hung down, blocking off the left side of the building. Animal shit stained the path inside—my guess was probably bats—and the air was stale and moldy.

Alastair was examining a stone on the far wall with a hand on his chin. When I got close enough, I saw that carved into the stone was another Celtic knot. It was by far the largest one I'd seen in this place, but it had been exposed to the elements and was now covered in vines, spider webs, and almost-neon green algae.

Below the carving was a tiny miniature tree adorned with little red berries. Al had swiped a hand across it, clearing it off so he could inspect it.

It seemed weird to me that he seemed more interested in the tree than the Celtic knot.

"Are those berries edible too?" I joked.

Al's eyes stayed locked on the tree. "Sort of," he said. "They're rowan berries. Eaten raw, they can mess with your kidneys, but if you heat them up, they become edible."

I had to admit I was impressed by his knowledge of nature. "How do you know so much about all this stuff, *Nat Geo?*"

Clearly still preoccupied with the carving and tree, he said distractedly, "The internet and search engines haven't been around forever. When you live without the necessities we have now—well, you're forced to learn pretty quickly what you can and cannot eat." He added, "The Scots used to make a damn fine strong spirit using these berries. It's quite tasty. These trees are hugely popular in Norse and Greek mythology."

I gestured to the tiny shrub. "I sense you're going to regale me with the history lesson on this thing?"

And then he did regale me with the history lesson.

As if he'd rehearsed the story, he said, "The goddess of youth—Hebe—possessed a magical chalice. One day, through carelessness, she lost the mystical cup to demons. According to legend, the gods sent an eagle to recover it. In the ensuing battle between demon and eagle, the eagle was injured—it lost some of its feathers and blood in the struggle. The blood and feathers fell to earth to later turn into what we now call—" he gestured to the shrub "—rowan trees. The rowan derives its shape from eagle feathers. The red berry is the eagle's blood. These saplings offer protection. People used to place them in front of gates and doorways for that very reason."

I nodded, finally understanding. "This is a gateway."

Suddenly more curious, I stepped closer to Al as he nodded to a circle of squiggly lines etched into the wall. At the center of the circle were two serpents intertwined, twisting end over end; forever tied to each other. It reminded me of the blade and me. In place of their eyes were two large slits.

"This place used to be a temple," he explained as if he were a history professor. "No one comes here anymore because of technology advancements." He gestured around us. "Hence the dilapidated state of this place; only a handful of people even knows about its existence. It was my condition on keeping you safe. There were too many risks to just bring you through the front door."

"Have you seen *The Temple of Doom?*" I said nervously. I guess if you're going to make a ballsy move, throw a vampire hunter into the midst of a clan full of bloodthirsty vamps. I swallowed heavily.

Al finally took his eyes off the wall to meet my wide-eyed stare and to throw a nod across the room. I turned to see what he was looking at, and noticed for the first time the long rectangular stone table in the shadowy corner—on the opposite side of the dilapidated roof. It was covered in a thick layer of moss and bird crap. Rip Van Winkle's final resting place.

"It's an altar," he said.

"Alters are used for sacrifices." I cleared my throat in apprehension. "I think I'll hold my next Halloween party here."

I had curled my fingers around the hilt of my dagger without even knowing it.

Al took note of my hand placement, and something passed across his features: determination, and a gritty impulsiveness. It was a look that definitely did not suit him. Unyielding icy blue eyes met mine, and then he stuck his hands into the empty slits of the snake's eyes—all the way up to his elbows.

I shot forward, planning on pulling him free, but he shook his head violently, and I skidded to a halt beside him. My own eyes were just as round as that ouroboros I saw earlier.

"It's okay," he hissed. "This is how you gain entry."

"Is this the part where giant spiders eat your hands?" I snapped. "Because I don't think we should do that …" I let the sentence trail off, right as my mouth fell open at the sudden sound of gears whirring to life behind the wall.

Al rocked back on his heels. The unexpected movement sent the birds roosting in the thatches above us to flight. It wasn't until they took off, a sea of black wings and tiny terrifying shrieks, that I realized they were indeed bats. I shivered.

Placing a shaky hand on his shoulder, I murmured, "You're pale—I mean, *really* pale, even for you."

When he saw me open my mouth to shout for Larna, he shook his head. "It's designed to recognize our genetic makeup." He must have seen the disturbed look on my face, because he clarified. "It won't kill me."

"That's comforting," I said slowly, unconvinced

The device relinquished its hold. Al stumbled back, falling to his knees and pressed his injured wrists under his arms to staunch the bleeding. I reached out, and after a second, helped him to sit up, noticing the cuts had already started to heal by the time Larna had arrived beside us on a puff of wind that buffeted my hair to the side.

Glancing between us, her voice edged in concern, she barked out, "What happened?"

But before we could answer, the whirring had started up again, our heads collectively swiveling back to the wall as it slid open on surprisingly well-oiled hinges—a sign of technology certainly made in this century.

"These people have vast scientific resources, not to mention the best and brightest minds available." Al's gaze landed on Larna's neck where I'd nicked her with the dagger and then rested on me. I noticed she'd taken the bandage off. "When we get in there, you're under my protection. They said if you choose to go through tests to find out more about your *situation* ... it would be strictly voluntary. All these people want to do is help, but—" he jabbed a finger at me "—you only trust who I tell you to trust—you got that?"

"You couldn't have told me this before?" The flapping of my heart against my chest intensified, and suddenly I couldn't regulate the sound of my breathing. "A little bit of warning goes a long way."

"This is serious, Corinth." He looked me square in the eye, dropping his voice so I would hear the resolve in his tone. "Do you trust me?"

I nodded. There was no turning back now.

Chapter 27

Larna

THE FACT THAT WE'D been plagued by a cloud of mosquitoes before we entered the corridor seemed to make for the perfect opening to a horror movie. If locusts had flown down to greet us too, it wouldn't have surprised me in the least.

After we'd entered through the opening, a long passageway stretched out before us. At the end of the corridor, we found an elevator. Once inside, it silently whooshed closed. The disintegrating exterior was in stark contrast to the inside of this place. There were no buttons displayed on the elevator door. I assumed this meant it only went one way. We were on the longest elevator ride down to what Corinth kept saying led to the pits of hell, and all I could think about was all that strange, uncontained lightning in his eyes—with each flash, it had exposed a black void of nothingness—as if the light had sucked his eyes right out of his skull.

His white-knuckled grip on the blade was proof of how much he didn't want to be here. Corinth was covered in scrapes and bruises, and the dark circles under his eyes had returned. I sensed he knew he had reached a turning point with the blade. He kept giving me surreptitious glances when he didn't think I was looking, as if he were afraid he'd done irrevocable damage to me. It broke my heart to see him lose himself in this way. But underneath all of that fear lay a conviction that surprised me.

Back in the cavern, when Corinth had accidentally cut me with his blade, there had been a flash of pure rage on his face. Seeing such an intense reaction out of him, well, he might as well have clamped a fist around my heart and squeezed it to a bloody pulp. The prospect of throwing Corinth to the very thing he wanted to annihilate was also worrisome. It was Alastair's words of warning that had sealed it: *They said if you do choose to go through tests to find out more about your* situation ... *it would be strictly voluntary.* What was that supposed to mean? What kinds of tests?

Alastair seemed antsy as soon as we entered the elevator; he kept bouncing on the balls of his feet, and his eyes had taken on the color of the churning ocean we'd left behind.

As we hit the ground floor, Corinth mumbled, "Well, that was fun."

We followed Alastair, me taking up the rear behind Corinth. It was my job to watch his back. An ice-cream parlor filled with screaming kids could still be a lion's den in disguise. Make note of the entrances and exits, and always stay alert, that's what Dad had taught me. I tugged on the end of my long shirt-sleeves, making sure my vambraces were safely tucked away.

A light scent of bleach and orange citrus assailed me. What I didn't expect, however, was the fresh scent of the outdoors. It was earthy and fresh and oddly comforting, not at all like being in a tunnel underground.

Alastair seemed to read my mind. "Not what you expected?"

I shook my head as he led us through a set of double doors at the end of the hallway, into a reception area with a stern-looking woman sitting behind a desk. She had a head full of curly dark hair, and a jawline that could cut glass. I was pretty sure she had been patiently awaiting our arrival, because when she saw us, her sharp eyes zeroed in on Corinth first, whose hand rested near his blade. I knew that cautionary look she was giving him, because I'd worn it many times before.

We were led into a comfy-looking reception area filled with chairs that were arranged around small tables and overly stuffed sofas. It had the charm and quaintness of a coffee shop. Mini trees in pots, like the one that marked the way here, lined the walls. Their red berries added a touch of color that made it feel even more welcoming and homey. The thing that surprised me most, though, was the panoramic view behind the receptionist's window: a dark and swelling ocean, ebbing and receding with the undulating tide. I could almost smell the salt, feel the water hitting my face …

The woman behind the desk must have seen the impressed look on my face, because she said, "I like the desert better—more expansive and hot and uninhabited." She inclined her head at a remote sitting on top of her desk. "It's a projection."

Corinth inched closer, examining it with interest. "It looks like I could just walk right on out for a swim."

The receptionist turned her beady eyes back to him,

and her frown returned, eyes skimming over his worn and muddy clothes—then back to the dagger strapped to his thigh and to the blood coating his elbows. He did look a mess.

She pushed clipboards at each of us. "Alastair Iszler, your visitors need to sign in."

"What's this?" I asked, eyeing the paperwork.

Her dark, impenetrable eyes pierced right through me. "An agreement that states we don't condone weapons or violence. We are a peaceful clan." She pointed at Corinth. "No *riffraff.*"

"Forget it—I can't guarantee that there will be no riffraffery." Corinth turned to leave, but Alastair caught his arm, stopping him.

"No weapons are allowed inside. We deal with rule breakers accordingly, or you can head back to where you came from." She inclined her head again. "*That* especially includes the dark, tall one with the knife."

Alastair spoke up, trying to stop the onslaught before it even started. "Stephanie, It was agreed beforehand that we keep our weapons. Please check with Sozo directly before you kick us out."

The woman's gaze could melt titanium, but Alastair wasn't backing down either. I was only mildly surprised that he knew her name. I assumed he met her the last time he was here. His eyes were just as steely as Stephanie's. Eventually, when she knew he wasn't going to give up, she nodded and then reached across her desk to a small, round device.

Pushing down on the lid, it opened with a soft swoosh. She lifted a tiny earpiece to her ear and shoved it inside. Whoever was on the other line must have been expecting her call, because she didn't say a word.

After a second, she only nodded, pulling the earpiece out; then dropped it back into its holder. The woman straightened her blouse in agitation, apparently not used to being told no. With an indignant sniff and a nod in Corinth's direction, she said, "He still needs to sign the paperwork. And you two don't have clearance to bring in weapons." She pointed to Alastair and then me. "If he chooses to use the dagger on anyone, we will hold Alastair accountable. He is the one who vouched for the *tall* one."

Corinth gave a reluctant nod. "It's Corinth, ma'am."

She waved her hand as if she didn't think it was important enough to learn names.

After signing all of the paperwork, dotting all of the i's, crossing all of the t's, Alastair and I opened our backpacks so that she could search further. Once satisfied, Stephanie moved to another set of doors and motioned for us to follow.

Corinth's hand never left the blade's handle. I didn't let her know my pocketknife was hidden inside the interior of my vest, and my vambraces were still at my wrists. No one was taking them from me.

As soon as we walked through another set of expansive double doors at the end of the corridor, I heard an alarm sound so loud it could boil ear-wax. Red lights flooded on overhead and the doors slammed shut behind us. Several guards arrived to block our entry into the complex. All of them were wearing white pant-suits with gold trim on the sleeves. Even though the guards looked feng-shui-laid-back, they all still had stern looks on their faces.

I knew what they were after, so I held my hands up,

showing compliance as soon as they focused all their attention on me.

One of the first guards stepped up, pulling out a device that looked a lot like a baton, except this was powered—he had his thumb on a trigger, like a gun. Something told me I didn't want to find out if it worked like one either.

Alastair's hands were balled into fists by his sides. He had inched his way into my line of sight, his eyes hard, just like the night Gabriel had come into my room-turned-prison-cell at his manor. I gave a minute shake of my head, indicating Alastair should back down. He shook his head vigorously to let me know his extreme disagreement.

Corinth had his dagger in hand almost as if by magic. That's what gave me pause. I knew he could take out these guys if he wanted to. We didn't need to start a war before we even got inside though.

"It's okay," I said evenly. "There's no problem here, guys. I just forgot to take out my pocketknife." I pulled the small blade from the inside of my vest, holding it up for them to see.

By now there were five more guards circling us like vultures, all of them looking more nervous and jumpier by the minute. One younger man who looked to be in his twenties, accidentally pressed his thumb down on the mystery button, and it crackled to life, sending sparks shooting out of one end. He jerked back in surprise, as if he hadn't pressed the button in a really long time and had forgotten what it did.

I guess we all know now.

Their eyes kept darting back to Corinth and the blade. I think they'd come to the same conclusion that it hadn't been a good idea to show force right away. I'm sure they'd heard enough rumors to make him a cautionary tale. They seemed confused, frightened, and agitated all at the same time.

"Wow, you guys really take this no-weapon thing seriously," I muttered. "And apparently the X-rays are impeccably well hidden," I added under my breath.

An authoritative voice broke over the rest of the guard's grumbled murmurs. "Leave them be. I am sure our guests meant no harm." A man materialized from behind the security detail. He stood regally tall, wearing stately robes that had a pearlescent sheen to them, and the end of his sleeves were striped with intricate silver filigree patterns that suggested a leadership role or dignitary. He had a thin, angular face, with jet-black hair swept to one side. He looked like a horse had kicked him in his jaw—it appeared to be off-kilter, but strangely, only seemed to make his appearance that much more striking. I couldn't decide if he was attractive or the exact opposite. I decided to go with attractive.

In order to keep the diplomacy, I said, "I am sorry. It was not my intention to pull one over on you."

"No apologies necessary," he said smoothly. "As a sign of good faith, please, keep your weapons."

I inclined my head in thanks and the guards, realizing we were no longer a threat, dispersed accordingly to let us pass.

Corinth sheathed his blade back at his hip. The tension left Alastair's shoulders but I could see the alertness in his eyes, as he had appeared on edge ever since we'd stepped off the elevator.

"I am Sozo." He turned his attention immediately to

Corinth, his gaze slowly sliding down to the blade in curiosity. "You must be Corinth Taylor. I've heard a lot about you. You and your group are welcome here."

Corinth looked around at the surrounding security detail and to more guards behind him. "We appreciate your hospitality. I know it couldn't have been an easy decision to let some guy wander in off the streets with a dangerous weapon …" His hand lingered near the hilt of his dagger. I couldn't tell if he was trying to make a point, have a dig, or if he was truly sincere—maybe all three. Corinth did babble when he was nervous.

But if Sozo felt threatened, he didn't show it. "It is a pleasure to meet you all. I must warn you that there are a lot of curious people who want to know all about you. I have chosen to speak in front of them today to allay any fears you or *my* people might have toward one another." He took in our ragged and filthy appearances. "But if you'd like to get cleaned up first—"

Corinth stepped forward, suddenly a lot more sure of himself than I thought him capable of right now. "No— let's get this over with."

A nervous, prickling sensation bloomed in my chest at the thought of being introduced to a crowd of people without being properly prepared for it or cleaned up. I tried to smooth my hair back down. I'm sure I looked a fright. I pulled a face at him as he passed, wondering why he would want to rush into this. I guess I didn't blame him. If you were going to decide to stay in a place full of vamps and you had the one weapon designed to hurt them, well, I'd also want to know right away if I would fit in.

"Excellent," Sozo said, sounding pleased. "If you would follow me into our meeting hall, we can get the introductions out of the way. I am sure you are tired from your long journey. I have your quarters set up and ready to go once we are done. There are extra clothes in the wardrobes as well."

"A warm bed and meal sound great," Corinth piped up quickly.

We fell in line behind Sozo, and then his detail fell in line behind us.

I whispered to Corinth on our way out. "Are you trying to make yourself a target? You're covered in blood and about to enter a room full of vamps that drink blood."

He let out a deep sigh. "I'm already a target—I *need* to know what I'm walking into here." His eyebrows drew together. "At least this way, I can decide if we need to turn right back around and leave in a hurry."

I didn't want to say it out loud, but I was pretty sure we were both thinking it: *if they let us leave*. One thing bothered me: for a society claiming to be peaceful, they had already shown an unnecessary amount of force. It reminded me of winding my way through gravestones at St. Owens with Gabriel's clan gawking at us like we were freaks. Why had my dad sent us here in the first place? There had to be a reason—I just couldn't see it yet. That's why I'd been studying his journal more closely. Maybe there was something else in it that I was missing.

The corridors were exceptionally white, and the floors scrubbed clean. Nothing was out of place; not even a speck of dirt or piece of trash littered the hallways.

As we entered through a set of large wooden double doors, I found myself marveling at the intricate designs and Celtic knots carved deeply into the ancient wood. I wanted to study the symbols more closely, but we were being ushered through quickly and I needed to keep an eye on Corinth, now more than ever. If something was to happen to him, it would probably be in a room full of a hundred pairs of prying eyes, where opportunity lay.

Glancing around, my mouth hanging open, I realized this was no ordinary meeting hall. It was like walking into a courtroom the size of a stadium, except instead of the podium or a giant iron throne center stage, there was a massive rectangular iron table—and it was standing room only. There were hundreds of people filling the room. From the young to old, small and large, all races, sizes, and ethnicities. The seats were higher up in the back so that people in the nosebleeds could get a bird's eye view of the proceedings.

As soon as we entered, a buzzing of nervous, excited chatter filled the room. Panic, curiosity, fear; all emotions as palpable as anything I'd ever felt before. Their whispered words hung in the air: "*slayer*," "*hunter*," "*threat*".

Your entertainment has arrived.

I found myself immediately disoriented by the crowds surrounding us on all sides. *We should have gotten cleaned up first.* People were packed in close, making it harder to work our way through the throngs of onlookers. Fortunately, as they saw us approach, they fell silent and parted to let us pass.

Corinth's shoulders were pushed back, his posture rigid and guarded as he stopped behind Alastair.

On any normal day, I'm sure Sozo commanded the attention of every single person in the room.

But today, Corinth was the main attraction.

The walk from the giant oak doors to the iron table seemed to last forever. As soon as it became visible through the parting of people, I was able to see the seven-foot-tall man wearing a stylish tan linen suit and a fedora on his head. Right away, by Corinth's description, I knew this man was Dave—the healer who had shown up in Corinth's dream. My gaze landed on him as an unexpected and overwhelming hush fell over the entire assembly. I heard Corinth inhale as he laid eyes on the tall stranger at the same time I did.

He stopped to let me catch up, and as soon as I came up beside him, he said, "That guy in the linen suit … that's Dave … the dude from my dream." His mouth fell slightly open. "He's real … I mean, I hoped he would be, but I still wasn't sure …"

If we could get answers from this Dave guy, it might have been well worth coming here.

Everyone was curious to hear about the new arrivals now standing dead center in front of the iron table. The murmuring and excited chatter died down as everyone seemed to realize that the sooner they quietened down, the sooner they'd have answers.

People collectively took their seats as my eyes scanned the overcrowded venue. I felt the twist of trepidation in my gut as I saw the flickers of emotion cross people's faces. They all had the same look in their eyes: curiosity, fear, and apprehension. Our arrival had apparently been filled with much speculation. We'd been warring with Gabriel's clan for eight long months, and in those months, Corinth had made a name for himself. Running, hiding, fighting—we'd been so out of touch with the outside world that we didn't know what kind of impact we even had on it.

Surrounded by all these people, I kept thinking about the price on Corinth's head and how far some might go to get a payday. Alastair's caution had definitely been warranted. These rampant thoughts made the hairs on the back of my neck stand on end.

So consumed with everything going on, I didn't notice the swell of excited chatter begin once again, as if the spectators around us were witnessing something we couldn't see. The excited buzz of hundreds of people all talking at once increased until we couldn't hear anything else. I found myself looking around in curiosity, to try and find out what everyone thought was more interesting than Corinth.

Alastair's hand shot out, and he was pulling me roughly back, his grip so firm on my arm it hurt. My eyes narrowed in concern and annoyance. I started to question him, but as soon as I saw the look on his face I stopped, my heart leaping into my throat.

He had gone from watchful and cagey, to panic-stricken and ashen. It was like the wind had been sucked right out of him. Seeing that look on his face made my inner voice cry out: *Don't look. Don't follow his line of sight. You don't want to see what he's staring at.*

I couldn't help it—

There was no option *but* to look.

When my eyes locked on what Alastair was glaring at, the world around me faded, then folded in on itself like a collapsing star. Somewhere in the back of my mind, I knew Alastair's hand had tightened around my arm to a bone-crushing degree, but right now I only felt a sort of shocked numbness.

Suffocating and all-consuming, I suddenly found that breathing felt like a foreign concept.

His scar was the same as I remembered: an uneven

line zigzagging down from his left eye to his cheek, standing out against copper skin. He wore a well-tailored suit and had a nauseatingly sure-of-himself smirk that matched it. Aside from the scar, his skin was so smooth he looked like he was carved out of wax. Dark hair curled just over the tops of his collar. Tyrant. Killer. Deceiver. Gabriel Stanton. I didn't know what I expected him to look like when I saw him again, maybe for those ink-jet eyes to hold a healthy dose of fear, but it proved to be the exact opposite. I'd been waiting a long time to look him in the eyes again.

We'd been warned not to do any harm to anyone here. Unfortunately, there was no question I was going to hold back. The vambraces burned at my wrists: an itch to spill blood. *His blood.*

Chapter 28

Larna

SOMEWHERE IN MY HAZE-addled brain, I knew Corinth was just as upset. Alastair was too, but I had already committed to killing the man who had so boldly decided to show his face here. My breath came out in ragged gasps. I had just started to move when I felt someone weave their fingers through mine—as if in a dream, I found my eyes gliding to the hand and then to its owner. Alastair's piercingly blue eyes met mine. They burned bright with his *Sight*. He crushed my fingers together, as if to quell my desperation to flick my hidden blades free. I wondered why he was holding me back.

Everyone and everything around us had gone eerily quiet, no hum or whisper or noise from the gathered audience, as if they knew how dire this situation was. They could smell the unbridled rage in the air, as pungent as fresh vamp blood. What had Sozo expected to happen? A gladiator fight to the death? Sozo betrayed us. What if Alastair knew? I shut down that line of thinking quickly, noticing how his expression had darkened considerably.

Sozo was standing at the head of the table. We had all

stopped in our tracks, right smack in the center of the meeting hall. It was a spectacle to behold, I assumed.

Out of the corner of my eye, I knew Alastair was still staring at me, imploring me not to go after Gabriel, but all I could focus on was Gabriel.

My skin crawled, as if a thousand tiny insects were running up and down my body.

It was the way he was gazing at me, as if there weren't five hundred other people in the room. No one else existed. I stood rooted to the spot, paralyzed by shock. He disgusted me. The monster had killed my father, and here he was, goading me with that sardonic grin, his lips curling up at the corners. I could almost hear his whispered words in my head: *your full attention is anticipated and duly warranted.*

I tried to throw heat behind my glare, to prove I wasn't scared, but the fire in me seemed to wilt as an overpowering pull to go to him struck—as strong as if someone had placed an invisible magnet between us. So strong, in fact, that I felt myself drifting forward.

Alastair pulled me back, his whole body tensing up like a coiled spring. "He's trying to get a rise out of you—don't let him," he hissed. "Now is not the time to go after him."

"Now is the *perfect* time—"

Sozo put his hands up, his voice booming out with complete authority. A politician used to giving speeches, he had a voice that was smooth and commanding, imploring for silence so he could speak. "There are many grievances that *must* be worked out between our clans. That's why I called everyone here." He said evenly, "There will be no bloodshed. I gave my word of protection and I mean to honor that. Mr. Stanton has come here on a parlay. I have given him my word he will be treated fairly while here, and he has agreed to do the same. No harm will come to you or your group. We, as a whole, need to work through our problems—"

Corinth bolted around us, ignoring Sozo's plea for diplomacy. As he passed, I felt the smoldering fury coming off him in his wake. The air felt thin and full of a kinetic energy; it smelled of ozone, and I tasted copper in my mouth. His fingers crackled with threads of that eerie silver light. I watched in awe as an electrical current ran through his entire body, arcing portentously out of his hands and spilling down onto the blade in his white-knuckled grasp.

Lightning, as deadly-looking as it was luminous, swallowed his eyes whole.

This new threat was the only thing that could rip Gabriel's gaze away from me.

Alastair yanked his hand out of mine and went after Corinth, who was already halfway around the other side of the iron table.

Alastair was behind Corinth in an instant, his hand closing around his arm. It only took one light touch. Blinding golden light burst out of his body, a shimmering sphere expanding around him like a gigantic crystal ball. Corinth was a super-charged lightning rod.

The shockwave was so powerful that it blew Alastair backward across the hard stone floor where he rolled to a stop a few feet away, unmoving. A jolt of terror tore through me at seeing Alastair fly across the room to land in a motionless heap.

Finding I could suddenly move again, I ran toward him, my heart galloping with renewed fear. But by the time

I reached his side, he was already recovering, his blond, sooty locks sticking up at every angle as he sat up in a daze.

A collective gasp ran through the crowd of onlookers. Sozo's face morphed from stony indifference to panic, his eyes widening as half his guards rushed to protect Sozo while the other half encircled Corinth, training their weapons on him; effectively cutting him off from reaching his intended target. I felt dread rise up in me at seeing Corinth's less-than-happy smirk about this new turn of events.

Alastair's normally lively indigo eyes were glazed over with pain.

"You okay?" I breathed.

He shook his head as if to clear it and then locked eyes on someone across the hall. I followed his line of sight to see he was staring at Gabriel, who had his arms crossed over his chest with an omniscient grin playing on his lips. I tried to control my erratically beating heart as his gaze remained glued to mine.

Alastair ran a hand through his hair. "I'm okay," he wheezed. "Has Corinth ever done that before?"

I shook my head, still dumbfounded. "No. That ability is a new one."

Some of the color had drained out of Alastair's face. "I need some time to recover. Go—make sure Corinth doesn't blow us all up."

I stood slowly back to my feet, hesitant about leaving him. "You sure you're okay?"

He nodded, even though he still had a pinched, strained expression on his handsome features.

When I got close enough, I could see why the guards gathered around Corinth were all looking at him with trepidation. The state Corinth was in wasn't helping his case. His cheekbones looked gaunt and contoured in shadow; his muddy T-shirt was stained in dried blood and caked-on mud, and damp, dark hair hung down in clumps over storm-riddled sockets pooled with silvery lightning. The red tops of his Converse were surprisingly the only clean thing on him. He was grinning wickedly, as if he enjoyed a new challenge. I took note that fiery silver sparks crackled out of his fingertips, bouncing onto the blade he had pointed at the swarm of terrified guards. I wouldn't want to go toe to toe with him, that's for sure. The look he was giving them said it all. He wanted blood on his hands.

None of them seemed excited to be the first to take him down. They kept giving each other worried glances over who would be the brave soul to approach him first.

I inched closer to a woman with ebony skin. Her long dreads were combed into a tight ponytail, and as soon as I was close enough, her hard eyes met mine.

I held my hands out in front of me to show her I was unarmed. "Let me through," I said slowly. "I can talk him down. That display of power you just saw—it will get much worse if I don't."

One side of her face corkscrewed up into what I interpreted as a grimace. "Worse than those eyes?"

I nodded. "*Much worse.*"

After she studied me for a minute longer, she finally relented, letting me pass through a small opening into the inner circle. I guess she figured if Corinth was going to kill somebody, it might as well be the person who brought him here in the first place.

Corinth saw me approaching and swung his blade up, pointing it directly at my heart. I could hear a low growl of warning at the back of his throat as I inched closer, cautiously putting one foot in front of the other. One day, I might not get through to him, but it wasn't going to be today. My mind immediately brought me back to the dark cave, and my throat itched where the cut had started to scab over. A slow shiver worked its way down my spine.

"You can put the blade down. It's okay…" My eyes flicked to the corner of the hall where I knew Gabriel had been standing moments before, but he was no longer there.

Thank goodness for small miracles.

Bringing my attention back to Corinth, I said, "Gabriel is gone." I swept a hand at the overcrowded hall of people. His head seemed to follow the direction of where I pointed. I couldn't be sure, with those lightning bolts for eyes and hollow sockets, if he saw what I saw.

Someone coughed way high up in the stands, but it was the only sound in the entire place.

"These nice folks took us in," I whispered. "You're being rude, Taylor." I turned to eye the lady with the dreadlocks, feeling like I'd made a connection with her, and nodded. "They'll put their weapons down if you do. Okay?"

I gestured for them to drop their weapons. They glanced around at each other like I'd just asked them to do the impossible. All the while, the audience was getting a good show. I suddenly felt like a ring leader at a circus, taming the out-of-control lion.

"Put your weapons away," Sozo said, moving through the line of guards at the back. He was tall and imposing, his silver robes standing out against the whites of their uniforms. They shuffled aside immediately as he passed. And then slowly, one by one, they obeyed, dropping their batons back down by their sides.

Even though I couldn't see Corinth's eyes, I knew his gaze had landed on Alastair, who was still crouched on the ground, recovering, moving his head from side to side as if shaking off a vivid nightmare.

I could see a flicker of hesitation from Corinth, so I pressed harder. "I know you don't want to hurt anyone. You *can* control it. Remember what Alastair taught you about breathing? Your katas and training—do you remember the poses he showed you?"

The light in Corinth's eyes flickered and ebbed until I could see the warm honey brown of his irises once again. He sagged in relief, dropping the dagger down by his side right as I closed the distance between us to snatch the blade from his hands. Hot breath hit my ear as he threw an arm around my shoulder, looking utterly drained. "I'm so sorry … I didn't … How bad is Al hurt?"

Corinth took in all of the hundreds of faces all blinking back at him in fear and awe, and I felt a tremor run through his body.

Sozo spoke, his voice carrying around the hall once again as he asked for calm by spreading his arms wide. "I feel like the time for introductions has passed—that being said, everyone here is a guest. Please welcome Corinth Taylor, Larna Collins, and Alastair Islzer into the fold. They are to be treated with the utmost respect, just like any of us. You are all safe."

I wanted to interject the words *for now* after that sentence.

As if the crowd were roosting pigeons being disturbed from their nests, they erupted into a chaos of noise—voices screaming, talking, and jabbering over one another in excitement from the scene they'd just witnessed. Even though their words were unintelligible and garbled, their meaning was clear. They were ready to kick us out. Maybe this was Gabriel's plan all along: getting them to throw us to the wolves—to clan Deimos.

If that was his plan, it was ingenuous and it was working.

My eyes flitted from one scared face to another; all the while, the room felt like it was closing in around me from all sides, like a collapsing tunnel.

What have we done?

"We were brought here under the impression that this would be a safe place." Alastair pointed a finger at Gabriel. "From him."

Once the giant hall had been emptied, it was just Gabriel, Sozo, and our group left, making the great hall feel that much larger. I wasn't sure where Dave had disappeared off to, and I knew Corinth was chomping at the bit to inquire about him.

For what had just occurred, Gabriel looked strangely nonplussed as ever. Now that things had calmed down and my initial shock had worn off, I had time to study him. He was wearing a gray suit with purple tie and matching checkered pocket square. If first impressions were what mattered most, he would win that battle. If it came down to it, I knew that mob of people would side with him. He was enigmatic, charming, and ridiculously good looking. Anything that holds a certain amount of charm can be used as a weapon or an advertisement. These qualities were meant to numb us of all rational thought. He'd been doing it for over a century and getting away with it.

We were the stragglers who'd brought a real threat into their midst; the motley crew in dirty rags, reeking of desperation and an unappealing air of mystery. Gabriel had played us. He knew we would act on our hate. No wonder we hadn't encountered any of his people on the way here. He knew we were coming.

Gabriel wanted to make Corinth look as dangerous as possible.

Alastair pointed at Corinth and then me. "Gabriel Stanton must pay for his crimes. He murdered Larna's father, kidnapped Corinth's sister, and tried to kill me. We offer our loyalty to your clan, Eleutheros, but we require something in return." He turned to Sozo, beseeching. "Corinth can be a very powerful ally. You've seen what he can do. That's just a taste. If you allow him to use the dagger—against Gabriel—we can show you just how strong he truly is."

Corinth shot Alastair a look that said, "*What are you doing? Are you crazy?*"

Gabriel opened his arms in supplication to step up to the head of the iron table in a grand gesture only he could get away with. When he turned back around, he looked at no one else but me. And I was sure to hold his gaze, unwaveringly. My heart sure wavered though, hammering like a runaway locomotive against my ribcage. I felt it might turn to ash just by that severe look he was giving me.

Alastair, upon seeing Gabriel staring at me, ground his teeth together so hard I heard something crack.

"*Larna* ..." Gabriel purred, silky and smooth with a hint of venom. "I'll let Corinth strike me down" —he spread his arms wide—"once and for all, if after hearing me out, you don't find what I have to say useful." He held up a finger. "*But* my one and only condition is that I speak with you alone. If you aren't convinced of my truthfulness after we speak, you are free to have your minion do your dirty work for you."

Corinth vehemently shook his head at the same time as Alastair shot forward, his knuckles turning white as he balled them into fists by his sides.

I moved with my gift of foresight to place a gentle but firm hand on Alastair's shoulder. His eyes were burning. We both knew why Gabriel wanted to speak with me alone. He was going to try and compel me.

Gabriel arched an eyebrow in challenge, and it tugged his scar up with it: *What are you going to do about it?*

I licked my dry lips, but before Alastair or Corinth could say anything, I surprised even myself by nodding yes in answer. *Time to finish this once and for all.* If there was a chance that Corinth could finish what he started, I was going to take it. Something else inside me prickled at the opportunity to take him out all by myself—a fierce bravado brought on by my *Sight*.

"Fine, Gabriel, I'll meet with you alone, but our group needs one day to recuperate from our travels." Turning to Sozo, I said, "That is, if we are still welcome to stay?"

Gabriel seemed overly pleased by my agreement, his grin widening devilishly at the corners of his mouth as he cooed, "Excellent. I will see you tomorrow, *Larna*." And just like that, because he'd gotten exactly what he wanted, he turned on his heels and floated out of the hall like the ghoul he was.

Alastair nudged my side angrily. "No way in hell will

you *ever* be alone with Gabriel," he growled, "because I will drag you out of here before that happens."

It was my turn to grind my teeth together, but I only managed to give him one nod in response. We'd wanted to hunt Gabriel down for almost a year now, and here he was, almost gift wrapped and ready to go. There was no full weight of his clan here. No matter how we looked at it, this was the opportunity we'd been waiting for—Alastair would just have to deal with my decision.

Sozo said, "As I stated before, you are still welcome here as our guests. But I must caution you, please, no violence or bloodshed, or we will be forced to take action." I could sense Sozo's security detail inching closer, itching to make good on that threat.

"It's settled, then. Rest and replenish." Sozo held his arms out wide, dismissing us. "Thank you for your attendance; for now, the meeting is adjourned. When you are all more rested and cleaned up, Alastair, I would like to speak with you and your group in private." Sozo gestured to a mousy-looking man in a long white robe who appeared next to him as if out of thin air. "Caesar, would you give our guests the tour and show them to their quarters?"

I was going to follow Gabriel just to see which direction he had gone in, but Caesar moved into my personal space, blocking my way. His lack of social skills caused me to inch back a step as he pointed in the direction of the two large oak doors we'd come through.

"We'll be heading in that direction," he said, making a grand sweeping gesture. The wide sleeves of his robe smacked Corinth in the back of the head as Caesar passed. He turned around, giving Corinth a sheepish grin. "So sorry, sir, I lose control of them sometimes."

A lot of the crowd had waded into the corridors and were still openly gawking at us as we passed by. I suddenly felt like we would be swallowed up by the crowd if we didn't hold on to each other.

Corinth rubbed the back of his neck, casting me an apprehensive glance over his shoulder. He stopped to let me catch up and whispered, "I'm sorry about that ..." his voice hitched. "I know I messed things up real good back there. But what the heck were you thinking agreeing to that jackwagon's request to get you alone? Please tell me you have a well-thought-out plan, and you knew exactly what you were doing when you agreed to that."

I shook my head, mouthing the word *later* at him. There were too many people milling about, and things had gone colossally wrong so far. I was trying to conduct damage control as best as I could.

As we marched our way out through the wooden entryway, I got a glimpse of some of the carvings that I was sure had been whittled into these doors a millennium ago. The craftsmanship was nothing short of amazing. Dark lines curved and swirled and looped around complex-looking Celtic knots. I was so awestruck by the detail, I didn't realize everyone had left me behind until I glanced back up to see their dwindling forms.

Caesar turned back, waving for me to catch up as the throngs of people started to close in around me. "This way," he urged, clearly concerned by the crowd still lingering in the hallway.

As soon as we moved further away from the gathered mass of people, Caesar relaxed more—and then he even seemed delighted to be able to show us around, bouncing on the balls of his feet in excitement.

I, on the other hand, was only concerned about getting food of the enriched-iron variety back into my system. I felt sluggish and weak after everything we'd been through to get here—especially after discovering Gabriel was here under the same roof as us. I shivered, thinking about his manor. No home court advantage here though.

I was starting to think we were a particularly disturbing exhibit on display at a museum—the kind meant to lend itself to controversy by shock and awe. Even though most of the vamps here were afraid to approach us, I still felt weird by their incessant ogling. As we followed Caesar, I began to study our surroundings more closely. Most of the people here wore attire that consisted of white robes and matching sandals. It was all very New Agey and hip, leaving me with the feeling that we'd entered some weird cult.

The walls were intricately painted flowers and vines in pale shades of green and gold. Caesar gestured at them like a tour guide as we passed. "The walls were painted by a man named Michelangelo di Lodovico Buonarroti Simoni."

Corinth stopped abruptly and I almost ran into the back of him. "As in *the* Michelangelo?"

Caesar had continued on as if it were nothing, until he realized we were all still standing there gawking at the masterpiece on the wall.

"You know of him?" Caesar asked, clearly perplexed by our reactions.

"Are you kidding?" I said. "*Everyone* knows of him."

"What would a kid have to do with this?" Caesar smiled like he had to correct a child. He acted like we shouldn't be surprised that the most famous Italian Renaissance painter of all time had etched his painstaking artwork into these very walls. This place had been here for who knew how long; vital history hidden from the rest of the world. I felt a pang of sadness at how this was kept away from everyone else above our heads. We were walking through a private collection not many people had ever laid eyes on.

Corinth spoke quietly from beside me, tearing me away from my thoughts. "You realize we're trapped underground with a psycho, right?" he said. "You showed incredible restraint back there … Did you see the way Gabe was staring at you? He barely even noticed the rest of us."

I knew he was just as angry with me. This was going to be a fun conversation.

"You, however, did *not* show restraint," I whispered, glancing around. "We should talk about this later."

My gaze leveled on Alastair's back as he led the way, hands balled by his sides. Corinth was right. Gabriel didn't seem to give two flips about Corinth or the dagger strapped to his hip, which was incredibly odd considering what we'd just witnessed from Corinth.

"We should discuss this *later*, okay?" I insisted.

There were a lot of people with the ability to hear everything we said. I didn't want to risk saying anything with the chance that it might somehow get back to Gabriel. Corinth knew me well enough to leave it alone for now.

Moving through each labyrinthine corridor only revealed more sculptures, photos, displays, and hallways.

All I wanted was to take a shower and wash away the caked-on mud, not to mention the lingering feeling of

Gabriel's eyes on me.

As we rounded another bend, a sign pointed in the direction of "Kitchen A," and I felt a surge of hope at the prospect of getting sustenance. I guessed they had multiple kitchens in different wings. It didn't take long to notice stragglers trailing behind us—people who had been following us since we'd left the hall.

Three blond children with curly hair and dimples, a brother and two sisters, I presumed, finally plucked up enough courage to run up to Corinth and tug on his hand.

Caesar turned to see the little girl at Corinth's side. He immediately tried to shoo her away. "Go away, Cora."

Corinth waved Caesar off. "It's okay, Caesar." He knelt down beside the small girl, who had a big smile on her face. I knew he was thinking about his sister, Zoey, back home. She grabbed his finger like she was holding on to a balloon, while the other two kids decided to join her, hanging back as if extremely shy.

"Hi, Cora." Corinth glanced between the other children. "There's no way you guys are related, are you?" He winked at them, eliciting a fit of sudden nervous giggles from the group. "What are your names?"

The boy, who looked to be about three, stuck his thumb to his chest. "I'm Tanner."

Corinth turned to the little girl, who shyly shook her head, and Cora answered for her. "That's Stella."

"Hi, Stella," he said. "I like your pretty dress."

She smiled and then took off running in the opposite direction.

Corinth gave them a rueful smile and, to the untrained eye, it almost looked like he was enjoying himself ... *almost.* "I tend to have that effect on the young ladies." He was good with kids, but I could see his smile was more sad than happy. I think he missed his siblings.

Cora, who still held his finger, pointed with her other hand to his hip. "Are you going to hurt people with that?"

He glanced down, noticing the tarnished bronze handle sticking out of its sheath, and then shook his head adamantly. "No … no way. I'm not here to hurt anyone. I promise."

I thought back to his show at the meeting hall and shuddered, thinking otherwise.

Once she'd gotten the answer she was looking for, Cora turned to her brother, Tanner, and stuck her tongue out, taking off after the boy, yelling, "*Told you so!*"

A fair-haired woman with a flowing white dress rounded the corner, shouting, "Cora!" Once her gaze landed on Corinth, her eyes stretched wide in fright. She ran up to Cora and grabbed her hand, throwing a hasty glance back to Corinth. "You stay away from that *boy*." The woman ushered her kids away, her head swiveling back just to be sure he wasn't following her.

Corinth stood back up, dipping his head, his eyes hardening around the edges. I put a gentle hand on his arm, but he shrugged it off. I could hear the hurt in his voice when he spoke. "Caesar, the children here aren't …" Unable to finish the rest of his sentence, he let his voice trail off.

"Aren't what, sir?"

Corinth shook his head, frowning. "Vampire?"

Caesar opened his mouth as if finally comprehending what Corinth was insinuating. "No, those children are not vampire. This clan is open to those who seek shelter; and for anyone who plays a part in the furtherance of our society. There are humans here, of course, and some children that reside here too."

He ushered us through a set of censored sliding glass doors that glided open to reveal a cafeteria. The tables were set up much like any other ordinary restaurant. There was a long row of spigots that looked a lot like soda fountains, attached to a network of dispensaries across the room that drew my attention immediately. I didn't see any markings or signs indicating different flavors, so I assumed it only dispensed one thing—blood. Mugs and Styrofoam cups were neatly stacked next to the fountains for added convenience.

We shuffled closer to get a better look, right as an older man approached us. The stranger was mumbling animatedly to himself, gesturing wildly around the room to no one in particular. It looked like a good conversation was taking place inside his head, because he kept smacking himself with the ends of his robes. Tufts of wispy white hair stood on end. If I had to give him a nickname, it would be Gandalf.

Grabbing a mug from the counter, he started yanking on the handles attached to the spigots.

Caesar jumped into action to try and stop him from turning them all on at once. "Benny! You're in Kitchen A, again. You want to be in Kitchen B—it has that perfectly infused black tea you like so much ... remember?"

Caesar latched on to the handle of the mug Benny had in his hand, right as Benny pulled at the same time, his toothless grin making him look that much loopier. The old man was more than determined to get his own way. The porcelain cup flew out of Caesar's outstretched hand to land on the tip of his toe, bouncing off and then skidding across the floor all the way to the other side.

Caesar gave a yelp of surprise, while Benny took the fortuitous opportunity to pull down on the rest of the handles.

A dark, thick liquid spewed out from the nozzles, oozing into the drain catchers and confirming my suspicions. My stomach did a somersault. I didn't realize how hungry I was. And it looked like they kept it at the optimum temperature. Blood was best served warm.

Benny cackled in satisfaction at his act of defiance, cast us a wide, crazy grin, and skipped out of the cafeteria in triumphant glee.

Caesar grimaced as he fumbled with the handles. "Can you help me with these?"

Alastair and I worked to shut each one off while Corinth stood back, looking uncomfortable and grossed out. I didn't blame him. I had felt the exact same way before I was turned. It was sustenance to us, but to him, it was a symbol of life, pain, illness, and infection and being hurt.

Caesar said, "Benny's harmless, but he's gone a bit strange these last few years. He used to be the head of our engineering department for over forty years; he was sharp as a tack—that is, until his mind started deteriorating." He lowered his head in regret. "Very tragic indeed."

I glanced down the now-empty hallway where he'd darted down, and felt a pang of sympathy for the old guy. At least he seemed happy, making mischief whenever he wanted. That didn't sound like such a bad life to me.

Corinth said, "Caesar, do you mind if I ask you a personal question?"

He shook his crown of curly dark hair, his eyes earnest.

Corinth cleared his throat. "Do you turn … uh … humans, I mean, who want to become a part of your clan? How does that work? Take Benny for instance; could he have requested to become vampire?"

Caesar rocked back on his heels, locking his hands together. They disappeared into the long sleeves of his impeccably white robe. "We have a ranking point system here. Humans who have been vetted and have lived among us for at least ten years are allowed to request a turn." He glanced between us each. I found myself curious to know the answer to Corinth's question as he continued. "The hierarchy determines if a human has contributed enough to our cause during that time frame. And it's strictly voluntary—there is an age limit put in place. No children."

I watched Alastair grab a mug and fill it to the brim, trying not to lick my lips as my stomach rumbled. He handed it to me, and I took it gratefully while he poured himself a cup too. I couldn't help but notice how this topic of conversation seemed to put Alastair on edge.

I stared at the dark red inside the cup. It was still warm. "Where do get your supply from?"

Caesar said, "We donate."

He threw those words around a lot. *Voluntary* and *donate.* I guess it made sense. It was better than forcing it from unwilling participants like so many other clans out there. I was starting to think this was the way to go: peace and quiet, everyone coexisting with one another, *humans* included. If Sozo hadn't let a homicidal maniac in here, I might admit that this place wasn't so bad. I wondered how humans came to live here though. It didn't seem like they abducted anyone. Everything appeared legit—on the surface. Alastair had done enough homework to make sure we hadn't walked into an enemy minefield. Except for the part where Gabriel was invited to the party too, that is.

I felt myself starting to relax, the tension going out of my shoulders as I refueled. It felt like ages since I'd had a decent meal.

"You may take a cup to go if you wish—while I take you to your rooms—or you can stay and I'll show Corinth to Kitchen B. You are all perfectly safe here."

"No—" I said quickly. "We don't separate." Even though I was starting to get the tiniest bit comfortable, it didn't mean we threw caution to the wind. Gabriel was still out there, walking free after he killed my father, and that thought made my blood boil.

Chapter 29

Larna

THERE WAS A MEDICAL lab somewhere on the premises, as well as a science wing, classrooms, a gym, and guest housing in the subterranean complex. It was a maze of corridors and sterile cleanliness. We were all too tired and dirty to worry about exploring any further.

As we followed Caesar to our rooms, I listened to Corinth grill him. "So, Caesar, do you know who that tall guy is? Dave?" Corinth asked. "Or where I can find him?"

Caesar was wearing a frown, his forehead creased in apology. "Again, we must respect our guest's privacy. I am merely here to attend to your needs."

Corinth rubbed a hand over his mouth. "Well, Caesar, I *need* to know who this guy is … so technically, if you don't answer, you're in direct violation of your orders."

Caesar clasped his hands together, clearly alarmed by this contradiction. After a minute longer, he finally nodded, inching closer to us. "Your logic is sound." He searched the empty corridor before he said, "I can see you have a way with words, Mr. Taylor. All I can tell you is that he is part of a group called the Watchers."

The Watchers? I was pretty sure I had never heard of them before. Maybe we'd get some answers about what this guy wanted from Corinth. He'd been oddly quiet since we'd entered this place, but now his interest seemed peaked by this new bit of information. I shot Alastair a look, wondering if he had heard of them before, but he seemed just as puzzled as we did.

Corinth said, "Are the Watchers a vampire clan?"

Caesar held up a finger. "That's all I know, sir," he said. "And all I will share. If you would like to know more, I suggest you speak with Dave personally."

We wound our way down another long corridor, according to Caesar, the last one.

A custodian almost blended perfectly into the background, wearing all white, so when she bustled around the corner, Corinth ran right smack into her. She stumbled back in apparent surprise and fright, dropping the mop she'd been clutching. The handle fell forward, and Corinth grabbed it at the last second before it could hit the ground.

The startled woman's dark, close-set eyes honed in on Corinth. As soon as she saw the blade at his thigh, she turned on her heels and ran in the opposite direction in a blur of motion—*vampire*. In her hasty exit, she left her mop still in Corinth's outstretched hand.

These people had to have been terrified after his performance. I didn't know if it was a good thing or a bad thing, everyone being afraid of him.

"I can't even manage to scare this many people on Halloween in full costume," Corinth muttered.

Caesar's apologetic grimace was back. "People fear

what they do not understand." He cleared his throat and turned away, pulling out a keycard form his pocket. He seemed more subdued as he stopped in front of a seemingly smooth, blank wall space.

I glanced around, looking for a door or a sign indicating room numbers, and that's when I noticed the small plaque on the wall that read "C2."

He swiped the keycard through a gap in the wall where the plaque was located. It melded seamlessly within the design. If you weren't looking for it, you might miss it. I could barely tell there was even a door there.

A glowing green light lit up the outside of the door, outlining the almost-hidden entrance. It flashed once and slid open onto a darkened room. Once we filed inside, soft lights flickered on by motion sensor. Caesar pointed out the adjoining rooms on either side of the one we'd just entered. They were all connected, which meant we could get to each other in a hurry if need be.

A white down comforter was tucked into a floating bed frame, lit by pale green light, having also been triggered by motion sensors. The floor was polished white tile, and a gray fluffy rug covered half the room, giving it a modern but homey feel. There was a reading lounge in the corner and an end table beside the bed.

I turned to Corinth. "Take this room—it's in the middle."

Corinth snorted. "Just where I like to be … right in between you two." But he gave me a quick nod, surprisingly not arguing any further as he tossed himself onto the bed, kicking his feet up. He looked downright exhausted, having already closed his eyes.

Caesar reached down to hand the keycard to Corinth,

who sensed movement. He cracked an eye open, and stretching out a hand, accepted it with a grateful nod. "Thank you, Caesar."

Caesar showed us his card. "It has your room number on it." Pulling aside a thin tab on the back of the card, he revealed a small circular thumb-print pattern. Caesar pressed his thumb against the symbol, and the card flashed red. "Once you program it to your fingerprint, you no longer need the key to open your door. You need only to press your thumb against any part of the doorway, plaque, or wall, and it will open. It is a security measure for your safety so you don't have to carry a card with you. If you would all please do this now, I will be on my way and let you rest."

"That's handy," Corinth said, clearly impressed as he sat up again.

We all did as he asked, each of our cards pulsating red with acknowledgment of our new homes for the foreseeable future.

Caesar smiled once he knew we were all set, and then gave us a formal bow. "Should you have any questions—" he swept an arm over to the nightstand next to Corinth's head "—you can push that button. The round knob is an intercom. Whatever you need, we will supply with just a push of that button. We can clean rooms upon request, for privacy concerns and security."

"Thank you for everything, Caesar." Alastair ushered him out with a final wave and shut the door behind him, blowing out a deep breath. Blue eyes shined bright in the low-lit room. When he turned back, a look of relief washed over his features. "Well we made it this far." He swiped a hand across his brow. "Looks like you've made a friend, Corinth."

"I think I'll be in short supply of those around here." Corinth mashed his lips together and then added, "First order of business, though, find that guy Dave and learn about these so-called Watchers. He has answers. I know it. What if he can teach me how to control my powers? Or give me information about the blade?"

I ran a hand over my neck, only to realize it was the same spot Gabriel had chosen to drain me dry, and also, unnervingly, the spot where Corinth had cut me with his blade. I dropped my hand, swallowing past the newly formed lump in my throat. Alastair watched me with a frown on his face.

Corinth swung his long legs back over the side of the bed. "Al, did you know Gabe was going to be here?"

"No," he snapped angrily. I think he was more annoyed at himself than anyone else. He blew out a long sigh, adding, "I didn't give away any information. If something was leaked, it had to have been on Sozo's end— from someone here on the inside."

"Who knew we were coming?" I asked slowly.

Alastair bit his bottom lip. "Only the higher-ups in this clan, but I don't even know everyone—they're a very secretive bunch—as you can imagine."

"What if no one leaked the information?" I said quietly. Both Corinth and Alastair's heads whipped around to me. "It doesn't take a genius to figure out we needed support. What if Gabriel had already anticipated us coming here?"

"It's possible," Alastair murmured in thought.

I said, "Corinth, I know you want to find Dave, but we need to find Gabriel first. I've got until tomorrow—I bought us twenty-four hours before I meet with him. If we start digging now, we'll be able to turn the tide—"

Corinth twisted around to face me, looking offended. "What is it with you two? Are you trying to get us killed? Have you both lost it?" he said, frustrated. "First Larna agrees to meet a madman alone, and then Al decides to volunteer me to kill Gabe. 'Cause … you know … I'm a killing machine." He raked a hand through his hair. "I'm trying to control this and not make it worse."

Alastair's frown deepened and he gave a grunt of indignation. "I would have thought differently considering the light show you put on earlier, going after Stanton the way you did." He rubbed a hand absently across his chest as if remembering the pain it had caused.

"I don't want him prancing around, plotting evil— don't get me wrong—but these people are terrified of me as it is," Corinth said. "And, yes, I lost it when I saw that smug, smiling jerk again. But right now, while I have my wits about me, I'm not going to perpetuate that fear. Have you thought maybe he wants us to go after him?"

"You started it," Alastair said irritably. "Look, this might be our only chance at taking him out. You've seen what he's capable of—what if he's got something in the works that's end-of-the-world bad? Wouldn't you want to take him out if you had the chance?"

Corinth shot to his feet, hands on his hips as he started pacing. "Not like this—not until I have something more concrete to go on. I literally have no control over anything anymore. That's what I keep trying to tell you guys."

Alastair's eyes flashed. "You didn't see the way Gabriel was looking at Larna? You're telling me you wouldn't take him out to protect her?"

As if he'd said the one thing Corinth was worried about most, he sank back down to the bed with a hand over his eyes.

I spoke up, interrupting their argument. "When y'all are done arguing about who gets to kill Gabriel, keep in mind I'm the one who is meeting with him in private. You're going to have to trust me—let me shoulder some of the weight." I gestured to Corinth. "Why does he get to be the only one who takes him out? I have the perfect opportunity tomorrow." With a flick of my wrists, the thin blades inside the vambraces shot out, as quick and deadly as when my father had used them.

Alastair said, "I'm playing a game, one that Larna's father"—he glanced at me—"and I started a long time ago. Those people were gathered in that hall for a reason. They were witnesses. You want people to fear you, especially since we can't trust anyone here. You can bet Gabriel has his moles planted here too."

"Calm down, Jon Snow," Corinth muttered.

I moved to one of the connecting doors and it slid open. "Corinth, don't wander off without me. Alastair— we need to talk, *now*."

Corinth gave me a sarcastic salute. "Yes, ma'am."

My room was exactly the same as Corinth's: crisp white linens were tucked into the corners of a queen-sized bed sitting atop a sleek silver accented bed frame. It looked like it was floating. I knew it wasn't, but the effect was still impressive nonetheless. It was elegant, modern, and clean.

"You need to start filling me in on your plans," I

snarled, turning around to face him.

Alastair paced the small room like a caged tiger. "I had no idea Gabriel was going to be here." His eyes burned bright as a branding iron, almost blinding me, but when he glanced down and then back up at me, his eyes had softened considerably. "I'm trying to stay ahead of Gabriel. As much as I hate to admit it—I think his being here might be to our advantage."

That was what had been bothering me the most, and now that he'd cleared it up, the tension started to finally drain out of me. "I was thinking the same thing—it levels the playing field."

He was nodding, and my face flushed at how intensely he was looking at me, like he was more than impressed.

I dropped down onto the soft comforter, my head in between my hands until he joined me, his shoulder brushing against mine. My eyes snapped up to meet his. They were unblinkingly fixed on me—but unlike Gabriel's unwanted attention, this was totally wanted. He had this look filled with worry, frustration, and confusion—all conflicting emotions warring for his attention at the same time.

He ran a finger lightly over mine; my skin tingled and my heart swelled at the meaning behind his touch. It was intimate.

"No more surprises, okay?" I said, my voice suddenly hoarse.

He pulled his pocket watch out and laid a hand on top of it. "I promise, no more surprises, at least from my end. But you can't see Gabriel alone," he pleaded. "Promise me, Larna?"

My eyes flitted down to the watch—a symbol of how strongly he felt about me not going to see Gabriel. There was a sudden twist of nerves rising up in my stomach at the seriousness with which he'd addressed me. Even with those incredibly Robin's egg blue eyes staring at me like that, I still found I couldn't make him that promise. I had made up my mind. It was my turn to do the protecting. Sometimes you had to make a tough choice for your team. Alastair was trying to do the same. I just needed to get him on the same page in order to believe in me.

I cupped a hand over his pocket watch that still rested in his palm. "I need you to trust me—just like I trusted you when you left … I—I can't make that promise."

"You can't go see Gabriel alone," he insisted, and this time, there was a frosty firmness in his voice. "I trust you, but I don't trust *him*—he compelled me, and I'm older and stronger than you are. You can't underestimate him, Larna. Not ever."

I ran a hand through my hair. "I know that—don't you think I know that?" I couldn't hide the hurt in my voice. "My dad paid the price, but I won't lie to you, Alastair; if I get the chance to wipe Gabriel off this planet, I'm going to take it."

Alastair pressed his lips together in a thin line, clearly unsatisfied with my answer. "I guess I better keep a close watch on *you*, then." He dropped his gaze to the timepiece in his palm. When he looked back up, his eyes were roiling like the gray-blue ocean before a storm. He was *so* beautiful. I could see how truly concerned he was for me. No one had ever looked at me like that—not even Corinth. As if he'd wade through forty thousand miles of molten lava to make sure I was okay. I loved him. For the first time, I realized this was true love. It was a fierce desire to protect and comfort your partner.

My stomach flipped as I played that word over and over again in my head: *love*. I liked the feelings that word evoked.

Suddenly there was nothing in this world that I wanted more than to confess my love for him—let it roll off my tongue, experiment with the feel of it on my lips— but before I could spill my guts, he was pulling me to my feet and wrapping his arms around my waist. His warm breath hit the side of my face and neck. He smelled earthy: of salt, smoke, and trees and dirt. After a second, he pulled back, as if something else weighed on his mind.

I wrinkled my forehead, curious and concerned. "What is it?"

His cheeks flushed with a soft pink tinge that made me want to kiss them in turn. I'd never seen him look so full of hope and longing and happiness before.

He leaned in toward me, his face inches from mine, and barely above a whisper, said, "There's something I want—"

But he cut himself off abruptly, tilting his head to the side—and then he was jumping up and moving to the connecting door to Corinth's room in order to crack it open. Something was wrong. I felt it as soon as he did. We flew into Corinth's room and then into the bathroom, where the shower was still running with no one inside.

Alastair shut the water off, shaking his head as if his luck had just run out and this was exactly what he'd expected to happen. "Corinth's gone."

Chapter 30

Corinth

NO PIECE ON THE chessboard is expendable, but sometimes you have to sacrifice a pawn. If the pawn were a person though, would it still be okay? Nothing else matters except checkmate. If you look at it that way, I'd say every piece on the board is as vital as the next. Why other people can't see that logic is the problem with politics and hierarchy. Those two very things are something I was never good at. I didn't particularly like taking orders—so there was that too. Maybe that's why this damn dagger chose me out of the billions of people out there. I had a different way of looking at things.

Or it could just mean I was expendable.

Larna had once again chosen to leave me out of a conversation with Al. That part wasn't what angered me. I knew they were both trying to help. I'd decided I didn't want to be used. Even if you had the power to do something and you were really, really good at that something, does that still make you obligated to do it? The crazy thing about all this was the fact that I had to argue with myself *not* to kill. I was still reeling at the way that mother had said, "Stay away from that *boy*." Coming to this realization was what scared me. I needed to think, but thinking required rest. Unfortunately, rest wasn't my strong suit ... so I settled for getting my caffeine fix on instead, which meant I needed to find Kitchen B. I had cleaned up quickly before heading out, cleaning off the dried blood on my elbows and knees so I wouldn't tempt the blood-craving villagers into sampling the goods on my first day here.

I'd been wandering around for ten minutes, managing only to find empty classrooms. I should have paid more attention on the tour. I tried to stop several people for directions, but they had all either stared at me with open mouths or run away screaming like I was a monster. I sniffed at my shirt. Yeah, it did need laundry service.

I wasn't surprised in the least when Caesar found me on a comfortably cushioned bench in one of the hallways.

He rushed up to me. "I've ... been ... trying to ... find you." He put his hands on his sides, trying to catch his breath. "Your friends are worried sick about you."

I waved off his concern. "Can you tell me where I can get a strong cup of joe around here?"

He smiled and gave a curt nod, straightening back up. "Of course. Yes, sir, very well." He switched gears quickly, going from concerned about my safety to happy to be of service.

I followed him as he opened his arms and pointed me in the opposite direction of where I'd thought about going next.

"Are your rooms to your satisfaction?" he asked, leading the way.

"Most satisfactory, thank you, Caesar." I peered at him out of the corner of my eye, noticing he was studying me with deep curiosity etched on his face. "Spill it."

"Oh, sir, I would rather not spill anything. We've had enough of that from Benny—"

I put a hand to my forehead and laughed. "We really have to work on your figures of speech and literalness."

He grinned awkwardly back at me, clearly unsure about what I'd just said as he fussed with the ends of his sleeves. "I was just wondering what other types of abilities you might possess. I mean, besides that remarkable light that came out of your body—back at the meeting hall. That was something else."

I started to open my mouth, but closed it again, unable to decide where to begin. I didn't even know there had been a weird light coming off me. It was slightly concerning. I thought it must have happened when I'd thrown Alastair back by accident. It had felt like some sort of force field or impenetrable wall shooting out of me. If I could somehow access that ability, it would definitely come in handy.

He must have taken my silence as a sign I wasn't going to answer, because he added, "I'm sorry if that's a rude question."

I shook my head. "You don't need proper etiquette around me, Caesar. It's okay." I scratched my chin in thought. I wasn't sure how much I should tell him, so I asked a question of my own. "What have you heard?"

He shrugged. "Only rumors—you can compel vampires. And you possess the gift of *Sight*." He threw a finger in the air. "I heard you can fly too!"

I noticed how intently he was watching me. I

suddenly had a feeling I should tread lightly. Al had told me not to trust anyone, so I settled on the partial truth for now. "All true. Except for the flying part. I can't do that—I'm not Peter Pan."

His stopped in his tracks. "By the *stars*—that's amazing." His eyes glittered brightly back at me. "*You're* amazing. Is this Peter Pan a friend of yours? I'd really like to meet someone who can fly."

I raised an eyebrow. "Oh yeah. Peter Pan and I are real tight," I answered seriously. After a second, I drew in a deep breath and exhaled. "It doesn't feel amazing though." I found that Caesar's easy-going manner made him easy to talk to. It felt good to finally get some of this off my chest.

"It doesn't?" he said, "Sozo must trust you"—he pointed at the blade at my hip—"to let you carry that around."

Deflecting the topic away from my dagger, I asked, "What's Sozo like?" I didn't want to talk about it anymore, and I wasn't sure I wanted to give him any more information.

"S-S-Sozo?" he stammered, then he was turning a corner, power walking away so fast I almost had to jog to keep up with him. "He's a great leader. We have everything we need here, and we thrive because of his protection and guidance."

"That sounds a bit rehearsed," I prodded slowly. "And a lot cult-like."

"It is not meant to sound rehearsed. We are all truly happy." He seemed to notice the change in my temperament and stopped, turning to face me, reiterating, "He is a great man."

The crinkles around his eyes told me he seemed genuine about how he felt toward Sozo. I realized our conversation was over as he ushered me around one more bend in the hallway and into Kitchen B, tucking his hands into the large sleeves of his robe and bowing. "Please, help yourself to anything. The chef can whip up anything you'd like, as well."

"Thank you, Caesar. Once again I am in your debt," I said. "But could you do me one more favor?"

He nodded enthusiastically. "Of course, sir."

"Don't tell Larna or Al where I am." I felt bad and I didn't want to worry them, but I needed time to think on my own, without them breathing down my neck.

Caesar glanced around us as if afraid of being overheard and then reluctantly nodded.

Before I could thank him, he scurried out of the doors, leaving me on my own. I turned toward the giant buffet, which consisted of, thank goodness, deliciously *cooked* food. The buffet was filled with ham, turkey, and potatoes. On the other side was a giant salad bar. Everything smelled intoxicating. But the best thing was the large machine serving latte and coffee—including espresso shots. *Bingo*. I must have caught it at a lull, because only a handful of people still milled about. Some of them began shoveling food into their mouths with reckless abandon as soon as they saw me—all too eager to leave at seeing my presence, no doubt. Apparently I didn't belong with the humans either.

By the time I started to go through the line, the cafeteria had emptied. The three or four people in front of me changed their minds about eating to hurriedly dash out of the cafe.

Wow, social pariah—table for one, please.

I guess that was a good thing; I didn't have to worry about anyone coming after me. They were all too scared. I made a beeline for the coffee, selecting the espresso, and then decided on making it a double. Tapping a foot impatiently, I was waiting for the machine to finish filling my cup when I felt a hand on my shoulder.

Expecting it to be Larna, I turned, ready to defend myself, but my retort died on my lips as soon as I saw who it was—

Imani had one hand on her hip, and the other still on my arm, a voracious look on her face. I interpreted it as being a cross between rueful and coy and famished. My eyes flew unconsciously to that smirk, and then to those insanely dark red lips. I took an involuntary step back, hitting the coffee machine, and spilling hot liquid down the backs of my legs. I let out a yelp of surprise.

Smooth, Corinth.

When a guy is approached by a beautiful, dangerous woman wearing a red dress, with long muscular legs, smooth dark skin, and high heels... well, he usually doesn't play it cool.

There was a tiny surge of emotion that rose up inside me—a sensation that I had to admit was pleasure at seeing her still alive. I cleared my throat and said gruffly, "You sure are a hard one to kill."

"And you're still mouthwatering as ever." She inched closer, taking in my full appearance.

"Get in an eyeful—this is as good as it gets," I muttered under my breath. I gestured to the now-empty cafeteria. "Would you like to join me for coffee?" It was out before I could stop myself. *Idiot.* She'd tried to kill my friends, worked with Gabriel, and if Larna knew Imani was here, she'd probably kill her. But I liked to live life dangerously, apparently. Wasn't there something to be said about the air of the inexplicable surrounding her? I also needed what was inside her head.

Besides, she wasn't going to try and kill me here; I was about eighty-five percent sure.

"That's very civil of you," she murmured.

"'Civility is not about dousing strongly held views. It's about making sure that people are willing to respect other perspectives,'" I quoted idly. Her eyebrows rose in astonishment as I added, "Oh, don't look so surprised … I used to rank high in my debate class."

Plus, I still had my dagger. The steady thrum (real or imagined, I wasn't sure) coming off the blade was my reminder that it was practically begging to do my bidding—at any time.

Imani nodded once and then gestured for me to lead the way.

Once we had our coffees in hand, we glided to an empty booth in the corner of the dining hall and sat down at the same time across from each other. I realized, with a strange sort of relief that I was happy someone had chosen not to run away from me. Decent conversations were so hard to come by these days.

"I didn't think I'd ever see you again," I confessed. "I thought you were toast back there. I have to grudgingly admit, I'm glad you're not toast."

She took a sip of the dark liquid, puckering her lips in disgust, and then set the cup aside. "I don't understand why anyone likes this drivel."

"I survive on drivel."

"That explains why you're so skinny." She lifted a dark, well-manicured eyebrow at me. "I'm a survivor … as you are aware." I felt her eyes rake over my muddy and soiled clothes and then travel down to the dagger at my hip. I knew my hair was a frightful mess; my plan had been to grab a coffee and some food to go and then rush back to my room to change clothes. I was stalling on changing because I'd seen the attire around here, and I wasn't a fan.

I let the sarcasm fly, speaking in a hushed tone. "So, you're here with *His Majesty*. I wondered which lackey he'd bring with him." I said dryly, "I was also wondering when you plan on dropping that dude like a bad habit."

She inclined her head, taking the warm cup back between slender fingers. They looked delicate, but I knew they were anything but—they were lethal. I had an image on the backs of my eyelids of her stabbing Vinson with the sharp point of her heels.

She didn't say anything, only scrutinizing me with those deep-set ebony eyes of hers.

"How did Gabe know we were going to be here?" I pressed.

Imani picked at the rolled edge of her paper cup with a long red fingernail. It was irritating how she ignored my questions, only to keep dissecting me in sullen silence.

I would wheedle answers out of her. I was ready to start in again when she finally said, "I saw what you did back there when Alastair tried to stop you in the meeting hall. It was quite the display of power … that force field surrounding you …"

It was my turn to not answer. If she wanted to be coy, I could too. "So, Gabe clearly wants us here. Why? To hug it out?" I mused. "We did a lot of damage to his clan. What does he want?" My temper started to rise and I couldn't prevent my voice from cracking. There was a moment when I thought I was going to drop my mug and grab my blade to force the answers out of her. Instead, I took a long, slow steadying breath and growled, "If Gabe goes anywhere near my friends—"

She laughed at my bravado. It was a tiny trill of a sound and not at all unpleasant. "This is what I missed about you … that overly inflated ego of yours. It really is quite refreshing."

I felt blood rush to my cheeks and immediately glanced away to take a slow sip of my still-molten coffee. It was just enough caffeine to take the fuzziness off the edge of my vision. I took a few more sips, realizing how much I needed something in my system, even if it was just coffee. My stomach growled, telling me food needed to be next.

"Gabriel wants to speak with you—"

I cut her off. "This is about what you told me back at the warehouse, isn't it? About my blood being the key or something."

She sat back and I took it as a sign of acquiescence.

"Can't we just cut through all this BS?" I pleaded.

Her forehead wrinkled in confusion. It almost made her look adorable, except she wasn't the type of person I'd ever use the word *adorable* to describe. I assumed this was just how most guys reacted around her.

Her eyes darted away from mine, tracking something or someone she saw behind me. "Come to join the party?" she asked, sounding sweet and menacing at the same time.

I tensed, swallowing heavily. "Larna's right behind me, isn't she?"

Imani tossed her long black locks to the side and

smiled as I twisted around to confirm my suspicions. If steam could come out of a person's ears, it would have. Larna's almond–green eyes had been replaced by the blazing light of her *Sight*.

And that deadly gaze was leveled on Imani.

"Corinth, if you don't want blood all over you, I suggest you move," she hissed.

I realized this was my one and only opportunity to stop the onslaught of bloodshed, so I slammed my hands on the table, causing my cup to teeter precariously close to the edge. "*Remember the 'no violence' contract?*"

"Remember when she stuck her heel into Vinson's thigh and I got skewered."

"Yeah …" I put a hand to my head. "But that's been a minute. Look, we all need to just calm down for a second. Imani has answers—"

Imani had that taunting smirk on her face again. She cocked her head to the side, black hair falling over her shoulder as she glanced at me and then back to Larna. "Is this what you meant by *hugging it out*?"

Larna pushed her chest out, stretching to her full height, which wasn't saying much, but before I could step between them, Imani exploded to her feet.

I jumped up—the cool, unforgiving steel, an extension of my own hand, pressed to Imani's throat, quicker than a blink. The itch to use violence to end this debate wasn't lost on me. Civility had come and gone. I shivered in both delight and repulsion. This was what Al had been talking about. *What's one more enemy?* I was surrounded by the very thing I was trying so desperately not to kill.

Imani's eyes honed in on me. I noticed the slits of her

pupils looked almost catlike as they shimmered with her *Sight*.

My hand tightened on the blade, squeezing through the rage coursing through me, thundering in my ears. "We are all walking out of here with our heads, arms, and legs intact. Is that clear?" I swung the dagger back toward Larna, the blade quivering in my hand. "Is that clear?"

Both Larna and Imani nodded, their eyes cautiously fixated on the dagger pointed at them. Their fear wasn't lost on me, and I was ashamed to admit I liked it. It wasn't until I glanced down to see what they were looking at that I saw the electricity sparking out of the ends of my fingertips, onto the blade. It reminded me of an arcing live wire.

I dropped the blade down by my side, breathing heavily, my chest heaving up and down. "Let her leave, Larna," I begged. "*Please.*"

The desperation in my voice must have gotten her attention, because she reluctantly relented, letting her *Sight* go as she clenched her jaw tight. I had just threatened her with the dagger *again*. The next time, I might not be able to stop myself from hurting her—worse than I already had. Guilt roiled in the pit of my stomach, making me suddenly nauseous and not so hungry anymore.

Once Imani knew the threat had subsided, she traced a measured finger along my shoulder on her way out. "See ya soon, *Sparky*."

Once she was gone, I slumped back down into the seat, gingerly placing the dagger on the Formica tabletop, next to my hand, still upset at myself for threatening her with it. This time, I really had felt it was the only way to prevent them from killing each other.

Larna collapsed onto the seat beside me. "We're

gonna need something stronger than coffee."

I ran a hand through my hair. "*Take it.*" My eyes flicked down to the blade, and my throat tightened with raw emotion. "You have to take it away from me before I do something I'll regret."

She reached across the table, pulling my hands into hers, ignoring the blade. "You're learning to control it—I saw it in your eyes this time. You *won't* hurt me," she said confidently. "You just have to believe it."

Chapter 31

Corinth

WE WERE SEATED AROUND an oval-shaped table. I couldn't help but notice how elegant, classy, and oh-so comfortable the wing-backed leather chairs felt against my backside. If there had been a contest for sitting still though, I would have lost already. They shouldn't put rolly wheels on chairs if they don't want you to spin yourself around in them.

Al placed a hand on my chair, stopping me mid-whirl. I was pretty sure Larna was mad at me. I didn't blame her, having coffee with the enemy was probably not the best way I could have handled that situation. Of course, if you think about it, politics were never in Larna's wheelhouse, and she wanted to meet with Gabe alone—so we were technically equal in dumb ideas.

Waiting was not my strong suit, especially since I'd had three cups of coffee, a Mountain Dew, and some chocolate chip cookies. Also, laundry service was efficient and speedy around here, so I felt immensely better after a shower and changing into clean clothes. Extra caffeine in my bloodstream was making it harder to sit still. I was trying really hard to ignore the urge to draw the blade back out and slaughter everyone with it. *Totally normal thoughts.*

Al was moody and quiet, his hands clasped together, resting on the table. He seemed to be in his own world, as he'd been staring off into space since we'd walked into Sozo's conference room.

"Penny for your thoughts," I asked him.

He glanced at me, blinking rapidly past his musings. "I'll be very interested to hear what Sozo has to say about why he invited Gabriel Stanton here, especially because we were looking for asylum *from* him and his clan."

I was wondering the same thing but before I could respond to Al, Stephanie, the receptionist from before, bustled in. She looked sharp in black-rimmed glasses and a high-waist skirt, with a yellow blouse and perfectly made-up face. She provided us with a pitcher of water and cups for the table. I eyed the decanter of dark brown liquid that I assumed was whiskey.

Sozo swept ceremoniously into the room a short while later, wearing a sophisticated heavy-looking white robe. His sleeves were lined with silver thread, and his dark hair was swept back in a short ponytail. He looked like Loki, the god of mischief.

Stopping at the opposite end of the table, he said, "I trust you are well rested?"

I opened my mouth to speak, but Larna beat me to the punch. "We need to know what Gabriel's intentions are."

Sozo reached across the table, grabbing a glass to pour himself a drink from the decanter. "Gabriel is here because he believes he can contribute to our way of living. He has vast resources and his clan is far-reaching. We would be fools not to listen to what he has to say."

"Let me guess, he's talking merger ... and what does he want in exchange? *Us?*" I asked sardonically. "His pockets are deep."

Sozo took another long, slow gulp of his drink, repeating, "We would be fools not to consider his offer."

"I expected the Druids to be smarter. You *are* being played for fools," I said. "I mean, you guys *are* Druids, correct?"

Sozo's hawk-like eyes zeroed in on me. "Some called us that a long time ago."

Al and Larna turned to stare at me, mouths agape as I said, "The internet really is a handy tool. Information right at your fingertips twenty-four seven. When Al described this place to me, I knew it was time I did some research of my own. Bits and pieces about history ... stories from strangers along the way. For example, oak trees are a symbol of the Druids. They say those who possess knowledge of the oak possess knowledge of all the trees. Those Celtic knots and intricate carvings are also signs of Druid occupation."

Alastair and Larna shared a surprised glance with each other as I continued. "The labs and classes—all signs of higher education. Your advanced technology is truly impressive," I said, "Your washing machines alone could save so much time and water and energy—"

Sozo pulled one of the wing-backed chairs out and sat, interrupting my train of thought. "All correct assumptions thus far."

"I'm not just a pretty face," I quipped. "Y'all live for centuries, maybe even longer—all relying on each other's blood to survive. What happens when your supply runs out, or you have a group of vamps that takes advantage of that supply? Maybe they steal it or sell it on the black market? Or there's something else going on—maybe there's an outside threat." I pressed, "There's something worse than warring clans out there, right?"

Larna's eyes were wide as she turned back to me. "What are you talking about?"

"Clearly, you know a lot more than I have given you credit for," Sozo said. "Yes, Mr. Taylor, this is part of the reason why I wanted you here. Also, I have been profoundly interested in what you can do. Your display of power back in the meeting hall was most riveting." Sozo splayed his hands out on the tabletop. "Please, grant Mr. Stanton an audience. He means you no harm. There are things you need to know, and he can provide the much-needed answers you've been looking for. Yes, there is a bigger threat out there. But you are wrong about one thing. We don't want to hand you over to Gabriel. We want you to join us."

Chapter 32

Larna

ON OUR WAY BACK to our rooms, I turned to Corinth. "Why didn't you share any of that stuff with us? Did it sound like they were building an army to you?"

"I had my suspicions. Gabriel has a solution to Sozo's problem, and Sozo must think it's worth us hearing it out." Corinth pointed out. "I bet I can guess what that solution might be."

"Well, would you like to share with the rest of the class?" I asked quickly. "You seem to be full of ideas these days."

"Your sarcasm is duly noted … but technically, I did share *mostly* everything with you…" He pressed his lips together. "I'm sorry, Larna. I should have said something, but I feel you and Al act like I'm going to break, like I'm fragile." He shrugged. "Plus, I wasn't completely sure about everything. The bigger issue is, what if Gabe wants to start turning people who don't volunteer to be turned? Sound familiar?"

Worry laced my voice as I rubbed a hand along the

back of my neck. "That's a chilling thought and not out of the realm of possibilities. Look, about Alastair—"

"*Alastair!*"

We all turned to see a striking young woman running toward us. She looked to be around Alastair's age, curly light-brown hair bouncing off her shoulders as she stopped in front of us. Intelligent pale green eyes, as light as sea-foam, locked on to Alastair.

I found myself glancing to Alastair, wondering if he knew who she was, because it was apparent she knew him, and then froze as soon as I saw the way he was staring at her. His face was pasty, his chest heaving up and down like he'd just sprinted through an entire marathon in thirty seconds. I heard his sharp intake of breath as he whispered, "*Sarah.*" It was barely audible—the way he said her name made it sound as if his mouth was full of razor blades. He opened and closed his eyes, as if desperately wanting the illusion to be real. This was more than just spooked. Alastair looked like a spirit had risen up out of the ground to escort him into the beyond.

When he swayed on his feet, my hand shot out to help steady him. He never swayed on his feet, ever.

The young woman's olive eyes flicked briefly to my hand on his arm before she said, "*Alastair Iszler*—I wasn't sure it was you; it's been such a long time." She reached out toward him but then thought better of it, dropping her arm back down to her side. "When I saw your"—her eyes darted to Corinth and then me—"entrance, I knew I had to find you."

I'd never seen Alastair look so shocked.

It was a strange feeling, knowing you were on the verge of learning something significantly important about the person you loved. Whoever this woman was, she had definitely meant something to him. The pain buried deep in his eyes was enough to make my heart skip a beat. I wanted to take it away for him.

"Are you okay? You look pale." My eyes darted back to the green-eyed girl. She looked just as taken aback as he did. I couldn't help but notice her eyes were a shade of green unlike anything I'd ever seen before: froth straight from the ocean's tide.

There was something oddly familiar about her. I knew I was missing something, but I couldn't quite put my finger on what it was. Alastair had only shared a few stories of his past with me. I could tell there was some serious history between them. I was suddenly very curious as to what that history was... former girlfriend maybe? A prickling sensation danced through my chest. I wasn't the jealous type, but something about those green eyes, that small frame, and larger-than-life smile bothered me.

Okay, so maybe I *was* a little jealous.

I shouldn't have been worried about it. I had never seen Alastair so affected by anyone in this way, not even Gabriel. I guess I just never considered the possibility of Alastair having an ex-*anything*. This was probably how he felt about Corinth and me and our past history together.

In a strained voice that didn't sound like his own, he gasped, "How is this ... *possible*? *Sarah* ..." His voice cracked as he choked on her name. "I thought you were dead. All these years ... I never knew ..."

He thought she was dead.

It hit me like a bolt of lightning, as shocking as ice water injected into my veins. This was Sarah—the girl he thought Wrentmore had killed on the night he'd been turned. My eyes widened to the point where they threatened to pop out of their sockets.

Corinth was caught just as off guard by their emotional reunion as I was, a puzzled expression on his face as he glanced between them.

Sarah tore her gaze away from Alastair, murmuring, "I must apologize to you both for the interruption. I just haven't seen Alastair in over a century."

Corinth held up a finger. "That's crazy because you don't look a day over seventeen."

A giggle bubbled out of Sarah: sweet and innocent and decidedly appealing.

Corinth grinned back at her, already smitten—and judging by the fact that he hadn't considered unsheathing his dagger to stop a possible threat, she must have made quite the impression on him.

"Corinth," he said, sticking his hand out.

Sarah pumped it enthusiastically. "I'm one of your biggest—" she put a hand to the side of her mouth, lowering her voice considerably "—and *not* your only fan around here. What you did in that meeting hall was pretty extraordinary. I've been dying to introduce myself." She gave Corinth a playful wink, adding, "But what everyone failed to mention is how ridiculously good-looking you are. I was in the nosebleeds back in the hall, and even sitting that far back, I noticed."

Corinth's cheeks flushed at her compliment.

I stuck my hand out. "I'm Larna."

Sarah gripped my hand in hers. She had a firm, confident handshake that belied her petite build. She also wasn't wearing the usual white garments everyone else wore. She had on blue scrubs like someone in the medical field would wear.

"So, you know Alastair from … New York?" I asked hesitantly, refusing to meet Alastair's gaze.

Sarah rocked back on her heels, grimacing at the words *New York*. "Yeah... I haven't been back there in a long time."

Having sufficiently recovered enough, Alastair stepped back, folding his arms across his chest, clearly uncomfortable. "It's a long story."

He still looked green around the edges; it was weird seeing him wear his emotions on his sleeve.

Sarah glanced between us all. "Do you guys have dinner plans? I'd love to catch up with Alastair—"

Alastair was still visibly shaken, and when she mentioned getting together, he seemed to fall apart all over again. I could hear it in his voice as he said quickly, "I … uh … just need some fresh air … I'm sorry …"

And then, just like that, he was gone before anyone could stop him.

Chapter 33

Larna

I FOUND ALASTAIR ALONE in his room, his attention completely absorbed by the polished marble at his feet. After a second, he extracted something from his pocket and uncurled his fingers from around it. My breath caught in my throat. He was studying his watch, as if it would start spilling its guts after all these years. He had kept this memento because it reminded him of the night he had been turned. All of his horrific memories were being dredged up all over again.

"I wish there was something I could do to make the pain go away—you don't have to face this alone, you know."

Without taking his eyes off the timepiece, Alastair said, "You know who Sarah is?"

I nodded, finding my voice had fled me.

His eyes met mine briefly before locking back on the pocket watch. "Where's Corinth?" he asked softly.

I inched my way into the rest of his room through Corinth's connecting doorway. It slid closed behind me. "He's resting." I traced a finger on the end table and then turned to face him, but this time he wouldn't look me in the eye.

"Want to talk about it?" I asked slowly, gently.

I caught the flicker of something in his eyes and I sucked in a breath and held it. He looked so forlorn—as if he were dealing with the recent loss of a loved one. I wanted to comfort him and take away that pain. It was why I found myself standing beside him to lightly brush a knuckle down his arm. When he looked back up, he regarded me in silence. I reached out and pulled him into a tight embrace, his arms hanging down by his sides. It was like the first time I'd ever hugged him—as if he were confused by the thought of being comforted.

And I thought he might push me away, but then he was winding his strong arms tightly around my waist, hanging on as if I were his only lifeline that threatened to blow away in the wind. We sat like that for a long time, neither of us saying anything.

Eventually, he spoke. "Do you remember me telling you about Wrentmore?"

I nodded against his chest, listening to the strong, solid thump of his heart beating against my cheek.

"Sarah was—*is* the green-eyed girl ... the one I told you about. The one I couldn't save on the night he turned me ..." His voice faltered, and he gritted his teeth as if forcing himself to get it out. "I thought he had killed her, all this time, but it turns out he had turned her like he turned me. I just never knew."

I nodded in understanding. "Alastair ... what it must have been like to see her again after all this time. I don't even know where to begin." I drew back from him, consumed by a surge of emotions. "When my dad disappeared without so much as a goodbye, there were times when I thought he was dead. For years, I came up with all sorts of scenarios in my head on how he could have died. Like maybe he went hiking in mountainous terrain and slipped and fell to his death. Maybe he messed with the wrong people and they shot him, or maybe he witnessed a murder and he was shut up. But when I saw him again after all those years—having never aged since the day he disappeared—it shocked me to my very core." I laughed softly at the memory. "You were there … I passed out. After you imagine someone being dead for so long—well, you must have thought she was a ghost."

He pulled my hand into his, kissing the backs of my knuckles, and as he came to some realization, said, "You *do* know what I'm going through."

I wondered how many times he had pictured her over the course of the last century, torturing himself over her death. If that didn't mess with your head, nothing would.

"You should talk to her—when you're ready. Find out what really happened," I said, catching the sliver of light glinting off the watch still clutched in his grasp.

Chapter 34

Corinth

I HAD DECIDED TO let Larna have her space with Al. I had witnessed the spooked look on his face. Whatever happened between Al and Sarah was some serious next-level history. I couldn't imagine knowing someone for the better part of a century. At least vampires are slow to age—I think Larna said they age once every seventy-five years. It looked like someone had danced a jig on his grave. We did have some heavy issues to consider, though, with Gabe and Imani running around with no supervision. They were bound to try something, like steal a certain dagger from my hip. Although, I was pretty sure Gabe had us dead to rights. He needed to behave for now or he'd get himself kicked out—unless Sozo was already on the take. For now, I felt my only threats were the locals, and most of them had seen what I could do.

I suddenly realized how tired I was. The problem with a dream is that it sneaks up on you quickly, because one minute you're awake, and the next you're not. I was standing on cool Saint Augustine. The sky was a cloudless blinding splotch of light that reminded me of a hot summer day in Texas. I turned in a slow circle, admiring the view and enjoying the fresh breeze that gently ruffled my hair. When I arrived back at the original spot I'd started in, I noticed a bench had appeared from out of nowhere and Dave was sitting perched atop it like a yoga master, defying the law of gravity.

If I hadn't been expecting it, I might have jumped out of my own skin.

"I saw you at the meeting hall, but you disappeared. You owe me some answers," I said, striding over to him—barefoot and all. "What are the Watchers?"

His eyes seemed to twinkle unnaturally as I stopped in front of him. Upon closer inspection, they looked like the Milky Way, swirling in a cosmos of endless space. There was a light behind his eyes, revealing something other than just a higher intellect. Something alien. I hadn't been able to put my finger on it until now.

"You're not a vampire, are you?" I observed, suddenly cautious about how flippant my attitude had been toward him as of late.

Without hesitation, Dave said, "No. I'm not." He gestured to our surroundings. "This is the only way I can assure our conversation remains private—by meeting you in your dream. The risk of being overheard is too high. I have come to warn you that you are in grave danger."

As I stood there, the space around him began to glow white hot, light bursting out of his body like a disco ball, and then something dark unfurled, extending out of his back, that looked unbelievably like wings. *Impossible.* These wings weren't fluffy and white, they were black and singed and war-torn.

Wings?

The sudden and dazzling light forced me to take a step back—a potent demonstration of power if I'd ever seen one. It shook me to my core. A million different thoughts hit me at once, but I couldn't force myself to focus on any one of them. By the time the brilliant light faded around him, my chest was rising and falling in time with my heartbeat. I could feel my pulse thundering in my neck. "What the hell *are* you? Were those *wings?*" I panted, "This is a dream. Nothing in it is real …"

Dave seemed to find my reaction amusing, because he laughed softly. I circled him, eyeing his back with a healthy dose of caution and admiration. There were wings protruding out like a dragon from *Grimms' Fairy Tales*.

He crossed his legs as if this type of thing happened every day. "Sorry … but I figured the only way you would believe my warning is to show you what I am." He regarded me in silence for a few seconds longer and then lifted a hand as if in a twelve-step program to confess, "I'm an angel."

This was all in my head. It wasn't real. Vampires are one thing … but *angels?* I was in the presence of an *angel?* Except a small part of me couldn't help but think about how he'd miraculously healed me by a single touch. Goose bumps pebbled my flesh.

I dropped down to the bench, feeling suddenly light-headed. "Wait—th-th-this is all too much." And then, because I still felt like I needed something solid to ground me, I sank down to the dew-soaked grass. *Please don't collapse in on yourself like a black hole.*

After taking a couple of deep breaths to gather my thoughts, I said, "Let's say I believe you … in this *dream,* anyway—why are you telling me all of this? Why am I in danger?"

He pulled his hat off to pat his sandy-blond hair back down. "A long time ago, two hundred angels descended from Heaven in a voluntary exploratory mission to help provide guidance to humankind. I was part of that original two hundred. We were supposed to lead—to educate and teach—to spread kindness to all mortals. But some of us who descended didn't see it that way." He cast a glance down. "Because angels didn't come from corruption, or even understand it, we ended up falling victim to it. So, the original two hundred split off to form two different factions: the Watchers and the Grigori. The Grigori blame humans for their corruption. Their mission is to cleanse the world of it, in whatever destructive ways they can to achieve their goals." Dave stopped. I could see an infinite amount of pain and sadness in his gold-flecked eyes. "The Watchers, like me, came to realize that humans are amazing, intelligent, free-spirited individuals who make this world go round. Some of us ended up falling for them—having kids, getting married, starting lives with each other ... like any ordinary human family would." He cleared his throat. "But it wasn't long before the Grigori found out about what they considered to be immoral and irresponsible acts. Their solution was simple and yet devastatingly cruel ... to kill all of the offspring of angels and humans—Nephilim, the by-product of ultimate corruption."

I suddenly felt sick, my stomach churning as acid hit the back of my throat at the thought of the Grigori killing innocent children. My younger sister and two brothers were the first people to pop into my mind. There could never be justification for killing innocent kids—especially if you couldn't control what you were born into. I shook my head in disbelief, rooted to the spot. The only thing I knew for certain was that the story he had just painted for me sounded a lot like aliens coming to our planet for world domination.

"These Grigori—they're murdering zealots, and the Watchers are our allies?" With wide eyes, I said, "I'm trying to stay with you here, I promise, but you're throwing a lot at me—and I'm still in shock about the whole *wings* thing …" I rubbed my eyes. "This is the trippiest dream ever."

Dave tipped his head to the side. "An oversimplification of everything I just told you," he said. "But essentially, yes."

"I don't like the look on your face, like you're about to give me more bad news other than the fact that I'm in danger."

"Because I am." He ran a hand along the brim of his hat in thought. "The Grigori want chaos—the more the better. They will try and swoop in at the last second to reclaim Earth: To be its saviors. A long time ago, the Grigori created a virus. This virus changes humans—forces them to crave each other's blood." I sat up straighter at the mention of '*blood*' and '*crave*' as he continued. "The Grigori sat back and watched their creation spread. And in turn, the demand will *always* increase. The world will feed upon itself. This need for violence and savagery will never end. Your race will be threatened by actions put in place long ago—until the Grigori reveal themselves to the world and bring with them a cure for vampirism. People will pay any price for peace of mind and health," he said. "If this happens, earth is in for a rough ride. Millions will die."

My heart thumped wildly against my ribcage; actually, I was pretty sure it was going to sprint right out of my chest at any second. All I could think about was Larna. She was right in the middle of this mess—she had … a *virus*? *All* vampires had a virus. That was all it was?

I held up a hand. "Does that mean there is a possible cure I can get my hands on?" I asked. "Please tell me my best friend has a chance of being human again." I felt the beginnings of hope bloom in my chest, and I spoke softly at first, until suddenly my words began tumbling over each other. "Vampirism is a virus? All this time … there's been a cure? Where is it? How do I get it?"

Dave squinted as if considering which question to answer first, tilting his head to the side. "There is a cure and you are the key."

I wiped a hand across my mouth and then held it up as a thought struck me. "If the Grigori created this virus, why can't y'all just undo it? You're all-powerful, right?"

"I wish it worked like that." Dave's eyes met mine, glowing like liquid nitrogen. I sucked in a shocked breath at how mesmerizing they looked. "You were chosen by the blade. Because of this, we might stand a chance of destroying everything that they have created."

"Hold up." I barked out a frustrated laugh. "Destroying? You think I can help against a bunch of rogue angels? Seriously, I don't even know how to control the blade. How am I the key? Why are you being so evasive? What about the danger?" There was an overwhelming tightness in my chest that had worked its way up into my throat.

But before he could answer my slew of questions, he cocked his head, suddenly looking more than a little concerned. "*Something's wrong.*"

The lush meadow shifted and tilted around me and

then flickered from vivid green to black, enveloping and then folding itself around me—

And I woke up, spread-eagled on my bed with my plastic keycard stuck to my forehead. I had forgotten I'd left it on the bed. Soft light filtered in through the main door of my room right as alarm bells went off in my head. Something *was* wrong. The outer door to my room should not have been standing open like that. I was trying to reorient myself to my surroundings when I saw a flicker of movement off to my left, a dark shadow at the foot of my bed, and a flash of something glinting in the darkness.

A spike of adrenaline tore through me as I came fully awake, my brain finally registering what that flash was: *knife.*

I bolted upright at the same time as I felt that weird pressure at the backs of my eyeballs that told me a vampire was nearby. Instinct had my dagger in my grasp right as something heavy dropped down on top of me, knocking the wind from my lungs, our two blades meeting with such force sparks shot off them.

Hot, ragged, and metallic-smelling breath hit my face.

Bony arms dug into my ribcage as my attacker tried to ram their razor sharp-looking knife into my heart. I had a second to take it all in, including the fact that my attacker was wearing a mask.

With growing dread, I realized the only thing standing between me and certain death was my blade. Every ounce of my strength was focused on holding off the vamp on top of me—leaving me unable to even scream or cry out for help. I pushed up as they pushed down, a mirror image of our bodies tangled in sheets, fighting against one another. I did manage a small gasp as the biting pressure on my forearms increased. My only goal was keeping them from killing me swiftly, because they were going to kill me, of that I was certain.

My strength was already waning.

I had a fleeting thought of how it was just my luck that Larna and Al were in the room right next to mine and they had no idea what was going on. Beads of sweat popped up along my forehead, but no matter how hard I strained and pushed against them, I still lost ground, little by little—inch by inch—they had all the leverage. I inwardly cursed my mortality as the tip of their knife sliced through the top layer of my thin shirt, and then in excruciating slow motion, I watched as the blade slid home. Closing my eyes, I fully expected to feel the final push of cold steel sinking into my heart—

And then I heard the most gloriously sweet sound of the connecting door to my room whooshing open, signaling the cavalry's arrival. The vamp on top of me growled something under their breath, and then the burning pressure on my chest lifted, and I was sucking in painfully deep breaths of air.

My attacker slipped out of the open doorway to my room, as fleeting as a shadow as I sagged back against the headboard, panting like I'd just sprinted a few hundred miles uphill. After another second, coming out of my stupor, I clawed at my chest where their knife had penetrated my shirt, not knowing the full extent of the damage.

Al flew past me to disappear though the open doorway in hot pursuit of my attacker, right as Larna appeared beside me.

She saw the rip in my shirt and said quickly, "Are you hurt?"

I still found breathing to be a challenge, but her hands were already exploring my chest as I fell back in complete exhaustion. "No … just …" I panted, "nicked me …"

"I'll be right back." Larna gave me a stern look. "Stay here until I get back, okay?"

And then slowly the conversation I had with Dave started to return. *There was a cure for vampirism.* But before I could tell her about it, she disappeared through the open doorway my assailant and Al had vanished through. And then it was slamming shut behind her, flashing red. I assumed this meant I was on lock-down.

After I'd recovered enough to stumble to my feet, I lurched toward the door, placing my thumb against it. The red flashing increased, and Caesar's voice broke through the silence as a soft whine coming out of the device on the nightstand. "Sir, we've had a security breach. Your room is locked until we can get security over there."

"No kidding..." I clutched at a painful stitch in my side. "Where are Imani and Gabe?" I panted, still breathless. "*Tell me now.*"

Caesar's voice crackled out of the device. "Um—I do not know, sir …"

"Open the door, Caesar!" I shouted. I had to help Larna and Al. What if they caught up with the attacker? I felt angry for having been caught so off guard. If I had been thinking rationally, I would have listened, stayed put, but I wasn't happy about the assassination attempt on my life. The dagger was still painfully tight in my grasp, and a sudden flood of anger coursed through me.

After a moment's hesitation, Caesar's voice crackled to life once again. "Sir, you can't leave your room until we have the situation—"

"Open the door, Caesar. *NOW!*"

I wasn't sure if it was Caesar or not, but there was a delayed response met by empty static and then by some miracle, the door slid open in a rush of air, granting me passage.

Without thinking, I dashed outside and was immediately met by an elbow to the face.

Whoever hit me had thrown their full *in*human weight into it, because blood gushed out as badly as any nose-bleed I'd ever had. Tears blurred the edge of my vision. Someone grabbed for my blade, and even though I still couldn't see, I instinctively kicked out, my foot connecting with someone's shin.

I heard a yowl of pain, followed by hands loosening on my wrist.

As my vision cleared, I noticed who'd elbowed me for the first time.

Unbelievably, it was not the knife-wielding intruder from earlier, unless they had removed their mask. This was an older woman wearing a long black robe with thick sandals. She stumbled back and then lost her balance. As the cobwebs in my head started to clear, I realized I'd seen her before: the cleaning lady who had run away from me in a panic earlier. If she'd had a weapon or been better trained, I might have been dead by now. It told me this was probably an attack of pure opportunity.

She flew at me again in a flurry of motion, black hair floating out behind her like a cape, long, sharp fingernails raking down the side of my cheek, all the way down to my chin. They felt like hot coals on my skin. My blood was her catalyst. Once she saw it dripping down my face, she came at me with renewed vigor and wild eyes.

"*Demon!*" she cried.

I brought my hands up, the dagger still clutched in a fist, and struck out, clocking her on the side of the face. She rocked back on her heels, momentarily stunned at the power I'd managed to put behind it. This was survival—and it was what Larna and Al had been trying to teach me from the get go—except now I felt bad for hitting a lady.

This time, I was ready when she threw herself at me. Slashing out with the blade, I sliced through one of the heavy sleeves of her robe. Her eyes flashed blue with her *Sight* as she easily avoided my next jab. Screaming at the top of her lungs, she flew at me. Again I scrambled out of the way at the last second, and that's when I noticed the opening, right below the base of her armpit. Exposed ribs made for a perfect place to bury a blade. So when she propelled herself forward, I sprang, sinking the dagger into the meaty part between bone and ribcage.

Her pain-filled eyes widened. Time slowed down then stilled. The rush of blood in my eardrums roared—and in that moment, an image of me standing atop a pile of skulls and bones crashed its way through my mind's eye. *Kill or be killed. Kill or be killed. Kill or be killed.* A deep sense of calm satisfaction washed over me as I realized what I had to do. Kill her. The thrill of violence was too strong to waste on the inept.

It was this kind of thinking that shocked me to my core, stopping me dead in my tracks as I hesitated.

It was also going to get me killed.

I knew if I was ever going to put an end to this violent cycle, I'd have to start making decisions just like this one. Destiny could listen to me for a change. I refused to succumb. The only way I knew how to do that was by pulling back. And it was in this moment's indecision that she managed to knock the dagger from my outstretched hand. The blade skittered down the hallway, scratching polished marble along the way.

With a final terrifying wail, she went for my throat as I fell backward. *This is it.* Death had finally come for me, and it wasn't knocking on the door, it was blasting it off its hinges.

But before she could rip me to shreds, her wild eyes widened and her back arched like a cat's, her body giving one final spasm as she fell to her knees as still as a corpse.

Behind the dead vampire stood Imani, her eyes blazing bright and terrifying, her slender fingers curled around my bloodied blade in her death grip.

Chapter 35

◆

Larna

I
T TOOK ME ONE millisecond to take in the tableau in
front of me as I came barreling around the corner back
to Corinth's room. Imani was standing over him,
clutching his dagger in between bloodied fists. Corinth had
a huge gash running down the right side of his cheek all
the way to his chin and a bloodied nose. This image sent a
fresh bout of adrenaline coursing through me. My eyes
burned, matching Imani's in intensity. Hate was a good
motivator. It was also blinding. If I'd taken a moment
longer to take in the rest of the scene, I would have realized
that there was a dead woman lying at Corinth's feet. Imani
and I had unfinished business, so nothing mattered more
to me than taking her head off.

With a flick of my wrists, the hidden blades inside my
vambraces slid free. I jumped into the air, aiming them for
the nape of her neck, right as Corinth threw himself in
front of Imani at the last second. He had one hand held to
the jagged cut on his cheek, and the other out in front of
him, and by the way he squeezed his eyes shut, he was half
expecting to be skewered by my blades.

I stumbled to a halt an inch from his outstretched hand as he cracked an eye open. "Don't kill her ..." he rasped. "She saved my life."

Imani turned around slowly and then handed the blade back to Corinth, a look of submissiveness on her face. It surprised me how easily she would just give it back—after our experience in the warehouse. Maybe I'd misjudged her, or maybe she was just playing us. I gave her a nod as she inclined her head at me. We hadn't quite made peace, but it was a start.

Corinth, accepting his blade back, sheathed it at his hip nodding his thanks at Imani. His eyes flicked back to meet mine. Still out of breath, he said, "Did ... you catch ... the masked intruder?"

I shook my head. "No," I said. "Alastair and I chased them through several connecting corridors, but they gave us the slip." I glanced down to the dead woman at his feet. "I told you to stay put. Who is this, and how many more people are trying to kill you?"

I emerged out of Corinth's bathroom, the first aid kit provided by Caesar in hand, only to find him blocking my path, towering over me. His feverish body heat radiated off him in waves, the sensation so strong it almost knocked me back. Corinth's body ran as hot as the sun. I imagined this is probably what it felt like to stand next to Superman. "Are you sure you don't want to check out the medical wing here? I'm sure it's hi-tech," I said. "Or better yet, find your friend Dave to heal you right up?"

He pressed his lips together and shook his head adamantly. "Unless you have a way of tracking Dave down,

I don't think I'm going to see him again anytime soon." He sounded distant as he added, "He came to see me in my dream but vanished as soon as I was attacked. He was trying to warn me about a threat. He was right about that part …" He shuddered. "And I don't want to go near a lab in this place until we make sure we can trust these people."

I craned my neck to look up at his tall frame, noticing the extent of dried blood staining the entire right side of his face. It made him look rugged and savage and strangely striking—like he'd just come off the battlefield in a blaze of glory. There was also something in his eyes, a depth in them I'd never seen there before.

"What did Dave say?" I asked hesitantly. "Do you know why that woman attacked you? And why Imani helped you?" I edged my way past him to put the box down on the bed, and when I turned back to face him, he was wrapping me up in his arms. His skin was on fire, and his whole body shook from exhaustion … or maybe something else. The longing in his eyes made me suck in a surprised breath.

I pulled back, concern washing across my features. "Come here." I pulled him over to the bed, making him sit down beside me. "Tell me what's going on with you."

Keeping his eyes glued to mine, he gripped my hand in his and drew it to his chest. I felt the beating of his heart through my fingertips. Corinth had this way of staring right into my soul. X-ray vision for the psychic. Maybe his real super-power was reading me.

"There's a cure, Larna."

My lips parted slightly. I couldn't tell if my shock was more from the look he was giving me—like we were the only two people left on the entire planet—or because he mentioned a cure. A part of me knew exactly what he meant by *cure*, whereas the other part was still playing catch-up.

He gripped my shoulders tightly, turning me to face him. "There's a cure," he repeated more insistently. "A cure for vampirism."

My first thought was that if what he was saying was true, I would never be able to give it to my father. He was beyond its reach now. I was suddenly overcome with emotion. I licked my lips, wondering how I would tell Corinth that I didn't want a cure. I didn't feel sick. I felt the opposite. What if this wasn't even what he meant by *cure*? I couldn't bring myself to even ask him, having been rendered momentarily speechless.

He was speaking in a rush now, not waiting for me to respond. "Dave came to see me in my dream. He's an angel. And I don't mean he's, like, a kindhearted dude ..." Corinth pointed to his shoulders. "He showed me his flippin' *wings*." His eyes were so wide and round and sincere. "*Wings*."

I held a hand up, feeling slightly dizzy. "He came to see you and told you there is a cure for vampires?" I scoffed at the idea. It was preposterous. It made *more* sense to believe that Dave intended Corinth to be the ultimate slayer of all vampires—as in *he* was the "*cure*" for wiping us all out. "Are you sure he didn't mean ... something different?" I couldn't hide the skepticism in my voice. "Say it, Corinth. You think I need a cure? That I'm ... *we're* ... a blight to humanity?"

He whirled back around to face me, his mouth hanging open, as he had clearly not been expecting that reaction out of me. "Are you kidding? Larna ..." He threw a hand over his mouth, stunned. "*No* ... There's more to it than that. Dave told me there's a group of rogue angels that call themselves the Grigori. They want control over the human race, and in order to do it, they created a plague—that started with the first vampires craving each other's blood, and then it spread like wildfire. This is the bigger threat we were warned about. The Grigori plan to swoop in with a cure after they reveal to the world that vampires are real—it'll be mass chaos." He blew out a shaky breath. "We're talking end-of-the-world stuff here."

My pulse quickened. "This is *so* much bigger than we first thought. Are you sure about all this, because ..."

Corinth grimaced and then winced, gingerly prodding at the wound on his cheek. "Yeah, I'm sure."

"You know, I'm getting really tired of patching you up," I said, motioning for him to move closer. "I'm sorry— I didn't mean to go off on you like that. It's just that there are a lot of unanswered questions, and I don't want you to get your hopes up."

"It's kind of been an emotional rollercoaster for us all," he whispered, scooting closer.

I pulled the medical supplies over and threw the lid open to dump out its contents. The kit itself had seen better days, but at least the bandages, gloves, and ointment all appeared to be up-to date. I wondered idly if they had tech that could heal a cut instantly—I mean, on a human, not a vamp. Suddenly I found myself very interested in wanting to visit the medical wing, even if Corinth wasn't as excited about it. Of course, there were more vampires here, and they wouldn't really have a great need for a huge medical wing ... except they struck me as the type of people who really liked to keep up with technological advancements.

As I worked, Corinth filled me in on the rest of what happened after he had awoken, but I found I needed to rehash everything with him all over again. "Do you think Gabriel was behind the first attacker? And what about this second one? The cleaning lady?"

He shrugged. "I think the first one had been well planned. My door was open when I came to. That would mean they got through Sozo's security somehow," he said. "And the second attempt—I think she attacked me out of fear and opportunity. She called me a demon. I don't think Imani and Gabe were in on either of them. It wouldn't make sense for Imani to turn around and save me if she were in on it."

I said, "So, this Dave guy hijacks your dream—for the second time—and tells you there is a group of angels out there calling themselves the Grigori. These Grigori want to rule the world, but in order to do that, they have to *out* vampires to everyone—which is meant to create widespread panic. Once there is mass chaos, only then will these Grigori come forward and essentially promise to end the 'blood-craving illness' if everyone on Earth agrees to worship them?" I said, "You realize how crazy that sounds." I dabbed at the cut on his cheek and he flinched. "Sorry," I said, wincing in empathy.

He nodded. "Yeah, but think about it—it would be like living in the Dark Ages all over again if people knew vampires existed. Can you imagine humans, angels, and vamps all actively fighting with one another out in the open?" He ran a hand through his unruly mop of hair. "And now I'm supposedly the key to finding this cure …"

That troubling thought seemed to weigh me down more than the rest did. If he was right—it meant he was in a world of trouble. *We* were in a world of trouble. For now, I stayed silent, trying not to let him know how worried I truly was.

I watched as he closed his eyes against the pain and let me work in silence. He was so much stronger than I gave him credit for. I knew that contemplative face well. I'd studied every inch of it back when we were kids—every line and freckle, even down to those dark-brown-flecked-with-lighter-brown irises. I knew the distinguished lines around his mouth meant he was scared—although he would never admit it.

"This might scar," I said eventually.

One side of his mouth curved up at the corner. "There goes my modeling career …" And then, as if realizing something important, his eyes popped open again. "We have to talk to Gabe—and the sooner the better."

My hand stilled on his cheek. "You think Gabriel knows there might be a cure?"

Corinth lifted his shoulders. "The guy knows everything—"

Alastair marched into the room, interrupting Corinth. His eyes stayed locked on him, and I noticed they had narrowed in suspicion. "Imani said you hesitated." I could hear the fire and heat behind his voice as he said, "Why?"

The way he asked it made me think he knew exactly why Corinth had hesitated, but he wanted to hear what he had to say anyway.

Corinth dropped his gaze to his fisted hands and, in a thin, shaky voice, said, "So now you're talking to the enemy and believing them? I take it you just heard everything I said."

Alastair gave a curt nod as Corinth breathed, "Yeah … I did hesitate. All I keep thinking about is blowing this place to kingdom come—standing on top of a pile of dead bodies … and I'm laying waste to everything … to y'all." He avoided our gazes, suddenly looking ashamed. "I can't keep doing this. Not if there's a cure out there." His voice hitched, and I couldn't ignore the pleading in it when he spoke next. "Did you just hear what I said, Al? There's a cure for vampirism. It's like you guys don't even care."

If he was surprised by this revelation, he didn't show it. "Unconfirmed by someone we don't know or trust," Alastair clarified, "and you didn't answer my question."

Corinth let out a weary breath. "You don't want there to be a cure. You're afraid Larna will go back to normal and leave you all by yourself. Am I right?"

Alastair squared his shoulders, his eyes shimmering like blue-colored lanterns. "I'm so sick and tired of trying to watch your scrawny hide," he growled. "You have one job and you can't even get that right—"

"*Stop it!*" I yelled.

They both turned to look at me in silent defiance; Corinth's face shone ashen through the blood still painting his face.

I cleared my throat. "Alastair had someone from his past show up … someone who he thought was dead. It's taken a toll on him, Corinth." Turning to Alastair, I said, "Corinth is trying to get a handle on this whole Chosen One thing. It's why you brought him here in the first place, to learn to control his urges so we can clan up … but ever since we arrived, there have been new problems and surprises around every corner. We *need* to work together—now more than ever. Alastair, would you please meet with Sozo and figure out how someone could breach his security? You vouched for Corinth—I don't want this to fall back on you. Find out how we need to proceed next … if we need new cards or rooms or both."

He gave a curt nod, and without another word, disappeared through the motion-sensored doors.

"I've never seen him look that shook up before." Corinth turned back to me, lowering his voice. "This whole Sarah thing … and that watch he carries around with him … what's their history?"

I shook my head, unable to think of where to begin. It wasn't my story to share. What would I tell him? That the psycho who tortured Alastair and murdered those girls in front of him had left one person alive—and turned her … and he never knew it until now. Sarah. The green-eyed girl was a vampire. She was the one who he'd compared me to before I'd been turned. Sarah had been his reason to continue fighting for those who couldn't. Wrentmore had turned Alastair and then turned Sarah without him knowing.

I had thought that maybe he would be able to get rid of some of that guilt he'd been hanging onto, but it only seemed to cause him to sink into a deeper state of broodiness. I hadn't had a chance to pry out of him why he didn't feel some sort of relief from the burdens he'd placed on himself. I desperately wanted to know what he was thinking.

"If Imani hadn't been there, you'd be dead." I gave him a maddening glare, but he refused to meet my eyes. I could tell he had way too many conflicting emotions roiling around inside him, so I decided to let it go for now. I gestured at him to move closer. "Let me finish bandaging that cut."

After cleaning him up, I applied butterfly adhesive strips to his cheek, using several longer strips to hold the deepest parts of the wound closed. It made me think of Gabriel's scar. He had been on my mind a lot lately—to my detriment. The moment I'd laid eyes on him again, I'd felt that foreign entity, or whatever it was, unraveling inside me as if in answer to a call. I couldn't tell Alastair or Corinth this but, as much as I hated Gabriel, there was still something that unconsciously drew me to him: A moth-to-a-flame scenario. I'd felt it when he was staring a hole through me back in the meeting hall.

I was going to confront him and get to the bottom of it. The guy was Moriarty-level creepy. I guess that made me Sherlock; although, I couldn't hide fear's icy touch on my spine at the thought of looking him in the eye again.

There came a sharp rap on the outside door, snapping me out of my trance. A screen lit up the inside of the door, revealing who was standing on the other side. I guessed that a sensor detected movement, like an automated door bell and security measure all in one. If they were so technologically advanced here, then how did someone compromise their system? It was unsettling to think that someone could get to Corinth so easily—and all within a day of our arrival.

Caesar was standing in the hallway, his hands shoved up those massive sleeves of his robe. He was speaking through the door as if we were in a conversation face-to-face. "Hello, Miss Collins. I wanted to apologize about the security breach. We have updated our system. The woman—" he cleared his throat "—that was killed was a part of our cleaning crew. We have taken care of it and are screening everyone more carefully. As for the security breach into Mr. Taylor's room—it is being corrected and handled."

When I pushed my thumb against the door it opened and he poked his head inside, glancing owlishly around the room. When his eyes landed on Corinth, he said, "I trust you are okay, sir? I feel horrible …" Caesar's eyes misted over when he saw the bandages on Corinth's cheek. "I am here to accompany you to see Gabriel, as requested."

I tried to step out into the hallway so the door would close behind me, but Corinth was there, blocking the path of the sensors.

Caesar swept a skinny arm out from his sleeve, straightening the nonexistent wrinkles from his robe as soon as he saw Corinth. "I am so sorry about your face. Will you be joining us, sir?"

"I'm sorry about my face too, Caesar, but it wasn't your fault. I made you open the door—"

Caesar's eyebrows drew together in concern. "Oh, no, sir—I did not open the door. I would never put you in harm's way."

Corinth arched a dark eyebrow at me. "What?" he said, sounding confused. "Then how did it open on its own? And how was someone able to get into my room?"

Caesar lifted his shoulders. "A most worrying concern indeed, sir. We are looking into it now. The intruder must have stolen a skeleton keycard. Only our top staff has access to them. Rest assured, we are investigating it thoroughly. I promise that you are safe now, and we will also place guards outside your rooms."

It would only complicate things to have a detail outside our doors, and who knew if we could actually trust them? I waved a hand, dismissing this idea. "That won't be necessary, Caesar."

His lips corkscrewed up in apology. "Sorry, ma'am. It has become a necessity."

"What's this mention of Larna seeing Gabe without me?" Corinth interjected quickly. "Does Al know, or is that why you sent him off in a hurry?"

"Remember our agreement?" I said through gritted teeth. "I'm supposed to meet with him—*alone*. I didn't tell you I was leaving, because people keep trying to kill you. I figured it would be a good idea if you stay put."

Corinth groaned, putting a hand to his forehead. "Seriously, Collins, you make the worst decisions sometimes. In light of recent events, I'm changing that deal. There's no arguing. We're all going together—" he clenched his jaw in stubbornness "—Al included."

Chapter 36

Larna

SOZO HADN'T BEEN HAPPY about blood being spilled in his hallways. So when two large men dressed in white began following us, I wasn't in the least bit surprised. I couldn't quite help but notice how they looked more like guards in a psychiatric ward than a security detail. They watched Corinth and Alastair nervously, remaining alert for any more signs of threats.

I could have warned them that there would be no peace while we were here. It was their fault for letting Gabriel stay as their guest. Trouble followed us no matter where we went—and so did he.

"Caesar, what does Sozo do with the people who break the contract?" I asked.

He turned to study me, his nose twitching like a mouse. "It depends on the severity of violence."

"Like in Imani's situation, she killed another vampire."

One side of his mouth quirked up at the corner in thought. "When death is involved—banishment or … *worse*, but in this case, she was defending Mr. Taylor. For which I am very glad." He swiped a hand toward Corinth, looking relieved. "So she only received a warning and will be remanded to her room until we can investigate further."

I could handle being banished or worse for getting retribution.

Alastair came up beside me, his shoulder touching mine. I could feel how tense he was in the hard line of his muscles. His back was rigid and straight as a rod. "Don't think I don't know what you're planning," he said. There was a hint of tenderness in his voice I hadn't expected, but his anger overrode everything else.

We had arrived outside the conference room where we were to meet Gabriel. I had a sudden flash of him shadowing me in the graveyard, his blood-soaked white satin shirt standing out bright against the moon's soft light—and then he was sinking his teeth into my neck. I would never forget Gabriel's whispered words as he turned me: "*My blood is like poison moving through your bloodstream ... Of course, in order to make this happen, I have to drain most of it from your body ...*"

Alastair was beside me, a hand at the small of my back. I jerked involuntarily, my hands feeling suddenly clammy at the dark thoughts floating around in my head. I realized he was still waiting on me to answer him.

"You don't have to do this," he insisted quietly.

My voice sounded small but confident as I said, "I'm doing this."

I imagined launching myself at Gabriel as soon as we walked in. If there was a cure for vampirism, I didn't care. My father was dead and he would never benefit from it. I felt sick at the thought. It was easier to convince myself that Corinth was wrong about all of this. Alastair was right—it was unconfirmed by someone we didn't trust.

I jumped when someone touched my elbow. Alastair was still looking at me with concern etched across his brow. If I hesitated any longer, I wouldn't have the nerve to face him and that wasn't going to happen, so I marched through the doors with Alastair and Corinth on my heels, suddenly glad for their company.

He was dressed as impeccably as ever, in a form fitting pinstriped black suit and silver tie. His shoulder-length black hair was swept back over the tops of his shoulders. Raven eyes bored into mine, tracking me as we seated ourselves at the table across from him. They were evil incarnate, darker than his soul, I imagined—if he even had one.

He smoothed his tie down, ignoring the fire from our collective gazes as we seated ourselves. My scalp prickled in warning when he wouldn't stop staring at me again. That's when I became painfully aware of the thing inside me stirring to life—a flutter mimicking a heart palpitation. I shoved that feeling deep down, aware of Alastair's own intense stare-down with Gabriel.

Meanwhile, Corinth was seated beside me, and I was pretty sure he was going to spontaneously combust. The intense heat coming off him was almost unbearable; his hand hovered inches above the hilt of the blade at his hip.

The guards' stares on the back of our necks didn't seem to help as the tension grew between us.

Gabriel was the first to break the silence, and he didn't even pretend to acknowledge anyone else in the room. "You're looking very *fit*, Larna."

I knew he didn't give two cents about me. He just wanted to dig his nails into an open wound. *Don't let him get into your head.*

"You've got two minutes," I hissed. "Otherwise, Corinth here is going to run you through with his blade."

"Don't you mean stab me in the back when I'm not looking?" he corrected. "You disappoint me, Larna. We were supposed to meet in private..." He clicked his tongue infuriatingly, his eyes darting between Corinth and Alastair before landing back on me. "I did predict it though—how they follow you around like puppies. That's okay. They need to hear what I have to say, anyway."

"That was before Corinth was attacked ... most likely by one of your people." I glanced at my watch and counted down. "Forty-nine, forty-eight—"

Gabriel held a finger up, turning his attention to Corinth. "Why would I want you dead? My bounty on your head was on the condition you were delivered to me *alive*." He eyed Corinth's bandaged face, and pointed at the scar on his own cheek. "It would seem you've decided on the same fashion trend."

"It's definitely not a trend," Corinth grumbled. "I wear Converse and you wear a-hole wingtips. Never compare yourself to me ever again."

"Times up."

I stood to leave, but before I could, Gabriel cleared his throat. "All right," he said. "Shall we get right to it, then?" Gabriel turned his attention back to Corinth. "Corinth, I am sure you are interested in finding a cure for the love of your life. A cure for vampirism, that is."

I heard Corinth's tiny inhalation of breath, an almost imperceptible sound. And it was the surprise in it that stopped me cold. Only someone with super-human senses would have noticed it. So it was true. There was a cure, and

Gabriel knew about it.

Corinth barked out an irritated laugh. "What are you talking about?"

My pulse thundered in my ears, in tune with Corinth's own erratically beating heart, until they seemed to meld together, leaving me feeling faint. Corinth was good at using his jokes to hide his emotions, but he couldn't hide the truth from someone like me—not something like this. I wondered who Gabriel was talking about—surely not me.

Corinth didn't love me.

This was another way for him to get under our skin.

Gabriel sure did love his theatrics, and he especially enjoyed the puzzled expression on my face. He raised a smug eyebrow in acknowledgment of my initial reaction. "Corinth, if you had done as I asked months ago and killed Alastair, I would have shared this information with you. Instead, you chose to stab me in the back. *Literally*." He laughed but there was no warmth in it.

I guessed Corinth would have a retort ready, but when I caught his eye, I saw a defensive edge hardened in them.

"This has always been about you, Corinth," he said, opening his arms wide. "I learned all I could about your family. Where you came from, where you went to school, what kind of student you were ... who you were dating ... who you *wanted* to date." His eyes lingered on me. "How you would steal flowers from your best friend's garden. It's adorable how much you really *do* love her." Gabriel's voice lowered to a whisper, and yet it still carried the same threatening tone as his gaze stayed locked on mine. "Surely you must know that you, Larna, are the love of Corinth's life."

Listening to Corinth's thundering heartbeat felt like an invasion of his privacy. Guilt welled up inside me, constricting my throat. I knew he had liked me when we'd gone out a year ago, but we'd only been out on one date. We hadn't even gotten to the boyfriend-and-girlfriend part of the relationship. I had no idea he *loved* me. This news blindsided me so completely that my mouth suddenly went dry, like cold ash in a fireplace.

Corinth drew an arm around his stomach as if he was going to be sick. He turned to me with a grin-turned-grimace that didn't quite match his eyes. "I'm going to stab him in the back, again."

I had been parading my feelings for Alastair in front of him this entire time. Corinth wasn't the only one who felt ill. Why had he never told me how he felt? It explained so much—why he wanted me to have the cure so badly, why he had always put me first. I dug my nails into my palms, hoping the physical pain would take my mind off of how badly my heart ached. Even though I was afraid of what I might see on Alastair's face, I still couldn't resist giving him a quick glance. He was staring down, his chest rising and falling heavily with each breath he pulled in. I couldn't tell if he was angry or horrified or both.

I turned back to see Gabriel's smile. There was a grim curl to his lip—it was taunting, as he knew he had us on his perfectly baited hook. "Corinth was dating a young girl. I believe her name was Madison Bristow. Pretty and popular, but he only had eyes for one girl. Did you tell Miss Collins why you broke up with Madison?"

Hearing Madison's name come out of Gabriel's mouth felt like the worst invasion of privacy so far. It was as if he'd inserted himself into every aspect of our lives.

Something inside me felt torn and ripped away, like how memory loss happens after compulsion. I thought back to high school, wondering how long Gabriel had been watching Corinth. This had to have been longer than six years. Had Gabriel been watching him for his entire life? I knew I had to look just as green around the edges as Corinth did.

Corinth's eyes widened, and his voice sounded raspy when he spoke. "I don't know what you're talking about."

I should have kept my composure, especially in front of Gabriel, but I couldn't control this reaction. A shiver worked its way up my spine as comprehension dawned on me. "You knew …." I licked my dry lips and tried again. "This was never about my family, was it?"

Alastair ground his teeth together so hard I was sure he was going to break them. I couldn't tear my eyes away from Gabriel though. I wanted to reach across the table and avenge my father, use my hidden blades on him—

Gabriel opened his arms wide as if happy someone was finally catching on. "In actuality, it has always been about you and your family, Larna." He glanced between us. "Madison could never make Corinth laugh like Larna could."

I didn't want to know where this was going or how it was going to end. But I couldn't make him stop either. My stomach was twisted into knots.

"Larna's father was a means to an end. I needed him to steal the dagger so he could give it to Larna. I had to make him think it was his idea," Gabriel cooed. "It was so easy to get Mr. Taylor to bend to my will. Everyone has a weakness. I knew if I turned you, Larna, Corinth would never say no if I presented him with an opportunity to find a cure later on."

Rage threatened to send me spiraling out of control. I felt the *Sight* flicker to life in me, the hate transforming into something more sinister. I didn't even know how I'd gotten to my feet. I had the sudden taste of iron in my mouth, and I realized I'd bitten the side of my cheek. "You used me and my family as a means to control Corinth—to recruit him to your cause. You tear apart an innocent family ..." My voice cracked with the flood of emotion. "You find enjoyment in pain and suffering. You make me *sick*."

The oxygen in the room thickened, lending itself a soupy feel as Corinth stood slowly to his feet, speaking with a deadly undertone. "You're a master at *using* everyone around you. You may think you know everything about *me*—who I love or don't love—who I dated, but you'll never know what it feels like to have friends watch your back. People who will never turn on you ... comrades in arms," he said. "Now *that's* love."

The guards were outside of the closed-door conference room, and I suddenly wondered if they could feel the charged energy in the air: a sign of his impending violence.

Corinth's hand hovered an inch over the hilt of his blade. He looked incredibly white, his fingertips sparking with lethal fire. "You did this to Larna because of *me*?" He growled, "You killed her father, kidnapped my sister ..."

Gabriel shrugged as if unconcerned by the way Corinth was stalking toward him now. He murmured, "I tried to convince your father to work for me, Larna. He did at first, but he was never one to play by the rules for long. That's why I had to kill him. That part was *fun*."

Alastair, who had been oddly quiet up until now, launched himself across the table at Gabriel, his hands wrapping around his throat. I knew what that look in Alastair's eyes meant. He was going to kill Gabriel no matter what happened to him in the process. But Gabriel had been ready, and his hidden blades slid out of his sleeves, stopping right before they pierced Alastair's windpipe. A pin drop of blood slid down Alastair's neck to his shirt collar. I wasn't sure how Gabriel had managed to get through security when I'd barely made it through with a pocket knife.

Maybe it was because he could compel vampires.

Gabriel gritted his teeth in annoyance, as if someone with their hands wrapped around his throat was only a minor inconvenience. "Now, now—you wouldn't want to kill me before I finish what I have to say, would you? It's just starting to get good. I have the answer to finding the cure. If you kill me, you'll never get it."

Alastair's voice shook with rage, his blond locks falling into his eyes, and his face turning an unnatural shade of purple. "We didn't come here to find a cure," he snarled. "We came here to kill you."

I turned to Alastair and said in a whisper-soft voice, "*Hey.*"

It was enough to get his attention and make him pause. He cocked his head, hearing the significance in the inflection I used in that one word.

"Alastair ... *please*—don't do anything reckless," I said softly. "That's my job. Plus, I'd never forgive you if you killed him before I got the chance to first."

Gabriel's eyes started to churn, transforming from coal black to a color as blinding as any precious sapphire I'd ever seen.

Corinth, unperturbed by Gabriel's display, drew his dagger and pointed it at him. "You try and compel Al and I fry you," he said icily. "You know I can."

"You aren't going to sacrifice yourself, Alastair. Not gonna happen." I inched closer. "I want him dead just as much as you do. But not like this. Both of you stand down. This isn't going to turn into a blood-bath today."

Gabriel's hate-filled eyes met Alastair's. "Alastair was the one hiccup in my plan—the wild card. It just goes to show that you can't plan for something as idiotic as *love*. It's why I wanted Corinth to kill him. Alastair used up his usefulness a long time ago." Gabriel twisted back to look at me, wheezing as Alastair's grip tightened around his throat. "You don't need distractions like Alastair, Larna."

"So, what, you're a sadistic matchmaker now?" Corinth said.

If Gabriel meant to goad Alastair into trying to kill him, it didn't work. His words proved the opposite. Alastair slowly loosened his grip, but he didn't drop his hands completely away from Gabriel's neck.

Maybe I was getting to him.

My heart gave a lurch. His blond hair, which was normally parted to the side, neatly combed over like a 1950s movie star, was damp from sweat. It still made him look that much more handsome. His square jaw was cleanly shaven, and I had the irresistible feeling I needed to run my hand along it. I could smell his old-man deodorant. I wouldn't settle for less than one more chance to lay my head against his chest, to let my troubles fade away while I got lost in thoughts of him, to listen to him regale me with tales of *Miracle on 34th Street*—his favorite movie. No way was Gabriel going to take another person I loved away from me. This wasn't going to be the last time I ever talked to him again.

I should have told him a long time ago how I felt about him. Just like Corinth should have told me. I wasn't going to make the same mistake though. Time was precious.

Admitting it in front of Gabriel wasn't ideal, but if this was going to be my only time to tell him, I was going to do it. My gaze locked on Corinth for a moment. There was a horrible knot in the pit of my stomach for what I was about to do next. I didn't want Corinth in here to witness what I was about to say, not after learning his true feelings about me, but I felt the only way to stop Alastair from getting himself killed was to jolt him out of his suicide mission.

I cleared my throat, trying to control the tremor in my voice. "You see, that's where you got it right, Gabriel. I *do* love Alastair." Turning all my attention to Alastair, I said, "Let him go, numbskull, and we can try again another day."

I never said I was any good at timing. It wasn't exactly a picture-perfect moment to tell someone you loved them, and yet Alastair's eyes widened and his jaw dropped as if he'd just grasped what I'd confessed. And then, just like that, he was loosening his grip even more.

It gave Gabriel the perfect opportunity to strike. I watched in horror as he dug the tip of his blade deeper into the hollow of Alastair's throat. Alastair stiffened, the fear evident in his eyes. I almost launched myself across the table. The only thing stopping me was the satanically cold look on Gabriel's face. He was ready to end Alastair with the flick of his wrist.

The pit of my stomach dropped out as I gestured to Alastair and then Corinth, who still had his dagger aimed directly at Gabriel. "You don't feel that static cling in the air?" I raised an all-knowing eyebrow. "Corinth's about to take your head off, Gabriel. Is that what you want?"

Gabriel sniffed indignantly. "It would appear Corinth has learned a few new tricks since I saw him last." And then, without another word, he slid his blade back into place with a sullen grin. "Very well, you win this round."

The guards, having just caught on that something was happening, filed into the room and surrounded us with their weapons drawn. One of them, a guy as big as a grizzly, said, "Sir, we need that knife."

"Try and take it from me," Gabriel cooed, straightening his tie back into place.

Chapter 37

Larna

WE'D BEEN ESCORTED BACK to our quarters and asked to stay put for "safety" reasons. I didn't really mind it at the moment. It meant I could have a chance to talk to Alastair.

Ever since the meeting with Gabriel, I had noticed Corinth had a strange glint in his eye: a blazing madness I'd never seen before, sort of like Clint Eastwood's squinty-eyed look in those old westerns my dad used to make me watch. I was worried about him. After admitting I loved Alastair, maybe I'd done something to make everything worse. Guilt still churned in my belly, making it feel as tight as a closed fist. I didn't like seeing Corinth so distressed. I wondered what he thought about my abrupt confession.

Caesar had provided us all with new security cards, and more guards were posted outside our doors. Thankfully, Alastair's injury was only minor, and it had healed. I was mad we'd let Gabriel live. Unfortunately, the threat of more violence had put Sozo on edge.

Alastair was sitting on the window sill in his room,

gazing out at the fake landscape with a faraway look on his face, his legs drawn up to his chest as he stared out at the snowcapped mountainside. It looked like you could step right through the window and ski off into the winter wonderland. I imagined myself wading through waist-high powder, leaving all traces of my cares behind in the process. Sometimes it surprised me how he didn't look a day over seventeen. Today, though, he looked as young as I'd ever seen him, gazing out at the faux snowdrifts and mountains.

An image of Gabriel's glittering blue eyes flashed across the backs of my eyelids. I put a hand against the bed in order to steady myself. Of course he knew about the cure, he knew everything.

"So, we still have no idea why Gabriel wants a cure," Corinth said, marching back into the room through his connecting door. His hair was damp and he had a towel over one shoulder. He didn't seem to notice me falter.

I said, "It *is* convenient that Gabriel suddenly decided to show up with a means for finding a cure, that's for sure."

Corinth glanced at Alastair, who was still captivated by the window, and said softly, "Can I talk to you, Larna?"

My eyes glided to Alastair. I was pretty sure he hadn't even heard Corinth come into the room, so I blew out a breath and said, "Yeah."

Corinth guided me back the way he'd come, through his room and then into mine, the last one at the end. As soon as my door slid closed behind me, he turned back with an uneasy look on his face, his hands shoved deep into his jeans pockets. "I'm sorry," he mumbled.

My heart ached at hearing all that guilt in his voice. We'd always been comfortable around one another, but now, in this moment, it only felt awkward. "You have nothing to be sorry about," I assured him.

He raked a hand through his hair. "Yes, I do … for all of this. *All* of this is my fault. What happened to your family—it's because Gabe had this sick idea that if he turned you, he could control me, to force me into getting this cure." He scratched absentmindedly at the cut on his cheek. "The irony is, he's right. I won't stop until I find it."

My eyes flashed as a stab of anger pierced right through me. "That's not what I want, Corinth." As quickly as the anger came on though, it subsided, and I found myself crumpling down to my bed in an exhausted heap. "What Gabriel said about you lovi—"

"Is complete lunacy." But the way he said it, with so much dogged determination, as if he was trying to convince himself, was what made me think otherwise. "It doesn't change the fact that if there is a cure out there, I'm gonna find it and shove it down your stubborn throat."

"How do you plan on doing that, by snapping your fingers?" I barked.

Corinth's brow furrowed. "Condescension noted—"

Before we could continue arguing, a knock sounded on Corinth's outside door, stopping me. I held up a hand to interrupt him. "Someone's knocking on your door."

He trailed wordlessly behind me, back to his room. The screen display had popped up, revealing that Sarah was on the other side, holding a tray of cups and two steaming kettles. The guards were still out there, but apparently, it was okay that we accepted visitors.

Corinth strode over to the door and put his hand against it. The door slid open and Sarah immediately bustled inside to unload her delivery. I watched her in brooding silence as she set the tray on the bed, then grabbed one of the cups to pour coffee into it.

She handed it to Corinth first. "I heard you guys were on lockdown, so I decided to bring you a care package." She eyed Corinth up and down, studying him with a finger to her chin. "I assume you like coffee? I brought a strong roast with some sugar on the side." She turned to me next, holding out a Styrofoam cup. "A positive."

I took the proffered cup, nodding my thanks, but I was still agitated from squabbling with Corinth only moments before.

"Where's Alastair?" Sarah inquired softly.

"He's unavailable." It came out more gruffly than I wanted it to.

Sarah glanced down at her hands, nodding. "Of course. I wasn't trying to pry. I just brought him something to drink as well."

I assumed she must have thought I was mad at her, so I softened my tone. "I'm sorry, that angry retort wasn't directed at you." My gaze flitted to Corinth momentarily, who now only seemed to have eyes for Sarah.

She gave me a small smile to let me know it was okay. I studied her, noticing the tiny freckles dotting her nose. The pattern sprayed out across her cheeks like butterfly wings. Her smile was kind, and even though I was still suspicious of her, I found myself relaxing a little. Someone from Alastair's troubled past was here. And then I'd gone and confessed to him in front of Gabriel, no less, that I loved him. It didn't take a genius to realize how overwhelmed and confused he must feel right now.

Corinth lifted the cup to his lips. "Sweet Christmas, I love strong coffee." He gave her one of his rare lopsided grins in thanks. "I like my coffee as bold as the *Enterprise*."

I rolled my eyes, but Sarah's eyes crinkled at the corners in amusement as she said, "You're a Trekkie … I've always been more of a Rebel myself."

Corinth took another sip of his coffee, blinking his surprise at her knowledge of pop culture. "I'm impressed," he said, smiling. "I was just testing you. Everyone loves *Star Wars* more than *Star Trek*."

I glanced between them. Corinth was looking at her like he used to look at me. I wondered if he was trying to make me feel better about confessing my love for Alastair by acting like he liked Sarah, so we wouldn't feel awkward around one another. Normally, I would have joined in on any conversation about movies, but I couldn't seem to focus on anything other than Alastair.

Sarah glanced between us. "Did I miss something?" she said. "Whose funeral is it?"

Corinth plucked the lid off his cup to toss more sugar inside. "We just had a particularly nasty reunion with a psycho," he responded. "How about you take our minds off it and tell us how you and Al met?"

Sarah's smile slipped, and Corinth, who realized what he'd just asked of her, corrected, "That was totally insensitive of me."

She chewed on her bottom lip in thought and then shrugged. "It was a long time ago. I'm not surprised he didn't mention me before now. It's not like I'm a blast from his past." Sarah turned emerald eyes on me, searching for something that seemed to be just out of her reach. Finally she said, "So he *has* told someone." She inclined her head. "You must mean a lot to him if he shared that with you."

People say the eyes are the windows to the soul and, in Sarah's case, that was completely true. She looked a lot more fragile and innocent than when she'd entered our room only a few short minutes ago.

Her mouth crinkled at the corners in a grimace. "A man named Thomas Wrentmore plucked me out of an orphanage when I was eleven. I worked for him in his kitchens." She clarified, "At his mansion. We, myself and the other staff, would sneak food from his elaborate dinners when his guests weren't looking." She gazed off into empty space as if remembering the distant memory. "No one bothered me as long as I did my job. It went on like that for years. Entertaining his guests, a roof over my head, and I got to eat whatever I wanted," she said, almost wistfully. "It wasn't a bad life. The day Wrentmore brought Alastair home, everything changed. Sarah's face blanched, her tiny freckles standing out against pale skin. "I fancied Alastair. He was so sweet and adorable, with those blond curls and ruddy cheeks full of food and life." She shook her head as if to clear it. "So, what's your story, Larna? How'd you meet Alastair?"

A sudden overwhelming pity rose up in me at what they had been through together. I couldn't help but see beyond that, to imagine the lavish mansion and ornate decorations, frilly dresses, and high-collared suits. Maybe they had been in love, even back then.

A strangled noise bubbled up out of my throat. "I'd rather not talk about that right now."

Corinth set his empty coffee cup down, giving me a fleeting glance. "I'm going to assume this Wrentmore guy was a grade-A jerk … and by the way Al stares at that damn pocket watch of his all the time, I assume it has something to do with this guy?"

Sarah's eyes snapped up to meet Corinth's. She opened and closed her mouth, floundering at words before gathering her wits about her again. "Alastair has Wrentmore's watch?"

Corinth shared a panicked glance with me, as if he'd accidentally given away too much information. "Uh … yeah … he's got an old pocket watch he carries around with him."

A flicker of anger flashed in her eyes, illuminating the green and blue fire in them. "That watch meant a lot to Wrentmore." Sarah turned back to face Corinth, the anger in her eyes fading as she regained control of her emotions. After a second, she said, "Enough about me. Corinth, what's your story?"

He cleared his throat, clearly affected by what Sarah had just told us. "Um … well, I'm the oldest out of two brothers and a sister. I grew up in Fort Worth, Texas; it's got a small town vibe, but it's actually a pretty big city. I'm a caffeine snob who loves video games and anything sci-fi. I recently came into possession of an ancient and decidedly finicky magical knife." He put a finger to his lip in thought. "And … oh yeah … I've also been told I'm a good listener."

Sarah laughed; it was bubbly and infectious and light, as if she'd recovered completely from her earlier grief. "And he's funny." She stood back up. "Well … I guess I better get going. Corinth, would you like to join me for dinner as soon as you're free-*er*?"

Corinth's head shot up, and his cheeks flushed at hearing the word dinner. "Um … yeah … I'd like that very much."

Chapter 38

Corinth

IT WAS AS IF Dave had just up and vanished. I'd fallen asleep on the small makeshift sofa in Al's room because neither Al nor Larna wanted to leave me alone. I found myself wedged between two people who had confessed their love for each other—which was *awesome*. It was annoyingly depressing how those two kept stealing glances at each other, but they wouldn't talk to one another. I think sometime during the night, Al had forced me to lie down. I hated sleep; it was such a waste of time. Also, I couldn't shut my mind off about what Gabe had said about me and my family. All of my suspicions had been confirmed. He knew everything about us. I was extremely thankful Vinson had volunteered to check on them. Some maniacal douche-bag was using Larna to control me and had ratted me out. When he'd told Larna I loved her, it had been a gut punch. I had planned on taking that bit of information with me to the grave. Larna finding out I loved her was at the top of the list of most embarrassing things to happen to me. Now things had gotten awkward.

I switched gears, thinking about Dave and what he'd

told me. Right now, I'd take the exception to my no-sleeping rule because I really wanted him to come back.

Larna, having heard me get up, appeared out of thin air with some aspirin and water in hand. The butterfly strips had come off some-time during the night. My cut had scabbed over, so I didn't worry about reapplying new ones right this second—even though it still hurt like hell.

"What, no coffee?" I asked, rubbing the sleep from my eyes. "Where's Al?"

"Meeting with Sozo about Gabriel. We aren't on lockdown, but in exchange, we had to agree to be shadowed by their guards."

"Anything I can do to help smooth things over?"

"As a matter of fact, I need you to work on controlling that blade of yours. There's a gym not far from here. How do you feel about getting a little workout in?"

I nodded slowly, giving it some real thought. "I think that's a good idea. I could stand to clear my head."

I looked her up and down, noticing the state of her clothes. Her black shirt was tucked into dark green cargo pants, a canvas belt cinched tightly at her waist. They were wrinkled, as if she'd been sleeping in them. Short jet-black hair framed her face, making her look edgy and hard—but no less hot. I could see the outline of her biceps and the cut of her abs through her shirt. It still surprised me how much she'd changed in a year. A pang of longing welled up in me at what could have been—and would never be. I'd only admit it to myself, but I was still reeling about Gabriel. No amount of therapy could take away my guilt. She'd been turned because of *me*—because I had a thing for *her*. I hated feeling this way. I had to learn to control my emotions. Learn to let love go. You couldn't just wash away the lingering doubt and regret. I needed to beat them out of my brain.

Physical pain was so much better than mental pain.

I could still make this right. It was why I desperately needed to talk to Dave again.

"Let me change. I'll come with you," Larna insisted, bringing me out of my musings.

I shook my head a little too adamantly, glancing at the scabbed-over cut on her neck where I'd accidently cut her in the caves. "I need to figure this out on my own; if I hurt you again. I don't know what I'd do ..." My voice cracked and I stopped. "Besides, I have a feeling you and Al have a lot to discuss."

Larna stepped closer to me. We were inches apart, and for one split second, I imagined myself pulling her into my arms to kiss her. I also imagined enjoying the warmth of her body as it melded into mine, like how protons and neutrons are held together in a nucleus by the strong force. The strong force gets its name by being the strongest attractive force—which is six thousand billion billion billion billion times more powerful than gravity. I didn't know how else to describe the chemistry between us. *This is exactly why I am a science nerd.* Since she'd been turned, her metabolism had increased tenfold. I had thought it would have been the opposite—the myth of vamps being the undead and all. She reached out to me, but seemed to think better of it and pulled her hand back. Things had changed so much between us in the last twenty-four hours.

Damn Gabe for meddling in my life.

"I don't like that glint in your eye," I observed. "You're *not* going after Gabe, right?" I raised a distrustful eyebrow. "You need to tread lightly—he's dangerous."

One side of her mouth tugged up at the corner as if to say, "You don't have to tell me that." "You concentrate on controlling that weapon of yours, and I'll concentrate on our enemies. We've been assigned a guard detail. They'll be stuck to us like glue." She jabbed a finger to my chest. "And you, Corinth, you stick to the gym *only*."

I put a hand on her arm, and a burst of static electricity arced between us. It was the first time I'd touched her since her admission about Al. I jerked my hand back as if I'd been burned, averting my gaze from hers. "What Gabe said back in the conference room—" I swallowed hard before continuing "—I used to feel that way, but not anymore." I stopped, finding I couldn't even say the word *love* out loud. It stung, lying to her, but I would not be the source of her not moving on. I could see it in her eyes: the conflict of guilt and pity. I wouldn't be that person clinging to hope that she might see me as something more one day. Maybe if I admitted I didn't have feelings for her anymore, I'd actually start believing it.

Her tone was gentle yet firm as she said, "I know this isn't exactly an ideal situation between any of us right now, but we need to stay focused. What I said—about loving Alastair ... well, I meant it, Corinth." She cleared her throat. "And I love you too. I'm just not *in* love with you." She cast a glance down, but not before I saw pink flood the contours of her cheeks. "Gabriel's reason behind turning me, though, is *not* your fault—it's *his*."

I nodded, feeling a swirling hollowness in the pit of my stomach. She wasn't *in* love with me. *Ouch.* It was hard to look her in the face and not believe her about Gabe. I whispered under my breath, "I guess we're both on the same page, then. And it still doesn't mean I feel any less shitty about it."

I knew it had to be hard for her and Al right now. I'd felt the growing tension between them. If she told me she loved me, I'd be vaulting over the moon. Why did things have to be so complicated? I think they were holding back because I was so far wedged between them they didn't want to hurt me. I wished I could tell them it was way too late for that.

Two big, burly-looking dudes were my security detail. One had a graying Gandalf beard, but he looked younger—and had bulging biceps. The other one had squinty eyes, a hook nose, and incredibly smooth dark skin and a shaved head. They were kind enough to point me in the direction of the gym, but not kind enough to tell me their names, so I gave them ones: Thor and Luke Cage.

Once inside, I realized this place wasn't really a gym at all. A giant dome over my head lit up an Olympic-sized track-and-field-type arena. In the center of the sports ground sat all of the workout equipment I would ever need. I took some time familiarizing myself with the gear while my bodyguards disappeared from sight.

It appeared I had the run of the place, which was great; it meant I could explore my powers without turning anyone into a crispy fried nub. An assortment of oversized tires, ropes, and medicine balls lined the white-washed walls. There was a jogging track that looped around the field, much like the one at my old high school. A plethora of jump ropes, yoga mats, and free weights sat in the grass. I found myself gravitating toward the equipment, inhaling the heady scent of freshly cut lawn. It was real. I wondered if the lights overhead were ultraviolet or something, replacing the sun's natural light with UV rays. I found I had missed the scent of dirt and earth and the outdoors. I inhaled deeply, enjoying solitude's comforting embrace. And even though it was obvious that I was probably being watched, I still found my alone time cathartic. Maybe I'd give my audience something to talk about in the meantime. It suddenly occurred to me that maybe Luke Cage and Thor were keeping people from entering the gym … or maybe everyone here attended classes during the day, which left places like this empty for the uneducated, like me.

This might be a good time to really let loose and see what I could do. It was nice not having to worry about hiding my abilities or holding back. It also could have something to do with the fact that I always felt like I was within a hair's breadth of frying everyone around me. There had been a lot keeping me in check as of late.

It was time to shake the cobwebs loose.

I wasn't someone who enjoyed working out. To be honest, I'd rather be sitting in front of a computer with a can of soda and some Cheetos. But if I wanted to give myself a fighting chance against stronger beings—like angels and vampires—I felt it best to try and keep in a good a shape as possible. I was only human after all. Every time I tried to clear my head, I kept thinking about reasons why Gabe would want a cure for vampirism. Whoever had control over the most powerful weapon on the planet had control over the playing board.

I wasn't the weapon though, the dagger was.

In the middle of flipping a giant heavy tire across the track, a very mundane task, I found it served the purpose of clearing my head. Too worried about breathing to overthink, I focused on moving the heavy object across the field, one foot in front of the other: *flip, stoop, lift … flip, stoop, lift …* Over and over again it went like this until I had to make myself stop for a sip of water. My arms were trembling, and the thin material of my shirt clung to me like a second skin. It felt good to pour myself into something other than the blade. And it wasn't until my legs started twitching with fatigue that I realized how spent I really was.

My fingers skimmed over the hilt of the blade at my hip. Ever so slowly, I drew it out. The sound of it clearing the scabbard filled me with an unexpected and light-headed wooziness. The world tilted around me before I realized the dizziness had come from me holding my breath. I expelled the oxygen from my lungs. *Come on, blade, work* with *me. I don't want to fight with you anymore; I want to work* with *you.*

Do you need a name? Should I name you? Holy crap, I hadn't named it. I named everything. I closed my eyes, concentrating on the familiar weight. *Evil's Bane? The Sword of Time? Menace to Society? Girlfriend Blocker? El Capitan? Pain in My Ass?*

One name kind of did stick: Thunderblade.

I kind of liked it.

I tightened my grip on the cool metal. It bit into my skin. "Why did you choose me? Tell me what you want from me, Thunderblade."

Widening my stance just like Al had taught me, I started practicing a basic kata practical in weapons use. Recalling the right number of steps in the right order was the hard part: tighten my core, center my balance, lean into each strike, and use my torso, because that was where the power came from.

I slashed out, sweeping the blade back and forth in a wide arch. Once I was comfortable with the balance and weight, I started to add more difficult techniques to the routine. Twisting, turning, and kicking, I moved to a tune only I could hear, the blade humming menacingly as it sliced through the air. The finale was me adding in some spinning kicks—some difficult moves, but I felt connected to the blade in a way I never had before. I felt limber and centered and skilled. Each strike and block and slash felt like I was shedding the dead-weight of doubt and fear and loss of control. By the time I was done, sweat was dripping off my forehead, and running down my arms and legs.

And then I heard the sound of mocking laughter.

My eyes popped open as I searched for the source. A group of five guys were watching me across the open field. They stood on the track, their hands on their hips. Once they saw me notice them, they moved out onto the grass, heading toward me. By the derisive sneers on their faces, I realized they weren't fans of mine.

I looked around for signs of Thor or Luke Cage. Maybe there was a reason for their sudden disappearance, or maybe these five guys took them out—in either case, my protection was now conveniently gone. These dudes looked like they were ready to rumble. I focused on the one standing in the front of the group with his arms crossed: most likely their leader—a shorter guy in the back, who had on a baseball cap with an original Yankees logo on it. The rest of the group was wearing basketball shorts and jerseys. Sports fans, I could use that to my advantage.

Still trying to catch my breath, I gestured at the guy

with the baseball cap. "Yankees fan, huh?"

He cupped a hand over his mouth and shouted, "*Best team in the world!*"

I took note of his thick New York accent.

"You kiddin'? Agreed, The Bronx Bombers are the best!" I shouted back. *Forgive me, Texas Rangers.* My dad was a baseball fan, and I had picked up enough over the years to get by. But I was definitely *not* a Yankees fan.

He smiled and then elbowed the guy next to him, who nodded in agreement.

"You guys catch any of the games?" I asked, stepping behind the giant tire I'd been flipping. It would offer little protection if they did decide to do something stupid. Their eyes kept shiftily darting to the blade in my grasp. I swiped a hand across my forehead and smiled, what I hoped was a friendly, unconcerned one. I *was* concerned. Being outnumbered by five vamps was bad, very bad.

"Sure—we get the games here," the Yankee fan said, eyeing my sweat-soaked shirt. "You looked like you were getting in quite the workout. Those were some crazy moves. Those high kicks you were doing looked like some kind of fancy dance routine." He laughed, his eyes swiveling back to the dagger still in my hand. "That blade looks pretty sharp."

I glanced down to it and then, as if making hopefully the right decision, sheathed it back at my thigh, shrugging nonchalantly. "It is."

He said, "You must be pretty sure of yourself—putting that blade away like that."

Again my eyes slid back down to the dagger and I shrugged. "I am."

The leader, who had a crewcut and a bronze skin tone like an Italian, stepped forward. "That tire there"—he nodded to the one I was standing behind—"is about five hundred pounds. We saw you flip it all the way over here. You're pretty strong, for being humanly impaired and all …"

I gave another shrug. "Just determined."

"I heard you hunt vamps," he said softly, a threatening undertone in his voice.

At the mention of the word *hunt* my heart began to thump wildly against my chest. He closed the distance between us. This was not going to end well.

I scanned the area, noticing I was right smack in the middle of the circular track, which was about a quarter of a mile around the entire complex. The rest of the guys had slowly maneuvered themselves to form a semicircle around me.

"I don't particularly like to hunt." I shifted on the balls of my feet, getting ready. "And I definitely don't want to hurt anyone—unless I have to."

The Italian shared a glance with his buddies and then thumbed a hand in my direction. He grinned, but it didn't reach his eyes. "This guy thinks he can hurt us."

There one second, and gone the next, he was in front of me, picking up the tire that had been the only thing between us as if it weighed less than a feather. Using one hand, he tossed it across the track like a shot put. The tire bounced a few feet, thudding heavily against the track, and then rolled sluggishly over onto its side as if it had seen better days.

"That was impressive," I said, and meant it.

"I'm John," he said.

I wiped my hands on my pants, holding out a hand toward him, hoping he wouldn't see it shaking. "Corinth."

His eyes flicked to my outstretched hand then back up, and they just so happened to be glowing with his *Sight*. "Are you a betting man, Corinth?"

Chapter 39

Corinth

"I DON'T REALLY BET—"

John inched closer, effectively cutting me off as he moved into my personal space. "You're not afraid, are you?"

I suddenly realized I wasn't getting out of this unless I could do some fancy talking or a lot of fighting. Sweat slid down the middle of my back. Why was Larna always right about these things? I was a shit magnet.

He was going to make me fight. I really didn't want to fight, especially since my arms and legs were fatigued from the workout I'd already done. Not to mention I hadn't even tried to use Thunderblade to its fullest extent. It was like being made fun of in high school—which I had actually managed to avoid. I had learned how to make people laugh. Something told me I wouldn't be so lucky now though.

"Um, what did you have in mind?" I asked, and by the looks on their faces, I realized I shouldn't have asked. They looked like wolves in sheep's jerseys.

John pointed at one of the guys behind him. "Irwin

here thinks he can take you."

I glanced at Irwin, who was a stocky guy; his legs were corded in muscle, and they looked like they could crush my skull like a watermelon. Irwin was right—he probably could take me.

"You lose, *well*—" John nodded at my blade "—then we help ourselves to that dagger of yours."

"What if I say no?" I asked brazenly.

He rolled his eyes as if I'd just bored him to death. "Then I guess you fight all five of us."

"And if I win?"

He shrugged. "Name it."

I figured I could use this to my advantage. Gabriel had a room that was begging to be searched—what better way to get information than from people who knew this place so well. I also had decided I'd rather fight one guy instead of all five of them.

"You know who Gabriel Stanton is?" I asked.

John spit on the ground, nodding.

I guess he didn't like him either.

"I need to get into his room under the radar … if you catch my meaning."

John glanced at the rest of his crew. "I think we can make that happen. But you're not gonna win, so it really doesn't matter."

Al had been teaching me ground control: a form of martial arts called Brazilian jujitsu. I wasn't an expert at it by any means, but I had a few moves down, and at least I would buy myself a little more time before Irwin snapped my neck.

"I won't hold you to the usual rules," Irwin told me.

"That's good, because I have no idea what the usual rules are."

They all turned to each other, laughing as if I'd just told them the funniest joke.

"I'm glad y'all find my lack of knowledge amusing," I mumbled as I followed Irwin to an open patch of grass. Everyone else lagged behind us to watch the show—and probably make sure I didn't make a run for it.

Irwin pointed to my dagger. "You can't use that."

My eyes flicked down to it. "Like hell I can't."

"That's not fair."

"I don't know your rules. I'd say that makes it fair," I said. "Besides, don't tell me you guys aren't even a little curious about how you stack up against it?"

They all nodded in unison—everyone except Irwin, that is.

I stretched my arms over my head, trying to loosen up some of the lactic acid that had built up, then unsheathed my weapon. The rest of the crew stepped back, finally looking apprehensive. I guessed they'd seen the fireworks show I'd put on in the meeting hall. Irwin cracked his knuckles, then his neck, and probably a few vertebrae as well. Now I wished I'd been dressed in something other than jeans and a tank. Like maybe an Iron Man suit. At least I had my Chucks on.

Key word: *had.*

It only took a fraction of a second to get thrown out of them.

Irwin hit me with enough force to crush the air out of my lungs and cause the world around me to explode in an array of psychedelic colors. Little black comets zipped across my vision. I shook my head, trying to reboot my system, realizing I had been flattened on the ground by a bulldozer. Still feeling woozy, I fumbled with the straps, forgetting I'd already removed it from the scabbard—and then I panicked when it was empty.

My dagger was gone and Irwin was bearing down on me, mere feet away. If I had to guess, I'd say he weighed more than that tire I'd been flipping. Mental note: don't make bets *ever* again.

I rolled painfully to the side, hyper-aware of how slow I was moving and how much it hurt to not have shoes on. Irwin barreled past me at the last second, the blast of wind whipping my hair out of my eyes. He was outmaneuvering me, changing direction so quickly my mind couldn't keep up. He meant to mow me down and he was going to do it.

Before I could even change tactics or run or raise my fists, he was on top of me, his eyes fiery and piercing with all-consuming alien light, pulling me in with his *Sight*. "You lose—" he started to say, but stopped as soon as my own eyes sparked to life.

There was a deep fire in the pit of my belly that warmed my soul at the same time as it sought to claim his. *No*, you *lose. Game over, man. Game over.*

Somewhere off in the distance, I registered the sound of gloating merriment as the cadre cheered in victory. Anger roiled in my belly like a red-hot poker left too long in the fire. It grated on my nerves. They didn't know Irwin had made a fatal error. I was still reveling in the flood of my anti-*Sight* as Irwin stood rigidly at attention, waiting for my command.

I put a hand to the back of my head, feeling the newly formed lump. *Ouch.* My shoes were a hundred yards in the opposite direction, in the same exact spot I had been tackled in. A wave of relief washed over me when I saw my blade back by my shoes.

None of them paid any attention to the fact that I was still in complete control of my own faculties.

They were still too busy celebrating as John roared, *"Hey, hurry it up over there!"*

I marched calmly past Irwin, commanding him to get my dagger. He disappeared and reappeared a second later, obediently holding out Thunderblade to me. I didn't take it back just yet; instead, I gestured for him to follow me. He wasn't going to give it to them. They all still believed I was compelled. So as they watched me approach, I gave them a blank stare, complete with glassy eyes and a slight limp, which was easy to pull off, since I'd been knocked senseless.

John glanced up from his belly laugh, the mild surprise apparent on his face as we got closer. "Hold up," he said hesitantly. "What's this about?"

John held his hand out to Irwin. "Well, mate, don't keep us waiting. Give us a look at this legendary blade."

Irwin's eyes sought mine for permission, and John took notice.

"No, Irwin," I ordered, my eyes flashing. "I'd like *my* blade back."

The group collectively dropped their jaws as I took the weapon from him, finally releasing my anti-*Sight* at the same time. I didn't feel as drained as before—and this time, the strength and stamina hit me with such force it was all I could do to hold myself back. For a second, I thought I was flying high above everyone else, on a buoyant cloud of delight. Even before John could react, I was holding the tip of my blade against his chest. The power swelled inside me, and sparks of light shot out of my hands, crackling with uncontained energy as John cast an uncertain glance to the rest of his group.

The point of the dagger rested right where I knew his heart to be. The sudden urge to kill was an ever-present force. *You're not in control, blade. I am.* I let out a deep, shuddering breath, pulling back on the supernatural reins vying to take control of my mind, body, and soul. Shaking my head, I let my anti-*Sight* slough away from me, imagining water running down a windshield.

Flipping the dagger, I expertly caught the handle before sheathing it back at my hip. "I'm not much of a gloater—but a bet is a bet." My eyes glided to Irwin, who was still standing in a dazed stupor beside John. My point was clear: *Mess with me again, and that's what will happen to you.*

John's eyes narrowed, and then he looked to the rest of his friends, who all had the same stunned expressions on their faces. None of them seemed as confident as they had before the fight. For one infinitely long second, I thought he was going to tell them to try and take me out, but then he was laughing.

The tension I'd been holding in my shoulders loosened, and I sagged in relief, suddenly feeling fatigued.

John pointed to Irwin's expressionless face. "Is he gonna snap out of that?"

"Probably."

He clapped me on the back. "You're all right, kid." He glanced down to my socks and, with a shake of his head, said, "You fight decent for a human who just got knocked out of his own shoes."

"I think that's the nicest thing anyone's ever said to me," I mumbled groggily.

Chapter 40

Corinth

MY SECURITY DETAIL CONVENIENTLY reappeared sometime after I left the training grounds. I'd catch glimpses of their white uniforms as they drifted down the hallway, following me like lackadaisical apparitions. I wondered if they would actually do anything if someone did attack me.

It hit me that they'd probably look for any excuse to take me out first. I saw the way their hands hovered over those cattle prods of theirs.

Training this morning had gone way better than expected. I felt more confident about using the blade than I ever had before. John and his crew had invited me to their game room to watch baseball. It seemed stupid and trivial, but it meant a lot to me. It never hurt to have allies. John also promised to give me access to Gabriel's room, so win-win. Even with all of these thoughts to keep me occupied, my mind kept wandering back to Sarah and those intriguing green eyes of hers. I don't know what it was, but I felt a little too comfortable around her, as in if she asked about the dagger and my abilities, I'd probably spill my guts. It felt like we had been friends all our lives. I craved to find out more about her. Maybe it was a good thing everything was out in the open with Larna. I could move on—I knew she had moved on from me.

Speak of the devil; as I rounded a corner in the expansive hallway, I barreled right into the person I'd been thinking about—*Sarah*. The large stack of books she'd been carrying was almost as tall as she was. Her armload teetered precariously as she defied gravity, balancing the heavy tomes in one hand and lifting her opposite leg in order to right herself. It amazed me how she pulled together strength and dexterity so seamlessly.

I reached a hand out, foolishly thinking I could help. "Sorry, sorry, sorry," I said frantically. "Do you need help?" I couldn't seem to wipe off what I'm sure was a huge, stupid grin on my face. "No, of course you don't need any help," I muttered more to myself than her. "You can defy gravity."

"Yogi extraordinaire here," she teased. "Don't worry about it," she said. "It's what I get for checking out the entire library all at once."

I glanced down, noticing the book on top of the pile, quirking an inquisitive eyebrow. "The study of alchemy?"

She hugged the books to her chest as her cheeks lit up the prettiest shade of rosy pink I'd ever seen. "Yeah. I couldn't find *Alchemy for Dummies*."

"You enjoy reading about chemistry?" I asked, unable to hide the look of disbelief on my face.

Sarah opened her mouth in feigned surprise. "Don't be so shocked." She pointed at herself and said in a deep voice, "Yes. Woman like science."

I imitated the same deep bass to my voice that she had done, most likely to make herself sound like a caveman.

"Woman smart."

"You may have heard of the scientific study of turning something ordinary into something special." She nudged my chest playfully with an elbow. "Sorta like the definition of you."

My mouth fell open. *Did she just hit on me?*

I found myself wondering if her hair was as soft as it looked. I wanted to run my hands through the curly-to-the-point-of-almost-frizzy locks to judge for myself. I cleared my throat, trying to ignore my own cheeks flushing, skillfully avoiding her wide, round eyes to glance back at her book. "That sounds like some heavy reading."

She shrugged. "It's light reading for a doctor."

"Wow … really?" I said, surprised. "You're a doctor? What do you practice?"

"On a good day, I'm an epidemiologist, hematologist, and an infectious disease specialist." She must have interpreted the look on my face as confusion instead of wonder, because she clarified, "I study diseases and I look for cures for those diseases."

It suddenly hit me how cool it would be to have all that time on your hands. Maybe being a vampire wasn't so bad after all. Or maybe I was just being swayed by a very pretty girl. Either way, I found myself inching closer into her personal space just to get a whiff of her. She smelled of lavender and lilacs and everything nice.

"That's a mouthful," I said. "*And* you're a genius. So clearly, you're off to save lives, then?"

Sarah blushed, and when she pushed a strand of hair behind her ear, she suddenly looked younger than she appeared. "Nothing as glamorous as all that … just a class on hematology."

"That was my second guess," I said. "Is that the study of blood?"

"Give this guy a cookie," she said with an impressed grin.

"I have occasionally been known to dabble in the art of science." I started ticking off my fingers. "Let's see—you're incredibly smart, funny, and you laugh at my jokes. What's wrong with you?"

Sarah let out an indignant huff and then, as if realizing she was late, started speed walking down the hall. She turned around when she saw I had lagged behind, and then motioned for me to follow. I had to jog to catch up. When I was beside her once again, she glanced at me over her tower of literature and started moving again. I found it was hard for me, even with my long legs, to keep up with her rapid pace.

"You forgot to add to your list 'has a knack for being late.'"

"Would you like to have dinner tonight?" I blurted out.

I don't know why I did it—maybe it was the way those exceedingly green eyes offset pink-tinged, glowing cheeks. Or maybe I needed to take my mind off current events.

Whatever the case, Sarah stopped in her tracks, turning back around to face me. "I've got a load of work to do tonight … but maybe I can give you a tour of the labs later, since you dabble in science—they're quite impressive. It's on a restricted level, so you'll need access …" Her voice drifted off as if she was working through a problem. After a second, she raised her eyebrows and glanced around as if confiding something important to me.

"Fortunately, I just so happen to have said access." She winked. "And it will be completely abandoned at that time of night, so we'll have the place all to ourselves."

For the first time in a long time, I felt halfway normal—and then a little voice at the back of my mind said, *Yes, going on a date with a century-old vamp is totally normal.* I tamped it back down, overriding that thought because it had been so long since I'd been hit on, and I really needed to get Gabe's monologue about me still loving Larna out of my head.

I saluted her gallantly. "I guess I'll see you later tonight, then."

She giggled and shook her head as she rounded the corner, leaving me in the dust.

I yelled after her, "I don't regret the salute!" I whispered, "Not even a little bit."

Several people walking by turned to give me strange looks, but I didn't care. I had a date.

I glanced down at myself, realizing I was still covered in grime and sweat from my earlier training session. Embarrassment for not having taken a shower sooner set in. I didn't let it steal the light mood from me though.

As I hurried in the direction of my room, Benny, the toothless ex-engineer, materialized around the corner out of nowhere. He seemed agitated, gesturing wildly with one hand and holding a steaming mug in the other. He was in animated conversation with himself, and it was at this time that I hoped he wouldn't see me.

I ducked my head to avoid him, and that's when it happened.

Something warm and sticky hit me in the chest, blossoming into a red Rorschach pattern across my tank.

At first, I couldn't tell what the substance was, until the recognizable odor of blood hit me. Benny cackled madly at his creation. Even his wriggling-caterpillar eyebrows danced in time to his jig of triumph.

I rolled my eyes in disgust, wringing out my hands at the mess. "Oh, that's just great. Thanks, Benny."

He leaned closer, giving me another gap-toothed smile. "'Well may it sort that this portentous figure comes armed through our watch; so like the king that was and is the question of these wars.'"

That last part wasn't gibberish; it was Shakespeare, maybe *Hamlet* or *Richard III*—I wasn't that great with literature.

"That's Shakespeare, right?"

Benny perked up, grabbing my wrist in a surprisingly firm grip. He opened his mouth to say something, but stopped abruptly when we heard the sound of feet slapping on polished marble. His hand stilled on my forearm, and his eyes went wide, the tufts of white hair above them rising in unison. His eyes, which had been glazed over, were now clear and focused and almost translucent. And there was fear in them. I followed his line of sight to see Thor and Luke Cage almost on top of us. Caesar was behind them, looking flustered and out of breath.

Benny leaned in close, pressing his lips close to my ear. When he spoke, there was no trace of his usual childlike glee; he seemed as lucid as I'd ever heard him, his eyes flicking to the rapidly approaching guards. "*They* are watching you."

My heart thumped madly against my chest and goose

bumps pebbled my arms at this sudden and well-articulated observation. I wondered if he was talking about my new security detail; he had been staring at them rather hard when he had warned me. They hadn't been that interested in protecting me as of late. Were they afraid Benny might know something and give it away during coherent moments? Was that why they had just shown up?

Before I could question him further, his hand fell away from my arm, and he disappeared into the now-crowded hallway.

Caesar caught up to me, panting heavily. "He gave me the slip again …" His eyes widened seeing the blood staining my shirt. "Are you hurt?"

My eyes flicked down at the mess and then back up to the burly men behind Caesar, watching for signs of subterfuge. The one with the long gray beard—Thor—had sharp, intelligent eyes, and he appeared younger than what the gray in his beard belied.

"No. I'm okay. I was heading to my room to change, anyway," I said quickly.

"I'll call for laundry service right away." Caesar glanced at the men behind him. "Dover, can you help him?"

I put my hands out to stop Caesar. I did not want these two lurking around if I could help it. "I'm fine, really."

"No, sir. It's unacceptable that he keeps doing this to you. I'm going to have to get him confined to his quarters."

"Please don't do that," I pleaded. If he did that I might not get to question him again later. Why would he have said *they* were watching me?

Caesar finally stopped fussing over me long enough

to nod. "Very well, sir."

"Would you stop calling me sir?" I put a hand to my forehead. "It's Corinth. I don't even like the word *sir*. It's pretentious."

Caesar stood to his full height, sticking his chest out as if I'd offended him. "No, sir. I shall use the proper form to address you."

I leaned closer, hoping the two guards wouldn't hear me, or if they did, hoping they wouldn't take notice. "Okay, fine, whatever makes you happy." I said quietly, "But can you please set up a meeting with Sozo. I need to talk to him as soon as possible."

He made a face like he'd just sucked on a lemon. "Oh, no. Sir, I am so sorry. He was pulled away unexpectedly— but as soon as he returns, I will set it up." He looked crestfallen when he spoke next. "Can I be of some other assistance?"

"You can accompany me back to my room, if you like."

Caesar beamed back at me as if I'd just told him he'd won the lotto. Maybe he was just that eager to help out, or maybe he had a crush on me. Either way, I didn't want the two goons to follow me, and I much preferred Caesar's company over theirs.

When I'd finally made it back to my room, with a pit stop at the kitchen along the way, I found an agitated and pacing Larna waiting for me.

Her eyes widened at seeing the state I was in. "Please tell me you aren't injured—*again*," she breathed, moving to examine me. "Do I even want to know?"

I glanced down with a grimace and held up a hand to stop her. "Probably not."

"You're going to give me a heart attack, you know that?"

"You can't have a heart attack," I quipped. "It's not like your arteries get clogged."

Larna plopped down onto the bed, sighing. "Dare I ask whose blood that is, then?" she asked. "Unless it's Imani's, and then I might be okay with it."

I put my plate of fried goodness down on top of the bed and pulled my ruined shirt off. As soon as Larna saw my chest, she gasped—not because she thought I was in phenomenal shape or anything, but because of the nasty bruise across my ribcage and chest.

She jumped up in distress once again.

"Hazards of the j-o-b," I told her, spelling out the last word.

Because Larna had lost my duffel bag on the climb up the cliff to the caves, I had been generously supplied with all-new clothing. I perused the outfits that were all neatly folded in a sleek dresser inlaid in the wall. There was only stuff that would make me look like I was a sixties cover band lead singer—white robes and slacks and basic wrap shirts that tied at the waist. Eventually, I settled on throwing on one of their karate-looking gis. Once it was around my waist, I cinched the sash tight around me.

After getting comfortable on my bed, I grabbed an onion ring form the plate and pulled it apart before popping it into my mouth. "That old guy, Benny, threw blood all over my shirt. I think he's starting to like me ... *but* ..."

"I don't like the sound of that *but*," she said slowly.

I shook my head. "Nothing. I don't know—it was

weird. He's old and has dementia, right?" I pursed my lips in thought. "He said *they* are watching me."

Two tiny worry lines appeared in the center of her brow. "I think it's a safe bet that people *are* watching you—and you're right, he's got a few screws loose." After a moment's hesitation, she added, "Did you get any training in?"

"Yeah, you could say I did some sparring."

Larna let out a deep sigh. "Jeez, Corinth, I'm never leaving you alone again."

"Relax," I said. "The blade and I are coming to an understanding. I'm making some headway."

Larna threw herself down onto the bed beside me, grabbing an onion ring off my plate absently, as if she was so used to our normal habits that she had forgotten she didn't like food—or me. I watched as she nibbled at it in thought. Things seemed to be okay between us. Maybe we could make this work out, without it being awkward, I mean. Even with Larna knowing how I felt about her … *had* felt about her, I corrected.

"Well, that's good news at least," she said, bringing me back out of my thoughts.

I leaned back against the headboard, closing my eyes. "I get the weird feeling this dagger has a mind of its own. Maybe it's not a *thing* at all," I said faintly. "You had it in your possession for a while." I cracked an eye open to peer at her. "You ever get any weird vibes back then? After your dad gave it to you, I mean?"

One side of her face corkscrewed up as she seemed to consider what I'd asked. Finally she said, "Back before you took the blade for the first time—right after you confronted me about the compulsion not working on you." She nodded. "I grabbed it from underneath my bed and had this sudden urge that I needed to give it to you." She gazed off, seemingly far, far away, on another planet. "It's almost like there was something else inside me ..."

I sat up quickly. "*That.* That right there is what I'm talking about. It's a kind of weird intuition or pull or body snatching. I feel it too."

Larna spoke and it came out in a breathy exhale. "You do?" She looked as innocent and sweet as the day I met her all those years ago. Maybe she didn't think I would understand, because she was a vamp. For the first time in a long time, I felt the connection between us rekindle, like a frayed string being tied back together. That sense of being altered and forever changed was what had brought her and Al so close. Maybe we had more in common in that way than I first thought.

"How did it feel when you stabbed Gabriel?" she asked softly, picking at the batter on the onion. Even though we'd always been honest with one another, this seemed different. More vulnerable. She had never asked me this before. It was a topic of conversation we'd both shied away from for obvious reasons.

"It felt good." There was no hint of sarcasm like I normally let myself fall victim to. This time, I meant what I said, and she knew it. "But that doesn't mean I want to be the one to kill him."

Larna nodded, determination setting in her features. "Good. Because that's my j-o-b," she said, spelling out the last word like I'd done earlier.

We sat in comfortable silence for a while until I wrapped an arm around her shoulders, not trying to make a move, but because this had been our routine for as long as I could remember. The warmth of her skin against mine was electrifying. This time, though, instead of melting into me, she pulled away. When I glanced over at her, she was chewing on her bottom lip. It reminded me of the girl I'd grown up with, determined yet awkward in her shyness—one of the many qualities I loved about her.

She tossed her feet over the side of the bed and stood back up, suddenly looking uncomfortable.

I found myself staring at the ceiling because I couldn't look her in the eye. If I did, I might try and shake some sense into her. To make her see that things didn't have to change between us. The awkwardness settled around us again, as heavy as a wet blanket. I hated the fact that Al had come between us. I wanted her to be happy; that's what mattered. Why did Al get to take my best friend from me?

"You think what Dave said about him being an angel is true?" she asked, changing the subject and bringing me out of my musings.

After another long, uncomfortable silence, I said, "I do."

"We really need to find him," she said adamantly.

"I'm pretty sure he'll find me in my sleep. I think Dave is worried about this place being compromised—too many chances of being overheard. And now I am too."

Larna spoke in a measured tone. "I think you should try and get some rest. See if he comes back. This time, I'll be here to make sure no one tries to sneak into your room uninvited."

I leaned back on my elbows and whispered, "Go. I'll be okay."

What I actually meant was, "It hurts too much when you're around me."

Chapter 41

Larna

G ABRIEL'S ADMISSION OF WHY he'd turned me made my stomach churn. My father had died by his hand while he sat on a cure. I didn't know why I had the sudden urge to find the bastard, but that need was all-consuming and very imminent. I moved toward the door to my room and found Alastair there, blocking my path as if he could read my mind. For a moment, I could only blink back at him, wondering if he had done just that.

He raised an unyielding eyebrow at me as if to say, *I'm everywhere.*

"Can you keep an eye on Corinth for me? I … uh … have an errand I need to take care of." *Like killing Gabriel.*

Alastair's expression darkened and he crossed his arms over his chest. "Are you going to do something stupid I should worry about?"

We hadn't discussed my admission of love. I suddenly found myself worrying that maybe he didn't reciprocate those feelings. I studied him. He seemed more relaxed since the day Sarah had come crashing back into his life.

His blond hair was parted neatly down the side. The tension in his shoulders had lessoned too, and he had changed into a black motorcycle jacket and jeans. It was the same leather jacket he'd worn the night he broke me out of Gabriel's manor.

There was a second where I pictured us lounging in sweats and enjoying a normal evening watching movies … or maybe he'd read a book. He was a great listener. I thought fondly about how he let me prattle on about my childhood while we were at Nan's place. What I really wanted to know was if he loved me or not. The thought that he didn't feel the same as I did about him was almost enough to bring me to my knees.

Unfortunately, even though Alastair was on my mind, so was Gabriel—him being out there made me incredibly restless. I wanted to wipe that smug smirk off his face. Ever since I'd seen him, something felt off, like Gabriel had been searching for a missing piece of a puzzle his whole life, and I was that piece. I didn't want to see him again, but I *had* to. There was no choice in the matter. Something was pulling me toward him. Even now, I felt the powerful urge to find him. I kept telling myself these feelings stemmed from my desire to know why he needed Corinth's powers so badly. I couldn't take him being under the same roof as my father's killer. Even though I knew this situation was completely different, it was as if I'd been transported to his manor all over again.

Alastair must have sensed the uneasiness in me, because he reached out and hauled me all the way into his room, the door closing softly behind him. His room was made up to look like an alpine ski lodge—cold and frost dusted and distinctly romantic. With a white fluffy comforter on his firm bed and a dizzying view of gorgeous ski slopes, it almost felt like we were on vacation. Almost.

My room was more tropical, with beachy themes and warm tones. I liked his better.

When he turned back to face me, his eyes seemed to pierce right through me like daggers. "What Gabriel said about Corinth loving you … is it true?"

My mouth dropped open and then I closed it, unsure what to say. Running a hand through my short hair, I ruffled it up on top in frustration, not caring how messy it looked. "I don't know … I think so. He won't come out and tell me …"

Seeing my face wrench, he took a few long strides across the room, and before I knew it, he was sweeping me up into his arms. It felt right and safe being in them. His shoulders were hard and corded in muscle. A soft moan escaped my lips as he pulled me tightly to him. He ran his fingers along my back and I shivered in pleasure.

"You always know when to hug me," I breathed against his ear.

He guided me to sit beside him on the end of the bed. "I understand if what you said back there about you loving me"—his eyes flickered down—"was just a ruse to get me to let Gabriel go," he said. "The last thing I want to do is get between you and Corinth."

Alastair's eyes were still cast down, but I could see the flash of hypnotic blue under his light-blond lashes. I reached a hand out, gently tilting his chin so that he was looking at me again.

"Are you thick?" I asked, frustrated. "I love you, Alastair Iszler. So much so that my heart feels like it's going to burst inside my chest. It would be an epic mess if that were to happen, but I am willing—"

Alastair crushed his lips against mine, effectively cutting me off as he hauled me closer, half lifting me from the bed, fisting his hands into my hair. I felt the desperation of teeth and tongue and lips meeting all at the same time. This wasn't a soft peck like back at St. Owens. If there had been a doubt over whether or not he loved me, it had now been extinguished. All of the added tension between us from the last few days melted away. I tried to pull him closer, my arms devouring every inch of his chest and arms and back, as if he could somehow fuse himself to my body. His tongue explored every inch of my mouth. I relished the feel of his smile against mine. A tug of pleasure rippled through me all the way down to the tips of my toes. I reveled at the way his hands, smoothing up and over my shoulders, felt on my skin—the way his chest heaved up and down against mine.

Being loved by someone—the need to protect and care for one another's feelings and well-being—was everything I thought I'd never have.

When we finally pulled apart, my cheeks tingled from the rush of blood. I put a hand to my mouth, speechless. Alastair's smile turned my insides to slush. Witnessing the amount of joy on his face was even better than the kiss. I'd never seen him so carefree. True happiness, if even for a second, was well worth all the heartache we'd been through together.

"I'm mad at you." He laughed softly as he brushed his lips lightly against my cheek. "I didn't get to say 'I love you' first." And then he was whispering those words against my forehead. "I love you. I love you. I love you."

Even though I wanted to live in this moment forever,

the ever-looming thought of Gabriel came crashing back to the forefront of my mind—a vivid and disturbing image of him pulling my pocketknife out of his neck hit me—

I staggered to my feet, pushing away from Alastair. *Why was he in my head?* I should be celebrating our love for one another, and here I was, thinking about Gabriel.

"What's going on?" he asked quickly, concern flashing across his handsome features. "Did I do something wrong?"

I reached a hand out and ran a finger lightly across his cheek. He closed his eyes as I said, "Never. You are decidedly way too perfect." I shook my head, trying to clear it of Gabriel. "All this stuff about a cure—we need to find it first. How is it administered? Lots of questions with no answers—and they all seem to reside within *Gabriel.*"

"I know you think you need to prove that he doesn't bother you, but he bothers *everyone,*" Alastair pointed out. "You don't have to put on a brave face for me. I promise I won't with you." He drew in a deep breath, his chest moving in time with mine. "You saw me make a colossal fool out of myself earlier. I have never been good at keeping my emotions in check around that guy." He locked his gaze on mine, and it was so full of hope and need and desire that I could only stand frozen in place, unable to look away from him even if I wanted to. "And admittedly, I have also not been able to communicate my feelings very well." His mouth set in a hard line. "You don't want a cure, do you?"

I searched his eyes, silently pleading for him to understand. "It doesn't matter what I want. What matters is what *they* want." I pointed to the door, indicating the outside world. "Once vampires find out there's a possible cure, what do you think will happen? Imagine all the vamps who don't want one. If word gets out that Corinth might be the key, someone who doesn't like that idea very much is going to try and kill him—or worse, use him. That's got to be why the angels are after him."

"So nothing's changed?" he remarked. "I think there might be a lot more vampires out there who want to be cured than you think."

"You want to be human?" I asked, surprise lacing my voice. It had never dawned on me. How could we be on opposite ends of the spectrum on this issue? It amazed me that he had even considered it.

He dropped his arms away from my shoulders, his blue eyes flicking to Corinth's closed door. "I want to be able to enjoy a normal life with my very stubborn girlfriend."

"You just used the g-word," I said. "What about Sarah?"

"What do you mean, what about Sarah? And technically, you used the l-word first—that usually comes after the g-word." Alastair seemed to put two and two together, and he raised a hand to his mouth as if finally understanding. "That's what's been bothering you? Sarah?"

I shrugged, unable to make eye contact with him. "She told me she liked you back when she first saw you. She's known you for a hundred years. I can't compete with that kind of history—I want that amount of time with you. It's all I've ever wanted."

Alastair pulled his watch out of his pocket—a constant reminder of his past, of what he'd been through. "We went through a traumatic experience together. I don't think I'll ever be able to let go of the guilt surrounding my lack of action that day. I can't even look Sarah in the face, because of it, so yeah, there are some unresolved issues between us, but I promise you, Larna, you and I still have an adventure ahead of us. No matter how much or little time is given to us, I can promise you one thing—it's going to be epic."

I reached up to touch his cheek gently, listening to the faint sound of snowfall through the portrait, committing the look of hope and longing in his eyes to memory. I wanted to remember that look on his face for the rest of my life.

He brushed his forehead against mine. I inhaled the scent of spice like aged scotch and leather.

"I don't think sweeter words have ever been spoken before," I whispered. It expressed my own sincerity for what he'd gone through. It told him I wasn't going anywhere and that I would see him through his own torment. "I am so sorry you had to go through that with Sarah. When you saw her alive for the first time, I'm sure it was quite the shock. I can't even imagine the pain you must have felt."

His chest heaved up and down, like a boat being swayed to and fro on a gentle ocean breeze. I found my own breath rising and falling, matching his in its spellbinding rhythm.

So softly I almost missed it, he said, "I thought I really had gone mad. That maybe she was a ghost coming to haunt me. After all this time, she was alive—and had escaped. I just never knew it."

He squeezed his eyes shut and a tear leaked out. I reached a hand up and brushed it away as he spoke. "Sarah is a cruel reminder of the worst day of my life. I know she doesn't mean it, but I can't bear to look at her even now. It hurts too much."

"I hate seeing you like this," I said. "You got your redemption. You know that, right? And you'll get it again. Maybe not today, maybe not tomorrow … but you *will*. Gabriel is going down." His eyes popped open as cold fury rose up inside me. "Trust me."

Chapter 42

Larna

I HEADED IN THE opposite direction of the wing our rooms were situated in—toward redemption.

Before I knew it, I was standing in front of a door with an oppressive weight settling in my chest.

I didn't need a map or someone to lead me to his room.

I'd been drawn to it since day one but had been refusing to acknowledge that compulsion until now. Knowing where it was without being shown meant the connection between us had been real. I'd just been denying it.

After speaking with Alastair though, something snapped inside me, like a string breaking on a tightly wound bow. Gabriel Stanton had to pay for what he'd done. Not just to me, but to everyone he'd hurt along the way. Whatever was going to happen was going to happen now. Alastair's pain was my pain, and I couldn't stand it any longer. Sometimes you had to protect your love no matter what the cost.

I took a deep steadying breath, trying to quell the

shaking of my hands. Then, with a determination that surprised me, raised a hand to knock, but before I could, the door slid open. I shouldn't have been surprised that he knew I was there, with the motion sensors in place, but as much as I had tried to steel myself against seeing Gabriel again, I still found that he rattled me.

Maybe it was that insufferable arrogant smirk of his.

The courage I'd built up seemed to drain out of me as soon as he stepped back so I could come inside, as if he knew I would be standing in this exact spot at this exact time.

I marched past him, resolute in appearing unafraid. I'd forgotten how tall he was. He looked to be either late twenties or early thirties, but looks were misleading; he could've been going on five thousand. Normally, the combination of high cheek-bones and bronzed skin would make a girl swoon. But those dark, soulless eyes only served to make him look that much more evil.

I stopped in the center of his ridiculously lavish bedroom as he shut the door behind him and swept back into the room, stopping in the hallway to lean causally against the door frame, arms crossed. The way he stood like that reminded me of the day he'd turned me. I felt the hairs on my arms start to rise and bile stir in the back of my throat.

He saw the chink in my armor, and his smile widened. Fear was a hard emotion to control. As far as bad ideas go, this one took the cake. It was too late to turn back now. The tug of self-doubt hit me—and also a tug of something else. It was partly the reason why I had finally decided to seek him out. I needed to stomp this feeling into the ground. Make it go away. Make *him* go away. I wondered if Alastair had felt something similar when Wrentmore had turned him. This was the only thing I felt I couldn't share with Alastair. I should have, but it was almost too much to even admit it to myself.

He waited for me to speak first, patiently giving me the floor. He was wearing that same damn expensive cologne. My skin crawled. I tried not to gag on the overpowering scent of it as he stepped closer.

I spoke past the sudden tightness in my throat, finding I couldn't tear my gaze away from his. "Tell me about the cure."

Gabriel chuckled, but there was no humor in it; he only looked wolfish and hungry. "You came alone," he whispered softly. "Considering you know what I can do... that was an incredibly bold move—especially for you. You're always hiding behind those boys." He tugged at the end of his jacket sleeve, where I knew his blades were hidden.

My blood started to boil. What he didn't know was that I had my father's blades tucked away too. I also had the small knife Alastair had given me, the one I'd stabbed him in the neck with the night he turned me. I thought about which weapon I'd use on him—

"And your entourage isn't outside, waiting to beat the door down?" He put a hand to his chin in thought. "I wonder why that is." His soft laugh was grating. "Is it because you felt the connection, like I did?"

I was about to ask him so many other questions, but this one sentence gave me pause. He knew he had my attention. "What connection?" I asked.

His eyes gleamed coldly back at me. "Someone such as myself"—he opened his arms wide—"is a lot more powerful than your average *ascended* being ... If you're at ground zero of a catastrophic event, you're bound to suffer the most damage. And in your case, you suffered ... a lot ... Of course, in this scenario, *suffer* means 'power.'" He said, "You're powerful beyond measure—you're welcome."

I felt pale and sick to my stomach as comprehension started to dawn on me. Would I always be drawn to him in this way? I wouldn't let that happen—I would kill him first. It was the only thing that made sense. If I did, it would mean the connection would be severed. It was why I'd come here in the first place. He was just giving me another reason. I felt the twinge of anticipation as the hidden blades on my forearms responded to the threat of violence.

I'm not sure if I was able to successfully hide the revulsion on my face, but I tried to keep it as stony as possible when I spoke. "I know you want this cure just as badly as Corinth does. Why?"

There was no arguing or avoidance; he looked me square in the eyes and said, "If I tell you, will you do whatever it takes to help me get it?"

Why was he so eager to have my help? It was Corinth he needed. Why did I feel this connection with him?

I should have considered my options more cautiously before saying, "If you can promise me that you'll leave Corinth and his family alone, and Alastair—let them be for good—then yes, I will help you get it."

He actually looked relieved, which was saying something, because I had never seen that look cross his face before.

"That's good ... team-work, Larna. I like it."

"You and I are finished after this. You leave us in peace—*all* of us." I crossed my arms over my chest and growled, "Do I have your word?"

"If that's what you want. But something tells me it's not." He ambled over to the minibar, unconcerned about turning his back to me. I had the opportunity to take him out right here and now. The thin blades at my wrists itched to be released. *Use them. Take him out once and for all.* Something stayed my hand—and then the opportunity was gone, as he was already turning back to face me. *Why did I hesitate?*

"Would you like a drink?" he asked smoothly.

Before I could tell him no, he was closing the distance between us. I accepted the proffered glass, and his finger brushed mine. The sudden contact was jarring and unexpected. It sent a shiver up my spine. This was somehow familiar, like a dream I had once. I didn't like feeling so out of control.

I tipped the drink back, swallowing it down in one gulp. He finished his and left me to refill it. When he was done, he sat down on the end of the bed, his legs crossed. "We both know why you're really here. What I told you back at the manor before I turned you. It's all true. You've gained strength, power—*control.* People wish they were you. Men fight over you. I know you don't want to give all that up …" He let the sentence hang in the air, an offer to join him, as if he'd known this moment would present itself once again.

I laughed at his audacity and the fact that he thought he knew me. How wrong he was. "You really are certifiable. You know nothing about me. You can choke on that silver tongue of yours," I hissed. "Tell me about this cure, now."

He moved as quickly as a lightning strike, past my defenses and into my personal space before I could react, his breath hitting the side of my cheek. "I know what you really want." Gabriel's eyes flew to my hand and then to the object resting in it. "Here's your chance to strike me down." I didn't even realize I'd palmed the bone handled knife until he was pulling it from my grasp. "This is why you're here," he said, disappointment lacing his voice. "To kill me."

He set his drink down first and then threw my knife to the bed, unconcerned. I watched him tear his jacket off and then his tie. His vest went next, and by the time I knew what he was doing, he had tugged his shirt off. Seeing his show had had the proper effect on me, he plucked my knife back up into his grasp, and held it out at the same time as I flicked my wrists down, ejecting the hidden blades. They slid free with a menacing click.

He barked out a laugh in mild amusement as his eyes glided to the thin blades at both my wrists.

"You better have a damn good reason for doing that"—I gestured to his bare chest, my blades glinting with lethal intent—"because whatever you think is going to happen—*won't*."

His chest was smooth, and surprisingly, well-defined abs lined his stomach instead of dragon scales, which I had thought might have been the case. A vambrace was attached to each of his wrists—much like my own. Seeing him with those devices brought back visions of my father, and it was enough to tear me out of my rage.

Gabriel rolled his eyes at seeing my violent reaction to him taking his shirt off. "Don't flatter yourself."

Unable to tear my eyes away, he spun around, and I was instantly drawn to the scar on his lower back. Corinth had stabbed him almost a year ago. A thick layer of disfigured scar tissue stood out starkly against copper-colored skin. The cut must have been a nasty one because it curved down along the edge of his spine, ending at his lower back and then disappearing below his waistline.

Gabriel let me get an eyeful before finally turning back to face me. He glanced at the armor on my forearms again. "I see you have your father's flair. Go ahead, now's your chance." His eyes flicked to my pocketknife in his outstretched hand. It had been gifted to me by Alastair—and seeing it in his clutches infuriated me. "Even as strong as I am … Corinth can still kill me. And I need him on my … *our* side," he corrected. "You can eliminate me right now and I won't fight you, but then you won't get the answers you so desperately seek. I only wish to protect him, much like you."

My eyes darted to the knife in his outstretched hand. "As much as I so desperately want to end you right now—why would you offer me the chance? Why now?"

"A leopard never changes its spots, Miss Collins. I dare-say I am disappointed you didn't take your chance when I gave it to you." He threw my knife back onto the bed when I wouldn't take it, and then slowly pulled his shirt back on, methodically buttoning it back up. "Have you heard of Thermopylae?"

I glared at him, uncertain where he was going with this, until I finally decided to hear him out. "Isn't that the place where the Spartans held off the Persians or something? Three hundred Spartans, right?"

"It was more like a few thousand Persians, and it

wasn't just Spartans, but, yeah, essentially. Before I was Gabriel Stanton, I was Ephialtes." He strolled back to grab his drink, seemingly lost in a memory from the past. I hoped they haunted him as much as he haunted me. "I haven't spoken that name in a very long time," he said slowly.

My mouth dropped open. If what he was telling me was true, he was extremely, extremely old—we're talking ancient. How long ago had that taken place? Over two thousand years? I couldn't even fathom living that long. I knew I shouldn't believe a word of what he was telling me, but I could see the truth in his eyes and hear it in his voice.

"Have you heard that name before?" he asked, carefully studying me.

I expected to recognize him from some history book I'd read in school, or maybe recognize the name he'd given: Ephialtes, but nothing came to the forefront of my memory. "Let me guess, you're the lead singer of a heavy metal band?"

"I am the son of Eurydemus." He glanced down, and I caught his eyes churning with his *Sight*—stony and impenetrable—a radical change from ink black to luminous blue. I stepped back, suddenly wary that he might try and compel me.

"So you're telling me you were around for the freaking battle of the Spartans. *The* Spartans?" I asked slowly.

He took a sip of his drink, eyeing me with glowing eyes over the rim of his cup. "I betrayed a lot of people that day to secure my own fortune and future. I've always been out for number one. *That's* who I love," he said. "That's who I am. You're like me. I can see it in your eyes. And there will come a time in the future when you'll need to decide how much you need me."

There was a tiny moment's hesitation right before I knew what he was going to do. It was the way he looked at me from under hooded brows—Red Riding Hood meets the Big Bad Wolf. Except I was the Big Bad Wolf in this scenario—he just didn't know it yet. I could feel the strange bond linking us together. This time, though, I didn't resist it.

"You wanted to test me—see if your theory was right, that I wouldn't kill you when given the chance," I said. "You feel it too?"

"You and I are connected."

Why didn't I kill him? I knew I'd never get the chance to again. The urge had fled me the moment he'd opened the door. I don't know why I did it, but I retracted the thin blades back at my wrists with a tap of a button. They locked into place, and as soon as he heard the ominous click, he struck—

Ice-cold hands wrapped around my throat. With dread, I realized he was going to compel me or kill me. He wouldn't let me keep so much information about himself. *This* very thing had been a possibility even before I opened the door, and I knew it.

His eyes sliced right through my resolve. An image of Alastair flashed across my vision. He was warning me not to go see Gabriel by myself.

My own eyes flared as cold and unforgiving as his, my *Sight* working in overdrive. I concentrated on the pungent smell of whiskey on his breath, on the expensive cologne he wore, and his overly starched shirt. I used these things to ground me. It would have been so easy to let him take over—

succumb to the feeling of oblivion … so easy, except …

I heard the sound of my father's voice. He was telling me to take him down—to fight with everything I had in me, to flick the blades free again. In a fight to the death with a two-thousand-year-old vampire, I knew I would lose. Gabriel was stronger, and to prove my point, his hands clamped down tighter on my throat, to the point where it hurt to even draw in a breath. But I was a nerd. Nerds are smart because we had to be. Mental fortitude and mind-set are worth their weight in gold.

"You will do exactly as I say," Gabriel cooed, trying to dig into my head like a tick. I could feel the magnetic pull, the way he tried to slide into my thoughts and feelings like rolling fog in a storm.

Sweat popped up on my forehead, and I hissed, "*NO.*"

Deep in the bowels of his mind, I curled around a shard of memory and clung to it as if my life depended on it. And then I couldn't separate my own memories and thoughts from his. His fears, desires, and manifestations hit me like a high voltage shock—flashes of images soaring through my mind—both he and I were connected to each other, as potent as a current of electricity. I couldn't tell if he was screaming or if it was me. It sounded strangely foreign to my own ears. I thought about the night he had turned me—the feeling of being doused in gasoline and lit on fire. This is what that felt like.

Fear swelled up inside me, and in a weird twist of fate, I felt him cringe.

And then an image did come into focus, my memories unraveling like a ribbon as I saw my dad teaching me how to hold a gun, a proud look on his face: my dad pushing me on a swing; dancing with my mom … Flashes of images fired through my head. I caught snippets of things that sent my heart soaring—like a vision of Corinth sprawled out across a picnic blanket on my mother's lawn. We were both grinning ear to ear at each other, pointing at the stars hanging overhead … and then it vanished, replaced by Alastair kissing me—the last kiss we'd shared—his lips moving fervently over mine, his hands winding into my hair. The feel of his heartbeat drove a hard rhythm against my chest. Everything was distorted, and when I came out of it, I was doubled over and panting.

The slight reprieve didn't last long.

An explosion of colors and light flooded my senses as a strange and unfamiliar memory crossed my vision: Gabriel standing atop a grassy hill, holding a short sword in hand. He was wearing armor and chain mail, and he looked glorious and fierce and not at all well-put together. The lines around his face were smooth. He looked considerably younger—my age. The vision swirled and changed—this time showing Gabriel holding an old woman's hand, aged by time. Blue veins stood out against bronzed and weathered papery skin. The woman shared Gabriel's stern inkblot eyes. She had been kissed by the sun many times over, the wrinkles around her eyes and mouth deep-set. Tears poured down his face, dampening long, dark eyelashes as he gazed down lovingly at the woman dying in his arms. I don't know how I knew she was dying, but I did. This was his mother. A strong feeling of love and remorse washed over me.

I tasted salt as I came fully out of my trance—and I realized the salt had come from fresh tears running down my face.

Gabriel looked just as shocked as he dropped his hands from around my neck and collapsed to the floor in complete exhaustion. His face had gone a shade paler. He had one hand cradled against an already rapidly healing cut at his collarbone, blood seeping through his expensive shirt. With the other hand, he traced a finger along his lips, seemingly lost in his own head. Something told me he hadn't revisited his own memories in a long time.

At first I wondered how he'd been injured, and then slowly the all-encompassing fog started to lift. I glanced down to the ejected blade on my vambrace. Somehow, during our struggle, I'd released one of them. I slid the knife back into place, swiping a hand under my nose. When I pulled it back, I noticed it was slick with blood.

We fell silent, and in the quiet, I could hear Gabriel's heart hammering against his ribcage. I finally managed to look him in the face, and what I saw surprised me. His black eyes weren't soulless; they were full of shock and sorrow and emotion.

Chapter 43

Larna

"ARE YOU—COMPELLED?" I rasped, my mouth going suddenly dry. "Tell me everything about the cure... *now*."

I could tell he was still trying to shake off the last few remnants of our connection. "Nice try," he panted, his breathing ragged. "It didn't stick—you're still not strong enough for that."

Intending to leave, I picked my knife up from the bed, but when I tried to stand, I found my legs no longer capable of supporting me. I hadn't managed to compel him, but I had somehow thwarted his attempt at compulsion. Even more surprising, Gabriel had a mother. I'd always imagined he'd been the exception to the rule—having grown up as a troll under a bridge or something. He had had a family at one point in time, and I'd tapped into one of his reveries. Knowing his heart wasn't completely devoid of compassion seemed to bother me more. I bit the side of my cheek, hoping the pain would help clear my head. *He wasn't human. He didn't feel.* He *was a killer.* I couldn't let myself believe he wasn't anything other than a monster.

"Well, that explains why you were so drained the night you turned me," I said slowly, shaking my head. "That's how I was able to stab you in the neck. You were weak."

For once in his life, Gabriel wasn't one step ahead, because he seemed unsure about what to say or how to proceed next. There was no way he'd seen this coming. I was equally horrified and fascinated by what had transpired between us.

He pulled his hand away and glanced at the red on his fingertips. "It is safe to say you were able to stab me again. I saw something I didn't want to ..." He let the sentence trail off, clearing his throat and then lightly, as if he thought he might burn himself, traced a finger along his lips. I could see the way his eyes darted back and forth, exploring the edge of a memory—possibly the one where I'd shared a kiss with Alastair. It was intensely personal, and extremely embarrassing that my mortal enemy had witnessed something so tender and heartfelt.

I felt the blood rush to my cheeks at the thought. That memory wasn't his—he couldn't have it—yet I was pretty sure he had stolen it.

I gathered what little strength I had left, my limbs heavy, and stood, standing regally tall. "Still strong enough to beat you." I shuffled to the door to jam my thumb against it. A light flashed red: access denied, I guessed.

Gabriel had locked me in. Big mistake. When I turned back to him though, I could see he was rubbing a hand across his brow and looking decidedly a lot less threatening than when I'd first entered his room.

I narrowed my eyes, vehemently hissing, "Open the door."

He put an elbow on his knee, but made no move to stand back up. "You weren't coded to my guest list," he said, still breathless. "Give me a moment."

I whirled back around, suddenly needing to know the answer to the questions that burned so deeply inside me. This would be the only opportunity I would have to pry it out of him. "Compelling me was your brilliant plan? Well, tell me, Gabriel," I said, "how does failure feel?"

This man who had lived for thousands of years, who had been in battles I couldn't even imagine and dealt with foes more powerful than anyone I could conceive, was looking at me with the tiniest bit of—impossible—*respect*. We had seen into each other's minds. I knew more about him than I cared to admit now. He'd seen some of my best moments on this planet, a shared kiss with Alastair after our declaration of love to each other … and I saw a fraction of his pain and vulnerability—one of *his* worst. I didn't like it. Sharing hidden, surreptitious thoughts and emotions; empathy, it wasn't meant for anyone else. It was invasive and terrifying and eye opening.

Something else had occurred between us when our minds had been locked. I saw myself in his eyes, touching on a foreign feeling of fondness—*for me*. I could never forgive him for murdering my father, but a tiny part of me understood him better now.

Gabriel, having sufficiently recovered, got slowly back to his feet and met me at the door. When he brushed past me this time, his touch didn't feel as vile or repulsive as it once had before.

Chapter 44

Corinth

I NOW HAD IN my possession a keycard that looked exactly like mine, except this one was already programmed to my thumbprint—and it opened Gabe's room. John had come through for me. Did I want to risk being caught? Hell yes, if it meant getting answers. I was ready to get back home and see my family again. What I wouldn't do to hug my brothers and sister. As much as they annoyed me, I still missed them. I knew the people here must have some way to connect to the internet or have access to a phone, but I hadn't gotten around to calling them just yet. For now, the outside world could wait.

After John and gang had told me where to find Gabe's room, I had casually made my way there, making sure I hadn't been followed by my security detail—Thor and Luke Cage. It had been easy giving them the slip with the help of John, who had been more than happy to assist in anything that required covert operations. I ended up losing them in the labyrinthine bowels of Kitchen A—in a maze of steel and high-grade-looking equipment that helped camouflage my movements.

I had changed into my freshly laundered jeans and a black T-shirt, all dark clothing, because that's what they did in the movies (if you were planning on breaking and entering), except I also had on my Converse—they were red stealth with a side of flair.

When I chanced a glimpse around the corner in the direction of Gabe's room though, nothing could prepare me for what I saw: Larna sneaking out of his room. *What the holy hell.* She threw a guarded glance over one shoulder, and I almost let out a startled cry in surprise. *No, no, no, no … Gabe must have gotten to her. Please don't let her be compelled. What are you doing, Larna?*

What if she was doing what I was doing? Beating me into breaking in to Gabe's quarters? Maybe he wasn't there. I clenched my fists down by my side, drew in a deep breath, and was ready to give chase—but as soon as I took one step around the corner, I saw Gabe slither out of his room. My heart gave a lurch. I watched, momentarily frozen in fear and shock, as he headed in the opposite direction Larna had gone in—straight for me.

It only took me a moment to recover as I ducked back around the corner. And then I was moving, arms and legs pumping as I bolted down the hallway to sprint into an open classroom I had passed earlier. I needed to take a second to gather my bearings, to figure out a game plan. What I really wanted to do was introduce Gabe to my blade, but I wasn't sure what he'd done to Larna. I had a fleeting thought that this would be the perfect opportunity to search his room, but everything in my being screamed to go make sure she was okay first. *How did he get to her?* When I fell inside the classroom, I felt the eyes of a hundred people turning to stare openmouthed at me.

Panting and out of breath, I grabbed my side, gesturing awkwardly at the door I'd just come through. "This isn't the bathroom," I said loudly as the instructor, a gawky-looking teen with glasses sitting on the very edge of his nose, stopped talking to stare at me.

After another awkward, everlasting second passed, I flashed everyone a wide grin and then flung myself back outside, fearing Gabe would walk right into me. Instead, to my great relief, I was only met by an empty hallway. Following Larna was out of the question right now. I tried to think through my options: *Larna is incredibly strong. If she's compelled and I try to confront her, she'll kill me.* I needed Al's help for an intervention.

Making sure the halls were clear, I tiptoed back to Gabe's room. A plaque on the wall read "A7"—exactly where John had told me to go. Holding my breath, I stuck my thumb against the side of the plain, smooth wall. When the light turned green and the door slid open, I expelled the breath I'd been holding and stepped inside. Irwin and John hadn't failed me.

The door closed with an ominously soft click behind me.

There was something to be said about the amount of adrenaline pumping through me at the prospect of getting caught. My hand hovered near the hilt of my blade just in case Gabe came sauntering back. At a glance, his room was way more extravagant than mine. No cool landscape with picturesque scenery adorned his wall though, unless he'd hidden it from view, which wouldn't surprise me in the least. Soulless guy like him probably didn't enjoy anything that evoked emotion.

He did have a minibar. Why didn't I have access to a minibar?

High-priced wingtips lined the inside of the closet. All of his suits were neatly pressed and hanging inside plastic zippered laundry bags. Ties were arranged by color, design, and thickness; even his socks were intricately matched and sorted by color. I rolled my eyes, thinking about how he probably had a matching diamond track suit tucked away somewhere. Douche level: premium membership.

The medicine cabinet proved to reveal more of his douchey-smelling cologne, a tiny gold bottle that, no joke, read: "Most expensive perfume in the world, created using the rarest and most precious natural ingredients." I wondered if the ingredients were soap and water. People spent an arm and a leg just for the little gold bottle … not what was actually on the inside. I sniffed the cap and scrunched up my nose. Gross. 'Eau de *toilet*.

Every other lavish-looking hair product or lotion was written in French or another language. I bet his toilet paper was made out of gold. I checked. It wasn't.

There was nothing of interest in any of his drawers, except for a gray-colored keycard with a purple stripe across it. I wondered why he would keep this lying around. Maybe he'd coded it to his own fingerprint … or maybe he hadn't yet, and this would give me access to somewhere highly restricted and private. I pocketed it and then hurried through the rest of my search, only finding a laptop and an old Bible. Pulling the laptop open, I noticed the screen was locked and password protected. Being a computer whiz, I felt pretty sure I could crack it, but it would take too much time, and I didn't want to be caught red-handed. He would be much more likely to report a stolen laptop than a keycard that he probably stole in the first place.

The rest of the room was unnaturally unlived in.

I really wanted to cut into his pillows, unscrew electrical sockets, look in the vents, but when I heard a knock on the door, I nearly jumped out of my own skin.

My face creased with sudden fear. I threw a hand to the blade's hilt, feeling the power surge through me. Gabe was back—except, why would he knock on his own door? With a racing heart, I took a tiny step forward, my hands suddenly clammy. When the knock came again, more insistent this time, I shuffled closer to see that the display screen was lit up. Al was there, standing on the other side with a scowl on his face, and he was glancing around as if afraid of being caught. I pressed my hand against the door and it instantly zipped open. Without another word, I ushered Al inside.

"Why in the world are you in Gabriel's room?" he hissed, not sounding surprised I was here in the first place.

"What are you doing here?" I countered right back.

"I followed you," he said simply, as if I should have seen this coming.

"So you know about Larna?"

A muscle ticked along his jawline before he slowly said, "What about Larna?"

"How much did you see?" I asked, careful not to give away too much information just in case Gabe had gotten to him.

He shrugged. "I saw you give your detail the slip; figured I'd better keep an eye on you. It took me a while to catch back up and find the right room. I showed up right when you were running from Gabriel, and then I looped back around in time to see you sneaking into his room."

"Oh boy." I glanced over to two lip-stained glasses on the table next to the bed. One glass was half-full, and the other one was empty. "Now, don't get mad, okay—" I swallowed hard "—but I saw her leaving Gabe's room … He left right after Larna, Al." I grimaced. "He was here with her."

Al's knuckles turned white as he squeezed them into tight fists by his sides. His eyes darted back to the two glasses near the bedside table as understanding dawned on him. "I really hate Gabriel Stanton." He murmured hoarsely, "You think she's been compelled?"

I let out a loud sigh. "What do you think?"

He started pacing; I noticed his face looked more drawn than when he'd first slipped into Gabe's room. "Did you find anything of interest?"

I started to shake my head no but then remembered the card. I yanked it out of my pocket and held it out for him to see. "Any guesses on what this might open?"

Al shook his head. "No. But we need to get out of here. Who knows what Gabriel has planned? Larna could be in a lot of trouble." His face screwed up in concern as I stepped over to him.

He looked so despondent that I found myself reaching out to put a reassuring hand on his shoulder. "Breathe," I told him. "Whatever you think happened in here—*didn't*." I glanced to the immaculately still-made bed and nodded toward it. "That's not Gabe's style. He'd rather program her to stab you in your sleep or something. He hates you because you're the anomaly—the wild card in his well-thought-out plans," I insisted. "You would be his next target."

"That's not comforting!" he snapped.

I shrugged. "Besides, Larna would never let that creep touch her."

Al's eyes snapped to mine and there was worry in them. "Not unless he compelled her."

"If she has been compelled, she'll try to go for my blade. It's what Gabe wants." I raked a hand through my hair. "I wasn't sure you weren't compromised. To be honest, my brain is fried."

"You could use your reverse compulsion on her," he said finally.

"If you haven't noticed, she's pretty strong. If she even thinks I'd try that on her—and she is compelled—she'll kill me. She knows what's in my bag of tricks."

He nodded, his lips set in a hard line. "This is my fault. I pushed her into it. I confided something to her—" his voice cracked "—and she went after him." He shook his head in desperation and at a loss for what to do next. I could tell he was just as frazzled as I was—maybe more so. But there seemed to be something else bothering him. I didn't push him about it yet though.

Al put his hand on my arm and caught my gaze. His eyes were steely and such a startling shade of sky blue that I'm sure they would blind anyone not prepared for it. "I know we haven't always seen eye to eye, but if Larna *is* compelled, we have to deal with it. Now." He cast a glance down, and I noticed he wasn't an impenetrable wall of stony indifference. I could see the emotion etched onto his face. "I can't do this without you—and to be honest, I don't want to." He murmured, "*Brother.*"

I was taken aback by his honesty and calling me brother. I'd never seen him so open before. Hearing him admit that he needed my help was unexpected. He wasn't such a bad guy after all. And suddenly it hit me: he loved Larna just as much as I did. When it came right down to it, she was our commonality. The need to fiercely protect her was ingrained in both of us. I felt closer to him than ever before. Of course, I'd never admit that to him; he wore his emotions on his shirt-sleeve—I didn't.

"I guess if Larna had to end up with anyone—I'm okay that it's with you." I slapped him on the back. "You have my approval. Now let's go get your girl back, Lancelot."

"I don't need your approval," he said, but he was smiling all the same as he gave me a nod, and for the first time in a long time, he truly seemed at peace. A thought struck me that maybe he did care about ripping my friendship away from Larna.

That was love, man.

I flashed him a wide, lopsided grin. "I love it when we work together."

"Yeah, well, don't get used to it," he quipped. "You know, if word gets out about a possible cure, all those clans out there, hundreds of them, are going to be gunning for you."

The hairs on the back of my neck begin to rise at that thought. We both knew the seriousness of the situation. "So no added pressure, right?"

He barked out a laugh. "No added pressure."

Chapter 45

Corinth

W E WERE ON OUR way back to our rooms when I heard someone shout my name. Al was a bundle of nerves, stiff and on edge as I twirled around to look for the source of the voice. Sarah was curled up on a beautiful curve-backed chaise lounge across the corridor from our quarters. This particular chaise didn't look like it was made for comfort. She was squirming anxiously, as if she'd been sitting for too long. Wisps of hair corkscrewed out from the tie at the high bun on top of her head. It made her look that much younger than she already did.

She waved us over.

"Are you stalking me?" I teased.

Sarah slid her book bag down so we could join her. "If I said yes, are you going to run away?" Her voice trailed off as her eyes landed on Al. She tucked a stray curl behind an ear, and her cheeks reddened. "Hello, Alastair," she said shyly.

Alastair pursed his lips and glanced away, unable to make eye contact with her. He did manage to mumble a formal greeting. He was definitely uncomfortable. He felt like a downed live wire beside me, uncontained and unpredictable, bouncing on the balls of his feet. Al had always been levelheaded and surefooted; it was weird seeing him anything but. I knew he had to be as anxious as I was to find Larna.

"I'm not really the running-away type," I answered brazenly, bringing her attention back on me. I was hoping to spare Al any more scrutiny, but then I put a hand to my forehead in apology. "Except for right now, that is. How long have you been sitting here?" I asked quickly. "Have you seen Larna pass by? It's really important we find her."

She marked her place in the book she'd been reading and studied us more closely, a look of concern passing across her pretty features. "I've been here for over an hour. I knocked on the door—but I don't think she's in there." Her eyes darted back and forth between us. "Is everything okay?"

For the first time, I noticed how tired she looked. Her eyes were red rimmed and glassy, as if she'd pulled one too many late nights studying.

"Not really," I murmured. "We really have to find her right now."

"Should we cancel our plans tonight? Do you need help looking for her?"

"Maybe." I said, grimacing in regret. "Not that I would ever want to cancel plans on you … Just let me figure out what's going on first. If you do happen to see Larna, will you let me know as soon as possible?"

"Of course," she said without hesitation. "Anything I can do to help."

I inclined my head gratefully and then thought about

the card I'd pilfered from Gabe's room. Maybe she *could* help. I pulled the stolen keycard from my pocket, hoping I could trust her. "I would really like to know what this opens."

She leaned in closer to get a good look at it. Her eyes widened, and she gestured for me to put it away quickly, glancing around in concern.

I tucked it back into a pocket as she said, "It'll get you into any room besides Sozo's offices. You just code your thumbprint to it—" Her eyes scanned the hallway again, making sure we weren't being eavesdropped on. "This is probably how the intruder got into your room. That's access to top-level clearance," she whispered. "Where did you get it?"

"We should really be going," Al interrupted.

And then I remembered the dire situation of finding Larna once again, but Sarah was suddenly and unexpectedly standing in front of him, blocking his exit back to our rooms. His cheeks burned bright red as he studied the floor as if it held the answers to the universe.

Her vivid green eyes were pleading as she tried to catch his eye. "You've barely said two words to me since you got here." She put a hand on his arm, timidly. "Please, let's just talk..."

I suddenly felt like the odd man out, so I turned to head back to my room to give them privacy and noticed Al reach into his pocket. He pulled his pocket watch out. Even though I knew the timepiece was old, it didn't look it. The shiny silver detailing was polished to a bright shine. I noticed the delicate floral pattern winding its way around a white clock-face. It was a breathtaking watch, and to my surprise, the mechanism still worked—I could hear the metronome-like ticking as I passed by him, planning on going straight to my room.

Al opened Sarah's hand, placing it gently into her palm. The meaning of the gift was evident on Sarah's face as she closed her eyes. Tears streamed down her cheeks. I couldn't help but feel a stupid twinge of jealousy rise up in me. Al had the girl of his dreams already; he didn't have romantic feelings toward Sarah, but this moment seemed special.

I shoved my hands deep into my pockets, thinking about how that guy, Wrentmore, must have been a real monster—maybe worse than Gabe. But before I left them alone, Al was flying past me, inhuman speed at its finest as the wind whipped my hair into my eyes.

Sarah gazed down at the watch nestled in her hands. I turned back, noticing her eyebrows drawn together, a far-off look on her face. The tears had left a salt trail down both sides of her red nose.

Finding I couldn't leave her in such a state, I whispered, "Are you okay?"

She sniffed and then, as if remembering I was still there, glanced up, nodding. "Yeah … I'm okay. It's just been an emotional day." She seemed to come all the way out of her trance. "Go. Find your friend."

The connecting door to my room opened. I was met by exceedingly blue eyes and blond, disheveled hair. I assumed he'd been running his hands through it one too many times.

"No sign of her—" he started to say, but the sound of Larna's door sliding open stopped him cold.

We both shot to attention, flying to her room right as she walked in.

Surprise was the best element.

If she was compelled, there would be no talking her down. I felt my gut twist with anxiety as I gave Al a fleeting glance, and we both lunged for her.

Chapter 46

Larna

THE SUDDEN FLASH OF movement and the way Corinth and Alastair sprang forward caught me completely off guard.

Gob-smacked was more like it.

I could sense the change in ozone as Corinth's super-charged energy filled the room like an approaching thunderstorm in the wake of summer's heat wave. It was muggy and humid and thick in the air. I had no idea why they were coming at me. My first thought was they'd both been compelled. It was why I reacted without thinking. Alastair was at my back and Corinth was in front of me—Corinth would try and distract me while Alastair would go for the submission hold from behind, or quite possibly— the kill.

I'd been training with both of them long enough to know their techniques, especially Corinth—I jabbed out at him, a straight shot to the nose. Collapsing to a knee, tears sprang to Corinth's eyes right as Alastair dove at me from behind. He tried to latch onto both my arms, to pin them by my sides, but I saw it coming from a mile away. I ducked out from under his grasp as if I were made out of vapor, his fingers clutching at empty air.

Adrenaline and sheer terror tore through my veins, giving me an edge as I reached out, snatching Corinth's blade out of its scabbard—all in the span of a few seconds.

But it still wasn't fast enough.

I caught an elbow to the side of my jaw, a glancing blow that made everything around me swirl in a nauseating tableau of distortion. Even though a fog of dizziness hung over me, I still managed to execute a spinning back kick, in hopes Alastair was still behind me in the same spot. He was, and it caught him right in center mass, knocking him off-balance. He hit the faux window behind him, his arms pin-wheeling out in front of him as he fought to regain balance. The picturesque landscape of a tropical paradise shattered, shards of glass flew into his hair, neck, and down his back like raindrops. Damp blond hair curled around the edge of his collar.

I pointed the tip of the blade at Corinth, my mouth papery dry, sweat dripping into my eyes. *How has this spun so far out of control?* My heart beat wildly against my chest, not so much out of exertion but fear: fear of hurting them or vice versa. I knew one thing for sure, I definitely did not like being on the other end of Corinth's omnipotent power. White bolts of energy crackled out of his fingertips, the light bending to his will, changing and morphing into whatever shape, I assumed, he wanted it to—in this case, lightning—and it looked deadly, arcing wildly out of his palms, snapping in anticipation as if it had teeth.

His dark eyes glided to the dagger in my outstretched hand, and then darted up to meet mine. When they did, I noticed the swift change from dark brown to black, and then, in a flash, they were gone, completely hollowed out, replaced by flames flickering in empty sockets where eyes should have been, like the inside of a carved-out pumpkin.

Corinth shook his head, trying to control it—and he sort of did, his eyes sputtering back to reform into two puddle-filled irises.

We all went very still.

If these two had wanted to hurt me, they would have. It was the only reason I was still standing. I had to let my head clear before I could think things through. I was still extremely drained after my encounter with Gabriel—all I wanted to do was to collapse into a heap on the bed and sleep for a week.

Corinth spoke between labored breaths, "Holy … crap. You're … Hulk strong …" There was a glint of foreboding in his eyes, which I found heartening, because he had come back on his own this time. His voice sounded sure and solid and human. "Can you put my blade down, *sweetheart?*"

Alastair's eyes narrowed as he inched closer, a hand on his chest where I'd kicked him. "Larna …" he rasped, "we know you went to see Gabriel …"

Glancing between them, I said, "Oh—*crap.*" My eyes swiveled to Alastair's. "I know how it must look, Alastair," I croaked. "I went to his room to end him once and for all." I spread my hands out, tossing the dagger back onto the bed to show them I was still me. They shared a quick glance with each other, the conflicting emotion evident on their faces. "I am *not* compelled … I promise."

"Yeah, sure. You just went to Gabe's room by yourself willingly," Corinth scoffed.

"As a matter of fact, yes, I did." I met Alastair's

penetrating gaze, silently pleading him to understand. "It was stupid. I went there to confront him about a cure." I wanted to tell Alastair how his admission about Wrentmore and Sarah had spurred me into confronting Gabriel. "He tried to compel me—" My voice caught in my throat.

"*See!*" Corinth leapt for the blade on the bed; once it was in his grasp, he deftly spun it up into his palm to point it at me.

I inched forward, forcing Corinth to take a step back. "I stopped him," I said evenly. "Somehow, as unbelievable as it sounds … I *stopped* him. This is all me. I am in control." I pointed to my face, which I was sure was as pale as I felt. "Look at my face. I'm drained beyond exhaustion. I beat his compulsion. I am not Temple-of-Dooming y'all."

"Let me get this straight … *You* bested Gabriel Stanton?" Corinth laughed incredulously. He might as well have said, "'I don't believe you'." "Alastair couldn't even do that … How is that even possible?" he said in disbelief.

"He turned me, remember?" I murmured. "When he did, he transferred some of his strength to me." I lifted my shoulders. "I'm not even sure how it works."

Alastair, still looking warily between us, said, "I don't know. It's not entirely out of the realm of possibility."

Corinth lowered the tip of his blade an inch. "Are you sure he didn't just try and convince you to say that?" he said. "And, *gross*—I bet his mind was foul."

"I want to take a bath in acid." I shuddered. "I'm sorry. I owe you both an apology. My hotheadedness won over and I went after him by myself. Please believe me …

my thoughts and mind are still my own."

"You realize I still need to make sure—to use my anti-*Sight* on you to verify."

I nodded. "Fine. If it convinces you, I'll do it."

After Corinth tested me and discovered I was telling the truth, I found myself back in Alastair's room. We were finally alone. Alastair had been oddly quiet ever since he'd found out I went to see Gabriel by myself. He stared intently out at the wintry wonderland through the fake window as if he contemplated stepping right through it. Alastair's hands were fisted by his sides, and his shoulders were squared and tight with tension. I knew he was angry and I didn't blame him.

"You went to his room *alone?*" Alastair whirled around to confront me. "He could have killed you. If he *had* compelled you, just think what he would have made you do. There are an infinite number of possibilities, and each one of them gives me the hives."

I pulled the covers back on his bed and hopped under them, feeling wiped after the effects of the fight and the battle of the minds with Gabriel. It was all I could do to keep my eyes open. It had been a rough twenty-four hours. I craved sleep more than anything else. The crisp, cool sheets lulled me into a rapidly declining state of consciousness.

I stared sleepily up at him, the covers pulled up to my chin. "After what you told me about Sarah—I had to, Alastair. He's a monster—like Wrentmore—and he needs to be stopped. If I'd had the strength, I would've made him tell me everything about the cure, but it was all I could do to get out of his room in one piece. I know how disappointed you are." I felt some of the fire in me return. "Let me help you."

Alastair joined me on the bed, letting out a deep sigh and when he spoke, there was a hint of fire in his voice. "I don't need help. And you don't get to use Wrentmore against me like that."

I glanced away from him. "Everyone needs help sometimes, whether they know it or not," I whispered. "Gabriel *has* to be stopped."

He curled up beside me, wrapping an arm around my shoulder. The warmth of his body against mine was most welcome. "I was worried about you. If he did anything—" His voice broke and he cleared his throat. "I don't know what I would do. You're everything to me." He turned his head to look me in the eyes. The intensity with which he was staring at me made my heart flutter.

He nuzzled my neck with his chin. "I kind of need you around."

I let my head fall into the crook of his arm and said drowsily, "That day we met for the first time, outside of the library in Bromham—seems so long ago." I thought about my encounter with Gabriel again and my pulse quickened. Suddenly overcome with emotion, I said, "It was horrible—being an unwilling witness to his memories. There was so much sorrow in them." I felt the icy finger of a shiver run down my spine. "And a sense of emptiness, the likes of which I've never felt before, but past all that ... Gabriel seemed ..." I paused, unable to vocally bring to light the rest of my confession. If I told him this, what would he think of me? How would he react?

Alastair, sensing my distress, pulled me tighter against

him. I could hear the curiosity mingled with concern in his voice. "What is it?"

"I don't know … Gabriel seemed almost … *human*. I saw that part of him that had been buried for so long; it's how I was able to break free of his hold, and that's what really bothers me—what if I did the same to him?" The more I talked, the more the truth came spilling out of me, like a dam bursting at the seams. The burning desire to get this off my chest was too much. "I think he witnessed a memory of you and I sharing a kiss." I stared down at my hands, unable to meet his eyes any longer. "He showed me his scar … the one Corinth gave him after he stabbed him in the back."

I felt Alastair stiffen beside me. "He showed you his scar?"

"Nothing happened," I said quickly, sitting up on an elbow, suddenly desperate to make sure he knew I was telling the truth.

"Oh, it is a damn good thing I wasn't there." His jaw tightened like impenetrable stone; he almost launched himself back off the bed in anger, but I grabbed his arm, lugging him back down beside me. "I'm going to end that guy," he growled.

"Gabriel wanted me to kill him with the pocketknife you gave me—but I couldn't bring myself to do it…" I broke off, rubbing the side of my neck absently. "After all the time we spent trying to find him—I just *froze*. It's like he's in my head and I can't do anything about it."

Alastair dropped his gaze from mine, but when he looked back up, his blue eyes were set with fiery determination. "I know what that's like," he said. "But don't forget, you're the one with all the power, and he knows it. It's why he's so focused on you. He doesn't care about me or Corinth … *or* the dagger. Not really. Maybe you tapped into his humanity and he's drawn to you like a magnet too … Sometimes the pain of an itch is worse than the itch itself." He kissed the backs of my knuckles in deep thought. I reveled in the feel of his smile against my hand as he whispered, "I can tell you one thing; after that spinning back kick you did earlier—I'd want you in my corner any day of the week."

My eyes slid shut and I smiled in contentment. Before I knew it, I was drifting on an endless wave of fatigue, utterly drained from the past few days. I was next to him and I was safe; that's all that mattered. With him beside me, we could face anything.

I let myself get washed away with thoughts of Alastair: the curve of his jawline; the way his forehead creased when he was brooding; how he hummed when he cooked; his incessant need to protect everyone. He was the silent ship in the storm and the unyielding anchor. I supposed when someone saves your life on more than one occasion, you tend to get a little attached.

Vulnerability was the best thing about getting close to someone, and also the hardest thing to give. I wanted this moment to last forever.

The sound of Alastair's voice brought me out of my semiconscious state. "What would you want to do with your life if we weren't in the middle of … well … all of this?" he asked quietly.

"I suppose go back to college, do something in the medical field, like my mom."

"Dr. Larna Collins has a nice ring to it." He whispered, "I think your father would have been proud of that choice … your mother, too."

He laid a hand on my head, and I sighed as his fingers wound their way into my hair. I felt a swell of pride hit me at knowing he was all mine and I was his.

I drifted off for a second and then I mumbled, "What about you?"

"A spy."

My eyes popped open, but when I shot him a glance, he had a teasing smirk on his face.

I hit his shoulder playfully. "You can cross that one off your list already."

He shrugged. "I don't know. I've been so wrapped up in taking down Gabriel, and before that, others just like him … that it never really occurred to me. I guess I wouldn't mind owning my own restaurant or a small bakery in France—" he twirled a lock of my hair between his fingers "—near the river."

"Hmmmm." I imagined him hunched over an old stove in the kitchen of some tiny bistro situated amongst a quaint boutique café, the birds soaring on a gentle breeze, the wind blowing off the waterfront. The smell of freshly baked bread seemed as tangible as anything I'd ever smelled.

I started drifting off, thinking about delicious pastry products and buns. He would be in the kitchen, kneading the bread shirtless … I wished I could have explored where else my mind was going with that image before I passed out, dead to the world.

Chapter 47

Corinth

HER EYES HAD FLECKS of brown in them. That's what made them shine like little jade jewels. Bright pink lips stood out against pale, freckled skin. I kept trying to discreetly stare at her when I thought she wasn't looking. It wasn't like I could take her to a steak house or a movie or a coffee shop—a jaunt to the medical wing was as close as it was going to get to a romantic evening. Did this count as a date? Larna was resting, and I had the chance to find out more about what these people were doing with my blood. It was a risk I had to take—and besides, I was in very capable hands with Sarah. She might have looked petite, but I felt pretty sure that if need be, she could pack a mean punch.

"This isn't exactly the spot I would pick for a first date—I mean, if you would consider this a date …" My voice drifted off as I looked around the lab in awe. There was a lot of sterile hi-tech equipment in here. "So, you don't have access to this part of the facility? Because I distinctly remember you saying you did."

Sarah met my quizzical gaze with an eyebrow raise, as

if to say, "Guilty as charged." "Only those with top security clearance have access to this level. But you have that nifty all-access keycard … so why not use it?"

These particular labs were situated on the floor below us. We had gained entrance to this level through a private elevator ride—one in which I had used the stolen card to access. The room we stood in was bleached to the nth degree and cold. It reminded me of being in a morgue or mortuary.

I gave her a small shrug. "I'm honored." I hoped it came out sounding cool and nonchalant, because on the inside I was cringing.

It was disturbing that they had squirreled away my blood, studying it without me knowing what they were doing with it. It seemed duplicitous, and because I'd been attacked on more than one occasion while here, not to mention warned not to trust anyone, it made it seem that much creepier. *What are they up to?* It made me wonder if Gabe had been down here. It would make sense, him having acquired this card I now possessed.

"You really know how to show a guy a good time— and not at all creepy in any way," I mumbled sardonically, tracing a finger across one of the steel surgical-looking tables to prove my point.

There was an expensive-looking microscope, Petri dishes, Erlenmeyer flasks, and jars filled with colorful unidentifiable liquids, along with medical masks, surgical gloves, and scalpels—all things that caused the hairs on the back of my neck to stand on end.

Sarah pulled herself up onto one of the empty tables and swung her legs out like a four-year-old on a swing, her eyes flicking downward. She pursed her lips, suddenly shy.

I couldn't help but notice the flyaway strands of hair tumbling free of the bun on top of her head. She looked almost angelic, sitting directly under an angled light that lit her up from behind.

When she didn't say anything, I said, "I'm sorry … I joke when I'm nervous."

"It's not that," she whispered so softly I almost missed it. "I just really like you."

Her admission both warmed and sent an ache of desire running through me. I'd thought I'd never be able to long for anyone else after Larna. So when these familiar stirrings came bubbling back to the surface, it surprised me in the best possible way. I glanced at her hands, planted beside her legs. It was chilly enough to leave a fine sheen of moisture around her fingertips, like a warm breath on a cold window. I wanted to swoop in for a kiss—the kiss that would end all—passionate, daring, and bold, except this sort of atmosphere wasn't exactly suitable for a make-out sesh. Being in this place gave me the willies. I wasn't good at reading signals. All of a sudden, I wasn't so cold anymore. I knew a moment when I felt one. But I let this one slip by me as I moved along the row of refrigerated shelving, pretending to be deeply interested in it. Realizing that this was where they kept my blood, I found I *was* deeply interested in it. I wound my way around another table to a refrigerated glass cabinet. Through the glass, I could read the labels on several vials.

I heard her voice echo hauntingly in the small room as my attention stayed locked on the vials. "Apparently, your blood is in high demand …"

My name was written on every single tube: "Corinth Taylor, white/male, 18yoa." That wasn't ominous at all. I tried to look for a handle to open the door and examine further, but couldn't find a way inside. When I turned to ask Sarah for help, I found myself nose to nose with her. I hadn't even heard her sneak up on me.

I sucked in a sharp breath. I could almost feel the soft pressure of her lips against mine, feel the chemistry bouncing between us. And then she was retreating, crossing to a closed door, to a part of the room that we hadn't been in.

"What you're looking for isn't 'in here," she said slowly, turning back to me. "Look, I'm not going to lie, a lot of us are curious about your blood—especially me. I'm a doctor, for crying out loud. It could be the cure to a lot of illnesses out there."

I didn't know what to think about that. Did she know about the rumors of a cure for vampirism?

She must have taken my silence for a bad thing, because she clarified, "I'll help you … if it convinces you that I'm not up to anything nefarious. This is my home. We aren't bad people."

"I wouldn't have come to you if I didn't trust you," I whispered. "But I have been attacked a few times since I've been here." I felt my mouth curve up on one side, along with the freshly applied butterfly strips holding the scabbed-over cuts together on my cheek. "You have to understand my reluctance isn't baseless. I just need your help in figuring all of this out … if you can help me find a cure—"

Before I knew it, she had my hand in hers. A prickling tingle went up my spine as she took my thumb in between her fingers and pressed it against the door. It whooshed open—all access granted thanks to the stolen keycard.

She shooed me inside first, and as soon as I got to the center of the room, I stopped dead in my tracks and froze, an icy dread welling up inside me.

There were rows and rows of ampules, and one of those chairs you'd see in a blood-donating facility. The kind you could stretch out on in case you felt the need to pass out. It looked nothing like the stretcher the bounty hunter had forced me onto; even so, it still reminded me of that day back in the warehouse. I shivered despite myself. Sarah was just as transfixed as I was, as she'd never been in this room before. Her mouth was gaping open as she slowly made her way toward one of the tables lining the far back wall. There were, like, a thousand microscope slides on top of the table, the kind like we used to use in biology class.

I gestured to them, my mouth slightly open. "Is that all my blood?"

She nodded. "It would appear so. Those are called blood films." Her overly bright green eyes slid to mine, wide in fascination. "What I wouldn't do to be able to study this more closely …"

"Hey … standing right here," I said, appalled. "I know I've said the word *creepy* a thousand times since we've been here … so I'll switch it up. It is incredibly *eerie* … being in a room filled with my blood. It's like *The Shining*, but a lot less cool."

She lifted a shoulder in apology. "Sorry. I just meant this would be so interesting … to see what answers your blood holds."

"Can you tell me what all this means?" I asked, casting another cautious glance around the room.

"It's like a blood panel you'd get at a doctor's office.

Kind of like when they check for blood count, disease, mineral count, glucose levels, cholesterol ..." She must have noticed the concerned look on my face, because she crossed to another table with a chart on top of it, her eyes skimming over the paper. "Don't worry; according to this chart, you don't have malaria."

I combed a hand through my hair, making it stand on end. "I guess that's good to know ... I get you're looking for a cure for cancer or something, but this makes me feel the teensiest bit uneasy. Did I tell you I hate needles?" Striding over to a machine in the corner of the room, I asked, "What's this one do?"

Sarah wandered over to a clipboard with more charts and papers to get a better glimpse of it. Preoccupied with reading, she said, "It reads for specific diseases by using cartridges packed with tiny beads of molecule coating."

I stopped to read over her shoulder, but the graphs and bar charts and numbers all looked Greek to me.

Her eyes glided over the paper as she flipped it to the next page. "These are fascinating results..."

I grinned nervously at her, thinking about winding up on the other side of that table as an unwilling volunteer. I kept hearing Imani's words repeated over and over again in my head: *Destined to be a lab rat for the rest of my days.*

It made me wonder if they did happen upon a cure for cancer, would these clan members really help humankind? Or would they use it to exploit us? Control us? Like the Grigori? Or were they searching for a cure of their own? I didn't know these people.

When I felt a cool hand on my arm, I jumped and swore under my breath in surprise. The contact was just as jarring as an exposed battery on bare skin. I hadn't realized how deep in thought I had been until she'd touched me.

"You're right—about me searching for a cure for cancer. Before you came along, I was working on breast cancer, specifically."

My mouth fell open slightly. "Did you find one?" I asked, stunned. "*Cancer*? I mean … seriously? That's huge."

She shrugged. "I felt like I was getting close. I wasn't getting anywhere with vampire blood … but with yours …" She let the sentence hang suggestively in the air as I circled the room, starting to feel queasy. It wasn't as if I didn't want to hear about her work—I did—it was just that concentrating on anything other than my blood in this overly sterilized place had become increasingly difficult.

I spun around in a circle. "Is that what this is all about? Or is something else going on here?"

Sarah's eyes flicked to mine and then darted back to the clipboard. There was a flicker of something in them, like a doctor trying to keep a neutral face in front of a terminal patient. I let her comb through the rest of the paperwork in silence. Maybe she could give me the answers I was looking for. This was why these people had invited me here. To be a living, breathing test subject; except, if that were true, I'd already be tied down to that chair in the center of the room. Al had told me it would be strictly voluntary.

My legs had unwittingly carried me to that very same chair that doubled for a torture device. I sank down to it on wobbly legs, suddenly overwhelmed. The cold leather hit the backs of my legs, seeping through my blue jeans. I didn't mind the frigid temps; it helped keep the feverish anxiety from taking over.

The blade seemed to sense my unease too, because it hummed in dangerous harmony against my thigh: *Danger, Will Robinson. Danger.*

"Think about how many lives we could save—*together...*" Sarah's voice seemed tiny and faraway.

I suddenly found myself in a daze as I looked up at her. "Are you asking me if I want to volunteer to be experimented on?"

I could sense her caution as she approached a sensitive topic of discussion. "Isn't that why you're here?" she asked slowly, carefully. "To help people?"

"Did you see something in those charts I need to know about?"

Sarah glanced to the dagger on my belt and then did something that surprised me: she ripped the paperwork from the clipboard, rolled it up, and tucked it into the back of her pants, hiding it. "I need more time to study this to be sure—and even then I don't have access to the full results ... but it looks very promising." She flashed me a teasing grin. "Big, bad, scary vampire hunter is afraid of needles?"

"I never said I was perfect or scary, or a *vampire* hunter, for that matter." I added, "And can we get out of here, please? Let's go someplace less *glacial* to go over everything. I need coffee and warmth and, most importantly, not to be here."

Sleep deprivation will do a lot to the human body. Such as hallucinations, memory impairment, mood swings. Take your pick. Currently my eyes were burning. With great reluctance, Sarah ushered me back to my room so I could get some rest while she went over the findings. She kept telling me I was only distracting her. It took everything I had to let her walk away with so much information about me. I couldn't drink any more caffeine for fear of turning into a coffee bean. And I had to trust someone who could read the scientific language in those reports.

Looking back, I realized I'd had maybe six hours of sleep in the last few days. It was not being able to shut my brain down. I didn't like feeling out of control. My attacker was still on the loose. Plus, I wanted to make sure I could make contact with Dave again. Maybe this time, I'd get some real answers.

After warning Larna and Al that I would be trying to get some shut-eye, I finally dragged myself over to the bed, throwing myself down on top of it in an exhausted heap.

I pressed the call button on the nightstand next, and Caesar promptly answered. "Yes, sir?"

"Hello, Caesar. I was wondering if you could do me a favor."

"I'm at your service, sir," he replied instantly.

"I'm about to sleep for a week … Is there any way you can lock my outer door? Make an alarm sound if anyone walks in or something? Can you do that? I don't want any surprises or unwanted guests in my room."

I heard a sudden rustle of material, as if he was fidgeting with the sleeves of his robe again, and then the outside of my door flashed a bright blue. "All done, sir. Just ring when you want me to unlock it."

His voice drifted through the line right before I lost consciousness. "But, please, sir, don't sleep for a week. That seems a bit excessive for a human."

I found myself smiling at Caesar's literalness as I

rolled over onto my side.

The last thing I heard was him telling me, "The guards are posted outside your door, sir. Pleasant dreams, sir."

"Thanks, Caesar. Good night," I mumbled.

I was still amazed that I had to look up at anyone. Dave was a giant. He looked like he'd just walked out of a 1970s beach ad, with bleached blond hair, tanned skin, and matching fedora.

I glanced around at our "usual" meeting spot in the open field. We were sitting atop a grassy hill in the same meadow. This guy was the essence of cool; he could get away with wearing sunglasses indoors.

"I have been trying to reach you," I said, stepping over to him immediately.

His eyes hardened around the edges. "I apologize," he said curtly. "Unfortunately, it has become harder to ward you from prying eyes; it would seem there are some spies within these very walls. I'm sorry about the intruder in your room. I had to wake you up before we finished our conversation." His eyes flicked to the cut on my cheek and my swollen nose. "Are you hurt badly?"

I cocked my head to the side. "Can you can heal me?"

He nodded. "I can—but it would take some of my protection from you. I am not as strong as I used to be …" He took his hat off and ran a hand through his hair. "Would you like for me to try?"

I shook my head. "No—" I ran a hand along my cheek. "It's just a minor inconvenience," I lied. "It'll heal. But thank you. And thank you for your protection …" I added, "I don't mean to rush you, but I need to know where this cure can be found."

Dave's golden eyes met mine. "What I am about to tell you might be hard to process." I snorted as if to say "duh", as he continued. "I have already told you about the Nephilim."

"Yeah—half human, half angel. I got that part. You said these offspring have been wiped out by the Grigori."

He nodded. "This war of ours has finally reached its apex."

"What does any of this have to do with me?" I pressed.

A faint smile played across his lips, but there was no humor in it, only a grim resolve at what he had to share with me. "We—*Watchers*—have found a way to fight the Grigori and give them a dose of their own medicine at the same time." He flicked a hand out, and my blade suddenly rested in his outstretched palm. I had to admit, it looked even better in his hands than it did in mine.

My mouth fell open. "Is that my blade?" I asked in awe. "Where did it come from?"

Dave raised an all-knowing eyebrow. "This dagger is more powerful than you can ever imagine. Seven of us poured our souls into this very blade. The Blood Dagger." He tested the weight and balance, nodding his approval as if he'd forgotten what it felt like to have it in his grip.

"*Blood Dagger*," I repeated, testing the words. They felt heavy on my tongue—as if I weren't worthy to say them out loud. I didn't think I was worthy to wield it either.

"Yes," he said. "By combining our strength into one blade, we gave ourselves a fighting chance. Our resources, power, and strength dwindled throughout the centuries and millennia. We were losing. So the Watchers decided to stack the deck and add a dash of retribution."

My legs felt weak. This Blood Dagger held the power of seven angels. I suddenly didn't feel worthy of carrying the blade any longer.

"Why in the world would this thing choose me? You're *angels*, for Pete's sake! You're clearly more powerful than I am …" I rubbed a hand down my face in aggravation. "I don't understand—you must have trained warriors—why use a teenager with little skill or knowledge as your savior?"

Vampires, angels, Nephilim … it was all too much.

Dave gave me a terrifying grin, as if I should know the answer to the questions already. "Don't you get it? *You* are more than just human. You're Nephilim," he said sagely. "And you are the last. I took great lengths to protect you until you were ready for this very moment. Don't you think it's fitting that a *Nephilim*—part angel and human— is the very thing that can take the Grigori down *and* enact a cure for what they created?"

My heart thundered in my chest at hearing that word: *Nephilim*. Actually, it was more like there was a stampede of horses inside my chest, all clamoring to get out at once. I would have joined them to run for the hills—but something told me I couldn't outrun this.

I ran a hand through my hair, too astonished to say anything. Even though I could feel the truth of his words all the way down in my soul, I still shook my head, willing it to not be true, until finally I managed, "You're lying."

I could see the pity and empathy all rolled into one expression. "I'm sorry I'm throwing everything at you at once. Great lengths have been taken to ensure no one knew where or who you were—until you took the mantle of the blade. It was designed to seek out the last Nephilim as soon as you turned eighteen. But the dagger was stolen and hidden away by the Grigori. They thought they could keep it out of your hands, but as you can see, that was a nigh-impossible task. It can't be destroyed or buried or hidden or locked away."

I swallowed past the massive lump in the back of my throat and croaked, "*I am so royally screwed.*" Then I thought about my family. "My dad, he had to have known …" The color drained from my face. "Is he an angel? Or is it my mom? I don't even know where to begin." I pulled in a breath so deep my abs contracted tightly as I held it in. I let it out raggedly, gasping, "How do you expect me to process all of this?"

I'm not human. Things started to make more sense as I thought about my dad's evasiveness on the phone—the way he looked at me that night I went to get my sister back. How I felt different when the power of the blade took me—as if I were something altogether alien. A deep shiver worked its way down my spine. *I am part angel!*

"I wish I could share the rest of the information with you right now—about your family, about everything—but we have been sworn to secrecy to protect all those involved. I have been protecting you ever since you took possession of the blade. It has become increasingly difficult though. My strength is waning. I must teach you how to use the Blood Dagger and guard your mind for the coming—"

"Whoa, whoa, whoa … What makes you think I won't chuck that damn blade into the ocean right now?" I grumbled. "I don't want any of this. I reject your angel blade—Blood Dagger, whatever. Why should I believe anything you say?"

Something crossed his features, hurt and sorrow and anger maybe … I couldn't tell which, because his eyes started glowing fiercely with that golden light I'd been witness to before.

I shielded my eyes as he held the dagger out. "This blade isn't just a powerful weapon; it holds the answer to a cure for vampirism. Take it," he said firmly. "You believe the blade, right? It will confirm everything I've just told you. We created it for this very purpose."

I licked my lips and then slowly reached a shaking hand out to take it from him. Right before I curled my fingers around the hilt, I hesitated. The certainty and confidence in his face told me he knew what was going to happen and it wasn't going to go my way. I pulled it into my grasp and went tense all over, suddenly breathing hard. The bronze hilt thrummed with power. It flooded through me, sending what felt like ice-tipped needles shooting through my bloodstream. I threw my hands over my ears as a sudden ear-piercing ringing started in my head. Taking a knee, I found the pain almost too unbearable—as if it would rend my skull in two. The blade was speaking to me—somehow I knew it to be true—except there was no speech—it was only a feeling—the words coming to me on a thrum of vibration … whispered through the sands of time perhaps, from a plane of existence I'd never know or understand. I don't know how I knew it, but *it* told me to trust Dave, that he was telling me the truth.

Unable to take it any longer, I crumpled at Dave's feet, curling into a ball as the dagger fell from my grasp. And then everything went black—the agonizing pain vanishing as quickly as it had started. Ever so slowly my vision cleared. When I came to, Dave was staring down at me as if he understood the pain of the blade's speech.

His eyes crinkled at the corners as he kneeled next to me. In a whisper-soft voice, he said, "I believe you are interested in saving a fellow friend. The Grigori won't leave you alone—no matter how hard you try, where you go … or how much you might want to reject your lineage. If you think vampires are bad, just wait until you meet the leader of the Grigori—Angela."

I wanted to tell him that even though I knew he was telling the truth, I still didn't plan on jumping on the bandwagon just yet, but speech and spit and my tongue had dried up like ancient parchment.

After a second, I came to the realization that he was going to hand me the very thing I wanted most in this world—a cure for Larna—but in doing so, I had to claim my Nephilim half, which just so happened to be the obstinate half. Or was that the other way around? To be fair, I couldn't quite get the human half down either. I was only eighteen. I felt like maybe I'd lost all of the color in my face, until my temper started to rise and blood rushed back into it. "That was Gabe's bargaining chip as well. You two clearly know how to play me." I scoffed, "If I was going to choose one group to work with though, I guess I'll choose the Watchers—for *now*."

Dave opened his mouth before he clamped it shut. After a second, he implored, "Stubbornness isn't always a bad quality. Look, kid, it's not a bargaining chip. It's about your survival. I don't want to see you hurt. The Grigori want to wipe you off the face of this planet. They hate Nephilim … You're the only one left." The pleading in his voice increased. "I am only trying to help you. You are their greatest threat—not us."

I grabbed the sides of my head, gritting my teeth in resolve. "Okay, tell me how this cure works. Do you want me to snap my fingers or click my heels? If that's the case—whatever you need me to do—let's get it over with now. If we have the cure for vampirism, it defeats these Grigori's plans for world domination, right?" I cracked my knuckles. "Let's do this."

He shook his head. "I appreciate your gusto, but it doesn't quite work like that." He cast his eyes down as if ashamed about something. "I need to talk to the Grigori first... and I need you to be there with me."

At the mention of talking to the same people who really wanted me dead, my heart rate increased. And then it was beating too fast, and I felt sick to my stomach all over again. "Excuse me?"

"I am sorry, Corinth." And he did sound sorry as he added, "I haven't exactly shared everything with you—Angela is the only one who knows how to get the cure. We have to get it from her."

The earth started to spin sickeningly as darkness threatened to swallow me up. I felt a steadying hand on my shoulder. Looking up into Dave's eyes, I saw overwhelming concern in them. Whatever his intentions were, I felt like maybe he did care about what happened to me next—and the blade had been pretty damn convincing of that fact. Even though I was deathly afraid of Thunderblade's power, I trusted that it wouldn't steer me wrong.

Dave said, "I promise I won't leave you alone while we meet with them—but there isn't much time left."

I reached out a hand so he could help me back up.

Once on my feet, I straightened to my full height, which wasn't saying much when standing next to him. "Are we talking imminent—as in tomorrow—or are we talking months of preparation and training so I can become a badass warrior—?"

His eyes snapped down to meet mine. "Hours."

"*What?*" I felt the beginnings of panic start to rise in me all over again. It would do me no good to argue now or point out to him that he should have been training me since I was four. Except he couldn't have, according to him; he'd had to protect me—by staying away until I took up the mantle of the blade. "Why have you waited so long to tell me this? We could have been training … doing something … *anything* …"

"I am sorry, but as soon as you started drawing on the power of the dagger, we have been working to protect you. We found Larna's father first—or rather, he found us. He was fiercely protective of you and her. He wanted us to meet on neutral ground—here. The plan was for Jack to arrive with you so that we could all work out a plan … but Jack was killed…" He bowed his head, taking his fedora off as if paying his respects. "My warding is failing … and they can feel it too—the Grigori will soon be able to track you anywhere."

"Larna's father knew?" I felt the pit of my stomach drop out at this revelation. This whole time—he was only trying to *protect* me? "How? I need *more* answers … *more* time. You're talking about the end of the world here," I said in a rush. "Have you seen me fight? I don't even know how to control the blade. If there is a slim chance of getting this information out of the Grigori … how do you expect me to do it?" I shook my head. "They know I have the blade. They don't know I can't use it. I used to think my super-power was talking a big game—"

Dave's gaze landed on the dagger clutched in his fist. "You let me do the heavy lifting. All I need to do is convince Angela to meet with us, which she will undoubtedly do—to get a look at you. I can get into her head—search it for the answers we are looking for. I just need you and the blade with me to draw power from. She is stronger than I am."

I threw a hand to my forehead. "That's comforting!" I cried. "Have you tried to talk to them—convince them to see reason...? Maybe try a little diplomacy?" I asked, sounding unconvincing even to myself.

Dave shook his head slowly. "There is no peace or reasoning with them—only death." He must have seen the look on my face, because he added, "Don't worry. I will be there to protect you."

I exhaled in resignation, unable to think of another solution and also feeling utterly helpless, like I was falling down a never-ending tunnel of doom with no way to stop myself. "Once you get the answers from Angela—I'm out. This ends and you tell me how to cure Larna. Deal?"

Dave closed his eyes and then opened them again. "Deal," he said. "Keep the blade close. I'll be in touch."

When I woke, the room was dark and I was covered in sweat. The faux window, which had afforded such stunning views before I had fallen asleep, was now shut off. Maybe it was set on a timer or something. Goes to show how much I'd been in my room lately. My whole body shook as a tremor racked through me. I reached up to feel fresh tears stinging my cheeks. This was what I was waiting for—to have a meltdown in solitude. My first thought was about my family. Was Dad my biological father? I wondered the same about my mom. Did that mean my family wasn't even my family? Was I adopted? Had they been duped into thinking I was theirs all these years? Maybe I'd been switched at birth. The questions slid through my mind as slick as oil, staining my perception of a once-upon-a-time ordinary life. Everything was a lie. A tiny voice kept telling me Dad and Mom would always be there for me, but the haunted look on my dad's face that night before Larna and I left still plagued me. If he knew anything—anything at all—he should have told me. I felt betrayed. I also felt like my mind might break at any moment. I was half human. Half angel. A Nephilim. *What the hell?*

My eyes were heavy, and so was the dagger strapped to my hip. I glanced at my watch. Five o' clock. Wow. It was the most uninterrupted sleep I'd gotten since I'd been here. I didn't feel well rested though. I felt like a guy on his last day before being sent to his execution. Seeing as how I only had mere *hours* left, I wondered what my last meal would be.

Chapter 48

Larna

THE SOUND OF HAPPY whistling woke me up. I'd never heard Alastair whistle before. I rubbed the sleep out of my eyes, focusing on his face. It was the most beautiful face I'd ever seen. I wondered if his mom had known how handsome he was going to be when he grew up. Alastair had his shirt sleeves rolled up to his forearms and a wide grin on his face.

Actually, I'd never seen him in a better mood. I felt myself matching his infectious smile as he hopped onto the bed to flip himself on top of me, his elbows on either side of my head to hold himself up. He gazed down at me and then very slowly lowered himself so he could plant a quick kiss on my lips. I arched up to meet him. After we both shared the moment of just being in each other's arms, he stretched back out onto the bed beside me. He acted like we'd just had sex. We hadn't. He just seemed exceedingly happy that I was waking up in his room. The topic of sex hadn't been broached as of yet.

"Why are you looking at me like that?" he asked finally.

"You're cute," I said with the tiniest of shrugs.

"I've been called many things before, but cute hasn't been at the top of that list. I'll take it."

I found myself curled up at his side like a cat, my head against the crook of his arm, exactly where I wanted to stay forever. He glanced down and closed his eyes. We stayed locked like that until a soft knock came from the other side of the door from Corinth's connecting room.

"Guess who's finally awake," Alastair muttered. "The guy never sleeps. I swear he's part vampire."

I rolled over and swung my feet off the side of the bed. "I can feel your eye roll without even looking at you."

Alastair gave an annoyed huff and got up to open the door.

Corinth shuffled into the room, dragging his feet as if he had cement blocks attached to them. He eyed my disheveled appearance but didn't say anything. When he came all the way into the room, I noticed how haunted he looked—his feet barely lifting off the ground as he moved. Dark half-moon circles stood out under his eyes, almost the color of a bruise.

Alastair stopped behind Corinth, looking just as worried as I felt. "Did you see Dave?"

There was something in Corinth's eyes—a resigned deer-caught-in-the-headlights look that unnerved me. It also put me instantly on edge as I jumped to my feet.

"What happened?"

Corinth ran a hand down his face. "You could say that." I watched him slump down onto the edge of the bed, and I traded a concerned glance with Alastair.

Concern contoured the sharp lines of Alastair's face. "You're white as salt."

The silence seemed to drag us all down, replacing our

pleasant morning with a more somber mood. Alastair edged closer to look Corinth in the eyes. After a second, he disappeared and returned with a cup full of dark liquid, shoving it into his hands. "Drink," he ordered. "It'll help."

After Corinth managed to choke down a little bit of the liquid, his glazed-over look seemed to dissipate.

"He's in shock," Alastair clarified. "I've given him some brandy. Corinth, tell us what happened," he coaxed.

I sat in stunned silence as Corinth explained everything that had happened in his dream. From the Watchers and Grigori—two warring factions—to the meeting he'd been asked to attend with the leader of the Grigori—Angela, he had said her name was. He spoke of the dagger being infused with angel magic, which made sense considering the power he harnessed when he possessed it. It wasn't until the end of his long speech that he seemed to take a minute to steel himself before continuing. He took another swig of the brandy and coughed. A flicker of something I couldn't quite decipher passed across his features as he told us he was the offspring of an angel and a human—a Nephilim. I felt a shiver go up my spine when he admitted he was the only one left in existence.

I wasn't sure how much I could process at the moment. At first I wanted to deny the truth, to argue and tell him I didn't believe it, but I kept thinking about his ability to control lightning and how he didn't need the blade to use his anti-*Sight* or all of his other powers— including that weird force field he'd conjured. My eyes slid to the blade at his thigh. There had been so much strangeness when it came to that thing.

Rubbing the sudden cold from my arms, I said, "These Grigori ... they want you dead?"

Alastair's eyes had darkened alarmingly. The rest of his face remained impassive and as impenetrable as a block of ice, but I could see he was thinking the same thing I was. Corinth wasn't just in danger from vampires—these angels could be an even bigger threat.

It wasn't until the room had suddenly gone quiet that I realized everyone had stopped talking, all of us too absorbed by this new turn of events to comment.

Al slow-blinked back at Corinth and finally said, "Well, I can see why you made that long face when you came in."

Corinth's shock quickly turned to annoyance. "What? No barrage of questions about why I trust Dave? Or about the Nephilim blood running through my veins? Or why the dagger chose a scrawny half human like me in the first place? Why do Dave and his legion of angels need me?" He blew out a frustrated breath. "I get none of that from y'all?" His eyes darted to me and then back to Alastair, his chest heaving up and down.

He wasn't angry at Alastair, he was angry at the world. At the hand he'd been so unexpectedly and abruptly dealt.

"Do you trust Dave?" Alastair asked quietly.

Corinth ran a hand through his hair, and then he gripped the back of his neck. "Not enough to take him on an all-expense paid vacation with just the two of us, but enough to believe him about this. We've always known something was off about me. Now we know why Dave knows about the cure. He says only Angela has it." His determined gaze locked on mine. "The only thing I can think of is to go with him—to talk to these Grigori. Put a face to the enemy and find this cure before they kill me first."

I scooted closer to Corinth, putting a gentle hand on his arm. "As scary as it sounds, we'll figure it out—take it one problem at a time. I think it's time we rally Sozo for help." I looked between them. "If you both agree, that is."

Alastair rubbed his chin in thought. "Sozo lost my confidence as soon as we got here," he admitted finally. "He will need to earn it back in the future. I'm going to talk to him. I have to admit, this meeting is rushed—I don't like it. I don't think Corinth should go forward with it."

Corinth avoided our concerned gazes, looking past us to stare at the winter wonderland. The way he was rubbing his hands together, I was pretty sure he'd start a fire. "I appreciate you both for everything you've done for me … for coming here with me. I found out what I needed to know about myself—no matter how outlandish or wild it sounds, I believe it. And I also believe the right thing to do is to meet with these Grigori," he said. "With that being said, are you sure you guys want to be involved in all this mess? It's not like you both don't have anything else going on right now, not to mention we don't even know how powerful these angels truly are." He swallowed hard. "If you want out … I understand. This is my problem now—I kind of dragged you into it in a roundabout way. We finally know how the blade fits into all of this, and Gabe is still a threat— maybe you guys can focus your attentions on him while I take on the apocalyptic Revelation stuff." He mussed his hair up, chuckling softly to himself. "Saying it out loud makes it sound even more unbelievable..." He let the sentence trail off and then finally risked a glance back up at us.

I was about to tell him that we were in this together and that he was family and that my dirt is his dirt and vice versa, but Alastair beat me to it, grabbing a chair and pulling it toward him.

Knee to knee with Corinth, Alastair planted his hands flat on his thighs and spoke with a firmness and resolve that surprised me. "When one of us can't carry the load anymore, the other one takes it up. That's what family does for each other. I have to admit, I didn't have a very high opinion of you when we first met. You were too cocky. Too scrawny. You didn't know how to fight or listen. Over time, though, *you* managed to change my mind … and not only did you change it, you turned it upside down and dumped it over my head like ice water. Not many people can claim to have had that effect on me." His eyes flicked to mine for the briefest of moments before zipping back to Corinth. "You two are important to me. So when you tell me I can bow out of an apocalyptic-end-of-the-world scenario, you are in actuality offending me. Besides, this is all connected. If these Grigori created a virus for the purpose of taking over the world, don't you think it's a good idea that *we* stop them before it happens?" He glanced between us. "There's a bigger picture at play here." Alastair extended his hand, waiting for Corinth to shake it.

I could tell Alastair's words meant something to Corinth; his eyes were brimming at the corners as he reached out and clasped hands with him, and then he unexpectedly pulled Alastair into a hug. "Vinson's getting one of these too when I see him next," he muttered under his breath. "Jeez, Alastair, you're a sentimental one," he said wryly, but he was grinning as he pulled back. "Larna, got any other sage words of advice? I don't know if you can beat Alastair's pep talk—"

I launched a pillow at him from across the room; by using inhuman speed, he never saw it coming. It struck him square in the face, and a lock of his dark hair fell across his forehead. "Not fair," he bellowed.

I raised an eyebrow as if to say, "Get used to it," and added, "I think Alastair covered what I was going to say. Mush and all. You're not doing this without us."

Chapter 49

Corinth

D AVE MET ME IN person this time. His presence in real life was no less electrifying and charismatic. We sat in a small conference room in Sozo's private office. I was standing perched against the side of the table with my arms crossed. Larna sat in a wing-backed leather chair, and Al was pacing behind us with a stoic expression on his face. Sozo, of course, was seated regally at the head of the table with his fingers steepled in thought. We had called the meeting hoping to gain their allegiance in taking down the Grigori.

Sozo's long black hair was slicked back, and the contours of his high cheekbones stood out starkly in the soft light of the conference room. He looked almost skeletal in this light. "The Grigori have given us an ultimatum: turn Corinth over or risk war with their kind." His eyes, which were equally as dark as Gabe's, met mine. "We have weighed all of our options. Our council has discussed the impossible position in which Corinth has unwittingly found himself." He spread his arms out in front of him. "We are a peaceful society. To even consider going to war is unthinkable; we do not have the means or desire to do so. I am sorry to say that if Corinth cannot convince them to stand down, we will not be joining your charge. We can, however, guarantee safe passage for Corinth to meet with the Grigori. Because we would rather not have the whereabouts of our location known, we think it pertinent to have the meet-up be in one of Corinth's dream states"—he glanced over to Dave—"which Dave has said can be accomplished. And Dave can also pull Corinth out if the situation becomes too perilous." His lips drew back, revealing gleaming teeth almost like a wolf's. I could see the sharp tips of his fangs just below the gum-line. He didn't look like he wanted peace at all as he said, "I can provide our most trusted guards as sentinels while Corinth enters his slumber. I realize there is an assassin still on the loose who wishes him harm. That *is* on us." Sozo inclined his head toward me. "I am sorry for not holding up my end of the bargain. I truly hope it ends with no more blood being shed for your kind."

I balked at the words *your kind*. It seemed cold and detached, like he was trying to distance himself from the angels and Nephilim altogether. He was telling me that they would turn me over before going to war. Anger surged up inside me, white-hot and uncontainable as I launched myself off the edge of the table. Reaching into my pocket, I tossed the keycard I'd gotten from John across the polished table. When it slid close enough, Sozo slapped his hand down on top of it. His eyes honed in on the card and then narrowed once he realized what it was.

"This place isn't as secure as you think it is. If I can gain all-access, don't you think that someone else can too? Y'all are tangled in the same web as we are—except you lot get the luxury of putting your heads in the sand." I met his gaze unwaveringly. "You should know, though, some spiders live in the sand. And that room full of my blood you guys are hoarding suggests different about your level of involvement. Before, you asked me to join you. Has all of that changed because things have gotten messy?" I leaned across the table to get closer to Sozo. "Trust me, you don't want to get on my bad side."

Sozo leaned back, taking in everything I just said, his expression impassive. If he was mad that I had admitted to breaking in to his top-secret lab, he didn't show it. After a few seconds, his dark, fervent eyes met mine. "I will take your words under advisement. It is not our intention to make an enemy out of you. But as it stands, nothing has changed," he went on, raising his voice. "We hope you understand."

"Well then, I want my blood destroyed," I insisted. "It's creepy and disingenuous. Why do you even want it in the first place?"

Sozo's face flashed with annoyance, all trace of diplomacy disappearing, replaced by a look of warning that said, "Tread carefully." I wondered how much needling it would take to draw this reaction out of him as he said, "Your blood was the price of admission. I am sorry to say we will not be destroying it."

Alastair, seeing my hand inching toward the blade at my thigh, jumped in front of me to prevent any further escalation. "We knew that was part of the deal coming into it." He stressed, "*Didn't* we, Corinth?"

I knew it had been part of the deal he'd made to get our foot in the door, but I was still angry Sozo had decided to keep us in the dark about the experimentation on it—

not to mention refusing to join our cause.

Larna's heated gaze darted briefly to Dave's as she turned to face Sozo. "We should stay focused on the meeting. This is happening tonight? You're able to arrange to speak with the leader of the Grigori ... this *Angela*?"

Dave nodded slowly, inclining his head. "Yes, it has been arranged," he said. "If Corinth agrees, the meeting will be held inside one of his dreams. Although, it does present another danger: once the Grigori have access to the inside of your head, it will leave you unprotected from possible future interference. I'm not sure how much strength I'll have left to protect you..." Dave pressed his lips together, glancing between us. "Corinth's body will be here, safely guarded by their security. He cannot be hurt in his dreamlike trance; hence why we want to try it that way first, even with the risk of future exposure—I can teach you how to block them."

"Are you sure about this?" Alastair interjected. "Why can't you let them meet up in *your* head, Dave?"

Dave grimaced. "I wish I could, but I don't sleep or dream."

"Convenient," Alastair said haughtily. "If it doesn't work, Corinth, you're taking a huge risk in exposing yourself to the enemy."

I said, "It's a bigger risk meeting in person. I think it's our best play at the moment." I met Larna's steady gaze, those dark eyes gleaming. "I was hoping Dave could give me some tips on control and clearing my mind ... or whatever they do, just in case it gets hairy."

"You think that will help against the Grigori?" Alastair murmured.

I said, "It might. I've shown promise in compulsion.

If the blade is designed to take them down, what if my *Sight* can too? I could end this whole thing before it even starts."

"Compulsion doesn't work on us, and our blood is toxic to vampires," Dave pointed out.

Well, that explained why my blood was like a toxin to the fanged crowd. Maybe it was diluted. I reminded myself to ask Dave later, away from the ever-scrutinizing watch of Sozo. I wondered if my blood or abilities were different from theirs, since I was only half angel. I also thought about what would happen to a full-on angel if a vamp got a taste of *their* blood. Thinking about how toxic my blood was to a vamp, I realized nothing good, that was for sure.

Dave's voice brought me out of my thoughts and back to the present. "The Grigori engineered vampirism with specific qualities so that they couldn't be defeated by their own creation."

Sozo's eyes narrowed down to two tiny pinpricks at this new bit of information. Dave must have a reason for bringing this to light in front of Sozo. It made sense now why I had the ability of anti-*Sight*. They were at a disadvantage when it came to fighting angels. Maybe this also explained why Sozo was so reluctant to choose a side— *or maybe he already had.*

"I think it's a good idea anyway," Alastair explained quickly. "If they can get into your head, you can bet they can get ahold of your memories too. Maybe manipulate them even."

"Well that's not terrifying," I said.

Chapter 50

Corinth

D AVE AND I SAT at a table at the back of an empty room in the library. They had one of the largest archives I'd ever seen. A fine collection of rare books lined the walls. It smelled of worn wood, aged paper, and mildew. Rich, dark cherry wood made up most of the shelving, wall panels, and pillars, giving it the old-world feel of law offices and court-houses designed in the early twenties. There were five levels of winding metal staircases inlaid in the wall that led up, up, up and away. I had chosen this place instead of my room because I needed a change in atmosphere. Sozo had assured us that the library would remain cleared for us while we trained.

I also came to realize their editions here had some of the most archaic handwritten tomes in history. Unfortunately, they were kept under lock and key. According to Caesar, you had to handle them in low-level lighting with a special set of gloves to prevent them from crumbling apart like ash. When I was younger, I'd gone to see the Dead Sea Scrolls with my family at a museum. We had to view them under safety glass and a backlight. The ancient manuscripts here were untouched by nature or human interference, which meant if you had the ability to understand Aramaic, Greek, or Latin, they might be a titillating read. My curiosity was starting to get the better of me. I tried to imagine what kinds of blueprints the Druids had come up with that long ago. I was mad at myself for not setting foot in here earlier.

It was still and exceptionally quiet with us being the only people here—even though I knew libraries were usually quiet, you could normally hear pages being turned or fingers clacking on keyboards or the occasional cough. The stillness in this place felt portentous.

"So, you can't tell me anything about my family? Because I'm dying to know something … *anything* about them. Is my dad really my dad?" I begged, "*Please.*"

Dave averted his gaze from mine. "I wish I could tell you more, but unfortunately, this information has been kept secret and closely guarded. To know anything about your family would only put you *and* them in more danger."

I nodded in frustration. Even though I knew this was going to be his answer, I was still disappointed. I didn't press him any further, though, because the last thing I wanted to do was to endanger my family more than I already had.

He crossed his arms steadfastly over his chest, glancing to the blade at my hip. "Unsheathe it," he instructed. "The key is finding the balance of power within the blade and power within you."

I did as he asked, carefully placing it on top of the table. "There's something I need to ask you about the blade." I hesitated, trying to find the right words. After a brief pause, I said, "When I am under its influence, it's like it completely overtakes me. When I get like that, I'm worried it will use me—negatively—to destroy everything in its path." I shuddered as the blood rushed to my cheeks, an image of me slicing Larna popping into my head. "How do I control it?" I asked, praying he had an answer.

His eyes flitted to it and then back to me, silently assessing how much I could or could not handle. "You *can* control it—it takes incredible concentration and willpower and a concept of otherworldliness that comes from being Nephilim. The hardest part is coming to an understanding of symbiotic harmony with the blade."

I ran a hand through my hair. "No kidding," I said dryly. "What does that even mean, anyway?"

He tilted his head to the side. "Think of it as two very polar-opposite people being forced to live together. You're not quite sure how to benefit from each other just yet, but you know there is a purpose for your union. You are both fighting for control over the same thing." He lowered his gaze from mine. "Seven of us Watchers have imbued a part of ourselves into the Blood Dagger in order to make you, alone, strong enough to beat the Grigori."

"Seven? Where are the rest of the Watchers?" I asked slowly. "And why wouldn't one of you just use the blade yourselves? You aren't half human—which means you don't have a lot of the earthly restrictions that I do. If you can draw power from the blade *and* me, why not just take the blade and go after them yourself?"

Dave regarded me in silence for a second. "I was sent here as an emissary to represent the rest of the Watchers. In time, I am hoping you will meet all of them." He added, "And in answer to your question, we needed someone *with* earthly restrictions. The blade was designed with a

Nephilim in mind, and since you're the last one—it all comes down to you. I can use the power of the blade sparingly. Then it becomes too much for me to handle."

I stared at him, bowled over by this admission. I had to collect myself momentarily before saying, "So, what you're saying is that I am more powerful than you are?"

Dave inclined his head, his golden eyes glittering. "Now you're getting it."

I simply could not fathom being that powerful—that is, until an image of me standing atop a hill made out of gore and death and destruction hit the backs of my eyelids. Acid crawled up the back of my throat. I knew the truth in his words and it scared me to my core. The part of me that was afraid took a back seat to the part of me that really wanted to know more. I couldn't imagine giving myself over to something that powerful. That was my problem. I'd been holding back because I was terrified it would bend me to its will.

I wasn't just an empty vessel.

Then, with the blink of an eye, my blade disappeared from the tabletop in a crackle of energy and reappeared in Dave's grasp, fiery blue sparks shooting out from his fingertips.

I shook my head, eyes going wide. "Please tell me I can learn to do that."

Dave flashed me an all-knowing grin. "Oh, you'll be able to do a lot more than this." He put his palms up on the table and gestured for me to put my hands in his. I did so without another word or snide remark—which surprised even me. I needed to know how to do that. Another part of me needed to tell myself that if we were successful in getting this cure, I could go back home to

Texas—see my dad and mom, who may or may not be my real parents. I shut these troubling thoughts down quickly, unable to deal with them right now. I had barely started learning how to control the blade. What if I messed something up? What if I went all guns blazing and killed everyone instead?

His hands were cool and smooth, no calluses or rough skin marred them, unlike mine. I let out a nervous laugh as he said coolly, "Close your eyes and concentrate on the vibrations of the universe. Every pulse and beat and fluctuation is invisible to the naked eye. Angels can manipulate this space and also a very minute amount of time—by speeding it up or slowing it down. The laws of physics don't apply to us. For your first lesson, I want you to concentrate on getting the dagger to come to you when you call it. Draw it out with your mind, not your hands."

Jedi mind tricks abound. Noisily pulling oxygen in and expelling it from my lungs, I tried to focus on these elusive vibrations he was talking about. No matter how tightly I squeezed my eyes shut though, I couldn't connect with the blade or the universe. The only sound I heard was my own frustrated breaths. I stretched out a hand, palm up, and then beckoned for my blade to come to me. I thought about the cool, hard metal pressed into my skin, imagined the familiar weight in my hand.

But no matter how hard I strained or grunted or cursed, it would not obey. After what seemed like thirty minutes, I finally cracked an eye open. "Why can't I do this?" The hair at the nape of my neck was damp from the amount of effort I was trying to put into it. Maybe this wasn't about physical exertion though. "Everything I've learned about myself is a lie. My life has been turned upside down, and here I am, going off to meet some terrifying angels who all want me dead." I blew out a deep breath, frustrated. "If I don't get this down, I'll be turned over to these Grigori by a clan of vampires who don't want to ruffle any feathers."

I laid my head on the table-top, my fingers still annoyingly empty. Again, I tried to imagine the solid weight of the hilt in my hands: the steel hard and unforgiving.

Dave was oddly quiet, probably letting me work through it myself, but we didn't have time for this.

I heard the sound of his voice drift to me from what seemed like far away. "I wish I could've been there for you when you first took possession of the blade." I snapped my head up at hearing the regret in his voice. A light shone in his eyes that I couldn't quite put my finger on. It looked like pride wrapped in concern. "I'm truly sorry that I couldn't help better prepare you for this moment."

After a beat, I whispered, "You are?" I wanted to ask him why he felt this way, but I couldn't bring myself to.

He nodded resolutely. "I do not know you very well, but I wish I did. What little I do know about you shows your character and grace and charisma. Instead of embracing the half you don't know, embrace the one you do: your *humanity*. Be yourself. This is why you were chosen in the first place. Even if you don't trust yourself, I trust we can pull this off, together."

"We're out of time, aren't we?" I said.

"Yes, we are."

Chapter 51

Corinth

OLLECTIVELY WE HAD ALL decided that the meeting was going to take place inside one of my dreams. Because the assassin was still on the loose, the best place for me to fall into a deep sleep would be in Sozo's heavily guarded office. There was little else for Larna or Al to do but wait. Of course, they had insisted on being right by my side just in case something went wrong while I was under. I had this horrible feeling that if anything were to happen to me, it would be when I was at my most vulnerable—lying on a cot in a coma. I wasn't really being put into a coma, but it sure felt that way.

Two cots had been set up in the center of the grandiose office. Sozo had at least held up his end of the bargain. Crisp white sheets covered both cots. One for me and one for Dave, and even though he didn't sleep, he said it would be best to be in close proximity to me. I wasn't reassured by the fact that according to Dave, all I needed to do was show up.

I glanced around the office, studying Sozo's extravagant taste in greater detail. The chair at his desk was made out of gold. His desk carved from what I was sure had to be the most expensive slab of marble ever made. According to Sozo, the heavy-iron-looking doors were virtually impenetrable. He wanted to make doubly sure that we would be safe, locked away from any outside interference. Even though Sozo and I didn't see eye to eye on some things, he was still smart enough to understand the seriousness of the situation. I did have to grudgingly admit he was putting himself on the line for even having me here during this meeting of the minds.

Larna and Al checked the doors and the security detail outside. Both of them had severe expressions on their faces; Larna kept tugging at the ends of her sleeves, where I knew her leather vambraces were still hidden.

I had asked to speak to Sarah before I met with the Grigori. When she swept into the room, I noticed the worry lines creasing her brows. I drew in a sharp breath. She looked as stunning as ever. Brown wispy curls escaped out of the bun on top of her head. Those startlingly green eyes met mine. I was so focused on her face that I didn't notice the tray she was carrying until she stopped in front of me; on it sat a pot and a mug.

"What is all this about?" she asked slowly, glancing around. "Did you ask me here to take a nap?" She eyed the two cots, and then her gaze raked over the on-edge-looking guards milling about near the doors.

I saw Larna across the room; she was squinting at me as if I were about to vanish into thin air. I was thankful she had chosen to leave me alone while I spoke with Sarah. My heart had been broken recently, and I felt Sarah might help mend it back together again. As she stared at me, a small smile played on her pink lips. I noticed how they matched the tips of her rosy cheeks. A twist of something spiraled up inside me. We definitely had chemistry, but I owed it to her to keep her out of all of this mess with the Nephilim and Grigori. I was being selfish and this had gotten too dangerous. And if this meeting wasn't successful, I was about to get kicked out of here, anyway. It wouldn't be fair to her to start something I couldn't invest in. I was a hot mess.

There was no point mincing words, so I came right out with it. "I wanted to apologize," I started. "There are a lot of things I wish I could tell you—if I had time..." My voice wavered and I tried again. "I thought there might have been something between us, something special—"

I glanced away as Sarah reached a hand out to gingerly touch my injured cheek where the deep fingernail gouges had begun to heal.

I went still as her fingers grazed my jawline, my skin tingling in their wake as she said, "I felt it too. You don't feel the same anymore?"

My eyes slid to her hand, and then I looked away, avoiding intensely green eyes. They were too wide and round and perfect. I didn't know what else to say. This had all become so overwhelming; too many things floating around in my head about Nephilim and angels and the end of the world. A relationship would have to take a back seat, along with everything else good in my life, apparently.

"I found out some things about myself that I don't know how to handle. I don't expect anyone else to either."

She put a remarkably cool hand over mine. "If I wasn't scared away by your lightning show back in the meeting hall, do you really think I'll be scared off by anything else?"

I sighed, suddenly set in what I needed to do. "No.

I'm sorry. I can't bring you into any of this. It's too dangerous. I truly hope you understand."

I could hear the disappointment in her voice when she spoke next. "I think it should be my choice on what sort of risks I want to take. There might come a time when you need my help … What about the results, all the charts and paperwork we still need to go over?"

"I realize that—" I stopped to gather the courage to send her away, to be cold and aloof. "This *is* my choice. And I choose not to include you in any of what's about to happen."

"You sound as if something bad is going to happen." There was pleading in her voice now. "Is something bad about to happen? What's going on, Corinth? Let me help. I couldn't find anything of great importance in the paperwork about your blood work. At first it all looked so promising. Maybe I could get another crack at that lab. Please, let me help at least with studying—"

I gave her fingers a light squeeze. The sudden contact was electrifying. I had made up my mind. Larna and Al were in this with me because they were too stubborn to push away, but I'd only recently met Sarah. This would be an easier split. I felt a pang of guilt well up all the same. *Why did this feel so hard, then?*

I said coolly, "I am sorry—but you should go."

Her cheeks flushed bright red. I detected an undercurrent of anger as her eyes flashed, but then it was gone and she was jumping to her feet. "I'm sorry it couldn't be different between us," she glanced around, seeming to have noticed how somber Larna and Al looked now. "I brought some coffee." Her eyes flitted down to the pot, "I don't know if you want it now or if you need it, but I know how much you like caffeine... I guess this will have to be my *cheers* to your future and a goodbye all at the same time." She plucked the mug between nimble fingers and then poured me a cup of java, presenting it as a peace offering. I noticed how doll-like her hands were: porcelain and smooth. "Should you change your mind—" she drew in a shaky breath "—you know where to find me."

I took the proffered cup from her with a nod of thanks. It smelled delicious, and it was a form of comfort I needed right now. "Thank you." I held the cup up and drank the warm liquid down in one gulp. I wasn't worried about falling asleep. Dave would be able to put me out, so my caffeine intake wouldn't be a problem.

As it hit my taste buds, I found that the coffee grounds had a distinct and gritty aftertaste—a sign of some very strong java. "What kind of coffee is this—?" I started to ask, but Larna had appeared by my side, a grim expression etched onto her features as her eyes darted to Sarah.

"I don't mean to rush things, but Dave has finally arrived." Her gaze stayed locked on Sarah. "I suggest we have as few people in the room as possible, Corinth."

I felt like a total douche-bag for turning her away like this.

Sarah stood, wiping her hands on her pants. "I believe that's my cue to leave." Her green eyes slid to Larna and then back over to me. "I wish you all the best of luck— with everything."

She turned to go, but Larna caught her arm. When Sarah turned back, Larna said softly, "Thank you."

Sarah's brow furrowed quizzically as Larna clarified, "For everything you've done. I know we haven't had much time to talk—but if you're willing, and when things calm down, I'd like to get to know you better."

Sarah's usual light mood had chilled to a frostiness that suggested otherwise. I had a feeling it was my fault for this reaction. I felt my chest tighten, feeling horrible for pushing her away.

"Thank you, Larna, for your hospitality, but I don't think that's a good idea." She looked at Alastair, who was still across the room, checking on the security detail, and then dropped her gaze. "Would you tell Alastair thank you again for the watch?"

Larna said, "I think he'd rather hear that from you."

Sarah opened her mouth as if she wanted to say something else, but stopped herself short. After a beat, she turned around and gave us all one small sad smile before disappearing through the doors right as Sozo swept into the room with all the flair of a sultan, his presence commanding as usual. A bunch of surly-looking guards all dressed in white followed him, including the two who had shadowed me for a time—Thor and Luke Cage.

Personally, I thought it was all overkill. There was nothing they could do unless someone tried to break into Sozo's office. With this many people standing guard, it would be a death sentence for anyone trying to get in.

Sozo bunched the loose material of his robe into his hands as he edged his way over to me on the cot. "Everything is set," he said confidently. "Good luck, Corinth Taylor. I hope your meeting is successful."

I nodded my thanks, suddenly feeling a lot less confident now that Dave had filed into the room too, followed lastly by Caesar, who looked more flustered than I did, tripping over his own robes and coming to a lumbering halt beside me. I would have acknowledged

Caesar with a nod or something, but all my attention rested on Dave. I was gauging whether he looked confident or not. I finally decided he did. There was no trace of nervousness, unlike me.

He sank down to the cot beside mine.

Once everyone was in the room, Larna and Al gathered around me, along with Sozo, Dave, and Caesar.

"The way y'all are looking down at me like that makes me feel like I'm attending my own funeral," I said darkly.

Larna turned quickly to Dave, insistent. "I want to go with Corinth."

A spike of anxiety shot through me at the thought of Larna in my head. There was something to be said about that level of privacy invasion. Did I really want her traipsing around in my mind or thoughts? What if she saw those terrible images of me standing atop a pile of ash and bone and skulls? Or worse, what if she tapped into my emotions—she'd feel my glee at being surrounded by all that gore … she'd feel my heartache and pain and longing. *No, no way*. And then I thought about everyone else who was going to be attending my dream, and it only seemed to increase my apprehension.

Dave frowned. "I wish it were possible—but I can't bring a vampire through the dream veil. Not to mention your presence would only endanger Corinth. I can't protect your mind and his. It would take up way too much energy, even if I could take you with me."

Larna pressed her lips together into a thin line, clearly not liking the answer. It made me feel extremely lucky to have her on my side though. She would always watch my back.

She pulled me into a quick hug, seemingly reading my

mind. "I'll watch over you while you're under," she said evenly. "Promise me you'll cut and run if something goes wrong, Taylor?"

We stayed like that for a second longer until I finally nodded my head against her shoulder. "I promise, Collins."

I glanced up at Al next. If he was concerned, he didn't show it. He did, however, square his shoulders and stretch his neck from side to side, as if preparing himself for battle, which wasn't that heartening.

I turned quickly to Dave. "You're certain they won't be able to see into my memories or thoughts? Because none of you want to witness what's inside my head."

Dave's eyes flicked down to Thunderblade strapped at my hip and he nodded. "The Grigori have agreed to hear you out. I'll be there right by your side—my plan is simple, to get inside of Angela's head without her knowing. You shouldn't have to do anything but stand there and distract her." He flashed me a quicksilver grin. "Which, I have no doubt you can accomplish. If anything should happen, I'll pull you out of your slumber immediately."

Larna said, "Your plan—this drawing power from Corinth and the blade—it won't hurt him, will it? Or leave him unable to defend himself?"

Dave shook his head. "No—he will be very capable of defending himself. Actually, I'm counting on it."

Larna turned to me. "I don't know, Corinth. Something doesn't smell right here. Everything is too rushed. I think this is a huge mistake." She was squeezing her hands together so tightly I thought they might never come apart again. "I—"

Dave interrupted her, his voice sounding strong and

steady. "I will be there to help guide Corinth *and* protect him. I realize this feels rushed—because it is. When we have more time, I promise I will help him master the blade, *if* he wishes. Hopefully, by the time this meeting ends, we will have the answer for a cure. If I can get it—the Grigori will be forced to deal with us. We can put a stop to their plans. If we don't do this, they will hunt Corinth down. They will never stop until they find and kill him."

I suddenly realized we'd traded one enemy for another. I was really getting tired of being hunted down for something I knew next to nothing about. *Story of my life.*

Caesar rocked back on his heels, bringing me out of my gloomy thoughts. I'd almost forgotten he was in the room. When I turned my attention to him, I noticed for the first time how pale he looked, his dark curls damp at the collar of his robe. "Sir, so sorry to interrupt, sir … but we're all set here."

I rubbed a hand over my eyes, suddenly feeling bone-weary tired, which I attributed to extreme stress.

Larna said, "Dave, Alastair, and I will be the only ones in this room. The rest of you will have to wait outside." She planted her hands on her hips. I'd seen her give people that very same stare, the one where she dissected people using lasers instead of eyeballs.

At first Caesar seemed annoyed, but then he finally relented with a slight nod of agreement. I wondered if he'd grown attached to me. I felt like he wasn't such a bad guy after all.

I watched as everyone, including the group of guards and Sozo, filed out of the room, leaving only Larna, Al, and Dave behind. Sozo was troubled about his people. His concern wasn't lost on me—but him letting us use his personal office was a sign of his trust. I was pretty sure his office was the best spot to be in if a major catastrophe were to occur in this place.

Even with drinking all that caffeine, drowsiness still managed to curl its hooks into me—

And then a loud clang brought me out of my stupor, making me jump. I turned to see Al securing and bolting the doors closed, the sound resonating through the now-empty room. It almost felt like he was locking us inside a tomb. I shivered at the thought.

Once Larna and Al knew we were by ourselves, with the exception of Dave, they marched back over to me.

I ran a hand across my eyes, barely able to keep them open as Larna said, "Why are you sticking your neck out again?"

"We've been over this," I mumbled sleepily. "Clearly I'm the bravest, strongest, and wisest—and fairest—don't forget fairest—of them all."

She rolled her eyes at me, a hint of a smile playing on her lips. "When did you get so brave all of a sudden?" Her tone was teasing, but it was also mixed with something that sounded a lot like admiration.

"I'd like to think I was born this way—"

I started to say, but Larna bumped her shoulder playfully against mine.

Al pointed to the solid and very heavy-duty doors with fixed intent. "We've got this place on lockdown. That's the only way in and out." He inclined his head at me as he straightened to his full height. "We got your back. No one is getting in here."

"Relax, guys." I turned to Larna, smiling lazily up at

her. She looked saintly in the soft glow of all the flamboyant gold on the ceiling. "I'll be back in a jiff..."

The room started to spin.

As I lay back, Larna knelt down beside my cot. "I'll be right here. I'm not leaving your side. And even though I can't stand the fact that I won't be there with you, the blade chose *you* for a reason. Maybe *this* is that reason. If you can prevent a war from happening, it will all be worth it."

Larna's concern-filled eyes darted back to Dave, who was already leaning over me, reaching a hand out. He lightly touched a finger to my forehead. And just like that, darkness was folding itself around me like a security blanket.

Al's voice drifted to me on a cloudy haze of obscurity: "We'll see you when you get back, brother."

Chapter 52

Corinth

I WAS BAREFOOT JUST like every other time I'd met Dave. Except this time, he was standing beside me and there was no bench. Even though it didn't help ease my anxiety, the lush grass, cloudless blue sky, and gentle breeze were a nice touch. I squinted up into the blindingly bright sun, trying not to overthink how I should open up to a group of strangers who wanted to kill me. I'd probably start with a cool one-liner or joke to break the ice.

I glanced down, wriggling my toes in between the soft tufts of grass. "Really, Dave?" I said. "I'm going to need my Converse if I want to at least appear a little intimidating."

Dave peered down at my bare feet. "Oh, sorry." He snapped his fingers, and just like that, I was wearing my lucky red Chucks.

"Thanks," I said. And then suddenly the blade was sheathed at my hip. I gestured to it. "Is this real or imagined?"

His eyes flickered with that strange golden light. "Both. I am drawing power from it back in the waking world—I just thought you might be more comfortable with it here, beside you."

I laid my hand on the hilt, the cool metal soothing against my skin. "You were right." Looking across at the vast open field, I noticed that we were still very much alone. Blowing out a determined breath, I said, "Let's get this party started."

"They sensed your presence immediately. They should be here any second—"

And right as he said it, a ball of energy erupted out of nowhere, as dazzlingly bright as a bolt of lightning, except this wasn't a quick flash like a sudden weather phenomenon. It was a shockwave of energy that almost blasted me off my feet. I put a hand over my eyes as a shimmering ball of light appeared, hovering off the ground. It expanded and then hurtled toward us with deadly accuracy.

For a split second, I thought this was how I was going to bite it, but the shockwave of energy stopped just shy of our feet, right before vanishing into a clap of thunder that reverberated through my entire body. Splotches of light danced across my vision. When it dissipated, I was finally able to make out the two strikingly tall figures walking out of the sizzling aftermath.

Fear sliced through me at seeing them.

Dave's eyes stayed locked on the two figures that had started toward us. "Be quiet and let me do the talking." I heard the undercurrent of fear in his voice.

A dude as well toned and sculpted as any I'd ever seen stopped in front of us. His curly platinum hair and pale skin seemed almost translucent. He had sharp, intelligent blue eyes that pulled together that effigy look he had going on quite nicely. The living statue of David—I bet his skin was as smooth as Sozo's marbled desk.

The other one—I figured by process of elimination— was Angela.

I pressed the backs of my hands against my eyes and sucked in a shocked breath. I'd never known true perfection until I saw her. There was no human standard to describe the extent of her beauty. She was Aphrodite, the Greek goddess of love and pleasure: A true vision with long, flowing raven hair, and legs that seemed to go on forever. And when I say *forever*, I meant it. She was taller than Dave and adorned in a silk robe made from the richest shade of royal blue I'd ever seen. I watched her, entranced and drooling, as she glided to a halt beside her companion.

The way they both moved was hypnotic and distinctly alien.

Nothing could have prepared me for how attractive these beings were—and yet, even though they were stunning beyond imaging, something sinister seemed to seethe just below the surface, like how a shark cuts gracefully through water. Maybe it was the way their giant hoods rested on the crowns of their heads—Royal Reapers coming to steal my soul.

I intrinsically knew it wouldn't be an enjoyable experience if they did.

And the ironic thing was, there was a tiny itty-bitty part of me that wished they *would* take me … As soon as I thought it, I put a steadying hand on the handle of Thunderblade, willing it to center me.

The statue of David stopped in front of us, the disgust evident on his face as his eyes raked over me. Dread curled tightly around my chest, constricting it. He had never met me before, but his derision said otherwise. I was just like every other bug he'd stomped on. I'd never felt true prejudice like this before.

When he spoke, the corner of his mouth twitched and his eyebrows rose. "Such a pity."

Forgetting Dave was right beside me, I found myself stepping forward, my hand sliding closer to the hilt of the blade in a rare bout of boldness. "What's such a pity?"

Dave reached a hand out to haul me back behind him right as Blondie cleared his throat and laughed, his lip curling in disdain as if I wasn't worth addressing. He turned to the raven-haired woman. "*This* is the last one?" His eyes lingered on my red Converse a little too long. "*Pity* … I had so wanted to slaughter more of them. This one seems to be the scrawniest out o—"

Dave, sensing my rise in temper, stepped in front of me. "There is no need for derision." His gaze shot to mine and then back to Angela. I could tell he was strained, a muscle ticked out on his jawline. I wondered if he was working on trying to get through her defenses undetected even as we spoke. If he was leeching my power from me, I couldn't feel it.

"This is Corinth Taylor," Dave said more loudly than necessary. "He is the wielder of the blade. I would tread lightly if I were you, Turiel."

I felt my heart pounding in my eardrums; even in a dream, I couldn't control my own racing heartbeat. For a brief second, I wondered if these angels could just snap their fingers and fry my brain to crispy bacon. I think I remember Dave telling me I was safe in my own headspace. Being safe didn't matter right now. I really wanted to take out the Greek model.

Turiel laughed, but there was no humor in it. "Introductions are not necessary." With a soft laugh, he added, "We do not introduce ourselves to insects. And just because he—"

A lift of her finger from Angela was all it took to shut her dog up.

As she inched closer, she lowered her hood suggestively. I was able to get a good look at her eyes: frost-white irises swallowed up by storm-ridden gray pupils. I'd never seen anything like them before. I swayed unsteadily, and realized it was because I'd been holding my breath. I expelled the air noisily back out of my lungs.

She gave me a chilling smile, as if enjoying the thunderstruck look on my face. "My name is Angela—I am the leader of the Grigori." Her frosty eyes drifted over me, starting at my feet, she worked her way up until her eyes landed on the blade. "What did Danel tell you about me? Better yet, what did he tell you about *himself?*"

The way Dave went rigid, his back stiffening into a hard line, made me suddenly very curious what she meant by that. I wondered if I'd been duped all this time by Dave. What if I'd put my trust in the wrong person?

In the span of a second, Angela had gotten within an arm's length of me. "Who's Danel?" An alarm bell inside me went off as I gave Dave another uncertain glance, my throat bone dry.

"Angela, you know what Corinth is capable of. I only brought him here so you could finally see for yourself how powerful he truly is. Your end is nigh. Please, see reason. Stand down." Dave lowered his voice, his usual calm replaced by foreboding. "Leave him be and stop your foolhardy plan. You will lose."

My heart rate spiked as Dave put me on the spot.

"His true name is Danel," Angela's eyes shimmered and glowed silvery white, like sleeting snow in a blizzard.

"He's told me," I said with surprising calm, "that the Grigori are senseless murderers, that they kill women and children." I squeezed my fists tighter against my sides, feeling the blood rush to my cheeks and neck.

Angela's face twisted up in remorse and regret, much like someone might look after accidentally running over a squirrel in the middle of the road. "It was never senseless."

Even though I knew Dave owed me more answers, he had at least been telling me the partial truth. I was on the right side of things. The first thought running through my mind was that Dave had better hurry. The second was that this was no armistice. Thirdly, I was really terrible at keeping my mouth shut. I pointed at Turiel. "I think it's time I wipe that smirk off that guy's face."

Turiel snorted as if it wouldn't even be a challenge going up against me. He was dead wrong. He hissed between gritted teeth, "You are an abomination. Not even worthy to stand in our presence." He stepped up behind Angela, his shoulders squared. "Let me take him out once and for all."

Dave was speaking again. I was just having trouble focusing on what he was saying because that surge of storm-raging energy started crackling out of my fingertips. This time, though, it wasn't me controlling it. This is what Dave meant by drawing on my power. We weren't going to keep the peace. This was about Dave showing his full deck, his ace in the hole: me. He was going to use me to take Angela out, me as an unwilling puppet. And I was okay with this. Power flooded through me, swirled in my chest, and I let it—not resisting in the least.

Angela's semi amused gaze met mine, her milky eyes hypnotic. She wasn't intimidated by the lightning sparking out of my eyeballs. Still, seeing her forehead wrinkle in surprise and then scrunch up in anger was a nice sight.

Then she was bending over, clutching her head in between her hands. "*What are you doing?*" she snarled.

Dave's eyes were clouded over, darting back and forth as if he were reading something extremely quickly, completely zoned out. I wondered idly if his eyes, clouded over like that, are what mine looked like minus the lightning when I went atomic.

Angela clutched her head, clearly in pain as she hissed, "*Do it, Turiel.*"

Turiel's hands erupted in a ball of fiery light—the same kind of energy I conjured while using the blade. Before I could cry out a warning to Dave, Turiel had hurtled one of the deadly bolts right at him. Dave never saw it coming, his eyes still glazed over as he worked on stealing the cure from Angela. Now I knew why Al and Larna had been so concerned when I went nuclear.

Standing next to Dave, the force of the blast sent me airborne, arms flailing out beside me as I tried to stay upright. I watched in stunned horror as the ball of light hit Dave square in the chest, flames engulfing him from head to toe. His scream of agony lingered long after he was sucked away—into a void, disappearing as if someone had erased him with a pencil. The only thing left was a cloud of ash and dust.

Chapter 53

Larna

CORINTH WAS SPREAD OUT on the cot, his long legs extended out over the edge. Dave was sitting up on the other one, stiff as a board, his eyes moving listlessly to something I could not see nor hear.

I let out another loud, frustrated sigh as Al checked the doors for the third time. Once he was satisfied, he made his way over to me. "You going to stand over him the entire time?"

I nodded anxiously, kneading my hands in my lap, refusing to take my eyes off him. "You going to keep checking the doors?" I quipped.

"Touché," he answered. "You think this is going to go south on us?"

"Something doesn't feel right, that's for sure," I muttered.

I felt his eyes on me again as he said, "Well, there isn't much to like about—"

He broke off when we both heard the sizzling noise of melting metal, followed by the tang of something burning outside the main doors. I shot to attention, flicking the blades free of my hidden sheathes, giving Alastair an "I told you so" glare in the process.

Alastair's whole body coiled like a tightly wound bowstring, and then he was flying to the doors, with me right on his heels.

He put an ear to the door, listening. They were made of heavy iron, and even with our supersonic hearing, whatever was going on outside still sounded muffled. There was a moment of silence, like the calm before a storm, as everything went incredibly still. I shared a look with Alastair, both of us thinking the same thing: the silence was eerier than the sound of melting metal. And then, as if someone had snapped their fingers, chaos and panic broke out just on the other side of the fortified doors. There came frantic shouting and screaming and feet thudding heavily against the stone floors. In here we were protected. Out there, would the guards be able to hold them off? I thought about the kids: Cora and Bella and Tanner, all left unprotected. What if they were in danger?

I gasped at the sudden flurry of panic, pulling my ear away from the door. Smoke billowed up through the cracks around the door and then poured out of the ventilation shafts. The same metallic scent right before a thunderstorm hung in the air. My eyes snapped to Corinth, who was still dead to the world, sleeping soundlessly on the cot.

The Grigori were here.

Alastair pressed his lips together in a firm line, thinking, and then, as if a lightbulb had gone off over his head, he flew to Sozo's desk, punching the intercom on the device. We waited—me listening to empty static from my position still near the door across the room, a grim expression on my face.

After a few minutes, Caesar's muffled and terrified voice broke through the line: "They're here! The Grigori—"

At first, I thought he had been cut off, until I heard the sound of someone else's frantic breathing: "It's Sarah." Her voice shook as it came through barely above a whisper. "We've been infiltrated. N-n-not sure who these people are, but they're coming for Corinth. Protect him at all costs—" Before she could finish the rest of her sentence, a blood-curdling scream pierced through the intercom so loudly that a mechanical screech drowned out the rest of her cry. And then the line went dead.

Alastair staggered back as if someone had punched in him in the chest, his face draining of all its color. I knew what he must be thinking. He wasn't able to help Sarah once again. I could see how much anguish Alastair was in as his brows drew together. I remember him telling me how Sarah's cries for help back when he had been turned had rooted him to the spot in fear. Now, he stood frozen in terror, as if he was fifteen years old all over again, digging up the macabre memories of his past. I was beside him in an instant, my hand shooting out to steady him. *I sent Sarah out there.* She could have been in here with us—safe for the time being. Icy dread welled up in me.

"Alastair—" I said firmly, making sure I held his attention. When his clear blue eyes met mine, I said, "*Go help Sarah.* I'll try and wake Dave and Corinth from their trance. They can help us."

We both turned to Corinth, his eyes moving rapidly under muted, almost-translucent eyelids. Dave was still in the same exact state as before, sitting rigidly at attention, his eyes clouded over.

I retracted the thin blades back into my armor so I

could gently cup his cheeks. He felt fever hot. Turning his head, I forced him to look me in the eyes. His breathing was erratic, and his chest rose and fell as if he'd just been chased by the Devil himself—and by the look on his face, the Devil had caught up with him. This was his waking nightmare; I could feel it pulsing in his veins.

"Alastair, I need you to hear me," I whispered fervently. "You can still help Sarah. We'll be okay in here. I'll lock the doors. Once I wake these two up, we'll be right behind you, but we can't leave all those people out there to die at the Grigori's hands. The kids …" My voice cracked. I caught of a whiff of burning flesh—I could sense their pain, it was palpable and thick in the air. I'm sure he could sense it too, but Alastair was in another world, reliving what he thought were the sins of his past. Finally, he blinked rapidly as if he was coming out of his trance. Then he was setting his shoulders in determination, and something else—desperation.

After he took a deep breath, he suddenly pulled me close, whispering, "Lock the doors behind me. I'll try and get as many people to safety as I can."

"Go," I said quickly.

Alastair broke into a run, with me right behind him. As soon as I unlatched the doors, he slipped past me, out into the melee without a backward glance.

My heart skipped a beat as he disappeared into the raucous noise of chaos and combat and fire. The cries of terror mingled with the sounds of the guards shouting orders at each other almost brought me to my knees. Blinding light crackled and sizzled as electricity lit up the haze in strobe-like flashes. Smoke curled around the door as I slammed it shut and I bolted the latch back into place.

Why did I feel like I had just sent Alastair off to his death? The pit in my stomach dropped out at the thought.

A thousand different emotions crashed through me as I skidded back to a halt in front of Dave. Terror and guilt and adrenaline—I had let Alastair go out there alone, without me; I should be right there by his side.

I gripped Dave's shoulders and shook him hard. "*Dave!*" I shouted, "Wake up! Wake up! It's a trap. Get out of there. *Now!*"

His eyes were glossed over, covered in some kind of peculiar white film. I shook him harder, his head lolling to the side. He was completely unresponsive to my touch.

I crouched beside Corinth next, hoping I could wake him up, and thereby bring Dave back with him. "Corinth, I really need you to wake up right now." I ran a hand along his forehead. He felt feverish and clammy, and his eyes were still moving rapidly under closed lids. I put my hands on his shoulders, gently shaking him. "Hey, *Ringer* ... I really need you to wake up now." I shook him more forcefully; one of his hands fell limp over the side of the cot. "Can you hear me? Please, Corinth ..."

"Oh—he can't hear you."

I was dimly aware that someone had spoken right behind me.

My mind was in overdrive, as I remembered shutting and bolting the door back into place after Alastair had gone through it. Fear paralyzed me to the spot. No one else should be in here with us. In a deliberately slow movement, I relinquished my hold on Corinth's shoulder, hoping that whoever was behind me wouldn't think I was a threat.

To be clear, I was a threat, but I didn't want them to know that yet.

When I turned, I caught sight of a ball of blisteringly intense light popping into existence from out of thin air, and two figures dropping down into the room to land within an arm's length of me. I slid both my blades free right as the two figures stood from their crouched positions. I froze when I saw it who it was. Caesar and Sarah. Relief flooded through me at seeing them alive. Had Dave rescued them? Or maybe Eleuthoros had some fancy tech that I hadn't been made aware of. If that was the case, this would have come in handy a million times over.

I watched in stunned fascination as Caesar raised his hands, forming a globe of crackling blue energy, the same kind of power that looked a lot like what Corinth generated when using his blade. One stretched-out second too late, I realized what he was going to do. My mouth fell open as he hurtled the ball of light at me. It struck me with enough force to send me rocketing across polished marble—

I fetched up against the side of Sozo's desk, my heart rate slowing and then skipping several beats before stuttering to an agonizingly painful halt. This was it. I clutched at my chest, panting in misery as darkness threatened to pull me under. I had a fleeting recollection of Corinth telling me that vampires couldn't have heart attacks. I almost laughed, even though this wasn't funny. It was brutal. But then my heart rebooted, starting up again like a battery on its last legs. And then it was beating, if weakly—my body furiously fighting to heal itself as I dragged in a deep lungful of air. Why did this hurt so much?

As I lay there trying to recover, a dark shadow dropped over me—the first thing I saw were his wings.

They spread out wide, the span of them at least the length of the room. What surprised me the most was that they weren't soft and feathery; they were a shade of color that reminded me of charcoal burning in a grill. This was an angel of doom. *Caesar was Grigori?*

He stared down at me, a sneer on his face as Sarah moved to kneel beside me, a matching smirk marring her normally pretty features. *But I heard her scream*—except, here she was, and the voice inside my head was the one screaming: I should not have trusted her.

"I have been waiting to do that for a very long time." Fiery lightning crackled out of Caesar's fingertips as his hate-filled eyes slid to Corinth's still form on the cot.

"Don't even think about it," I wheezed, still winded and queasy.

Sarah laughed. "I drugged Corinth with the coffee," she said matter-of-factly. "We're going to keep you alive so that you can watch me kill your best friend, and then after that … your *boyfriend*."

A scalpel appeared in her hands and she flashed it in front of my face.

White-hot rage licked my insides. My *Sight* took hold, also taking with it immobilizing pain, but as soon as I tried to sit up, Caesar planted a blazing, crackling hand against my chest and zapped me again. I screamed in anguish as fire lanced through me, dancing up my arms, running through my veins, hurtling into my bloodstream, shooting through internal organs—the pain was debilitating and unending. I think my heart stopped again, because everything went black. When I burst back out of darkness, the sweat was slick on my forehead and my heart thundered erratically in my chest.

Sarah bent down, clearly amused at seeing me suffer. "Don't make this hard on yourself. Caesar can stop and start your heart all day," she cooed. "We lured Alastair out—the two of you would have been too hard to take down together." She grinned maddeningly down at me. "Have you noticed how out of sorts Alastair has been lately? All I had to do was bat my eyes and cry, and he was like putty in my hands, so easily manipulated." Sarah pulled Alastair's timepiece out of her pocket and kissed it. "He even gave me the pocket watch back." The usual shade of her pale green eyes had transformed to dark and dangerous. "I loved Wrentmore, and Alastair stole him from me," she hissed. "So now I'm stealing something from *him*."

All this time, Alastair had been tearing himself up over her death. She loved Wrentmore? I rolled onto my side, gasping for breath, and caught a glimpse of Dave. He was there one second, his eyes almost at the back of his head and then he wasn't. I watched in horror as he burst apart like dust in the wind, a cloud of ash and powder raining down onto the white sheet.

I reached down to the watch at my wrist, to press the panic button, and realized with growing dread that it had stopped working right along with my heart.

Sarah put a foot on my shoulder, pushed me flat onto my back, and then flashed the scalpel in front of my eyes again. "Corinth has to die a slow and painful death. Too bad really, I was just starting to like him. I guess he shouldn't have rejected me so quickly."

That was what did it. There was no way she was hurting Corinth on my watch. Suddenly everything was so clear—every action and thought and move I needed to make. Time slowed down and then crawled to a halt. In the space between one tick on a clock, I reacted, slicing upward with my razor thin blades. They slid home, one carving right through her shoulder, ripping through bone and sinew, all the way out of the other side—the other blade, slicing off several of her fingers on her left hand. The last thing I heard before Caesar stopped my heart again was her terrified scream of pain.

Chapter 54

Corinth

I WAS ALONE, STANDING in the middle of a picturesque field with two angels who wanted me dead. They slowly closed the distance between us. I thought about Larna and Al and all they had taught me over the course of the last year. Drawing on all those training hours, I had the dagger up and in my palm so fast it even surprised Turiel. His slow-blink of astonishment added fuel to my fire as the power churned through me—fueled me.

I lunged forward, igniting muscles into action right as Angela spoke, but her lips didn't move—her voice was inside my head like a pick axe to my brain. I fell to my knees in agony as her voice echoed painfully in my ears: *The blade holds enormous value—imbued with seven angels' power—it is not meant for half-breed, mortal hands.*

She was in front of me, her fingers wrapping around my wrist.

When did she even move?

I conjured lightning as if it had been at my beck and call all along; it sparked out of my fingertips, as easily as breathing—but Angela snuffed it out like a flame on a candle wick. A jolt of pain rolled through my body, so intense I released my grip on the blade. Dave was wrong, so wrong. I could be hurt in a dream.

Angela towered over me, making me feel as small and insignificant as an ant. *What happened?* Panic flooded through me, folding its ugly hands around my throat, constricting my airway, making it impossible to suck in a deep breath. *Was this still part of Dave's plan? He's not dead. Please don't be dead.*

"You shouldn't play with fire." Angela murmured. "You'll get burned." She bent down, and her sweetly whisper-soft breath hit my ear. "Nothing you've ever felt before, no? Now that I've gained access to your head, controlling you is as easy as opening a bottle of water— with Danel gone, that is. It is not you that is powerful, little one. You are only a tool. Part human, part angel—no matter how insignificant that part may be, it still came from *our* blood." Her voice dripped like honey. "You don't deserve to feel such divine influence."

I tried to pull in a breath. *Calm down. She can't hurt you. Dave has it under control.* Angela watched me as if she found my need to breathe amusing.

All they had to do was pull me out of my dream. *Wake me up.* "Wake me up, Larna!" I shouted it out loud this time, searching the overly bright sky for any signs that she had heard me.

There was a dangerous undercurrent in the way Angela laughed at me, mocking. "I would ask who Larna is—but you are not long for this life anyway, so it doesn't matter." She circled me like a vulture. "'For everything there is a season, a time for every activity under heaven: a time to be born and a time to die.'"

I staggered back to my feet, scooping the blade back up into my grasp. Even though I was in pain, I refused to stay down. Panting, I said, "'So whoever knows the right thing to do and fails to do it, for him it is a sin. And now these three remain: faith, hope, and love. But the greatest of these is … love.'" It was one of the verses from Corinthians I'd learned in Sunday school, which had stuck with me only because my name was Corinth. I wasn't some great speaker; I didn't exude power or evoke change based solely on popularity—I could barely convince myself to get up in the mornings—so being in a fight with an angel was new territory for me. My plan was to keep her talking so I could come up with a better plan.

She put a finger to her chin in thought, staring at me like she was deciding on what to do with me next. I refused to acknowledge the fact that it was probably how she was going to kill me.

"I can quote scripture too. Stand down, Angela." In the most silken voice I could muster, I added, "There is no more need for bloodshed. Because in the end, your blood *will* run down my hands if you don't."

Icy eyes flashed under her brow, unmistakable, cold and calculating. "You're not at all what I expected." When she spoke again, it was softer, almost kind. It was scarier than her frostiness—it sounded final, as if she knew the ending to a particularly tragic book and was about to share it with me. "I almost wish you had not been the last."

I fell to a knee, wrapping an arm around my stomach as fire curled up my belly, incapacitating me. *Is this her?* I gasped, stunned by the sudden pain. *What is she doing to me? Maybe it's Dave drawing on my power.* Air was ripped from my lungs as my blade flew from my hand and into hers.

Using my blade, she weaved her hands together, twisting this way and that, forming a weird pattern in the air that sizzled with fire and magic. I watched in dismay and fright and captivation as that magic flowed out from her fingertips—and then she was hurtling it right at me.

Unable to move or jump out of the way, it hit me square in the chest. I was flung backward, flat on my back as the twist of energy wound its way around me like a living organism, rendering me immobile, like two tons of invisible steel pressing me into the ground.

This was my dream. I had control.

Wake up. Wake up. Wake up.

Larna. Al … if you can hear me—WAKE ME UP!

Angela's whispered words amplified and ping-ponged around in my head: *I can't allow you to use this weapon against us.*

Why was she stalling?

The searing pain that had started in my stomach was now spreading to my chest. I tried to curl into a ball, but whatever was holding me down wouldn't let me. I was buried above ground. A thought hit me that maybe this was happening in the real world, where I had been blissfully sleeping. Angela was holding me here. *Stalling.* I'd been blinded by a race for a cure. Even though I could still feel my power, I couldn't connect to it. I fought against her hold, but the more I struggled, the more it felt like the life was draining out of me, sinking me into the cold earth like a coffin being lowered into the ground.

In the background, I tuned out the sound of Turiel's grating laughter, the sound of my prison snapping and crackling with supernatural energy, bearing down on me, and also the sound of the blood rushing through my ears. I was in a dream. We were in my head. This prison wasn't even real—I was Harry Houdini. I blinked back the sting of tears at the backs of my eyes as more pain flooded through me.

I ground my teeth together, imagining the blade in my hand.

Pulling in one last deep, ragged breath, a primal scream tore out of my throat. I was a force that was vaporous and untouchable as air. She couldn't hold me any longer.

And then that invisible force relinquished its hold. I had been so determined at freeing myself that as soon as the heavy weight on top of me let up; I bit down on my tongue, drawing blood. The pain was instant and piercing and—blessedly corporeal. I sprang to a knee, a hand curled around my stomach, the other one held out toward the blade still clutched in Angela's grasp.

I called to it and it came to me in a flash of blinding cobalt light, the sharp gleam of metal winking out of her hands and appearing in mine, right as her eyes went wide with panic.

And then I was vaulting back to the waking world, Angela's whispered words echoing hauntingly in my skull: *I'm sorry.*

Chapter 55

Corinth

MY DAD USED TO take me on train rides when I was a kid. I couldn't get enough of the chug of the engine and the puff of smoke pummeling from the caboose, and of course, the deafening blast of the train's whistle—my favorite part. Train yards have an unmistakable odor in the air: a metallic, coppery tang that rests on the tip of your tongue. As a kid, it took me a while to figure out what that smell was. Now, though, being older, I know it's from all that iron in the tracks. If you go to a construction site, you'll smell the same thing.

That's why, when I woke, I thought I was in a train yard. It was the distinct taste of metal in my mouth. As I came to, shaking the fog from my brain, it took me a minute to realize that what I was actually experiencing wasn't a cherished childhood memory; it was the taste of blood in my mouth. I'd bitten my tongue in real life too.

I opened my eyes to find I was back on the cot.

Sarah was leaning over me, staring with those intense green eyes of hers, so close I could now see tiny flecks of blue in them—a kaleidoscope of color I'd never even noticed until now. They looked like loose tea leaves. For a second, everything seemed right in the world. Her brows were furrowed in concern as she peered down at me, a cute dimple popping up in the middle of her forehead as soon as she knew I was awake.

My memory unraveled, as jarring as walking through a thick layer of cobwebs. *Angela.* The frosty-eyed angel. I shuddered as her whispered words came back to me: *I'm sorry.*

As the cloudy haze of slumber started to lift, I wondered why Larna and Al weren't standing over me right now, too. Surely they had a thousand questions they wanted to ask. What if they were in trouble? As this disturbing thought hit, I tried to struggle into a sitting position, only to find that I couldn't move. Even trying to lift my head was too difficult a task. It felt as if a giant weight was sitting on top of me, keeping me rooted to the spot and flat on my back. Even my tongue felt like it weighed a thousand pounds. But there was nothing holding me down that I could see, only a smiling Sarah, staring at me with those gorgeous eyes of hers.

She put a surprisingly firm hand on my chest, stopping my further attempts at getting up. "Shhhh, shhhh, shhhh ..." Her voice came out warm and soothing, melting my insides and calming all at the same time. "It's all right," she purred.

There was blood on her hands. It was sticky and slick. Was she hurt? Not only did my whole body feel sluggish, but my brain felt that way too. Several things clawed their way back into my memory: Why was Sarah here? Hadn't she left? I tried to warn her about Angela ... and then I remembered Dave ... I was able to twist my head just enough to see that he was gone from the cot beside mine.

I wondered if he was dead or if he was a traitor, except that didn't make sense. Hadn't he tried to defend me from Turiel? Why did my head feel like it was filled with helium and attached to a string? Slowly my mind struggled to play catch-up. All the while, Sarah watched me, a small curious smile playing on her lips, and infinite amount of patience in those eyes as she waited. But now that my head was clearing, I realized something was off about the way she was studying me. Her grin looked painted on, as if the crinkles at the corners of her eyes didn't quite meet up or match. Where had she come from again? The doors had been locked and bolted tight. Maybe Larna let her back in.

My mouth was full of cotton. I tried to tell Sarah to get Al or Larna, but all I could manage was a strangled gurgle. I closed my eyes, breathed in hard, and then cracked them wide as my chest rattled painfully.

Sarah's grin stretched over white teeth and pink gums as she saw the beginnings of my comprehension. Her smile was no longer cute, mainly because it had been replaced by a satanic leer. The shadows around her face dipped and elongated as if she had horns.

Managing to turn my head an inch to the left, I got a partial view of the rest of the room out of the corner of my eye. Larna told me she would watch over me. Where was she? Even that small amount of movement hurt. If I could just go for my blade—

A prone figure lay on the ground, as still as a corpse. As soon as I saw her, the fight drained out of me. I was breathing in short quick pants now. Every fiber of my being screamed at me to turn away. *No ... she can't be dead. Please don't let her be dead. Larna, no.* This was what true agony felt like, staring helplessly at your lifeless best friend crumpled in the corner of the room, and not being able to help or cry out or scream her name. Tears welled up in my eyes. What was wrong with me?

Sarah followed my line of sight to Larna's very still and lifeless form. "She tried to save you. It was very heroic." She glanced down to her shoulder, and for the first time, I noticed the large amount of red staining her shirt. She swiped a hand across her face and I saw the grisly, bloodied stumps of three severed fingers on her left hand. I wasn't sure how I'd missed it before.

A weird half-chortle bubbled out of my throat as I wheezed, "Guess … vampires … don't grow limbs back—"

Sarah's eyes flashed dangerously. "Your girlfriend fought so hard we had to knock her out." She said it so nonchalantly it made me start to shake with rage. "We killed the security detail outside as a distraction to lure Alastair away, and then we slipped past. Larna never saw it coming—of course, I did hitch a ride with an angel." Sarah shook her head, her eyes welling in pity. "Don't worry, your girlfriend isn't dead," she whispered softly, "*yet.*"

Relief washed over me, so intense I closed my eyes against another flood of tears threatening to spill out. Larna wasn't dead. Sarah had used the word *we.* Someone—an angel—was helping her and whoever it was, wasn't in the room with her right now, which meant maybe Al was pursuing them. I still had a chance. I tried to concentrate everything I had on summoning my blade just like I'd done with Angela, but something inside me felt seriously broken—wrecked. I choked and coughed as blood trickled down my chin.

"I almost regret not giving you a fighting chance." She

licked her lips, her gaze drifting provocatively down to my throat and then chest. "I like you, Corinth. I wanted to make your death as painless as possible … so I drugged you. It's more humane that way, because of the mess I had to make—to leave for Alastair, you see. He has to feel the pain I felt all those years ago. I knew you wouldn't be able to heal—you had such awful scratch marks on your face from being attacked." She reached a bloodied hand out to run it along my cuts. I jerked away from her touch, disgusted.

The coffee had had such a chalky aftertaste. I was kicking myself now for not catching on quicker. Maybe the drugs had started to wear off, but I didn't think so, because all I could feel was intense cold. It was numbing. I heard it, the drip, drip, drip … of something leaking nearby, steady and uniform.

The clinical detachment in Sarah's voice was almost worse than not being able to move. She had been so convincing. Had she been compelled? What if this was Gabe? Where was Imani? I couldn't make myself believe I'd been this duped by her. Sarah was confessing a heinous crime as if it were as simple as stomping out an insect's life … I just had to snap her out of it.

And now that I was paying attention, I could see blood pooling underneath her feet, staining her blue scrubs and white sneakers—it hit me a little too late that most of it was mine. I was bleeding out, dying—that was why I felt so exhausted, why my heart was beating so hard, trying to pump what wasn't there. Why my stomach hurt so bad in my dream.

Larna had been abandoned in the corner of the room like a piece of trash—this was enough to spur me into action. With every ounce of strength I could muster, I bolted upright, but Sarah saw it coming from a mile away. Her grip was like iron and unforgiving as she pushed me back down. And then I saw it. A glint of something glittering off the walls, drawing my eye to it immediately— a stainless-steel scalpel rested in Sarah's good hand. I caught a quick glimpse of the blood and averted my gaze. *Concentrate on the ceiling instead of the blood on her hands. My blood.*

Patterns of Celtic knots stood out in vivid detail against pristine white walls. Intricate gold knots and loops wound their way through each other—a sign of singularity and strength that could not have been more lost on me right now. This couldn't be real. My life was being sapped … zapped … stolen from me, and there was nothing I could do about it. *Use your power, dummy! Thunderblade— now would be a great time to come to my rescue.* What was the use of the damn thing if it didn't help out when I needed it? But no matter how hard I tried to call on its power, it would not answer.

The one question that burned too deeply not to be asked broke through my cracked and swollen lips. "*Why?*"

She waggled a finger at me. "You're not the one I wanted to hurt, Corinth, not really. What I said about working with you to find a cure for cancer … all of that was … *is* true. My work is of the utmost importance." She pulled a vial out of her pocket. I could see my name written on it. "When you showed me the top security clearance keycard—and then gave me access to what I'd been craving to get my hands on—well, the opportunity was too much to pass up. I slipped this one out while you weren't looking."

I squeezed my eyes shut at the realization of what I'd done. *No. She has to be compelled …*

Sarah spit out, "I needed to get vengeance for my love." She yanked the timepiece Al had given to her out of her pocket as my eyes snapped open again. "This was all about hurting Alastair—exactly like *he* hurt me." Sarah pushed her face closer to mine. It swam in and out of focus as she breathed, "Thomas Wrentmore was my everything … and *Alastair* murdered him."

My throat constricted. How did this fit in with the Grigori? This couldn't be mere coincidence. I didn't understand why it was so eerily quiet outside either. There should have been scuffling or shouting or banging— someone trying to help me by now. No one was coming to my rescue. Was Sozo dead? Whatever Sarah had done, it was bad. Very bad. And I realized with dread that all of this had been planned out for quite some time.

Sarah, pleased that I was still following along, said, "I didn't even know sweet Alastair was alive until he showed up with you lot—"

She broke off as soon as a sudden blast of air stirred her hair.

A giant dome of light and electricity and lightning burst into existence right behind her. My mouth dropped open as the air thickened, became a bright ball of super-charged kinetic energy. I expected Dave to come to my rescue, to jump to action, but who popped out of the light completely threw me for a loop—Benny, the ex-engineer, darted out of the center of it in a clap of thunder, dropping down next to me.

His quick, sharp eyes assessed the situation—me lying on the cot, slowly dying, Larna unmoving, in a heap in the corner of the room, and Sarah holding a bloodied scalpel over me.

And then he took action.

Benny had appeared old and feeble when I'd first met him, but now he seemed exactly the opposite. Deadly lightning exploded out of his hands and eyes, blotting out the chaotic scene around me. I felt detached from my body—thin and hollow, like a dead seashell, whittling away—and even though I really wanted to join the melee, I found that too much life had drained out of me now. I did, however, have a front-row seat to Benny's awesomeness. I mean, I assumed he was a Watcher, because he bore down on Sarah with all of the gusto and flare of a vampire-slaying badass.

She whirled on him, her scalpel slashing right through his abdomen. What should have been a lethal shot didn't seem to slow him down though. His hands blazed bright as he traded blows with Sarah—she flew across the room, landing on her side near the impenetrable iron doors.

Once Sarah had been taken out, Benny turned those liquid-mercury lightning eyes on me next. I wondered futilely if he was here to finish the job for her. He lifted his hands, aiming them at the solidly built doors, and let loose his ultimate power. I would have shielded my eyes if I could have, because the doors exploded apart as he blew them to kingdom come, plaster and paint and smoke filling the air.

Hope flared in my chest as soon as I saw the movement out of the corner of my eye. Caesar was here, and he was only a few feet behind Benny. I wasn't sure where he'd come from—but seeing him made me want to whoop in joy. Caesar saw my brief glance in his direction. He put a finger to his lips as he inched toward Benny. I couldn't help but notice the blood staining the white sleeves of his robe. He had obviously been hurt or had managed to kill the second accomplice. Maybe there was a back way into this room that we didn't know about.

His eyes darted back to mine, and then he did something that made what little blood I had left in my body run cold. His eyes churned bright and crackled with the same kind of electrical energy I now knew all angels used. He formed the energy into a tight ball, weaving it expertly through his hands as I watched, mesmerized and horror-struck. I knew he wasn't here to help me—not when I saw his face morph from concern to hatred.

My eyes went wide as I managed to shout, "*Benny!*"

Benny was blown off his feet as Caesar's sizzling bolt pierced his chest, his eyes going wide as he collapsed to his knees like a puppet whose strings had been cut. This was something he would not recover from. His eyes were once again clouded and glazed, but this time, in death.

Caesar—the person who tripped over his own robes was the accomplice—and Grigori to boot? I had trusted these two. I had opened myself up to both of them. They had both played me.

Sarah lifted her bloodied head off the ground once the dust had settled. "It's about time you showed up," she spit, standing shakily back to her feet.

Caesar gazed down at me like I was a bug on a windshield and the rock in my stomach returned, twice the size as before. I wriggled my fingers, finding I could finally move them again.

Sarah was beside Caesar, looking decidedly less

energetic. "Too bad I can't sample his blood," she murmured regretfully. "It would be interesting to see what it tastes like … purely from a scientific stand point, I mean."

Why wasn't Al here? I had tried to avoid thinking about him, because if Larna was lying in a motionless heap—Al was most likely dead somewhere. That thought sent the shock of loss running through me as icy as the dark side of the moon. I almost wished Sarah had carved my heart out of my chest. Losing Alastair was not an option. I couldn't go there. If I did, I'd give up right now. I'd be happy to admit it would be nice if Al could save me life just one more time.

My eyes stayed locked on Larna's unmoving body across the way, willing her to wake up. Caesar followed my line of sight.

"Shall we wake her for the grand finale?" Caesar asked slowly, studying Sarah's handiwork with all the interest of a mortician considering their newest guest's arrival. "Mr. Taylor, it would appear this is the end of the line for you."

I had to live to grill my dad about my family's involvement in all this. I had to live for Larna. I had to live for Al. I had to live to take all of the Grigori down. They had made a terrible mistake.

It was now or never.

I pulled as much energy as I could from the still, ozone-rich atmosphere around me. It was thick in the air from Caesar and Benny's last encounter. There was power to take—just not my own … *theirs* … I would steal Caesar's. If what Dave said about me was true, I could draw energy from other angels, like he'd drawn from me. Even if I had nothing left inside me to use. I closed my eyes, feeling the thread of something strange and foreign wrapped around Caesar. I could see his power or halo or whatever it was outlining his body. It looked like tiny ripples in the water. I focused on stealing energy from him, imagined drawing the current into the dagger strapped to my thigh—imagined it strengthening me in the process.

I was the last Nephilim—

Thunderblade hummed at my side.

Sarah clicked her tongue like a babysitter might to a misbehaving child as she knelt down beside me. "Don't fight it, Corinth. Your friends aren't coming to save you." The scalpel flashed in her hand as she waved it in the air. "I wanted to show Alastair how much he hurt me. I think I've accomplished that task. I so want to be here when he finds you like this." Her eyes flicked to Caesar's hand, now resting on her shoulder. "Caesar laid waste to most of the guards outside." She flipped the scalpel over, curling it tighter in between bloodied fingers. "And then sent them running in the opposite direction. It was the only way to get them off your back. They've been stuck to you like glue. Sozo is in his panic room hiding—"

Sarah jumped in sudden fright as soon as she saw my eyes change and flare with glorious, almighty lightning: It was as deadly and unyielding as any power I'd ever drawn or felt. My fingers grazed the strap at my hip, where the blade rested—

I felt something pierce my side, and the searing pain came back tenfold. My eyes blazed with fire and flame and wrath.

I was destruction.

A look of terror crossed Caesar's features as soon as he saw me change. "Finish him," he hissed, and I could hear the fear in his voice now, too.

"You promised I'd get revenge," Sarah pleaded. "I'm not done yet."

"Of course you are," Caesar cooed. "You're taking away his love's *love*. It's a good start, *Sarah*." He patted her shoulder affectionately. "But it's time to go. Look at his eyes, his hands …"

I didn't know what was worse: not being able to wisecrack, or having to listen to their incessant babbling. The oxygen in the room thickened; the heady ozone tickled the back of my throat and passed through my body. I was about to light all of them up in an epic display of smiting when Sarah gritted her teeth and then plunged the scalpel deep into my chest.

It didn't hurt.

I thought it would, but the swiftness with which she'd done it only sent one final arctic spasm running through me. At first I thought it was my heart giving out, until I realized it was the rumble of someone's thunderous footfalls as they came running through the now-obliterated doors.

I blinked and almost missed it—Larna coming to … then I heard her strangled cry as darkness swallowed me up, mind, body, and soul.

Chapter 56

Larna

I AWOKE TO CHAOS and gore. Benny's burned and lifeless body was in the corner of the office opposite me, his eyes wide open in death. *No.* I squeezed my eyes shut briefly before glancing to Sarah standing over Corinth. She had a very sharp and pointy-looking scalpel in one hand, and Alastair's watch in her other, fingerless grip. Caesar was behind her with a demonic grin on his face: the purest form of evil. The room felt like I was inside a pressurized tank, the air now permeated with ozone, burned-to-a-crisp-wiring, and what was left of the smoldering remains of the iron doors. It was as if Vinson had used C-4 all over again.

At seeing Corinth lying as deathly still as a corpse, I let out a grief-stricken wail. The way his hand hung limply over the side of the cot, the gray pallor of his skin, filled me with a growing sense of dread. A tortured moan escaped from my lips. From my position on the floor, I could see very little of the rest of him, so I didn't know how badly he was hurt or if he was even still alive. My head was buzzing, and wisps of smoke still curled up from my body where I'd been repeatedly struck by lightning.

The sound of heavy footfalls broke through my train of thought as Alastair burst into the room through a recently scorched hole in the wall. I had seen that same look on his face before: the night he'd taken Jeremy down with an infantry sword at Gabriel's manor. His face had been blood spattered and ghostly white. His eyes locked on mine, and when he saw the state I was in, his *Sight* turned the most lethal, yet beautiful shade of sapphire I'd ever seen, probably releasing more energy than the sun would in its ten-billion-year lifetime. Corinth's eyes didn't have anything on Alastair's.

I should have been faster, reacted quicker, but shock and pain kept me flat on my back for a second too long.

Dave's cot was still empty. He was supposed to protect Corinth. So were the legion of now-dead guards outside—his first line of defense charred to a bloody crisp. The smell of burning bodies almost made me gag.

Caesar's hands erupted in blue flames. The air churned and crackled with power and charged energy. He gripped Sarah with a free hand right as she gave Alastair a wink and chucked the watch onto the floor next to Corinth's cot. And just like that, they disappeared into a spinning vortex of energy and vapor—a barrier of light much like what Corinth had produced back in the meeting hall when he had seen Gabriel for the first time.

I tried to stagger to my feet as Alastair closed the distance, catching me up in his arms before I could hit the ground.

I heard the undercurrent of rage in his voice when he spoke. "*Sarah*—she did this ..." His voice caught. "How badly are you hurt?"

I couldn't tear my eyes off Corinth. "Corinth. Help me over to him, hurry—"

Alastair was already guiding me to over to Corinth before I could even finish the sentence. I fell to my knees in front of his cot, slipping in the gory mess at my feet.

I listened to his vitals as Alastair dropped down beside me. He inhaled sharply at seeing the full extent of Corinth's injuries. Alastair's face crumpled, and for the first time I noticed the dark scorch marks and splotches of black soot across his cheekbones. "*Oh no …*"

This was just another patient. I could be clinically detached. Corinth wasn't bleeding out on this cot right before my very eyes. *Focus.* I assessed him, noting he was unresponsive and his pulse thready. His eyelids were blue and stark against waxy skin; his dark hair pasted to his forehead. I put a hand on his shirt and it came back slick with red. I found I had to steady myself against his cot at the sight of him—Alastair's firm, supportive hand on my shoulder. *Keep calm, Larna. Assess and heal. No time to get emotional.* I peeled his shirt up, the blood already clotted and drying and sticking to his skin in brown clumps. There was so much of it. I know any other vampire would have been salivating—but suddenly the sight of his blood only seemed to make me sick.

"He's been stabbed so many times—"

I broke off when I realized Alastair's hand was no longer on my shoulder. The sound of two people struggling, their shoes sliding across the polished marble behind me, was enough to distract me away from Corinth momentarily.

I turned to see Alastair seizing Gabriel's tie; he was shoving him toward the blown-to-bits doorway. Now that there were no guards to stop anyone from entering, Gabriel must have waltzed right on in—most likely to witness and gloat about his glorious achievement.

"Get him out of here, Alastair," I snarled through clenched teeth, turning my attention back to Corinth. I didn't have time for this. Looking for the deepest wounds, I grabbed the sheet from the empty cot where Dave had been sitting, and wadded it up, pressing the cloth firmly against his chest—using my inhuman strength to try and staunch the bleeding. A tiny exhale escaped his lips as I pushed down, expelling the oxygen from his lungs. Other than that, he showed no signs of waking.

My gaze flicked back to Alastair and Gabriel.

Alastair barreled into Gabriel, knocking him back a few steps. Gabriel stumbled, nearly losing his balance. His eyes narrowed in irritation as Alastair lowered his stance, and he was about to unleash his kung fu ninja fury on him when Gabriel put his hands out, hoping to stop Alastair's onslaught.

"I just want to help," he breathed, and then slowly, as if he had a practiced routine he couldn't ignore, adjusted his tie back into place. "I promise I don't want Corinth dead."

There was something in Gabriel's voice that gave me pause, as if he were imploring me to listen. Maybe he had information I needed to hear. At this point, I was grasping at any straw I could get.

"Wait, Alastair," I said, regretting it already. "As much as it pains me to say this, let's hear him out."

But Alastair was already leaping at him in a burst of speed and agility only comparable to a powerful jungle cat—surprisingly, managing to land a solid blow to

Gabriel's scarred cheek and jaw. Gabriel staggered back with a stunned look on his face, most likely because Alastair had gotten the better of him.

His eyes locked on Alastair as he put a hand to his cheek, moving his jaw up and down. "I'm not here to gloat. I'm here to help."

"Are you responsible for this?" Alastair growled. "Did you recruit Sarah and Caesar to do your dirty work for you?"

Gabriel shook his head adamantly, his dark eyes gleaming like an oil slick. "I've told you all along I don't want Corinth dead. That defeats everything I've been working toward. He's an investment; you know how I feel about investments," he insisted. "I don't waste them."

Alastair ground his teeth together, and then shared a quick glance with me. I gave a final resolute nod.

Alastair reluctantly relented, dropping his fists down by his sides, his tangled blond hair sticking to his forehead. "This goes against every fiber in my being," he muttered, joining me right as Gabriel did too, kneeling down beside me.

Gabriel took over, his steady hands next to mine, adding pressure, inspecting his wounds, and taking everything in. "The deepest wound is near his heart." I could feel Gabriel's body heat coming off him as his shoulder brushed against mine. "There's massive internal bleeding …" He put an ear to Corinth's chest, listening closely as he closed his eyes. After a second longer, they snapped back open and he sat up, wiping a resigned hand across his brow. "He is dying." He turned to me, anger lacing his voice. "Why did you do this without me?"

He actually had the audacity to sound mad.

Alastair took a knee on the other side of me, his eyes fixed on the bloodied watch at his feet. He put a comforting hand on my arm. It said, "I'm sorry for your loss." I refused to meet his eyes, because I knew what they'd show me.

"Don't do that. He's not dead," I said, forcefully. "He's got a pulse; he's breathing." I gave Gabriel more room to work, inching further back. "Fix him. *Now*. That's why you're here."

"There is only one thing that can save his life now." Gabriel met my unyielding gaze, pressing his lips together before saying, "Turn him."

I shook my head. "*What?*" My mind was still a scrambled mess from being electrocuted many, many times over, so I still couldn't wrap my head around turning Corinth. It would be impossible for a vampire to survive the process... or so I thought. "His blood is toxic; he can't be turned—it'll kill any vamp that drinks it. They wouldn't even be able to get through the process."

Gabriel gave me a look that said, *Why must I deal with your thick-headedness?* "His blood *is* toxic, yes, but he can *still* be turned."

"I don't understand—"

I started to say, but Gabriel cut me off.

"The ascended being who starts the process won't survive, that's true. But if another were to swoop in at the very last second and gave Corinth *their* blood, he could, in theory, be turned." Gabriel lifted his brows, imploring me to follow along. "There might be a chance he's too far gone already, but it might increase his odds of survival if *I* finished the process—my blood might be enough to get him over the healing hump."

My eyes churned and then burned bright with *Sight*. Even though I was weak and in an incredible amount of pain, I was going to try to compel Gabriel to start the process anyway. It was the only way. "Do it," I ordered. "You start it and I'll turn him."

Gabriel laughed softly at my bravado. "I don't think so."

"Are you here to help or not?" I added, "I'll compel you to do it." I breathed, "*You know I can.*"

Something passed across his face: pride mixed with anger and a smidge of delight. "You certainly can try, Miss Collins, but by the time you overtake me—" his black eyes flicked to Corinth, who was now a sickly gray pallor; his eyelids had a bluish tinge to them "—it'll be too late."

He was right; I couldn't fight him and then force him to turn Corinth before he died. I didn't have enough energy. I sensed remorse and pity in him—as palpable as anything I'd ever felt. The inconceivable notion he might actually have feelings in that soulless place called a heart surprised me into submission.

I nodded as clarity hit me. I would do it. It was the only way. I leaned over Corinth, ready to give my own life, but Alastair gently and firmly pushed me aside, still clutching his pocket watch in between his white knuckles. The white clock-face was bloodstained and tarnished, but it still ticked the seconds away while Corinth's life drained out of him.

I watched in growing panic as he threw his leather jacket off and rolled up his sleeves.

"*What are you doing?*" I asked, hating how desperate I sounded.

Stubborn, startlingly crisp, cool eyes met mine. I

could almost find myself swimming in them they were so crystal clear and refreshing. Eyes that showed his utter resolve about what he wanted to do.

"What do you think you're doing?" I repeated. A slow tremor of panic ran through my entire body because I already knew the answer. "Don't even think about it," I said in a measured tone. "If I have to—I'll compel you to stop."

Alastair reached out to gently cup a hand behind my neck. Slowly he drew me toward him until our foreheads were touching, his exceedingly blue eyes never leaving mine. I couldn't help but notice how full of light and life they were, like the lights of a thousand Eiffel Towers melded and formed to make up his irises. I knew that if that light winked out in them, a part of me would wink out too. I would never be the same. Never smile. Never laugh or love, ever again. I knew deep down I wouldn't want to.

His warm breath hit my face, rustling my hair. "This is my fault." He held the watch out for me to see as I glanced down to it. It was like I was looking through a blurry mirror, everything distorted and fuzzy. I didn't realize why until I felt the sting of tears hitting my cheeks. There were tears of anger and fear. Why would he give up so easily when I was fighting so hard?

"Sarah did this to get back at me for killing Wrentmore." He barely spoke above a whisper now. "You have way more control than I do." He said slowly, sadness etched on his face, "Teach him. Be his mentor. He has a much better chance of surviving if you're around. If you can change *my* life for the better—I know you can change his too." He put his hand on my wrist, encircling it with his fingers.

I shook my head, tears spilling down my face, burning my cheeks and chin on its mad dash to my collarbone— these fresh tears were out of something other than anger. Something else surged up inside me: loss and desolation and desperation. If I didn't take the watch, it meant he might change his mind. How do you choose between the two people you love most in the world?

That's why he was making the choice for me, because he unceremoniously dumped the watch into my palm. "*Get Sarah.*"

"*Alastair ...*" I begged. "Don't do this. *PLEASE*. I'll do it. I'll save Corinth. This isn't your responsibility. It's mine."

He bent his head, and a lock of blond fell into his eyes. "You wouldn't survive—you're too weak—you'd only be killing yourself and Corinth. I couldn't live with myself if that happened. You think I would sit idly by and watch that happen? I don't want to live with guilt any longer. This is how I can make amends for Sarah's actions—it was my fault she decided to take her sadistic revenge out on him." His eyes searched mine, imploring. "Besides, I don't have any remaining guilt about Wrentmore and Sarah any longer, and Corinth is my brother. I love him just as much as you do."

Something flickered in his eyes, as if he were playing out what our lives could have been like together if it had gone another way. Maybe he was imagining us huddled close in a quiet corner of a hole-in-the-wall café where they didn't speak a lick of English—nothing to worry about but poorly prepared food and a bad hair day. It sounded pretty good to me. Things I'd never have with him. I couldn't breathe. I didn't want to.

"Why aren't you angry? Why aren't you fighting for us? You're just giving up …" My eyes flicked to Corinth, who looked even worse now, his breathing barely even audible to my own super hearing ears.

Alastair's gaze fell on him too. He had the look of a soldier who had been in one too many battles. He'd seen so much loss and death and destruction that he couldn't stand to witness even one more death. He was seeing something beyond, on another horizon, something I couldn't even fathom. "I don't want to waste what precious little time I have left being angry … not when I'm looking into those big brown eyes of yours." He lifted my hands to his heart and then pulled them to his lips, kissing each knuckle.

My heart leaped into my throat, but my eyes burned brighter than an eternal flame. I wasn't going to let him do it—I couldn't—and he knew it.

"Just promise me one thing." He was giving me that damn half-cocky, half-teasing grin just like he had the first time I'd met him. "Don't marry Corinth."

"*Alastair…*"

"I love you." He said it with a finality that I couldn't bear to hear.

My tiny bubble of sanity popped as he pulled me tight, twisting his hands in my hair to kiss me. It was rough and abrupt, and when he pulled away, I still felt the pressure of his lips against mine.

And then his eyes were flicking to Gabriel behind me. "Hold her."

I whipped around, ready to rip Gabriel limb from limb, but his arms were already wrapped around me. He yanked me away from Alastair as I kicked out; trying to wriggle out of his grasp, fighting him with every scrap of energy I had left. His arms felt like iron bands, and no matter how hard I struggled, I couldn't break his hold.

Alastair's brows furrowed in anger and concern and sorrow. He gave Gabriel the iciest stare I'd ever seen; even Gabriel stopped short at the look on his face. "If you harm a hair on her or Corinth's head, so help me, Gabriel, I'll haunt you until the day you die."

By the amount of weight he put behind those words, I knew he meant it. Before I could tell him just how much of an idiot he was or how much I loved him, Alastair was already starting the process of saving Corinth's life and ending his own.

I writhed in vain, thrashing against Gabriel's embrace, screaming Alastair's name over and over again. It didn't take long. Corinth had lost so much blood already. All Alastair had to do was take what little was left. I knew Alastair was in excruciating pain. He handled the process better than I thought he would, proving just how strong he truly was. And all the while, Corinth didn't move or utter a sound, which meant his condition was worse than I had first allowed myself to admit.

I had to witness the love of my life dying. Something inside me broke. Eventually, I stopped kicking and sagged in Gabriel's strong grasp as he held me tightly against him. When I'd been turned, I had been in the worst pain in my entire life—this looked worse for Alastair.

"*Let me go,*" I said, barely above a whisper.

Gabriel, seeing that there was no reversing the damage already done, dropped his arms from around my waist right as Alastair stood shakily to his feet, wiping a hand across his mouth. I lunged forward, hoping against all hope that he would beat it. He gave one last grin of defiance, despite his pain, as blood dribbled from his mouth—his and Corinth's mixed together—and then he fell into my arms.

"*No! Alastair!*" I screamed. *He can beat it.* If anyone could, it would be him. For the first time ever, he proved me wrong. While I held him, his eyes, once the color of the ocean on a clear summer day, slowly clouded over. "I love you so much," I said softly into his ear over and over again; his chest barely moving up and down.

I had imagined a lifetime with him, and now all of those impossibly beautiful images melted away.

It reminded me of holding my father in my arms when he had died.

Why did bad things happen to good people?

Alastair had been good. He'd proven it time and time again. Yet this was where it had landed him. He'd died trying to save one more soul. Fresh tears slid down my face as I held him and wept. I'd never felt so much gut-wrenching misery in my entire life. It was worse than someone reaching into my chest and yanking out my heart. Actually, I would have preferred someone to do that so I'd stop feeling this way. The only way to survive was to seek out the very thing inside me that thirsted for vengeance: my *Sight*. And Sarah. Numbness settled over me.

I felt someone put a warm hand on my shoulder and, for one fleeting second, I thought it was Alastair.

Instead, I looked up to see that the comforting hand on my shoulder actually belonged to Gabriel. His eyes were filled with sorrow and sadness and sympathy. Caring didn't suit him—and it only served to anger me more. I was mad at him for not sacrificing himself. Mad at Alastair for being the insufferable hero. For giving his life to the cause as if he was nothing but an afterthought. It made me the afterthought. For once in his life, I wished he *had* been selfish.

"This is what you wanted, right?" I spit out.

Gabriel bent down beside Corinth, slowly taking his suit jacket off to finish what Alastair had started. "At one point in time … yes … but now …" He let the sentence trail off, shaking his head as if to clear it, maybe to rid himself of any emotion that had slowly started to take root. "There's no helping Alastair, but we can save Corinth."

Chapter 57

Vinson

SOMETHING HAD HAPPENED. HE felt it deep down in the desolate place he thought might be his soul—if he still had one. A gut instinct told him something was about to change. The wind picked up suddenly and unnaturally.

Vinson brushed his usually perfectly slicked-back hair out of his eyes—

And then it happened, two people popped into existence where there had been no one before. Spit from the fiery pits of hell—maybe the netherworld didn't want any part of them either.

Upon closer inspection, Vinson realized it was a man and a woman—or they looked like it, anyway. Looks could be deceiving. The man was wearing an oversized white robe, and the woman was in blue scrubs. Both of them were covered in blood—Corinth's. He knew that smell well. The woman had curly brown hair that stuck up around her ears, and her cheeks were flushed with exertion or excitement or both. There was nothing that would have gotten Vinson to go down into that pit of a clan with the kid and girl. He did *not* like tight, confining spaces.

Now he was regretting it.

Vinson recognized fleeing for your life when he saw it. The interlopers scrambled off and over the rocky terrain, scurrying away like cockroaches. From what or who, well, that was apparent. They'd done something very bad.

He'd done plenty of ruthless things himself, and he recognized the look and stink of it immediately. Vinson had been waiting at the opening of the cliff's side for a very long time after making sure the kid's family was safe. He had always had a certain amount of premonition for when and where bad things might happen next. This was the moment he'd been waiting for. Wicked things always happened around those three идиоты.

He hiked his rifle over his shoulder and followed the fugitives.

Time to go to work.

Volume Three – *Tree of Souls* coming December of 2019. Trust me—you'll want to stick with it…

Follow along – get updates and freebies, and be in the know about what happens in the next installment:

http://eepurl.com/dcl5ur

Acknowledgments

This book would not even be a blip on the radar without these people I'm about to mention. They're part of my *clan*, man. If I were to clan up, it would be with them.

As always, thank you, Misty Spitzer, for getting me through the dark times. Your constant support and guidance and "feigning" how much you liked my first drafts of all three volumes—even in their infancy—were what I needed to go the distance and finish.

An ever bigger shout-out and thank you to my copy editor, Leonora Bulbeck—I don't even have the words—your knowledge of Cornwall and rock-climbing, and everything in between has been invaluable. Thank you so much for helping shape this book into what it is.

Becky Pruitt, my sister, proofreader, manager, and self-sacrificing "'Joy'" who let me have my mental breakdowns, to sob on her shoulder—THANK YOU for being there when I needed you most. This year was a doozy, and I know I wouldn't have made it without you—*Watch for God*, sista. You loving Volume Two as much as you do means the world to me. Just wait for Volume Three.

My family is the glue that keeps me together. Thank you

and much love to you all for accepting my brush-offs, the rude and clipped manner in which I answered your phone calls—"I'M WRITING!"—and for understanding how important it was for me to finish this volume. To Robert Hayes (Dad), Annie Hayes (Mom), Christy Leonard (sister), Sherry Daugherty (vampire/sister), Becky Pruitt (sister), Oscar Pruitt (brother), and a very special thank you to Paul Leonard (brother/taxi driver) for letting me use your name—for taking me around London all those years ago; to Jeremy Daugherty (brother) and all my nieces and nephews. Oscar K. Pruitt for going over the first drafts of The Outcasts—and Susen Pruitt for being so supportive.

To Eric Skinner for joining me on some of my crazy adventures and never complaining, and for all of your help at the Florida Indie Bookfest.

A HUGE thank you to my editor—Naomi Hughes, I could not have gotten this far without your know-how and experience.

To Shannon Knight, thank you for your quick, fantastic edits and proofreading skills.

Juan Arriaga, we have many more nights of *Chuck* left to watch—and I expect the Tardis, time-jumping to continue in the near future.

Thanks go to my cover artist, Mark Reid and book formatter, Lorna Reid. Without you both, I would be lost.

To all my proofreaders and those who support me in my

book signings, conventions, and the general hub bub of my hectic life, and also my support team at FWPD. You guys rock.

Special ultra-thanks to these folks for their countless hours of support and encouragement:

Stephanie Hancock, June Owens, Oscar K. Pruitt, Amy Tillery, Debra Lockhart, Renee Wesbrooks, Monique Schomp, Paul Irwinsky, and David Marchioni.